PRAISE FOR *CROW MOON*

'Dark, gothic, and dripping with dread, this spellbinding debut is a triumph' C.J. Cooke

'*Crow Moon* is a hugely accomplished and extremely creepy debut from Suzy Aspley' Trevor Wood

'A page-turning plot, beautifully realised setting, and characters that are still walking and talking in my head, *Crow Moon* is an impressive debut from a compassionate and captivating new voice' Emma Styles

'*Crow Moon* is an extraordinary debut: intriguing, unsettling, heavy on atmosphere and with a formidable leading lady, investigative reporter, Martha Strangeways. Suzy Aspley is one to watch' Mari Hannah

'Exceptionally atmospheric. Excruciatingly tense. I cared SO much about the cast that I keep thinking: "No! Don't do that! Don't go there!" It's a belter' Emma Christie

'A gripping piece of contemporary gothic, *Crow Moon* signals the arrival of a hugely promising new talent' Kevin Wignall

'I read Suzy Aspley's *Crow Moon* with a creeping sense of dread and an unwillingness to put the book down for even a moment. A compelling story, beautiful descriptions of a fearsome wilderness setting and unforgettable characters make this one of my books of the year' Alison Belsham

'A nerve-tingling thriller set in the Scottish wilds with beautiful descriptions that enchant and terrify. Deeply moving with superb characterisation, this masterful debut will ensure you never look at a crow the same way again' Eve Smith

'A creepy story of folklore and grief' Heleen Kist

'Wow... what a debut! Deliciously gothic – dripping forests, terrifying disappearances and a haunting resolution' Heather Critchlow

'Combining thrills, horror and the occult, this will most certainly appeal to fans of Stephen King and C.J. Tudor' *Mature Times*

'A really engrossing read. Certain scenes are told from the point of view of the perpetrator of the crime, scenes that add a chilling tone to an already brooding narrative ... leading to a series of red herrings that keep the identity of the antagonist perfectly hidden right up to the dramatic, high-stakes conclusion. A brilliant start to this series ... I can't wait to see what trouble the author leads Martha Strangeways into next' Jen Med's Book Reviews

'An accomplished debut that grabbed me from the first page and simmered in my mind long after finishing it. It's not only an engrossing thriller and a riveting mystery but it also broke my heart a couple of times. It has a cast of wonderful characters that I hope will all be back for more, 'cos I most certainly will! Highly recommended' From Belgium with Booklove

CROW MOON

CROW MOON

A MARTHA STRANGEWAYS MYSTERY

SUZY ASPLEY

**ORENDA
BOOKS**

Orenda Books
16 Carson Road
West Dulwich
London SE21 8HU
www.orendabooks.co.uk

First published by Orenda Books, 2024

A catalogue record for this book is available from the British Library.
ISBN 978-1-914585-50-0
eISBN 978-1-914585-51-7

Typeset in Garamond by typesetter.org.uk
Crow image by Freepik

Printed and bound by CPI Group (UK) Ltd, Croydon CR0 4YY

For sales and distribution, please contact info@orendabooks.co.uk

For my mam, Mollie, always an inspiration.
And in memory of Crowzier. We miss you.

Her moondial rouses dead again
While ashen feathers fall from sky
Under a ghealach làn Feannag fly
Her craws cry end of season soon
As Ostara rises at Crow Moon.

—Anonymous, Strathbran, 1642

PROLOGUE

The Book of Shadows

It is cold out here beneath this bright moon. I exhale breaths in shallow plumes of fear. A hunting owl screeches. Her ghostly outline catches my eye in the moonlight as she glides by. I don't fear her; but I do fear what is to come.

I have done all I can to safeguard my child, but now dread that this feeble circle of protection will not hold. I am sorry for you, my son. I've tried so hard to appease him. I hope that one day you will read this and understand. Be brave, my love. Stay true. I hear him coming now and I am afraid.

CHAPTER ONE

FIRST FULL MOON

March 2018

A full moon glittered bright in the ink-black sky. A February moon that had slipped into the start of March, trailing winter's frost-tipped fingers across dormant ground. An owl, eyes like beacons reflecting the lunar glow, glided with quiet menace across the tree line. Hunting for prey. Its soft ghostly call – 'whoo, whoo' – reaching the ears of the boy who lay nearby.

Fraser's eyes shot open, pupils blooming in confusion as his eyes instinctively tried to absorb every available sliver of light. He blinked several times, but the teenager's usually pin-sharp sight failed, the monochrome gloom leaving him muddled. The bird screeched. This time nearby. A frightening echo in the dark. Fraser had no idea where he was. His head was spinning as though he'd been drinking. He didn't recall having enough last night to cause a hangover; he'd just been for a few beers with the lads in the village. He remembered getting home. Falling into bed. Wherever he was now, though, it sure wasn't home. His throat was dry and raw, a metallic taste on his tongue.

He'd been running. He remembered now. He'd got up the next morning. Thursday. The first day of March. The usual 6K route down Station Road hill before doubling back along deserted forestry trails, across the meadow and home through Black Wood. His routine. He'd been looking forward to a shower and one of his mum's bacon butties, lathered with spicy brown sauce. It made his mouth water just thinking about it. He remembered setting off, blood pounding in his ears as he ran up the steep hill through the village. He ran every morning before school, loved the feeling it gave him. Every muscle ached and throbbed, his chest tight as he gulped in cool air.

The air in here was damp and earthy. And there was another smell. Rancid, like something rotting. Heart rate and fear increasing, his breathing was suddenly heavy. He could smell stale, yeasty beer on his own breath, the fuzz of unwashed teeth on his tongue. A hint of the musky scent from the girl he was kissing the night before still lingered in his hair. He tried to focus. But where was he now? Fragments of memory combined: his running music booming in his ears, turning for home when he'd reached the path where copper-fringed bracken grew high, then back onto the main gravel road, a trip and a fall. His phone had fallen from his pocket as he tripped and he scrabbled his fingers in the gravel to locate it. His knee throbbed, ankle twisted so bad he wondered if it was broken, and as he lay back, winded, he tapped out a message on the cracked phone screen: *HELP* swooshed off as he pressed send. The phone slid from his fingers on the path. He couldn't recall whether he'd picked it up again.

The fog in his mind shifted: a man had appeared from somewhere. He'd ridden up on a rattling quad bike with a trailer attached. Come just at the right time with a friendly greeting. Had helped him up, given him a drink and offered a lift home. He recalled lying back in the trailer, watching the clouds scud overhead.

As his eyes adjusted to the low light, he could see something in the corner of the space. He sensed this was where the rancid smell was coming from.

And then a terrifying reality crept in. He couldn't move his limbs. 'What the fuck?' His words sounded sharp. He looked down. His hands and feet were bound together. Knotted loops of rough twine sliced into the bare skin of his wrists.

Eyes wide, he called out, 'Help!' in a voice that didn't sound like his own.

There was a slight blast of air as a door opened, bringing a shaft of moonlight into the place. Blinking hard at the sudden change, he registered he was in a shed. Timber-framed and watermarked tin walls. The foul, rotting smell was now so bad he could taste it. Torchlight suddenly flashed across the room – illuminating horrors. Just six feet away a heap of dead birds was piled against the wall. Black, shining feathers streaked with blood, opaque eyes staring and legs sticking out stiffly from the pile, beaks open as if gasping to breathe.

He recoiled, trying to pull himself further back, but his feeble body wouldn't do what his head demanded. Why would anyone keep piles of dead crows in a shed?

'Help me?' His weak voice was laced with fear, and the words seemed to drawl, as though he wasn't in control of them.

Someone had entered now, and another dead bird was thrown on top of the rotting pile. Then the light was shone into his face, blinding him. It seemed to come closer, and he tried to call for help again. He couldn't see the figure behind the harsh light.

A sudden searing pain hit him.

He saw his wordless assailant in the corner of his eye as his head met the floor.

CHAPTER TWO

Jane MacDonald was smaller than Martha remembered.

Having knocked tentatively on Martha's door, Jane now hesitated on the doorstep. 'Hello, Martha. How've you been?' she said at last.

Martha hadn't seen much of anyone since the fire at Blacklaw, but her son Dougie spent plenty of time over at Jane's house with her son, Fraser. Dougie and Fraser had been fast friends since they'd moved to Strathbran.

Noting the crease of anxiety on the other woman's kind face, and sensing her need for reassurance, Martha smiled. 'Aye, not bad, Jane. Would you like to come in?' Martha moved back from the door.

'No, you're alright. I just wondered if you'd heard from our Fraser? He's not been here with Dougie, has he? Didn't come home last night and I'm starting to fret.'

'No, he's not been here,' Martha said. She opened the door wider. 'Do come in. I'll make you a cup of tea. Please.' She realised how distant she must seem to folk in the village. She hardly ever stopped to pass the time of day with anyone now.

Jane MacDonald hesitated for a moment longer, then nodded.

In the kitchen, Martha cleared a pile of papers from the table. 'Here, take a seat,' she said. 'I haven't seen Fraser, but Dougie's been at his dad's. Is Fraser not just away to pals in Aberfoyle?'

Jane frowned as she shook her head. 'I haven't seen him since he went out for his run yesterday. I left a bacon butty warming in the oven for him before I went off to work, but it was still there when I came home. You know he can be a bit of a tearaway, that lad. Not like your Dougie...' She tailed off.

'Teenagers. A law unto themselves don't you think?' Martha sat down at the table with Jane. The woman's anxious face was still pinched, so she reached out, gently squeezing her arm. 'Have you checked with the school? Or on his social-media accounts?'

'I've spoken to a few of his friends, but no one seems to know where he is. And you know how secretive they are with social media.' Jane smiled slightly.

Martha rolled her eyes in solidarity. 'I'm not even on Facebook,' she admitted.

'Oh, Martha, I'm sorry to be bothering you with this, after everything you've had to go through.'

'I'm alright. I have good days and bad days.'

'I can't imagine...' It was clear Jane didn't know what to say. 'And here's me being daft about my lad going off for a night. I'm just a bit het up about where he's got to.'

'Hey, no worries at all,' said Martha, absorbing Jane's concern.

'You're not being silly. Listen, I'll give Dougie a ring. He's due back here later, but I'll check now and see if he's heard from Fraser and let you know. I'm sure you'll find he's just holed up at a girlfriend's or something and has lost track of time. You know what they're like at this age, always pushing the boundaries.' At the same time as she tried to reassure Fraser's mum, she couldn't help thinking how worried she would be if Dougie were to go AWOL.

'I'd better be off then,' Jane said. 'Thanks for the tea.'

As she saw Jane out, Martha wondered where Fraser could have got to. He was a lively teenager, much more outgoing than her own son, but the boys had been close since they'd met at school when Martha and Jamie first moved to the village.

She closed the door, pulled her phone from her pocket and called Dougie.

'I did get a message from Fraser yesterday,' Dougie said. 'It just said *HELP*, but when I tried to call him there was no answer. He was probably just pulling my leg though, Mum. You know what he's like.'

Martha didn't like the sound of that at all. It seemed an odd kind of prank to play. And the fact that Dougie had heard nothing further from Fraser made her antennae twitch. She told Dougie she would pick him up from school later on. It would give her the chance to ask some of her son's friends if they knew anything about where Fraser might be.

'And text him again, will you?' she told Dougie. 'Let me know if he gets back to you. He's not responding to messages or calls from his mum.'

'OK. See you later.' Dougie rang off. He was a good lad. She was lucky she had him.

Weak sun was trying to break through the cloud, but the breeze was chilly as Martha walked up the hill to the shop half an hour later.

Built on a hill with a church at its centre, the village comprised a square, a hall, the school next to the kirk, and the shop she was heading for. It was originally an estate village for Strathbran House with some of the cottages dating back to the sixteenth century. Over the years, a few smaller new developments had sprung up as nearby farmland was sold off, and a small council housing estate was also built. When she'd moved here with Jamie, it was because they believed it was a good place for children to grow up – in a close-knit community where they'd be safe, but not beyond commuting distance for Martha. That had been the plan when they moved out here, anyway. She thought of her twins and the fire that had ended their short lives, and then of Fraser, and her throat tightened.

She caught sight of something black flapping over the road by the church gate. Kirk Minister Reverend Locke. His dark robes catching the breeze. Maybe there was a funeral on today. He caught her eye, acknowledging her with a slight nod. She always felt a bit uneasy in his presence. He'd conducted the memorial service for the twins, which she'd endured with a numbness that reached deep into her soul. No comfort in the words from a god she didn't believe in. She hadn't spoken to Locke since.

'How are you, Martha?' he called. Moving closer, she noticed the five o'clock shadow grazing his jaw and was surprised to see a cigarette smoking in his left hand.

'OK, thanks, Reverend. Yourself?'

He nodded, taking a long drag. 'Got to have some vices, right?' His wry smile was unexpected.

'You haven't heard anything about Fraser MacDonald, have you?' she asked.

'Haven't seen that lad for quite a while. Why, what's up?'

'It's probably nothing, but he didn't come home last night. His mum is worried.'

'Just out with a girlfriend or something, I'd bet.' He seemed dismissive. 'Haven't seen him at church for ages, or your Dougie, for that matter.'

Martha didn't like the way he'd brought her son into the discussion, his tone insinuating his absence was some fault of hers.

'Well, if you do hear anything, could you let his mum know please?' she said.

He nodded, mouth pressed into a slight smirk.

'Be good to see you at church too sometime soon.'

Martha turned, ignoring his pointed remark, and walked away. There was something about the man she didn't like.

She arrived at the school ten minutes early and parked up, hoping to catch the pupils as they came out and boarded buses bound for home. At 3.45pm the bell rang. Martha got out and stood by her car. A warm feeling spread in her chest as three boys emerged, her son Dougie amongst them. His hair was growing. He pulled off his school tie and rolled up the sleeves on his shirt as he walked, eager to embrace the weekend, she thought.

'Any chance the lads could get a lift back to Strathbran, Mum?' he asked.

She nodded, and George and Hamish piled into the back of her Subaru.

'Apologies about the smell,' she smiled. 'Usually just the two dogs back there.'

'You cannae park there.' The voice behind her was less than friendly.

'I'm just about to leave.' Martha turned to see a small, skinny man, his hair pulled back into a greasy ponytail. Squinting eyes looked her up and down, the tip of his tongue briefly protruded from his lips.

'Aye well, that lad of yours should know the rules, eh Dougie?'

Martha saw the look that passed between her son and the man before she got into the driver's seat and started the ignition.

'Who was that creep?' She grimaced.

'That's Joe Gallagher,' Hamish piped up from the back seat. 'Works in the tech department.'

'What? Is he a teacher?'

'Nah, just support staff, but he watches everything we do on the computers and makes sure everyone knows it too.'

'Any news on Fraser?' she asked tentatively – not wanting to create a drama at this point.

'Nah,' said Dougie. 'He wasn't in school, and he's still not replied to any of my messages.'

'Boys...?' asked Martha, catching the eyes of the other two in the rearview mirror. But they both shook their heads.

'Christie might know, though,' George said. 'He was sweet on her for a while, wasn't he, Doug?'

Dougie shook his head, muttering they'd all just been friends. There was more to that story Martha thought, but she didn't want to embarrass her son in front of his pals. The mention of Christie interested her though, so once they'd got back to the village, dropped off George and Hamish, and reached their home, she told Dougie she was going out for half an hour for a walk, not telling him she was heading straight for the girl's home.

⨀

'Mrs Strangeways.' Christie looked surprised to see Martha when she answered the door.

'Hi, Christie. Have you got a minute?'

'Er, yeah, I suppose so.' She moved back, inviting her in, but Martha shook her head.

'It's OK. I just wondered if you'd heard from Fraser at all. His mum is really worried about him. He didn't come home last night.'

A rabbit in the headlights described Christie's look perfectly.

'No,' she gulped. 'I haven't seen him for ages. Not since this time last year, to be honest. I haven't been to school for a long while.'

Martha recalled now that Christie had dropped out of school some time ago.

'That seems very precise,' she said. The girl's face stretched with apprehension. 'To know the date when you last saw him – it was so long ago.'

'That's because it was the Crow Moon, Mrs Strangeways.' Christie glanced up at the sky, where the rising full moon was emerging as a pale disc in the sky. 'It'll be almost a year to the day when it comes around again.'

Martha shook her head, unsure what Christie was talking about.

'So you haven't heard from Fraser, either? No messages or—'

'You ask your Dougie,' Christie said.

A crow flapped down, making the girl jump, and landed in the tree in the front garden. It swung about in the breeze, watching them.

Christie stepped back, seeming nervous now. 'Dougie'll be able to tell you more about it. I'm sorry, but I have to go now.' She pushed the door closed.

Puzzled, Martha walked away, the bird taking flight as she came close. The dusk was drawing in, and the moon was now low on the horizon. She wondered where on earth Fraser could be.

CHAPTER THREE

The man had to be flexible with the plan. He'd watched Fraser running the trail for a few days and had done all he could to prepare. He knew the forest well, or at least this part of it. He'd been brought here as a child, had become used to the silence. No one to hear you scream but the ghosts. The Queen Elizabeth Forest Park stretched from the Trossachs hills and majestic Loch Lomond, all the way to the village of Crianlarich further to the north-west. Visitors flocked to the area. Studded with clear lochs and towering mountains, it was the Highlands within reach of Scotland's biggest cities. Friday was the start of the weekend here.

The nearby village of Aberfoyle was steeped in folklore, and the famous Fairy Hill on the other side of the broad glen drew families from far away. Sometimes, if the wind blew in the right direction, he heard bells chiming. Not church bells, but offerings to the pagan forest spirits from folk who should know better. But there were also lonely areas of dense woodland where you could easily lose yourself; and where he knew he would never be disturbed.

People believed there was magic in these woods, and local tourist guides still told tales of witches. They knew nothing, he thought. But the stories meant they didn't want to be here after dark, which was just as well.

He didn't think the teenager remembered him. It was a while since they'd crossed paths, but he could take no risks. He wore his heavy coat and dark glasses, just in case. Fraser was a strong young man, almost an adult; easily capable of getting away if he suspected anything, so the man had found a way of putting the teenager on the back foot. A rope slung low across the track had done that; Fraser hadn't seen it and had rolled to the ground. Then a friendly helping hand to get him onto the trailer. The boy looked relieved. Someone had come to save him. He was too trusting though. No sense of danger. At that time in the morning, no one else was about, but it was important to get him out of the way, off the main path, leaving as little trace as possible. He'd checked the forecast in advance. There'd been a run of dry days, so the quad wouldn't leave tracks through mud. It had all come nicely together.

The Risperdal was prescribed for him, but he hadn't been taking it. He'd just kept stocking up the supplies, sure they'd be useful for something. It was a stroke of luck finding the other drug stashed in the old railway buildings. He'd felt as if someone was helping him, knowing he needed to knock Fraser out for a while. But in the end he'd been forced to use a more brutal method – the stick still had the teenager's blood on it. He'd get rid of that later.

Do it. Hit him. Make sure he stays still.

She'd told him to take the boy. Said it was the only way.

All three would have to pay for what they had unbound with their ceremony that night. He had to make sure the thing that pursued him was sent back. He didn't want it in his head, talking the way it did. And he knew a way to rid himself of the curse. It was in the lines he'd been forced to write, over and over as a child. If he did what those lines told him, the voice would be gone for good.

He knelt down next to the boy. Blood trickled from the gash in his head. Despite the shadow of pale hairs across his jaw, he looked younger now, his face relaxed in uneasy slumber. Faint, shallow breaths came from his nose; his eyelids flickered in the gloom.

The man sighed, feeling her menace hovering. He wanted to take his time. This was the first one, after all. It was important to get it right. He'd been practising the writing on paper at home; the old ink had worked well on it, and he'd thinned it by adding a few drops of fresh crow's blood, still warm. His own magic. He'd even bought a side of pork from the butcher's and tried the writing on that. It had worked surprisingly well. Afterwards he cooked the joint till the fat crackled, and ate it with apple sauce. No point in wasting good meat. He'd heard human and pig skin had similar textures, but the flesh needed to be cool and dry.

He expected her to say something else, something unpleasant, but all he heard was the noise of the wind whistling through the slatted tin sides of the shed as he prepared.

He had no idea how long the drugs might last; once the ink was dry, he would have to haul Fraser out and back onto the trailer. He collected his equipment, pen and ink bottle clinking inside the bag. It was time for the next stage.

The teen was still as he approached. He rolled him over so he was face down on the earth floor, his left cheek pressed into the dirt. He pulled the cord lighting the single dusty bulb that hung from the ceiling of the abandoned forester's shed. Under the dull light he used his knife to slice away the lad's running top, exposing the muscled flesh beneath. Then he began, the words drilled into his mind for so long translating onto the pale back in front of him. He concentrated hard on keeping a steady hand so the message was clearly visible on the skin. His mother had made him repeat the lines out loud when he wrote them as a child. Over and over again. Sometimes she'd told him a Bible story about God sending ravens to help the prophet Elijah in the desert. She said they were his birds. But then she'd change and mutter about the Feannag Dhubh. When that happened, he always knew to hide if he could. There'd been black shadows in his life ever since.

'Are you pleased?' He said it aloud as he worked.

No answer. But displeasure fermented in the air close by. It was hard to focus, knowing what lurked. It had clung to him since the night of the ritual.

As he wrote, he pressed hard with his other hand, encased in a latex glove, to keep the skin taut. He continued until the job was done. Mouth set in concentration. Lines and lines of neat black script, straight from his head and onto this pristine human page. The boy's skin was cool now. No longer sweating from his earlier exertions. The ink mingled with the dried sweat and made a pleasing picture. Satisfied, he sat back, admiring his work. He'd done his best. He recited the words in a low voice. It was like a hymn. He didn't need to read it.

> *For every ill that bade this way*
> *She's shunned, chased off by night and day*
> *In ink-dark forests, floats mountain witch*
> *Her feathered cloak black as pitch*
> *Fear manifest, how near she comes*
> *To strip all things of flesh and bones.*

He looked around. He'd worked all night and daylight was shining through the door now and lighting up the stinking birds,

as newly emerged flies buzzed around the putrid pile. His pre-
occupation with his plans for the boy meant he'd left the mess for
longer than he should have. There'd be maggots now, crawling
over the black carcasses. He needed to get them outside and tied
to the fence, before the smell got any worse – or he could set fire
to them. He enjoyed that too. Watching things burn, the feathers
and then the flesh, until there was nothing left but ash and
fragments of bone.

The boy stirred, no longer fully unconscious, his breathing
rapid. The man watched as his chest began to heave, watery vomit
flowing from his lips and nose. He coughed several times, eyes
flickering as though about to wake, then he made an awful
choking sound before he stilled. The man watched, waiting for
the fit to pass, hoping Fraser wouldn't roll over onto his back
before the ink had properly dried. There was a little movement.
Then nothing.

CHAPTER FOUR

Martha was uneasy about the cry for help in the text message her
son had received, even though he'd dismissed it as a prank, and
Dougie still hadn't heard from his friend.

'I'm sure he'll be home soon, Jane,' Martha said in a Saturday
morning call to Fraser's mum trying to sound more reassuring
than she felt. Since the death of her three-year-old twins, almost
two years ago now, she lived with a constant underlying anxiety.

'Has anyone been out and checked his running route?' she
asked.

'The police said they were going to, and my husband has
walked his usual track, but couldn't see any signs of him. I'm really
starting to worry now.'

'Has his brother heard from him at all – he might have seen if
Fraser has posted on social media?'

'He says Fraser hasn't been active on anything, Martha. That's worrying in itself as he's usually glued to that phone.'

'Let me know if there's anything I can do. I'm around all day if you need any help.'

After lunch, Dougie went out, and Martha sat down to read up on how to locate a phone. Her journalist skills were rusty, but she knew where teenagers were involved, phones were key, and it sounded like Fraser was no exception. And based on what she now learned online, she thought she had to get Dougie to set up a 'find your friends' service so she could find him if he wasn't contactable for any reason.

But so far she didn't feel she learned much more about Fraser. Nothing that would help her work out where he was.

She spied a cobweb outside the kitchen window being buffeted by the breeze. A trio of pale threads glued the gauzy web to the window box. No sign of the spider though. Tucked away, waiting for an unsuspecting insect to trap in a tiny silken shroud for later. Birds chattered in the garden; the kitchen clock ticked gently. Outside, the late-winter sky darkened as cloud shadows crept across distant hills.

Silhouetted in the trees outside, birds cawed loudly, reminding her of that night. She'd heard it said that crows were the souls of murder victims; that they warned of evil to come.

That November night more than two years ago had been dark; the hard, cold land around Blacklaw gripped tight by mid-winter. Martha was bathing the twins, and little Freddie was chattering on about some 'strange lady' he'd seen around the house. Outside the window Martha could hear the calling of the crows that had gathered in the trees nearby. The racket grew so loud, it began to upset both twins. Martha looked out of the bathroom window, hoping to shoo the birds away, when she saw a dead crow lying below, its glassy eye staring at the sky. She rapped on the pane and the birds rose in a swarm of rough *craws* then headed off to roost in the trees on the hill behind the house. That night the hill was shrouded in icy fog, the moonlight giving it a spectral glow.

Her phone had buzzed then in her pocket, interrupting both her reverie and the twins' bath time. It was the newspaper she worked for. Her presence as their key investigative journalist was demanded urgently; a press conference had been called. She quickly put the boys to bed, breathing in their woody talcum-powdered scent, kissed their dad, Jamie, on the cheek, then headed off into the dark night.

She'd never see her babies again.

A shiver brought her back to the present. She instinctively reached into her jacket pocket, searching for the precious box that was always tucked safely against her heart. Her fingernail caught the rough edge as she slid it open, swallowing hard against the lump forming in her throat. Carefully she unwrapped the contents. Scared, as always, of what she knew was inside. If only she'd been there. If only she could have held them one last time.

A tear spilled down her cheek, dropping silently onto the small piece of cloth, an edge cut from the blue comfort blanket the twins had shared. She lifted the matchbox to her face, hoping their scent might still hide amongst the folds inside. It was all she had left to love. To remember them. If only she could bring them back.

Pushing the box back into her pocket, she looked at the torn envelope in front of her. It had dropped onto the doormat an hour ago, and it had taken her almost that long to open it. Postmarked Newcastle, she knew straight away it was from her old friend Orla. They were at school together in the eighties and were inseparable for their teenage years. They'd even signed up to journalism college at the same time, both fresh-faced and idealistic. Martha had rapidly branched off into newspapers, while Orla's perfect features were always made for the TV screen. She'd headed south, for the bright lights of London, and landed a job doing the weather on regional BBC, but her career progressed quickly, and before long she was presenting the news for the same region. They'd drifted apart, as people often do, but every few years they'd meet for dinner and usually ended the night drunk somewhere, reminiscing about old boyfriends.

It's been so long, Martha thought. Maybe it won't be the same anymore.

But when she'd opened the envelope, it turned out Orla was making a thinly disguised plea for help – which was perhaps why she'd opted for an old-fashioned handwritten letter and not an email or phone call. Her husband had dumped her for a woman half her age, and she was devastated. She was back at her parents' in the north-east, but said she'd rented a house near to Martha for a month and was coming up to stay. She'd be arriving at the weekend. Martha smiled. Typical of Orla. She'd not asked if it was OK, just announced her arrival and expected Martha to fall in with her plans. Maybe it was what they both needed though. An old friend and a good catch-up.

Two faces peered up at her, the smaller dog whining, his bright eyes expectant. Pushing back her tangled hair, Martha got up and poured away her now-cold mug of tea. She turned on the tap to wash the stain from the white porcelain. Pulling a worn green dog lead from the inside pocket of her jacket, a crumpled paper hanky and the small matchbox came out with it and fell to the floor.

'Bugger,' she said, bending down to pick up the battered yellow box, the swan's head hardly visible now. She heard the dull rattle of its contents as she pushed it safely back into her pocket and tightened the zip.

The mutts chorused their usual manic barking as she opened the back gate. Piling out in a clatter of fur and teeth, they playfully attacked each other. Martha pulled her hood more tightly around her face as the dreich, sticky air caught her skin. Underfoot, the track was sodden, a dense, earthy smell hanging about the place. Patches of fungi bloomed in dark corners amongst the trees. Later in the year there'd be trails of red-and-white spotted toadstools dotted throughout the forest. They looked pretty, but fly agaric fungi could be nasty if ingested.

Martha enjoyed her solitary walks. Saturday afternoons could be busy in the woods, but she hoped they wouldn't be today. It was mostly just her and the dogs who went out in this damp, dreary weather. At seventeen, Dougie was more often out with his mates or in his room practising music. He'd come home smelling of smoke after being out with Fraser a few times recently. She hadn't said anything, not sure if it was teenage rebellion, or a way of coping with the loss of his young brothers.

She wondered again about Fraser; she was glad the police were now making inquiries, but hoped he'd just turn up, grinning and asking what all the fuss was about. When Dougie was back later, she'd suggest to him that they take a run out through the forest in the car and see if they could see any trace of the lad.

Her sheepdog, Skye, and the daft terrier, BJ, belted about, diving under rotten tree stumps and through pools of thick, black mud. Martha wound her way downhill as the trees thickened and the light faded, stepping carefully over broken timbers that bridged the gushing brown waters of the burn. Cows called mournfully in the distance. As she went deeper, silence settled in the trees. A sense of unease gripped her – and she didn't quite understand why.

'River, Skye!' she called as they passed over the bridge. Her voice echoed back from the far side of the gorge. The sheepdog halted his mad dash and stared. Hazel eyes bright. 'River!' she said, more softly this time. The dog hurtled away, disappearing from view, the ragged terrier behind, running as fast as his small legs would carry him but with no hope of catching up. Hearing the dogs plunging into the tumbling water below, Martha headed down the steep slope, carefully planting her heavy boots. Leaves were heavy on the track, softly hiding tree roots, boulders and other traps.

Halfway down, she detected the scent of something sweet and slightly sulphuric. Something dead. Most likely a rotting sheep corpse nearby. Martha held her breath until she passed and was glad the dogs hadn't got wind of it first. They loved a good roll in something disgusting. From the second bridge, she watched them in the water below. Head cocked to one side, BJ stared, waiting for a stick to be thrown.

'Sod off,' she told him, but then gave in to his persistent whining and hurled a branch into the water.

She'd better drop Orla a line, she thought, and tell her to bring country clothes, wellies and a waterproof. Orla would want to spend as much time as possible with her when she arrived, so they would be out here walking a lot. Memories bubbled up of how they used to lie for hours together in her bedroom, talking about boys. She wondered what they'd chat about now.

After ten minutes, the light properly fading, Martha called, 'Come on, home, now,' and started to climb back towards the murk of the trees, heartbeat quickening with the effort of the hike. It would be almost dark by the time they got back, although there was a waning moon overhead. March had started with a full moon and would end with one too, she'd read on the BBC app earlier. Apparently it was a rare occurrence. She'd always kept track of the moon's movements, ever since she and Jamie had discovered the unusual moondial on the hill behind the house at Blacklaw. God, that seemed like a lifetime ago.

Feeling for her phone, Martha pulled it out. Full charge. But no signal. Shit. She didn't like to be out of contact. Especially with Fraser being missing. What if something happened to Dougie? She kept her eyes focused on the track, one step at a time. Her boot clinked as it caught against something. Something shiny. She bent down to look. A small bottle of heavy green glass, stoppered at one end. Shaped like a small hourglass, it seemed to contain something thick and dark. It was cold against her fingers as she picked it up. She put it into her pocket. She'd wash it later and see what was inside. The steep slope down to the river was now to her right. One slip and she'd be down in the water below. Concentrating on her the steep ascent, she recalled the dogs, her voice rising, 'Skye! BJ!'

She heard something in the trees above and glanced up. A shadow of some creature flitted out of her eye line. Looking for it, she misplaced her foot, and was abruptly thrown off balance. She reached out into the air and grabbed at nothing, her clumsy body weight tipping her over and down the steep slope. Her sturdy waterproof gave some protection from the fractured branches, but their edges tore at her face as she tumbled down. Teeth crunching together like they'd break, she piled down the muddy incline, her descent quickened by a carpet of rotting beech leaves.

'Shit. Oh God. No!'

She jerked to a halt. Her head near the rushing water, boots tangled in brambles. The air knocked clean out of her. She tried to move. A sharp pain made her gasp, the foul taste of blood and dirt in her mouth.

After a minute, she tried again, moving more slowly now. She'd landed on a slight ledge. And she noticed that the awful sweet smell was more intense here. She must be close to the carcass of whatever animal had previously taken the same route down. Gulping the air, she rolled over and pushed herself onto her hands and knees and looked up. Disorientated, her vision took a moment to clear. Everything stilled. Martha was staring into the upside-down face of a boy. Dark, matted hair hung over his battered, blackened cheeks. His clothes were torn and filthy. One milky eye was open. He was lying awkwardly over a fallen tree trunk, his upper back exposed. She could see something on his skin. Writing? A tattoo?

'Oh my God.' Her stomach pitched as the horror of what she'd found hit her.

For a second, everything was silent. The distant sound of the dogs' barking broke through, before pain overwhelmed her. She peered aghast through the undergrowth. It was Fraser. His dead gaze staring back at her.

CHAPTER FIVE

Laughter rang out in the playing field near his house. Girls with skirts too short and tops not long enough to cover their pale bellies. Talking too loudly, music from their phones blaring as they danced, almost naked, to tunes he didn't want to hear. It wasn't music to him; just noise. Intrusive, jarring racket, and there they were, shameless, shrieking and gyrating to the tinny drumbeats echoing from phones. Not a care in the world as they paraded themselves.

Where are their parents? Letting their daughters out after dark.

Ignoring the whispering, he stepped closer to the open window. Careful not to be seen, he stood behind the curtain. A girl with dark, glossy hair framing her face stood with her back to the wall. One leg was bent, her foot, clad in pristine-white trainers, resting on the stone. Her eyes shone in the blue light from her tiny phone screen. A short, tight skirt displayed ample white thighs and a dark string was tied around her ankle. No tights. No modesty. No respect. Her perfect white teeth glistened, illuminated by the phone, a spotlight she didn't deserve. The girl glanced up at his window and he quickly stepped back. A boy approached, pulled her close. One hand behind her head, his fingers threaded through her hair. The other hand around her ample backside; his tongue down her throat. The man watched, disgusted. His heart raced, seeing the young couple. Lines from the poem played in his head. Mother made him write it out, again and again. She locked him in for hours to do it, in the dark, afraid. Afterwards, over-affectionate, she'd held him tight, almost suffocating him beneath her heavy lavender perfume. She'd taught him respect though. He knew what was right and wrong.

The rattling of roosting crows in the darkening night sounded from treetops nearby, breaking the spell. Narrow-eyed, he stared at their ragged silhouettes outlined against the last remnants of sunlight.

They're watching you...
He heard her voice, but he kept watching the girl.

CHAPTER SIX

Martha opened her eyes a touch, just enough to let the light in. It was so bright. Peering through her eyelashes was like looking through sea grass; everything slightly blurred, her eyelids gritty. Her tongue stuck to the roof of her mouth as she swallowed, throat dry. Lifting a hand to her face, her fingers touched something grainy wrapped around her head. She traced the rough line of a gash in her cheek and wondered what had happened. A wave of nausea hit and, exhausted by the effort of looking even for a few seconds, she closed her eyes again. She wasn't sure where she was, and right at that moment she didn't care.

The soft padding of feet woke her. Gentle hands checking her wounds. She opened her eyes fully this time and watched a nurse bustling around the room.

'Hello, Martha. You're back with us. That's good.' Her lilting Scottish accent soothing. 'We've been awfully concerned for you. I'm Staff Nurse Susan Dean. I'll just let Dr Harris know you've woken up.' The nurse had kind eyes. Martha's gaze followed her as she left the room.

The doctor examined her for signs of concussion, taking her blood pressure and heart rate. She answered his questions with little effort or enthusiasm. He asked if she knew what day it was, and she shook her head.

'It's Sunday,' he told her, smiling. 'You had a few knocks, Martha, so now that you're awake, we'll send you up for a scan.'

She didn't protest. Martha wasn't sure she wanted reality to flood in just yet. But, she wondered, where was Dougie? And the dogs? What had happened in the woods? She remembered going out for the walk. Had she really fallen and woken up staring at

Fraser? In amongst the flashes of recall – rushing water below, birds calling overhead, dogs barking from a distance – were images of that lad. Horrible recollections she didn't want to believe were real.

'You've suffered a bump to your head and may have fractured a couple of ribs,' Susan explained. 'Those spectacular bruises make you look like you've been in a road accident. You'll need to take it easy for a bit.'

Martha felt like her whole life had been a car crash recently. And if she was honest, it felt quite good, just lying there, surrendering to other people's care. Unusually for her, she didn't have the energy right then to resist, or worry. So she just lay, staring out at the clouds crossing the grey sky, dozing and listening to the background buzz of a busy hospital, watching Susan coming and going, knowing that soon the world would crowd back in. Susan told her Dougie had visited with his dad, and again with his stepdad, but she'd been asleep both times. 'He's fine, and he says the dogs are too. He knows you'll worry about them. So you just rest and you'll see them all in good time.'

Relieved of any need to worry, Martha moved from long periods of unconsciousness to dozing half awake. In recent months, she hadn't let herself dwell on what had happened with the twins. But in the calm of her hospital bed, her defences were down. Life had always been busy and Martha had never planned to have more kids. She'd never known her birth family. Before she was one, her sister had died. Her mum too. Her adoptive parents, Denise and Oliver Halliday, brought her into their family, and she grew up believing their son was her real brother. They were still close, but as soon as she was old enough and had discovered her family history, she had taken her birth mother's name and become Martha Strangeways. A fling at college when she was twenty-one resulted in Dougie's birth. Orla said she was mad to keep the baby, but, as usual, Martha went her own way, determined it wouldn't sideline her plans to become a reporter. She immediately loved Dougie with a fierce power she hadn't realised she had in her. But between bringing him up as a single parent and pursuing her career, she had little time to herself. As Dougie grew older, he often spent weekends with his dad, and weekdays with her. Her life had settled into a satisfying rhythm of caring for Dougie, work and the gym, where she pounded her body until it was strong and lean. No pain, no gain. Her motto for more than just exercise.

The doctor advised she remain under observation until the full effects of the concussion from the fall had calmed down, but after a couple of nights in hospital she'd had enough. No one had told her what happened to Fraser, and as her strength and clarity returned, she began to feel like she couldn't just lie back and wait. She became restless, the memory of what she'd seen when she found him in the woods now more painful than her injuries.

On the second afternoon, she awoke in a panic. Where was the box? Her eyes scanned the room. How could she have forgotten? There were cards on the bedside. They had been opened and displayed. She picked a couple up and saw they were get-well messages from people in the village – and one from her old newsdesk. Someone must have been in and opened them for her – probably Dougie, or maybe Jamie. But where were her clothes? Anxiety gripped her, head spinning as her fingers scrabbled at the cupboard door. But it was empty. The events of the last few days – was it really just two days? – began to crowd in. Where was her jacket with the precious box inside? A few cards toppled off the cabinet as she slumped back, and she recalled the matchbox dropping to the kitchen floor, then picking it up and safely zipping it away, just a thin layer of Gore-Tex and her own warm skin between the much-repaired box and her heart. Panic building now, she jabbed at the buzzer to the nurses' station.

Susan arrived within seconds.

'Martha, what's the matter? Are you in pain? Do you feel dizzy?'

'My jacket. I need to know where my things have gone. I need them, now,' she gabbled.

'Don't worry. The police took your outdoor clothes, and boots and jacket, because, where you landed ... well, where you came to a stop... ' Susan's voice tailed off. She bent down and began to pick up the cards from the floor.

'Where's my stuff?' Martha whispered. 'I need my jacket, please.' Tears spilled over and down her cheeks.

'It's safe,' said Susan, reassuring. 'I'll go and call the police now and ask if you can have them back. They'll want to speak to you anyway. Dr Harris wouldn't let them in until he was sure you were feeling better.'

Martha nodded. She just needed to hold the box, to know that its contents were safe.

CHAPTER SEVEN

Jamie watched Martha sleeping. All the worry lines in her face had melted. It had been hard on them both, after the fire. They were so caught up in their grief, they lost sight of each other. At first, Martha had been there every day, visiting him in hospital as he recovered. But she had gradually withdrawn into herself, and he'd found it hard to break through to her. The fire and its aftermath still too raw, too awful for them to contemplate together. He hoped in time, they'd reconnect, but they hadn't been in touch much over recent months, although he was still named as her next of kin, as Dougie was still under eighteen.

'It's Mum,' Dougie had explained in the hurried phone call on Saturday. 'She's had an accident and is in hospital in Glasgow. Can you visit her with me?'

Jamie didn't hesitate to say yes.

Martha would never admit she was struggling. That wasn't her nature. She rarely made mistakes either. They'd been going out for about a year, in a relationship that seemed to suit her fine, with no hint of a deeper commitment, when a couple of weeks of intense sickness turned out not to be an inconvenient virus. She had seemed genuinely shocked when she found out she was pregnant, this time with twins. Jamie was secretly pleased about the news, although it wasn't immediately certain she would go through with the pregnancy. He'd always wanted more from their relationship than she seemed prepared to give. Where he yearned for commitment and family, Martha was focused on her career and her son. But she'd decided she would have the babies, and he was relieved, and had also been surprised to learn that she'd had a twin sister who died before they were both a year old. It was something she'd never spoken about before, but when the scan showed twins she told him about the sister she'd never known.

'I sometimes wonder what life might have been like,' she'd said in a rare moment of reflection, 'if I'd grown up with her by my side.' The fact that she had been a twin had influenced her decision to go through with the pregnancy. It seemed to Jamie that the prospect of twins had touched something deep inside Martha.

They'd bought a place in the country, only thirty miles north of Glasgow. Definitely, Jamie thought, a better place to bring up children, and somewhere he could work in a local GP practice. A new start somewhere else with Martha could be the answer to everything.

The place they had chosen was a croft, with five acres of rough grazing. It had been abandoned a generation ago and was pretty much a ruin when they bought it. The views were incredible though, with mountains and forests all around, and only a mile and a half to the village of Strathbran, as the crow flew.

Not long before the twins were born, they discovered something unusual on their land. It hadn't been mentioned in the property details when they'd bought it. It was a scorching hot day, and Martha was determined, despite the advanced stage of her pregnancy, to get through the overgrown bushes on the small hill some distance away from the back of the farmhouse. He'd found her hacking at the undergrowth with garden shears. There was something about the place, she'd said. She needed to see what was there.

He'd laughed, blaming raging hormones, but sure enough, after a couple of hours of work, they'd uncovered solid stone steps that looked like they'd been carved from the rock. And at the top of the hill, in a cool clearing beneath a circle of trees, they'd discovered an unusual stone structure. Tall and shaped like an obelisk, it pointed to the sky, and carvings in the stone seemed to chronicle the path of the moon. It had fascinated them both, although when, after some research, Martha discovered the story attached to this 'moondial' – a tale of a shape-shifting witch who could turn into a crow – she had scoffed. Jamie wasn't so sure though. The overwhelming feeling of isolation he sometimes felt might not just be due to the location of Blacklaw Farm.

They'd hoped that people in the local community, possibly some descendants of the former residents of the farm, would be pleased to see the place brought to life again as a family home. Their children would, in time, go to the village school, and Jamie would hopefully become one of the area's family doctors. It would be good to be part of a community. As Martha's belly swelled, their home seemed to grow too. They moved in just a month before the babies were due.

'Hello, Dr Bain, back again?' The nurse interrupted his train of thought. He'd been to visit Martha with Dougie several times since she'd been admitted three days ago. She'd been mildly sedated with a bad concussion, and in and out of consciousness, so he and Dougie had done little more than greet Martha and give her delicate kisses and placed reassuring hands on hers, before she slept once more. He knew she needed rest more than anything. But God, he'd been desperate to see her.

Dougie appeared at the door. He had Martha's green eyes and dark hair, but he now wore a haunted look that worried Jamie. He cared deeply for Dougie. The lad had always been good at putting on a brave face – again, like his mum. Martha had never worn her heart on her sleeve, which probably came from her upbringing. It had made her insular; afraid to commit. Dougie was similarly quiet and reflective at times. Their darling twins were much more like Jamie, though, with his fair hair and sunny temperament.

He put out his hand and gently touched Martha's smooth cheek. Her eyelashes fluttered open.

'Jamie?' Martha squinted. For a moment, she wasn't entirely sure he was really there.

She turned her head and saw Dougie was in the room too, standing awkwardly near the door. Had they both just arrived, or had they been here the whole time since she last woke up to see them in the room? And when was that?

'How are you feeling today?' Jamie asked.

She winced at the pain from her ribs as she hauled herself up in the bed.

'Better ... I think. Like I need to be out of here,' she answered. 'What day are we?'

'Tuesday,' Dougie said quickly.

She let herself settle a little. She definitely felt more clearheaded. She examined the faces of her son and partner. Jamie offered her a smile. She could see Dougie was struggling to do the same. She patted the covers at her side, and he immediately came over and took a seat beside her. She took hold of his wrist and looked into his eyes. The smile he gave her was real now, and relieved. They sat in comfortable silence for a while.

Finally, she couldn't hold back. The face she had seen was haunting her.

'So ... that was Fraser I saw that day, wasn't it?'

Dougie and Jamie exchanged a nervous look.

'What happened to him?'

Dougie stood up. He looked twitchy.

'I'm going to get a coffee,' he mumbled. 'Want one, Jamie?'

Jamie said yes, and Dougie left the room, just as shadows appeared outside the frosted glass. The nurse came in again, rubber-soled shoes squeaking against the linoleum floor.

'The police are here,' she said. 'They're wondering if they could speak to you. I can ask them to leave if you're not up to it.'

'No, no. Tell them to come in,' Martha said, smoothing her hair, and wondering what she must look like.

The nurse went back to the door and beckoned, and a large policeman entered the room, accompanied by a smaller officer holding a bag.

'DI Derek Summers.' He held out a beefy hand, but shook hers surprisingly carefully. 'How are you feeling, Martha? Up to answering a few questions?'

Martha nodded. 'I'll do what I can. Still a bit fuzzy, you know, but ... but I want to know what happened myself.'

'You're aware there was a body found near where you fell? A young lad. Fraser MacDonald.'

'Yes,' she said. 'I ... I saw him. His face...'

'When you fell, the rescue team called out to look for you found young Fraser close by bent over a tree. We...' Summers paused, checked the open door behind him. 'We don't think it was an accidental death. We're still waiting for the full results from the post mortem, but the circumstances suggest it wasn't a simple fall.'

Martha sat back, her dizziness increasing suddenly.

'Was it ... suicide?' Jamie said.

'We don't know yet, Dr Bain. There are some, shall we say, unusual aspects to this case, which we need to explore fully, but, as I say, we're not treating the death as an accident.' He turned to face Martha again. 'You were found so close to the scene, and you're our only witness so far. We need to know anything you can remember. Do you recall seeing anyone else out there?'

Martha couldn't believe Fraser would have wanted to end his

own life. He was always so full of life, had so much potential and energy. She'd rule out suicide – and it sounded like the police had too. She tried to focus her tired brain on what had happened that day. She could see the path, the river and then recalled slipping.

'So it really was Fraser. I keep having flashbacks of seeing his face, but my head's been so messed up, I wondered whether they were just because he was missing...'

Summers nodded. 'I'm afraid your memory's correct.'

Another image of those horrible moments dropped into her head.

'Was there something on his back? A tattoo?'

Summers sat up straight

'Yes,' he said. 'It was lines of script. Someone had written them on him.'

CHAPTER EIGHT

Stunned, Martha felt sick as the thoughts of what might have happened to her son's best mate began to spiral out of control.

'So ... so you think it was murder,' she said to Summers. 'Are you sure he didn't just fall?'

Summers shrugged. 'The lad had drugs in him. But we don't think he'd taken them himself. It looks like he'd ingested some, but there's also a puncture mark in the back of his shoulder, suggesting someone injected him too. And importantly, he has a head injury that he sustained *before* he died.'

Summers was clearly hoping she would know more about what happened to Fraser. But she had no idea how long he had been where she found him. She told the officer that his mum said he'd been out overnight when Martha last spoke to her.

'On Saturday afternoon I took my dogs for their usual walk,' she explained. 'It's a route I do most days. I'd been out there the day before and I hadn't seen anything.' Martha shuddered at the thought of what Fraser had been through. 'It's so awful. How long had he been there do you think?'

'Twenty-four hours, we think, but no more than that.'

She wondered suddenly about the strong scent she'd caught before she fell. Had she been able to detect anything in the air on her walk the previous day? The occasional whiff of a dead animal was nothing unusual in the forest, she told Summers, so she wouldn't have thought twice about it.

'There was a rotting deer carcass not far away from where you fell,' he replied. 'It could have been that.'

She prayed Fraser hadn't been there alive on the Friday, waiting to be found.

'People had been out looking for him,' she said. 'It wasn't part of his running route, according to his mum, but I'm sure someone would have found him before I did. Have you spoken to other dog walkers? We all use those woods.'

'We've been going door to door, interviewing anyone who might be able to help,' Summers said. 'Now, can you tell me what you recall of the moment leading up to your fall?'

She shivered and tried to focus. 'I was out for longer than I'd intended and started back when I realised it was getting dark. I was walking up from the river, calling the dogs, when I missed my footing on the slippery ground, and just went.'

'Do you remember seeing anyone?' he asked.

Martha shook her head. 'I honestly wish I could tell you more,' she said. 'I know I slipped and was trying to grab something to stop me falling, but I went down and must have bashed my head. When I came to, I looked up, and that's when I saw Fraser.' Her voice began to tremble. 'The next thing I knew, I woke up in here.' A deep unease had gripped her as she related her story, and some of the dizziness was beginning to return.

Summers sat back, placing his hands on his knees. It looked like he was about to leave it at that, but the journalist in Martha sensed a story and wanted to keep him here.

'What else do you know?' she asked. 'Are there any suspects?'

'We're at the early stages of this investigation, Martha,' he said. 'We're trying to determine more about Fraser's movements prior to going missing, and hopefully that will give us some leads.'

'What about the writing on his back?' She fixed Summers with her stare. 'Does that have anything to do with his death?'

But DI Summers wouldn't be drawn any further. 'We're looking at this death from all possible angles,' he said.

Martha frowned. There was no point pushing him for more. And she decided to keep to herself the feeling she had that she was being watched that day. Those ancient woods were full of stories, including ones tied to Blacklaw, which wasn't too far away from where she'd fallen. It was easy to let your imagination run wild if you were out there alone when the sun began to set. She had dismissed the feeling at the time and wasn't about to make herself look idiotic by admitting she might have been spooked in the woods.

'There's another thing, Martha,' Summers said. 'There was a break-in at your house sometime over the weekend. Your neighbour noticed that the back gate was open, and when she went to check it, she saw the window in the door was broken.'

'What?'

'There was a bit of a mess inside – drawers and cupboards were open, and it looked like someone had gone through them. But your computer and other higher-value goods were still there.'

'I'm shocked,' said Martha. 'Strathbran has always been such a safe place.'

'Our officers secured the property, and apart from the neighbour who had alerted them, no one else had seen anything unusual, or anyone around the place.'

Martha wondered what was going on. Why would someone have broken into her home, and not bothered to take any of the valuables? What had they been looking for? It made her more determined than ever to get back home.

'Oh, I almost forgot,' Summers said. 'DC Walker here has something for you.' He gestured to the other officer, who'd been standing by the door during the interview.

Walker came over to the bed and handed Martha a bag. Her things were inside. Martha relaxed as she took it from him, feeling the hard edge of the matchbox through the plastic. How easy it was for everything to change, she thought, as she watched the police officers leave the room after saying their goodbyes. One day you're fine, in control; the next: catastrophe and it's all gone. It made her think about her recent past, what she had lost. She'd kept the memories of the fire at bay for almost two years. But she still missed her little boys terribly. Woke often in the night, hearing their phantom cries on the wind, or capturing a hint of their sweet smell. But now, languishing in a hospital bed, her body battered and bruised, she couldn't hold her own tragic history at bay.

The day after the fire, when the police had eventually allowed Martha back to the farm at the end of the muddy track, even the sheep had followed her with sympathetic eyes. The heavy stench of chemicals and smoke still swirled in the air; she had smelled it as she got out of the car. She looked around, their home in ruins, the roof caved in, blackened timbers jagged against the sky. The fire had taken hold quickly, the heat so fierce there was little left of the building or its contents. Sorrow overwhelmed her, grief tightening around her, contracting her throat as she faced everything she had lost. Jamie was in hospital, fighting for his life, not there to hold her hand.

'They wouldn't have known what was happening,' the family liaison officer told Martha afterwards. 'The smoke would have been overwhelming pretty quickly.'

Her guilt and grief had made her angry. At herself. At the world. None of it was fair, and Martha blamed herself most of all. The news that the children would have died quickly was no consolation. Her beautiful babies gone, while she was at a fucking press conference.

CHAPTER NINE

It was Wednesday, and Martha was out of bed and gathering her things. She wanted to be home, although the doctor was still trying to persuade her not to leave the hospital. As she took down the cards and slipped them into a bag, a familiar voice pierced the air. Despite the obvious attempt at lowering her tone, she still recognised Orla.

'God, Martha. What the hell have you been doing?' She enveloped her friend in a tight, highly perfumed hug, which while comforting, knocked the breath out of her. 'Ow,' Martha said. 'Sore ribs.'

Behind Orla, Dougie appeared, wide-eyed.

She reached out her hand to her son, and Orla pulled back.

'I'm sorry, Martha. Dougie, go on, you can give your mum a hug too. Be careful though. I'm just so delighted to see you alive. What a shock I got when I arrived in the wilds and found out what had happened. I've been calling for days and had no idea what was going on.' Orla barely took a breath between sentences. 'Listen, I'll give you guys some time, OK?'

She strode from the room without waiting for an answer.

'Hello pet,' Martha said, as he scanned her face. 'The bruises are looking really good now, aren't they?' she joked.

He nodded, giving her a wide-eyed grin.

'I can't believe what happened to Fraser, Mum,' he said putting the hold-all he'd brought with him on the bed.

'I know. Me neither,' she replied. Then paused for a moment. 'Have you given any more thought to what that writing might have been and why he would have had it on him?' she said gently, asking the question casually as she put her things in the bag. She and Jamie had told Dougie about the black lettering on Fraser's back the day before.

'I've honestly no idea. He definitely didn't have a tattoo. He would have told me about something like that, and he was always taking his top off in the gym at school.'

Orla came back in, balancing three plastic cups in a cardboard carrier.

'So, I'm yours and Dougie's lift home,' she said. 'I've cleared it with Jamie.'

Martha took a grateful sip of the coffee, the caffeine and sugar giving her a lift as she watched her friend. It was such a relief to see Orla. It had been a while, and she realised now how much she'd missed her. She stretched her hand out and Orla took it, squeezing her fingers. 'Hey, it's OK, I'm here now.'

Martha's throat tightened. It wasn't just what had happened in the woods. She realised everything she had been through since the twins died had been held back, and Orla's sudden arrival might just cause the fragile dam she'd built around her emotions to flood out and drown her.

'Now, what the eff happened, Martha?' Orla said, in a brisk tone, toning down her language in front of Dougie. 'Jesus, woman, haven't you had enough drama in your life?'

'I don't know,' Martha said. 'Fraser's mother called the day before, looking for him. I thought he was probably out at a girlfriend's house, and Dougie hadn't heard from him either.' Dougie shook his head. 'We were all worried, but honestly, I was really hoping he would just turn up. I took Skye and BJ for a walk, like I do every day. It was getting dark, and I was on my way back...' Her voice trailed off, the sudden horror rushing in.

'He was dead,' she whispered, stifling a sob.

Orla wrapped her arms tight around Martha. 'Come on. It's OK. I'm sure they'll catch whoever did this.'

Martha shook herself and pulled her body out of Orla's arms. She wiped her eyes with her sleeve.

'And if they don't, I will,' she said.

CHAPTER TEN

Fraser's death was front-page news; the *Stirling Advertiser* carried a large photograph of the teenager in his footy kit, grinning out at Martha.

Finally back at home late on Wednesday morning, Martha picked up the paper from the doormat. Lying on her bed upstairs, she read the article under the headline 'Murder Investigation Launched into Teen Death'.

It reported that Fraser's phone had been traced and found, broken, in the forest. The reporter speculated he had dropped it while running, but no other traces of the lad had been found in the vicinity. At the end of the article there was a note about a church service taking place today. Not a funeral, as the procurator fiscal hadn't released Fraser's body, but a memorial service. The boy's family needed something to cling to. Martha wanted to go and pay her respects, despite having only just arrived home from hospital. It was coming on for a week since Fraser had last been seen alive, she thought. She wondered whether she'd hear from the police again today. If not, she would start asking questions herself.

'You ready, Mum?' Dougie shouted up the stairs a couple of hours later.

She'd had a good look round the house after she'd arrived home, and was relieved that Jamie had been in and tidied the place up after the break-in. Like the police, she hadn't found anything missing. It was weird. Unsettling. She looked out of the window. It was raining stair rods outside.

'Down in a minute, pet,' she replied.

She glanced in the mirror, pushed her hair back from her eyes, noting the dark shadows beneath, and that the bruising around her left eye was starting to change colour. 'Look at the state of you,' she said to her reflection. 'A face only a mother could love.' She glanced down at her nondescript black jeans and jumper. They would need to do, with a coat over the top. Clothes she hoped wouldn't attract attention.

'Are you there, Dougie?' she called as she walked stiffly down the stairs and into the hall.

He appeared at the door to the living room, eyes brimming.

'Oh, Dougie.'

'Mum, I don't know if I can go through with this,' he sobbed into her shoulder. 'I can't believe he's gone. I mean, it's Fraser...'

Martha felt her heart contract. 'We don't have to go,' she said, stroking the hair back from his tear-swollen face.

'We do. I need to be there, for his family. It's my fault,' he said.

She pulled him in close again. 'Dougie, something awful has happened, and we need to find a way through it. But this is not your fault, OK?'

She took his hand, and grabbed an umbrella and her keys from the hook by the door.

'Come on. I've got you.'

He still looked stricken as she pulled the door closed behind them. The umbrella unfolded with a snap, and they stepped out into the deluge. Martha braced herself. By her side, Dougie pulled his jacket collar up around his neck.

'Come under here, pet, you'll be drenched,' Martha said.

'I'm fine, Mum,' he mumbled awkwardly. 'It's only a five-minute walk down the hill.'

As they pushed through the gate into the churchyard, the rain seemed heavier, gathering in the old oak trees and coming down in a drenching glut, buffeted by the wind. The sound of Bunyan's 'To Be a Pilgrim' playing on the organ drifted out as they made their way between the ancient gravestones to join the queue of mourners entering the building.

The kirk was built in 1790 on the site of a former Pictish monastery. Standing stones from even earlier times could be found scattered across local farmers' fields. When they'd first come to the village, Jamie and Martha had attended a talk in the church on the history of the area and the pagan religion practised here in the past. The 'new' church building was constructed as a five-bay rectangular chapel of ease, with a bellcote and a porch. Gothic wrought ironwork and raven finials on the kirk roof stood out in silhouette. They were a nod to the earlier pagan traditions. Martha couldn't help looking up at them every time she passed the building. Real crows often perched next to their sculpted cousins. When they moved, it always sent a chill down her spine. Today was no exception. There was one sitting there now, and when it flapped its wings, she shuddered.

It was the first time she'd been into a church since the aftermath of the fire. She looked over at the corner of the yard, under the rowan tree, where the small stone marking her boys' grave stood. She could hardly bear to look and was stabbed by a shard of guilt; she should have been going every week and laying flowers to remember her babies. She wondered if Jamie went. Her hand moved involuntarily towards her pocket, where the box was safe.

Martha heard a voice and turned to see Orla, perfectly made up, her long blonde tresses ironed to perfection and wearing a figure-hugging black trouser suit.

'You came prepared for the country, then,' Martha murmured in Orla's ear, as she bent in for a quick hug in the church porch.

'Prepared for anything,' Orla replied, as Martha turned to greet Reverend Locke, who was at the door.

His hair was slicked back and although freshly shaven, there was already a shadow across his jaw. His ink-black cassock caught the relentless rain, and the gale billowed through the kirk door, but he still greeted everyone with a sombre handshake and a welcome. Dougie seemed to hesitate when he saw the minister, pausing before he took Reverend Locke's outstretched hand. It was only a second, and then he moved on. Martha squared her shoulders and held out her own hand, looking directly at Locke.

'You're very welcome in our church, Martha,' he said. 'I

understand this must be difficult for you, but we're glad you could come today.' His hand felt cold, odd considering it had clasped those of dozens of mourners already that afternoon. There was something about his eyes that unnerved her, and she recalled the moment last week when she saw him smoking. Not many people made such direct and unnerving eye contact – she felt as though he could see right into her thoughts. Locke's gaze moved on, his expression briefly changing to one of appreciation as Orla approached, giving him her most dazzling TV smile. So, the reverend wasn't made of stone after all, Martha thought, seeing a slight flush rise on his neck as he shook hands with her friend. He glanced back at Martha, and she simply nodded, saying nothing, and moved ahead, touching her son's soaking jacket as they were bustled onward by the queue of people eager to get inside and out of the storm.

A wave of recognition rippled through the assembled con-gregation as she and Dougie took a spare pew to the left-hand side. She breathed in the strong smell of flowers, dust and furniture polish. A woman caught her eye, smiling nervously. She remembered the last time she was in this church, at the memorial service for her babies. She'd sat at the front, with Dougie – Jamie still too unwell to make it. The weight of the pain she'd felt then threatened to rush back. She swallowed, steadying herself on the back of the wooden pew in front, and focused on the hymn book balanced on the shelf.

Soon, the church was packed. A busload of pupils from Glenview High School had arrived, bringing a buzz of teenage energy. Even in their uniforms, the girls were made up to the nines, Instagram-perfect. The boys were stiff in shirts and ties, expressions darting and wary. Finally, a large man entered. It was the detective who had interviewed her yesterday at the hospital. His eyes, unusually prominent, scanned the congregation, and she noticed him give a slight nod to the minister before he slipped into a seat at the back and the service began.

As Reverend Locke started speaking, Martha felt as though

she was watching a repeat of her own children's service – but from a distance, as if it was on a screen. Her fingers tightened on the back of the worn pew. She worried something inside her – feelings she'd kept contained since the fire – might break. A photograph of Fraser had been blown up and framed. It was propped up on a stand at the front, flanked by flowers and candles. Reverend Locke talked about what a great kid he had been, loved by many people; he spoke of the community's shock at his death.

'Aye, well, the police should be doing more to find out what happened to him,' someone behind Martha said in a loud whisper. A couple of people in front turned to stare at her, clearly thinking it was Martha who had spoken. She shook her head and looked at the minister.

'For such a young lad, Fraser packed a lot into his seventeen years,' Locke said. 'He loved music and sport, especially football and running. His friends, many of whom are here today, were very important to him. We must keep these memories alive in our hearts and hold on to them during the dark days ahead.

'We pray to our Lord Jesus to bring strength to Fraser's parents, Jane and Fraser Senior, his brother, Kyle, and his friends. His death was too sudden and too soon, but we know, and draw comfort from knowing, that he is in a better place.'

Fraser's mum let out a loud whimper. Martha recalled Jane sitting in her kitchen just a few days ago. The woman's anxious smile. Her fear for her son. How could they have known? Despair shook Jane's body, as she was held up between her husband and younger son. Martha was struck by how small Jane seemed. She'd had that thought when she'd knocked on her door, she recalled. But now she looked even smaller. Shrunken by grief. A part of her had disappeared forever – just as part of Martha had gone. Her life could never be the same without her boys.

She let out the long breath she had been holding, the knot in her throat painful now, and closed her eyes. Her fingers enclosed the small rough package in her pocket, its sandpaper edge now worn. She felt Orla squeeze her arm very gently. She opened her eyes to find them blurred with unshed tears. Beside her, Dougie's shoulders shook and, head bowed, he stared at the floor while silent tears slid down his face. She slipped her hand into his and squeezed his fingers. Someone coughed behind her.

The mourners, many heads bowed and tissues clasped in many hands, filed slowly out at the end of the service. A few were muttering about the police. They'd been doing door-to-door inquiries in the village, she heard, which was what Summers had told her.

Dougie turned in the pew, his face pale and drained, full lips pressed into a tight line.

'You coming, Mum? People are gathering at the pub.'

'No, I'm going to head back home. I'm still feeling pretty weak. I'll see you later?'

Momentary relief flickered in his eyes; he didn't want her there, she realised, her bruised face – and bruised heart – attracting awkward attention on what was Fraser's day.

'I'll come along,' Orla said. 'I'd like to ask the reverend for some advice, if he's got a moment.'

Martha shook her head, wondering what Orla would be wanting with their country minister. Pulling her coat around her, she stepped into the queue of people in the aisle.

'Martha?'

She turned around. 'Yes?'

'Detective Inspector Derek Summers.'

'Oh yes, we met at the hospital.' He had the bearing of a policeman. She'd met enough of them in her career to recognise it. He stood tall, confident, legs apart. Had she met him before? Somewhere else? A distant bell sounded in her memory, but she couldn't quite place him.

'Would you mind if we had another chat?' he said.

'No, of course. I was hoping I'd be able to speak to the police again,' Martha said. 'You can come up to the house, if you like.'

He nodded and she felt his fingers on her back as they were herded out into daylight. Reverend Locke thanked her as she dropped a twenty-pound note into the collection plate at the door.

'It would be good to see you here again, Martha,' he said. 'You're always welcome.'

Martha knew her smile must look empty. God hadn't been there for her when she'd lost everything. She felt no calling to any religious place. She had somehow got through the service for her boys in one piece, but her soul had been numb ever since and for her there was no crumb of comfort in religion.

It was a five-minute walk up the hill with the policeman at her side.

'Hope you don't mind dogs,' she murmured as they walked into the hallway. She could hear them fussing in the kitchen. He looked around, taking it all in, the stone flags into the kitchen beyond, the staircase up to the left leading to a dogleg. Light streamed in through the window halfway up. It must have stopped raining outside. She hoped the policeman wouldn't notice the dust and the flecks of mud scattered on the stair carpet. She hadn't noticed the muck until now.

'I'll stick the kettle on.' They went through into the kitchen, and he leaned down, allowing the dogs to sniff his hand. They accepted him, which for Martha was a good sign. She opened the back door to the garden and they tumbled outside.

'Beautiful view,' DI Summers remarked, looking from the window at the distant hills, where the tallest local mountain, Ben Lomond, stood against the sky. 'Now that the rain has cleared, you can see for miles.'

She made two mugs of strong coffee. He declined her offer of milk or sugar and took a seat at the table.

'Thanks, Martha. So – just to confirm what we discussed yesterday: we've launched a murder investigation. Have you remembered anything else from the day you fell?'

'Murder.' The word was heavy in her mouth. 'In this place.'

Summers watched her. She knew this was a technique – just letting her speak unprompted. But she needed prompting – and she wanted to find out what more they knew and hadn't divulged yet.

'Do you have anything more you can tell me?' she said. 'Anything that might jog my memory?'

'Well, I can tell you that Fraser didn't die from the fall. The actual cause of death was choking. He inhaled vomit into his lungs. The head injury and scrapes to his knees happened before he died.'

She examined him. 'Couldn't he have taken something in the woods and then fallen, like I did ... Although I'd not taken anything, of course.'

'We found traces of ketamine in him, a horse tranquilliser, but also another drug. An anti-psychotic called Risperdal. An unusual cocktail of chemicals, although ketamine is used recreationally in some circles,' he added. 'Anyway, we don't think he fell. He was dead already and was dumped where you found him.'

'And what leads do you have?' Martha had Summers talking now, and wanted to keep him going. 'I wouldn't have thought Fraser was into drugs. He was best mates with my son, Dougie...' She felt a sudden chill. 'His poor parents...' she murmured.

As a reporter, she'd spent years carrying out death knocks and dealing with bereaved families. Especially in her younger days on newspapers, when the juniors were often given the worst jobs, combing through death notices before the paper went to print to see what stories they could find. The age of the person or donations to an unusual charity often the only thing they needed to set them off on the hunt for a good human-interest tale.

'It's the writing on his back that we're trying to fit into it all,' Summers continued. 'His friends and family don't know anything about it. Is it some new craze that kids are into these days? A lot of them seem to be getting tattoos, but not like this. I mean, who would have poetry written on their back?'

Martha stared at Summers. 'Poetry?'

'The writing on his back – it was lines from a poem. I don't recall the title – something in Gaelic. We believe they were put there either just before or not long after his death.'

Martha realised her mouth was hanging open. 'What did the poem say?'

'Something about witches and crows. The ink is being analysed too, to see if we can trace where that came from. Anyway,' Summers went to stand up, 'I've taken up enough of your time. If anything else comes to mind, you will get in touch?' He pulled a card from his breast pocket and handed it to Martha.

'Oh, come on. You must know more than that,' she pushed. There was something about him that she warmed to. And despite the case being so close to home, her instincts were twitching at the prospect of an investigation. 'People will be frantic, you know, wondering what to think. Should we be keeping our kids in? And who is supplying these drugs if he'd been taking them?'

Wind raced down the hallway, carrying with it leaves and the distant sound of kids playing in the school field across the street. DI Summers looked up as Dougie appeared.

Dougie looked from Martha to Summers sitting in the chair. Like Martha, he was unaccustomed to people paying them visits these days.

'Hello, Dougie.' The boy nodded at the big man in front of him. 'I've just been chatting to your mother, and I'd like to have a word with you too, now you're here. I understand you knew Fraser very well.'

Dougie's face paled, eyes wide.

'We've recovered his phone,' Summers went on, 'and although it was broken, we've managed to access messages and calls from the cloud. It looks as though the message he sent you Dougie, asking for help, was the last one. We know you tried to call him a number of times too.'

'I did try to call,' Dougie said. 'But he never picked up.

Honestly? I just thought he was being daft.' Martha saw bewilder-
ment tightening her son's face.

'I think right now isn't the time to question Dougie,' she said
firmly, worried that a conversation with the policeman today
might send her boy over the edge. 'It's been a hell of a day, and my
son is in no state to be answering questions. We can arrange it for
another day?'

'OK,' Summers said reluctantly. 'But sooner rather than later
if you don't mind, and please let me know if you do recall anything
else, Martha. Sometimes it can take a while to remember details,
but they can come back, and we'd be really grateful for any
assistance you can give us. I can see myself out.' He stood and
looked around the room. 'Did you notice if anything was taken
in the break-in?' he asked.

She shook her head. 'Not that I can see.'

'Well, there'll be extra patrols around the village until we find
out what happened to Fraser, but make sure you keep your doors
locked if you're out.'

The door closed and Martha breathed out.

It was *poetry* that was written on the lad's back? That was crazy.
Should she say anything to Dougie about it? She glanced up, but
he'd left the kitchen and she heard his footsteps going up the stairs.
Crows and witches, Summers had said. She shivered, thoughts of
some kind of ritual killing making her blood chill. And to a boy
she knew, Dougie's friend.

They had to find whoever had done this, and quickly.

The Book of Shadows

He comes for me today, and I am so happy my heart could burst. It's true that I will leave my family here in Viborg, but what an adventure, and with such a man. I shall make the most of this summer with him. I've watched him with my father all these years and will take with me the treasures he has brought me during his visits. I'll return with him to his home, a place I cannot wait to see. Such history there, with castles and kings and queens. He has told me of great mountains and deep lochs.

My grandmother tells me the magic there is ancient and not unlike our own. She has given me instruction on charms for protection and to invoke love. I have written them in this book with the ink she sent with me, alongside rituals for the seasons and the cycles of the moon. I shall take the book with me, but she warns me to keep it hid. For she says he will not understand.

CHAPTER ELEVEN

They were all in church. They never usually came, but had turned out in force for the dead boy.

Hypocrites. They mourn him, but he didn't deserve their sympathy.

She was loud in his thoughts today, but she was right. Those girls in their short skirts again, even in church; they had no respect.

A disgrace.

What kind of parents let them go out like that? He couldn't show his outrage here, though. They played modern music that the boy liked. Ridiculous. What had happened to people these days? He watched their lips move as they sang hymns that meant nothing to them, having to read the words they should have known by heart. Fraser's mother was crying, her mouth distorted with grief. Her husband's arms tight around her; without him she would have crumpled to the ground. He regarded them all with contempt. They had no idea what their son and the other two had done, that night by the moondial. He'd watched them in the circle of moonlight, with their pagan candles and whatever the girl had laid down. Ignorant of what they would unbind with their chant. '*Crow they call her, trickster, shame, Feannag Dhubh to bear all blame.*' He shuddered at the memory. the shadow that had threatened to engulf them in the night. They had fled, screaming. But the thing had plagued him ever since.

He looked around. Wondering if anyone else could hear the voice that was so clear to him. But no one took any notice. It was him the shade had latched on to. In the kirk, they were all focused on the service, on their memories of the boy. Fraser was in a better place now, thanks to him. He watched her too, as she came in through the door. Her wind-blown hair framing her face and those startling green eyes. She was trying not to draw attention to herself, keeping her head down, but everyone's gaze followed her. Her teenage son, almost as tall as she was, stepped in with her and they sat together, staring ahead.

He had the same striking features, although he'd grown since the night he'd been with Fraser and that girl at the moondial. The mother had something about her that had caught his attention before. A strength she didn't know she had, perhaps. He could see a heavy weight lay across her though, no lightness at her mouth.

That day in the woods, he'd thought at one point, when she'd looked back and then carried on, that she sensed he was there. At the river he had watched from a distance, upwind, in case the dogs caught his scent. He'd enjoyed observing her, particularly when she fell. It happened quickly, and he had waited, listening to the voice.

Don't go near. Let her fall. Let her find him.

He'd waited, as instructed, until she stopped tumbling down the slope, and wondered if she was dead too. His heart lifted a little when she moved. Through binoculars he had watched the horror dawning on her face as her eyes focused on the lifeless boy lying over the felled tree trunk.

He looked around the kirk again. And back at her son. That girl would surely be here too somewhere; he scanned the congregation for her. Her bright hair stood out, despite her attempts to stay hidden between her parents. It was all their fault, the three of them. They didn't know what they'd done with their damned rite. They were all in danger. And he knew now there was still work to do. They'd pay.

CHAPTER TWELVE

Another day had gone by, but still no news. Martha had seen officers in the village after the service, going door to door. She'd heard the gossip. People were afraid – both of who had killed Fraser, but also that the police investigation might stall in a small place like this, miles from anywhere.

'They would have solved it already if it was in the city,' she'd heard a couple of young mums saying at the primary-school gates. They weren't the only ones sceptical about the investigation, and Martha didn't blame them.

She was both sickened and intrigued by the writing that had been discovered on Fraser's body. The idea that the killer might have done it was grim. Yet she felt a need to find out more. What did it mean? And why hadn't the police released information about it to the public? She powered up her MacBook, its first airing in months. Orla would be over later – she'd already sent a text message saying she'd be bringing wine. So Martha had better do her search now, before she was sidetracked for the rest of the day.

She keyed in 'witch' and 'crows' and 'poem'. The first page contained links to dozens of websites about corvids, ranging through everything from the birds in folklore, to the Tower of London ravens, right down to a few sites with dire poetry, one of which began 'Oh Crow, you know, I love you so'. Oh dear, she wasn't going to find out anything this way. She would need to dig deep and reawaken her story-hunting skills.

She'd always been good at her job and had worked hard to get to the top, ignoring the misogynistic dinosaurs that powered many newsdesks. In male-dominated newsrooms, where the smell of testosterone competed with that of printer's ink, women like Martha were sometimes not credited for their intelligence. But when she entered a room, men often caught their breath. Women, too, on occasion. Where others shied away from the hardest jobs – the door knock when a loved one had just died, or a kerb-side interview with the high-profile businessman who'd been caught coming out of a notorious city brothel – Martha had always stepped up without a second thought. It wasn't that she didn't care about how people reacted to her questions. But she turned their secrets and tragedies into newsprint, to be talked about in the pub or at the dinner table. That was the life of a tabloid journalist.

However, chasing stories in the pursuit of truth, which had always been so important to her, had faded since her boys died. But she felt the beginnings of something now. A strong sense that there was more to Fraser's death than any of them yet knew. The number for the police press office was still in her phone, and Martha banked on a junior media officer picking up when she dialled. She needed someone who wouldn't guess she was on a fishing trip.

'Police Scotland Press Office, Jodie speaking. How can I help you?'

'Hi, it's Martha Strangeways here from the *Evening Standard*. Hoping you can help me out, Jodie,' said Martha, friendly. 'Are you new in there? I don't think I've spoken to you before.'

'Hello, Martha. Yes, I've only been in here for a few weeks,' Jodie said, cautious. 'What can I help you with?'

'I'm trying to find out a bit of information relating to an investigation into the death of a young lad out in the Trossachs in Stirlingshire. His name is Fraser MacDonald. He lived in Strathbran.'

'I'm not sure there's any update at present...' The woman hesitated.

Martha cut in. 'I was speaking to DI Summers earlier on, and he told me about the poem. He couldn't recall the exact title, but said if I found out anything I was to share it. Sounds like a bit of an odd one, but I just need confirmation of the title. I'm trying to help by finding out background information, that's all.'

The media officer tapped away on her keyboard while other voices, presumably a bank of call handlers in headsets, were answering inquiries.

'Look, it sounds like you're really busy in there today, but if you could just check the name of the poem that DI Summers mentioned, that's really all I'm looking for. Then I can leave you be. It would be a massive help.'

'Ok, Ms ... what did you say your last name was again?'

'Strangeways, Martha Strangeways,' she replied.

'I suppose if you've spoken to DI Summers then it should be OK to confirm. I'm just checking now.' There was silence for a few seconds before she came back on the line. 'It looks as though the information you're looking for is "Feannag Dhubh",' she said. 'Not sure I said that right though.'

'That's great Jodie, thanks so much for your help.' Martha put the phone down on the table next to her. 'Bingo.' She now had confirmation she was on the right track. She stretched – her still-aching ribs nipped if she stayed in one position too long – then she got back onto her laptop and typed in the name of the poem.

Almost the first result she read astonished her:

'The Feannag Dhubh legend originated in the seventeenth century during the time of the Scottish witch trials. A young woman, born as the daughter of a church minister at Blacklaw Hill, near Strathbran (or the Glen of Ravens), was tried and executed as a witch at a site nearby.'

'Bloody hell,' she said out loud. Blacklaw Hill was the place behind her old farmhouse, where she and Jamie had discovered the moondial. So the poem and the moondial were connected. And someone had inked a poem linked to Strathbran on the back of a boy from the village. But why?

On the next page of search results, a link appeared to a website that looked homemade. There was a grainy, sepia-toned PDF file with the poem written out in a fancy-looking font. It read "Feannag Dhubh ('Black Crow')", with the text of the poem, and then 'Anonymous, Strathbran, 1642' at the bottom.

Feannag Dhubh

Through midnight haar she struts alone
Ancient spirit, twisted crone
Once revered braw and fey
Til cries of hex cast folk away
Crow they call her, trickster, shame
Feannag Dhubh to bear all blame

For every ill that bade this way
She's shunned, chased off by night and day
In ink-dark forests, floats mountain witch
Her feathered cloak black as pitch
Fear manifest, how near she comes
To strip all things of flesh and bones

In shadows Feannag Dhubh doth hide
While winter frosts o'er land reside
But as dark seasons yearn to turn
Through kirkyard murk grave worms do churn
Hide all treasures, Keep them safe
For things that gleam her eye will crave

Starvation months are nearing end
She'll strike new lambs where no defend
As fires blaze at Blacklaw braes
Her moondial rouses dead again
While ashen feathers fall from sky
Under a ghealach làn Feannag fly
Her craws cry end of season soon
As Ostara rises at Crow Moon.

She read the poem a couple of times, but felt none the wiser about why it had been written on Fraser's body. She wondered which lines had been used – not the whole thing, surely. She strained to recall what she had seen on his back before she fell unconscious. But the image of Fraser's face made her shudder. She looked at the poem again. She shuddered too at the line about fires blazing at Blacklaw. Had there been a fire there hundreds of years before? They can't have been uncommon back then, but she still felt a chill at the words. At the other bad memories it stirred.

She tapped the pencil she was making notes with against her teeth, trying to refocus on her task. During her years as an investigative journalist, she'd come across 'modern' pagans and witchcraft practitioners several times, and knew they were attracted to tales of witch trials like this, and to the places where they'd taken place. She typed in a few combinations of appropriate terms, and within a few minutes had found a group of practising Wiccans in the area – with a number to call. They had to know more about this very local legend – which appeared to have originated at her own farm. She dialled the number and after a couple of rings, a woman answered.

'Hi, is that the right number for the Forest Wiccans?'

'Yes, how can I help you?' The woman's voice was soft and melodic.

Martha introduced herself and mentioned that she'd recently lived at Blacklaw Farm.

'I've just discovered a poem called "Feannag Dhubh" and I'm keen to find out more about its connections to Blacklaw Hill. I found your website and thought you might be able to fill me in.'

After a brief hesitation, the woman said, 'Yes, I can help you with that, but it would probably be best to meet face to face if you've any time to do that?'

'Yes, that's fine. I'm free this afternoon.'

Half an hour later, Martha parked up near the ancient graveyard at the old kirk in Aberfoyle, where they had agreed to meet. While she waited she studied an information board telling the history of the place and of the Reverend Robert Kirk. He had supposedly been abducted by fairies, and was buried in the graveyard after his body was found on nearby Doon Hill.

'Hello there. Martha?'

Martha jumped and turned around. She hadn't heard anyone approach. The woman was small, slight, with long red hair tied in a plait over her shoulder. She greeted Martha with a warm smile.

'You mentioned on the phone that you lived at Blacklaw…' She gave Martha a sad smile. 'I'm assuming you are part of the family who moved there before the fire?' Her tone was gentle, empathetic, and Martha had the strange feeling she had met her before.

'I'm sorry, I didn't catch your name,' she said.

'That's because I didn't give it to you. I don't like to reveal too much of myself until I meet people.'

She took Martha's proffered hand in both of her own. Her grip was warm and firm.

'I'm Helen Horne,' she said. 'I'm sorry for being so mysterious, but we do have to be careful who we meet with. There's still a lot of suspicion directed at us, from those who don't understand our ways.' She paused, again with the sad smile. 'Shall we walk while we talk?' And she gestured at the gate into the kirkyard.

As they walked between the green-grey stones, Martha explained about discovering the poem – making no mention of the lines written on Fraser's back, of course – and described her astonishment at finding it was connected to her former home.

'There's more than just a connection Martha. Blacklaw is an extremely special and sacred place. The Feannag Dhubh was a young woman with many talents, but she was severely misunderstood. She was a healer and helped many local women, especially in childbirth. But she never took a husband, and over time, this made local people suspicious of her. A rumour spread that she could transform herself into a black crow and stalked the fields around Strathbran at night.'

Helen was a story teller, Martha thought. She could almost make you believe in her fairy tales.

'You'll be aware of the very special place behind the farm – the moondial up on the mound?' Helen said.

Martha nodded, recalling the day almost three years ago, when she and Jamie had discovered it. She remembered being drawn to the place. Even in her state of heavy pregnancy, she had been determined to get close to it.

'Well that is where the Feannag Dhubh practised her rituals,' Helen went on. 'She honoured her ancestors there, and made offerings to protect her family and friends.'

Martha thought about this for a moment, and tried to recall lines from the poem that she'd struggled with.

'The poem mentions "Ostara rising at Crow Moon",' she said. 'Do you know anything about that?'

'Ostara is spring and the Crow Moon is the last full moon of winter – when the crows can more easily find food and earthworms start to churn the warming earth.'

Helen stopped. They were under a tree at the corner of the kirkyard now. Everything was silent around them.

'This March has been very unusual, Martha,' Helen said, putting a hand on her arm. Her face was stern, almost as if she was giving Martha a warning. 'We have already had one full moon and the second, the Crow Moon, is due before the end of the month.'

'I didn't realise that,' Martha said, her mind working hard now. Whoever wrote the lines on Fraser had to have known what Helen had just told her. 'Does it have something to do with the poem?' she ventured, not wanting to reveal everything she knew, but certain she was on to something here.

'For some time, we have sensed an eidolon,' Helen replied cryptically. 'A spirit with a connection to Blacklaw, Martha. We have, of course, heard about young Fraser.' The sad smile appeared on Helen's face again.

She started to walk along the path, but Martha stayed where she was for a moment, thinking.

'I would urge caution on your part, Martha, given your tethers to that place. Be careful...' Helen looked over her shoulder with a knowing expression. Somehow she'd realised Martha was looking into Fraser's death. 'We will be making offerings at Ostara to calm the troubled spirit.'

Martha took a few quick steps to catch up. 'But why is Blacklaw important?'

'That is where the one they called Feannag Dhubh was executed. On the spot where the moondial was erected.'

They had come back to the kirkyard gate again. Helen looked out into the distance. Then pointed into the air.

'It's exactly nine days to the new moon,' she said, not looking at Martha now. 'Twenty-three days to the full moon. It is a time of powerful magic – the old spirits, who hold dominion over winter, are fading. It is their time to hibernate soon...' She trailed off and there was silence once again.

It was broken by a sudden, hacking *caw-caw*. A crow flapped down from the tree they'd stood under and landed on the roof of Martha's car. Its clawed feet clicked on the metal.

Helen pointed at the bird. 'It's heard everything we've said,' she murmured.

Then she gripped Martha's wrist, less gentle now.

'As the Crow Moon rises, Martha, you must take care. Fraser may not be the last to be taken.'

CHAPTER THIRTEEN

Although disquieted, Martha wasn't sure how much of Helen Horne's fey tales she believed. She had a quiet, determined manner, though. There were no hysterics – she spoke with a straightforward honesty that appealed to Martha. But it was the subject matter Martha found difficult to swallow. There was something about the landscape here – dense, ancient forests; deep, cold lochs, which no doubt held centuries of secrets trapped in their depths; sudden mists that rolled down from the brooding mountains that loomed over these insular communities. So she could see where the folklore was rooted. Why someone like Helen believed it all. But she refused to let herself be drawn into believing there was more to life than she could see, hear and feel. She hadn't mentioned the fact that Fraser had lines from the poem across his back, yet she had come away with the feeling that Helen knew more about his death than had been made public.

Martha favoured facts over magic though, and once she'd got home, she decided it was time to call her old colleagues on the paper. She was silent for a second when Janice answered. The familiar voice felt like it came from a place Martha had forgotten.

'Newsdesk, can I help you?' Janice said again. The heavy Glasgow accent was impatient at having to say it a second time. They'd be busy not just trying to get Friday editions over the line, but looking for an early edition Saturday splash for tomorrow's front page too.

'Hi, Janice, it's Martha. Long time, no speak.'

'Martha. Is it really you? When you coming back to work?'

'Whoah, slow down will you,' she laughed. 'I'm not sure if I will be.'

'Aw, bugger that, woman. We need you,' Janice said. 'There's none here can hold a light to you. The shite we've been printing recently. I heard about your accident. And you finding that young laddie. Christ, Martha, you've nae had much luck, eh? Must have been bloody awful.' Her words rushed out so fast it was hard to keep up.

Martha had always warmed to Janice. The eccentric newsdesk secretary was small and slight, still dyed gaudy orange what was left of her wispy hair and dressed in mismatched items gathered from charity shops.

'I'm alright now,' Martha said. 'But I'm not sure about coming back to work at the paper. I'm a wee bit rusty.'

'Bollocks. We need you back. It's not been the same since you left.'

It was good to talk to someone who knew her work and her history, but who wouldn't ask insensitive questions about her recent past.

'Anyway, who you wanting to speak to?' Janice asked. 'Neil's on holiday just now, and they've got Tom Preston standing in for him. Talk about elevated idea of his own importance ... heid up his arse, if you ask me.'

Martha knew exactly what Janice meant, and she was spot on as usual.

'It was actually you I was after. I'm looking for a favour. I'm trying to get some archive material, if there is any, on perform-ances of an old poem – a few hundred years old.'

She could almost hear Janice's brain whirring down the line. 'You're needin' to talk to the folk at the Mitchell Library then, not rake through our archives. There's a bloke there called Edward Purdue. He should be able to help you. He's an early-music and folklore specialist; sounds to me like that's what you're looking for.'

'That's great, but how do you know that?' Martha was surprised at her friend's almost instant knowledge.

'Ach, I didn't always work in this shit hole you know. I actually did literature at uni, then ended up getting temp work at the library. That's where I met Ed. What else do you do with an English degree? I'll send you Ed's email address. Tell him I sent you. He'll definitely see you then.' Her raucous laugh gave Martha the impression there'd been more to Ed than her friend was letting on.

Before hanging up, Martha promised to stay in touch. She meant it too. The friendly voice from work made her realise how isolated she'd become. Perhaps it was time to start thinking about getting her life back on track. The insurance money from the fire wouldn't last forever. She'd need to start earning her living again at some point.

Her phone sounded, the scratched screen momentarily lighting up the kitchen gloom. A text message had dropped in from Janice already.

Hey M. Great to chat. Contact you need is
edwardpurdue1@GML.org
Don't leave it too long till we see you again. J x

Martha considered what she had found out so far. She had read and reread the poem several times. She wished she could find out which lines were written on Fraser. The whole poem would have taken over the whole of his back, as there were several verses, and she knew she'd only seen a few lines. She felt slightly nauseous at the thought. But why that poem, why those words? From what Helen told her, there was a clear connection to Strathbran, Blacklaw, and perhaps to the current month, with its two moons. Maybe this Ed bloke would be able to tell her more – from a historical, real-life perspective.

She emailed him, asking for a meeting as soon as possible. The words sped off into the ether as the sight of the wine rack caught the corner of her eye. A few dusty bottles were slotted in, giving her a sudden strong urge to taste the tempting tang of a good Marlborough Sauvignon. Orla was due to turn up before long, wine in hand, and she'd want to talk about all the stuff Martha had kept hidden away. A bit of Dutch courage wouldn't go amiss, and she'd stopped taking the painkillers the hospital had sent her home with. She poured a glass, watching the bubbles gather and dissipate before breathing in the aroma. The wine was pleasantly cold and tart.

A noise announced an email.

Dear Martha, she read. *I'd be delighted to meet with you. Tomorrow 10.30am at the library? Regards, Edward.*

Holding her wine in one hand, Martha checked the date. Friday 9th March. Her calendar had tiny phases of the moon she had never noticed before printed on several squares of the month. She remembered what Helen had said. Twenty-three days to the next full moon. And then Helen's warning came back to her – 'Fraser may not be the last to be taken'. Was Helen just caught up in her own cryptic story-telling, or did she know something she wasn't letting on? Martha frowned. It made her more determined to find out what had happened to Fraser.

She took another gulp of wine and typed: *Great. See you then. M.*

She still had a few minutes before Orla arrived and wanted to put them to good use. She had the feeling that used to grab her in the old days, when she was on the scent of a story. She needed to explore every angle, ensure there was nothing she missed. She stood and looked out of the window, towards the glen where she'd been discovered. She'd not yet spoken to anyone from the rescue team who had brought her out. She should thank them. She supposed they'd helped the police recover Fraser's body too – maybe she could ask a question or two about that.

She knew a neighbour, Paul Mitchell, was a member of the team, and decided to give him a quick call.

'Paul, it's Martha,' she said when he answered.

'It's good to hear from you, Martha. How are you feeling? You were completely out of it when we pulled you out of that gulley.'

She assured him she was recovering well, and asked him to pass on her thanks to the team.

'I was wondering what happened to the young lad who was found near me. I haven't really heard exactly how he was discovered and what your team saw that day.'

'Well, we were only looking for you, so the lass who got to you first had a real shock when she saw that poor lad right by where you'd fallen. We'd done a few searches for him, but in the area where his phone was found which was a couple of miles away. No one expected him to be where you were. It's not that often we get a live rescue and a body recovery like that at the same time.' He paused for a moment, collecting himself. 'I'm not sure there's more to tell really. The police examined the scene and couldn't find any other evidence of what happened to him. We were as disturbed as anyone when they launched a murder investigation. But I guess, after the way we found him, and that far from where he'd gone missing, it wasn't a surprise.'

'So you didn't see anyone, or anything else around there that could explain how he got there?'

'It was pretty dark by the time we got to you, Martha. That sheepdog of yours was particularly frantic and led us right to where you were lying. It was only when one of the lasses swung the torch around that she spotted Fraser too.'

Martha thanked him again and said if anyone did mention anything else they'd seen, could he let her know. She didn't mention that she was conducting her own investigation; she would leave him to work that out himself.

She contemplated what she'd gathered so far as the wind outside began to whip noisily around the roof and the chimney. A dead boy, a poem on his body, drugs, and a possible, albeit supernatural, link to the place that gave her most pain.

The image of the burnt-out farmhouse formed in her mind. For a second she thought she could actually smell the charred remains. She shook her head. It must be the wind, sucking and blowing down the chimney. And then her mind took her back further in time, and once more she recalled uncovering the moondial, pulling back the brambles, standing at its foot and gazing at the glyphs and images carved into the stone. What had she felt at that moment? She'd stood on the spot where a young woman had burned to death. A young woman, it was said, who could turn herself into a crow and—

A loud knock made her jump, followed by a deafening bang as the front door hit the wall of the hallway. It was a moment before

Martha realised she'd leapt up and was halfway across the room, clinging to the back of a chair in fright.

'Martha!' Orla rushed in, her bag clinking with several bottles of wine. 'Sorry about the door – wind caught it.'

Martha dropped back into her chair. 'You nearly gave me a heart attack!'

'Sorry. But enough about that. I think I might have found the solution to my heartbreak. Nothing like a man in uniform to make you feel better.'

Martha gave her a bemused look, so Orla quickly filled her in. The target of her affections made Martha's head spin.

'You can't just decide to set your sights on the man, Orla. How do you know he's even interested?'

'Oh, I know he's interested. I spoke to him at length.' She arched an eyebrow. 'I got the vibe.'

'Oh, for God's sake. What next?'

'I'm hoping God won't come into it,' Orla laughed. 'And what might I find behind the uniform of a man of God?'

'I don't think it's called a uniform, Orla,' Martha said, trying to think of a way to deter her friend's distinctly unholy interest.

She couldn't bring herself to tell her that there was something about Locke that disturbed her – something eerie she couldn't put her finger on. But Orla was fickle – once she got bored, she'd head off and make new conquests somewhere else. A quiet country village was no place for Orla Reid to settle down.

CHAPTER FOURTEEN

She was roused on Saturday morning by the sound of a voice speaking sharply from above her head. It sounded like Dougie was talking to someone. It was rather early for him to be up. He usually kept teenage hours at the weekend. And the tense tone to his voice made her wonder who he was talking to.

She got out of bed and quietly opened her bedroom door.

'I'm sure she knows about it, Christie. She's been talking about the poem and asking people about Fraser.' Martha could hear the panic in his words now. 'I thought no one knew but us. I know we all ran off that night, but after, Fraser and me were never convinced there was anything there. I know you think there was...'

The mention of Fraser stopped her short. She wouldn't usually eavesdrop on her son; she liked to respect his privacy, but in this case, she'd make an exception, especially as it was clear he'd been listening in to her own conversations.

Straining to hear more, she stepped silently onto the landing and glanced up towards Dougie's bedroom in the attic. The trapdoor was open.

'I'm not saying you're lying, Christie.' Her son was clearly agitated now. 'I know you think you saw something, but Fraser reckoned we all just got carried away – you know, with the candles and the moon and all that. It was like being in a scary movie. Playing a part, you know? You were so good at the charms and stuff. But, I dunno if what's happening now has anything to do with that night. How can it? It was just a game, wasn't it?'

There was silence for a few seconds and Martha wondered if Christie had rung off.

'Honestly, Chris,' Dougie said finally, 'I know what you're saying about Fraser, the full moon and that, but do you really believe it has anything to do with us? It's almost a year ago.'

Martha heard him moving around. Had he heard her get up? She slipped back inside her bedroom and stood beside the door.

'OK, so what you're saying is, this Crow Moon is coming, and somehow Fraser's death is linked to some stupid local legend that I don't think anyone believes in anymore – except you!' His frustration was clear now. But why had he mentioned the Crow Moon? Had Helen Horne been talking to Christie, perhaps?

He was quiet again for a moment, then replied more gently. 'You know, I never liked being near that thing, even when we lived there. Those creepy trees and the moondial freaked me out, especially after dark. I wish we'd never gone there. I wish we'd never done all that stuff.'

It seemed they'd made up, because before he said goodbye she heard Dougie tell Christie to take care.

She slipped back into bed and reran her conversation with Helen Horne in her head – the significance she had placed on the two moons this month, and how the legend of the Feannag Dhubh was linked to Blacklaw. It was clear from the snippets she had just heard of Dougie and Christie's conversation that the two of them, along with Fraser, had been back there. But when? She didn't think Dougie had been back to the farm since the fire. And what did he mean about Christie and her charms and candles? She was torn, she couldn't ask him outright, or he'd know she had overheard him. But if this turned out to be significant in what had happened to Fraser, maybe she should admit she'd been listening in?

Awake now, she went down the stairs to the kitchen. She flicked on the kettle and checked the calendar again. Counted the days. Just over a week until the next new moon. But so what? What did it mean? Was it in any way connected to Fraser's death? The whole thing felt like a crazy mess, but Martha could see various strands of information weaving together and she didn't particularly like the pattern that was emerging. Especially, if her son somehow ended up at the centre of it.

The Book of Shadows

I have come to love this place as much as my home. Grandmother was right: there is magic here. There's a place near Aberfoyle where they say the fairy folk kidnapped a church minister centuries ago for writing down their secrets. His grave lies in the kirkyard beyond the Doon Hill, where he disappeared.

He took me to visit the grave of the kidnapped man. It was more as a warning than a reward. I wondered if his bones really lay beneath the earth. Had the fairy folk sent him back, or was the coffin empty? His headstone had a skull carved into it that made me shiver. Folk had left coins and offerings there. I felt the sense of it all. The connection to magic was in the air.

People had tied ribbons and bells to the trees on the way up to the hill. The place seemed enchanted to me, with faces of spirits carved into the trees. I felt we were watched. But I did not say so, for he wouldn't like that. So I write about it here and draw these sketches of what I saw.

CHAPTER FIFTEEN

A strange orange light drifted across the sky. According to the breakfast news, a storm had whipped up dust from the Sahara and brought it all the way to Scotland, tingeing the skies a weird, apocalyptic colour. It made the superstitious fear for their lives. On the screen, people predicting the end of the world were being interviewed.

Martha's head was still pounding after the conversation she'd overheard between Dougie and Christie, and after last night's session with Orla. She'd started by ranting about her ex, but the dangerous glint in her eye had returned when she had gone back to talking about Peter Locke. Martha knew Orla was single-minded when she set her sights on something. A revenge affair was clearly on the cards.

Downing the rest of her coffee, Martha took her bag and keys, signalling 'later' to the dogs as she walked out through the front door.

Approaching the outskirts of Glasgow forty minutes later, the same heavy sky frowned over the city. She parked in a multi-storey, the wind gathering the rubbish in a twisting knot against the doorway as she pushed her way out into the street. Within ten minutes she was walking into the reception of a magnificent building in Glasgow's Charing Cross. Its pale stone walls and copper-domed tower looked incongruous among the concrete-and-glass buildings all around, the busy M8 motorway nearby. The door slid shut behind her as she asked to see Edward Purdue.

'That'll be me then,' came a voice from behind her. The accent had an Aberdeen twang to it, although years in the arts world seemed to have weakened the Doric edge.

'Martha?' He grasped her hand in a warm and surprisingly firm shake.

'Yes, hello, Edward,' she said.

'The café should be quiet at this time of day.' And he led her away, through the building. 'Coffee?' he asked. 'I'll get them. You find us a seat.'

She took a table near the window. Students sat nearby, engrossed in their books. For a moment it all seemed so rational and normal, she couldn't believe she'd met a Wiccan yesterday and heard tell of witches and spirits. Across the road, she spotted two crows, pulling chicken bones from a takeaway carton lying in the gutter with jerks of their heads, competing over the scraps. Her skin prickled, as if someone had run a finger across the back of her neck. She ran her hands nervously through her hair. She was being ridiculous. Crows were everywhere. She was just noticing them more.

'So, how can I help you?' Edward asked, setting down a tray with two steaming cardboard cups and a packet of shortbread biscuits.

'Well, as I think I mentioned in my email, I'm involved in a police investigation. I had a fall out in the forest near to where I live in Strathbran.' She pointed at her bruised face. 'And in the same place, a boy was discovered. Dead.' She took a breath. 'I found him.'

Edward's stare was wide.

'I'm a sort of witness – in that the police don't seem to have anyone else. But the thing is, Edward, he was a friend of my son, so I'm desperate to help find out what happened to him. It's so awful.'

'But how can I help you?' he asked, puzzled.

Martha handed him a sheet of paper from her bag. He read it in silence, and recognition soon dawned on his pleasant features.

'I've discovered there's a connection between this poem and the boy's death,' she said when he looked up at her. 'And I'm trying to find out more information about it. I can't say exactly how it's linked to the case right now, I'm afraid. But yesterday I met with a local ... woman, who has some knowledge about this poem and the legend that supposedly lies behind it. She told me there's some sort of link between this poem and what she called a Crow Moon – and that there's one of those due before the end of this month. So, put all this together, and it just might have something to do with the case of this dead boy. I know this all probably sounds like mumbo jumbo, and believe me, it does to me too, but any help you can give me would be gratefully received.'

'Janice said you were a bit of a bloodhound when it comes to a story,' Edward grinned. Martha smiled back encouragingly. 'And you've come to the right place with this,' he went on. 'This poem was pretty well known in its day. It was even turned into a folk song. It has its origins in certain pagan rituals, which at the time of the Scottish witch trials were misconstrued and used against those who performed them. As I'm sure you're aware, hysteria over witchcraft spread right across Europe. It was a time when women were very much controlled by men, and many thousands were tortured for their so-called crimes. This poem is quite local though. Written in a village in West Stirlingshire.'

'Yes, I discovered that when I found out the name of the poem and ran a few Google searches on it,' Martha replied. 'The "Blacklaw" mentioned was actually a farm I lived on up until a year ago.'

Edward fixed her with a stare for a moment. She wasn't sure what she saw there. Was it pity – had Janice told him about her history? Or was it something else – something more like Helen's warning?

'We have a comprehensive collection of folklore literature here,' he said. 'So I'm sure I'll be able to find some more background for you in our archives. I've got your email address, so I'll send it on to you. Would that help?'

'Yes, thank you. It would.'

Martha smiled, and he gave her the same stare. This time she thought he was about to say something, then decided against it.

'Janice said to say hello,' she said, to break the silence.

'Ah, Janice. She's an old friend,' he smiled. 'Do come and see me again if you need any more help.'

Back outside, the orange sky still bore down on the city. Big spots of rain had just begun to hit the pavement. Martha's thoughts buzzed. Her brain hadn't worked this hard for quite some time. Pulling hard on the car park door, she walked into the grimy stairwell, where meagre light penetrated the filthy bubbled-glass windows. Glancing down, her eyes were drawn to something glinting. A tiny golden cross lay on the step in front of her. She looked closer and could see it was some kind of confetti – from a confirmation perhaps – and as she climbed the gloomy stairs, her way was guided by the trail of shining crosses.

She thought about the night she left the twins. Focused on the job. She'd never thought for a second she'd never see them again. She wished, for the millionth time, that she'd stayed at home, that maybe then she would have been able to protect them.

And then she wondered who might need protection next.

CHAPTER SIXTEEN

In the gloom of the car, Martha's phone started to buzz. Derek Summers, she noted the number on screen. So the police were working weekends after all.

'Martha,' he said when she picked up. 'I don't suppose you'd be able to come in to the station? There's been a witness come forward to say they saw a man in the woods on the day you found Fraser, and I've also got some images I'd like you to take a look at.'

'I'm actually in Glasgow just now,' she said, agreeing to meet him in half an hour at Police HQ.

It was exactly ten days since Fraser had gone for his run. She was hoping Summers' request meant that the police investigation was finally making some progress. A new witness was something positive. The connections she'd discovered between the poem, Blacklaw and the moondial intrigued her. But there had to be hard facts beneath it all. The drugs – that was something they could investigate.

Dougie and Christie's conversation and the information Helen Horne had shared were all swirling in her head though, trying to form a coherent pattern. Although she wanted to hear good news in the search for Fraser's killer, she was beginning to fear what all these connections might mean for her. They were simply too close to home. If the lines on Fraser's back were made public and journalists got hold of the poem and its connection to Blacklaw, the investigation, and the attached media circus, would drop right into the middle of her world. The tragedy of her life would inevitably be picked over. She knew better than anyone what journalists were like for making connections and sniffing out tragedies, and she wasn't sure whether she could handle that.

Martha thought about Fraser's mother, Jane. Right now, she was faced with the same wrenching misery that Martha had had to cope with. Fraser gone forever and now a police investigation to deal with; media attention on top of that. The whole situation was bringing back all those feelings Martha felt when she lost her twins. But it had also awakened something else in Martha, something she thought had gone up in the flames of her home. A fascination; a need for connection to the awful story. A need for answers.

✦

Taking a deep breath, Martha trotted up the steps of the police station, hurrying to get out of the rain. As she pushed through the revolving door, her fingertips left an impression on the glass.

The woman at reception looked up. Angular glasses balanced on her nose, she glared at Martha.

'I'm here to meet DI Summers. I've got an appointment,' she said.

'I'll see if he's free.' The woman was frosty.

'He asked me to come in.'

The swish of a wet umbrella being shaken out made her turn to look as someone came through the doors. The street was teeming with water. The famous Glasgow shower, her brother called it. Never go anywhere in this city without a brolly, cos it pisses down at some point in every day of the year. The thought made her smile. Even with his trendy Merchant City flat, her brother was always London-bound.

'Martha?' Summers had appeared from a door on the other side of the reception desk. 'This way please.'

She followed, throwing a tight smile at the ogress on reception as Summers led her to a modern glass-box lift. They weren't going to his office this time it seemed.

'How are you, Martha? Feeling any better?' His eyes were warm.

'Not too bad, except for a bit of a stiff neck and sore ribs. Is there any news? I'm assuming that's why you've asked me in.' An odd musky smell in the lift made her wonder if he was wearing aftershave.

'Toxicology confirms ketamine and the other prescription drug, Risperdal. We're trying to access medical records through the courts of anyone prescribed the latter. Without a specific suspect, it's unlikely we'll get permission though.'

As they reached the fifth floor, she paused at the floor-to-ceiling window, taking in Glasgow's stunning skyline.

'Rare view of our fine city,' DI Summers said, reflecting her own thoughts.

'You said there was a witness who saw something?' she said, still looking out at the panorama. Sometimes moments of pause like this, in a corridor, on the stairs, were the best time to get information from someone.

'A local man has come forward to say he was walking in the woods, sometime before you were there, apparently. He thought he saw someone further ahead of him, through the trees. Someone tall with a heavy jacket on, although he couldn't be sure as they seemed to disappear. He said it was more likely a man than a woman and he was possibly heading out of the woods through the north side and across into the fields. They weren't on the path. He was clear about that. Don't suppose you saw anyone on your way there did you?'

'Nope, it's still a blank I'm afraid. I didn't go in that way though. I entered by the south path, directly up from the village. If there'd been anyone around though, the dogs would have sensed it. They do usually, and I notice.'

He nodded, as though he'd expected to draw a blank.

'I think seeing Fraser will be imprinted on my memory forever,' she said, looking directly at him now.

'On that note,' he said, 'I'm afraid we want you to take a look at some photos. You'll need to prepare yourself. They're pictures of Fraser, showing the writing on his back.'

Martha turned back to look at the city before her. This was what she wanted, wasn't it? – to be involved in the investigation, to know what the police knew, to draw her own conclusions, but did she really want to see these pictures? She took a deep breath, then released it. She was here now, whether she wanted to be or not. They all needed to find out the truth. The same instincts that drove her to do her job for more than fifteen years kicked in.

'Are you OK?' Summers said.

She nodded, appreciating the moment he'd given her to gather her thoughts.

'If you'd rather not, then that's OK. Just say if it's too much. We've got the verse of the poem that we found on him and have had the handwriting analysed,' Summers went on. 'When you found Fraser, although the week before was dry, there was a heavy overnight mist that had soaked everything. Thankfully, it hadn't rained or the writing might have washed off him.'

Martha steeled herself, wondering now what exactly the photos would show.

'It was a bugger of a place, so whoever killed him must either have had help or some kind of vehicle to get him there.'

That was an interesting nugget of information. Martha had not thought of that. She was struck now by the surly detective's apparent trust in her. It sounded like she might be able to get even more from him.

'Of course, I'll do what I can on the photos,' she said, nodding firmly. 'What about other leads? Have you made any progress tracing where the drugs actually came from? I looked up the anti-psychotic and it didn't look like something you could easily get hold of without a prescription – especially not where we live.'

'No, we're no further forward with that yet. As I say, we're trying to get records, but unless we have a suspect, then it's a bit of a blind alley. But we're pretty sure Fraser wouldn't have taken it voluntarily.'

Summers turned. 'Shall we...?' He gestured to a door down the hallway.

She followed him into an open-plan office that looked familiar from her newsroom days. Police officers sat behind computer screens and no one looked up as they came in. In days gone by, Martha would have loved to have had access to a place like this, the heart of the police operation, to find out what stories she could find.

Summers pulled up a chair to a desk in the far back corner. The area was screened off. A young guy with round glasses reflecting the bank of four screens in front of him grinned at her, offering a slightly sweaty handshake.

'Martha, this is DC Ravi Cheema,' said Summers. 'He'll be showing you the images. You'll only see the shots of Fraser's torso, where the writing is. If you feel uncomfortable or want to stop at any time, just say. I'll leave you to it, and grab us a tea.'

As Summers retreated, Martha briefly wondered what his story was. Did he have a family? He was a big bloke, but overweight, and could be any age between forty-five and sixty. He had the demeanour of a beaten hound – maybe worn down by years of dealing with tragedies like her own. The young policeman signalled the pictures were ready. She sat down in the chair next to him.

Ravi pressed a series of keys, which brought images up on the large screen. 'Right, take a look. You can use the mouse just to scroll through them. If you see anything at all that rings a bell, stop and let me know.'

Although she wanted to help, she wasn't sure what they were hoping she'd be able to do. She'd known Fraser through her son, of course, but they were older now and looked after themselves mostly. She'd been wracking her brains for the past week, trying to remember whether there was anything else she had seen that day that could help, but there was nothing specific, other than the sense that someone may have been watching her in the trees. Was that the elusive figure the new witness had seen? Or could it be put down to an overactive imagination? Birdsong, rushing water and then the grisly sight of the boy's dead face. Perhaps the police wanting her to be involved was because they were desperate – they had no other leads.

Martha screwed up her eyes, squinting at the pictures. It was hard to make out what she was looking at – she wouldn't have thought it was a dead body if she didn't already know. Feeling slightly sick, she swallowed, steeled herself.

The skin was taut, yellow and tinged with bruising. As she scrolled up, she saw the lines of writing, bizarrely neat, considering where they were. She gasped and could feel Ravi's gaze on her. They looked a bit like a tattoo – one of those motivational quotes people put on themselves. Whatever the intention of this message, though, the writing wasn't permanent. Perhaps like life itself, Martha thought. Was that what the killer was trying to say?

'They must have really strong concentration skills,' she murmured.

'Aye, considering the lad was dead and they were writing poems on a body,' Summers replied, coming up behind her and saying out po-ee-ums in that peculiar Scots way she'd never picked up herself. He set a steaming cup in front of her. He put down a plate of biscuits too, but she certainly had no appetite. She turned back to peer more closely at the pictures.

Some words were slightly smudged where the ink had bled into the surrounding skin, but she could clearly read them. It was definitely a verse from the poem.

'There's more to this piece,' she said finally. 'It's actually the second stanza from the poem. There's one before it and two verses after.'

She paused. The significance of her own words just dawning on her. She thought about Helen Horne and her warning. She could almost feel Helen's hand, tight around her wrist. She thought of the crow that had landed on her car out by the graveyard at Aberfoyle.

She turned to look at Summers. 'That means we have a missing first verse and two more to come...' she said quietly.

His face tightened as he realised what she was hinting at. If there were more verses, would there be more victims?

CHAPTER SEVENTEEN

Christie's mum, Joan, was bustling around the kitchen, Sunday-morning TV on in the background and the kettle coming to the boil. Dressed for the stables, Christie's long blonde hair was pulled back into a rough ponytail and she wore tight-fitting black jodhpurs. They hadn't been washed in a few days and bits of hay and horsehair clung to the legs. The smell was unmistakably horsey too, but Christie loved it.

'Morning, Chris,' said her mum. 'Toast?' The girl knew Mum always hoped she'd ask for a full Scottish, or waffles piled with maple syrup and even ice cream.

Christie didn't want a lecture or a disappointed look. 'OK, just one piece, please,' she said. Her mum poured tea, added milk but no sugar, and when the toaster popped, scraped thick, golden butter onto the bread before handing it to her slender-framed girl. A delicate criss-cross of small white scars glinted on Christie's arms as she took the plate.

'Thanks,' she said, pulling out a chair and sitting at the kitchen table to eat. She knew it would please her mother.

It was a year since Christie and the boys had fled from the moondial. She'd had nightmares for weeks afterwards, dreaming about a suffocating black shadow chasing her; she'd wake in the night drenched in sweat, screaming about the witch. Her parents had no idea what the teens had been up to.

She'd been doing a school project, researching Scotland's infamous seventeenth-century witch trials, and had become obsessed with the subject – trawling the internet for information, joining discussion groups and signing up for newsletters, trying to find out everything she could about the women who had been persecuted centuries ago. She'd kept a journal too. Mum had found it in her drawer, and when she'd looked inside, discovered Christie had been writing down lines of poetry and things she had learned through her research – even spells and charms.

But then things had started to turn ugly. She'd started getting messages from people she didn't know, emails with horrible images that had frightened her. She'd confided in a pal at school – someone who, it turned out, couldn't keep a secret. The rumours had spread and the other pupils started calling her a witch. It was ridiculous childish stuff at first, but eventually had got totally out of hand.

'How are you doing, Christie?' Mum asked gently as she munched her toast. 'With all this stuff about Fraser, I mean.'

She had been close with Fraser, and with Dougie Strangeways too. The news of Fraser's death, a week ago now, had hit the community hard. Christie thought about the conversation she'd had with Dougie and about the approaching Crow Moon. Despite his scepticism, she'd always felt uneasy that they'd not managed to finish the ritual that night at the moondial.

'I just don't know how I feel, Mum,' she said. 'It still seems unreal. Do they really think he was murdered?'

'That's what the papers are saying, Christie. It's terrible if it's true.'

Christie nodded, her toast feeling dry and chewy in her mouth now. Police officers had come to the door last weekend, asking questions. She said that she hadn't seen Fraser for a while, and it was true. She'd felt herself drifting away from Dougie and Fraser after that night at the moondial. She hadn't mentioned anything about that to the police though.

Her mother was watching her closely now, as always these days, alert to any signs of distress. After the bullying at Glenview High School had got out of hand, Christie had dropped out of classes, her anxiety too much to cope with. It had taken months for her to get back on an even keel, but recently she'd returned to the riding school and had replaced her interest in witches with a renewed passion for horses and in particular her own. So things seemed to have been settling down, that was until Fraser had gone missing...

She stood up, her breakfast unfinished. She couldn't eat another thing.

Half an hour later, Christie was on her way to the stables. She tried to put thoughts of poor Fraser aside for now, but she knew she needed to speak to Dougie again soon. She walked down through the trees, and could hear the horses' excited whinnying. It echoed through the wood; her heart raced at the thought of a ride with her boy. As she got closer, the scent of horses in the air was intense. The sweet smell of haylage bales stacked ready for winter, fresh wood shavings and the muck heap steaming in the morning cold. With Walter's head collar and a carrot to entice him, she wandered down to the field.

'Come on, boy. Waltie!'

The horse galloped flat out from the far end of the paddock.

Safely haltered, Christie led him back up to the yard, washed off his muddy hooves and tied him to his stall with a hay net while she got to work scraping his coat, and brushing mud and straw from his multi-coloured mane and tail until his black patches shone against the white, talking to him in a low voice all the while. Christie never felt awkward or self-conscious when she was with her horse.

Finally ready, she brought out a saddle and bridle. When all the buckles were done, she tightened the girth and checked there were no bits pinching him before she put her helmet on, packed a few treats into her pocket and climbed on from the wooden mounting block in the yard, settling gently on to his back.

'You want some company today?' came a voice from behind her. Jan, another one of the liveries, had been trying to make friends for a few weeks. It wasn't that Jan didn't seem nice, but Christie just wanted time with her horse.

'No thanks, we're fine.' She gathered up the reins, ignoring the petulant expression on Jan's face, and squeezed Walter's sides as he moved forward down the track.

They walked carefully down the steep farm road, Walter's metal shoes clinking as they hit the tarmac. A few cars and a tractor slowed down when they saw her, and she steered Walter onto the grass verge out of their way. Reaching the turn-off into the forest, wind gathered in the dense tops of the pine trees as they walked along the stony track. It sounded like rushing water, but the river was miles away. Giant power lines crossed up ahead, mounted on robotic-looking pylons. The wind hit them, chiming loudly with an eerie, echoing sound.

Something called out high above them, and she lay back on

Walter's warm rump to look up. A bird of prey soared, diving and riding the wind currents above her. So graceful as it rose and dropped with the air, like a wind surfer on the sea. Its distinctive tail identified the creature as a red kite. She used to go bird-watching with her dad when she was a little girl. Christie smiled.

Watching through binoculars from a hilltop a mile or so away, the man smiled too.

CHAPTER EIGHTEEN

After seeing the pictures yesterday, Martha had been trying to figure out what would prompt someone to copy the verse onto a boy's back. It was an obscure text, but it clearly meant something to the killer. She'd read through it carefully several times. Perhaps Edward Purdue would be able to shed more light on it when he'd been through his archives.

With nothing else to go on, she decided to call Summers, see if she could glean any further information from him about the case.

'DI Summers here.' The detective answered his landline abruptly. She hadn't been certain he'd be in the office on Sunday.

'Hello. Martha here. I've been thinking about the poem since I came to see you yesterday. And it occurred to me: shouldn't we be warning parents to keep their kids in? It's clear someone else might be at risk, isn't it?'

'Are you calling in a professional capacity, Martha – on behalf of a newspaper, perhaps?' His tone had changed since yesterday. 'I've been informed you've been in touch with our press office...' That explained it, Martha thought.

'No, I'm not currently working at the paper,' she replied. She needed to tread carefully. She didn't want him to feel rattled about her doing her own digging. He would only clam up then. 'It was just that the poetry got me thinking. It's such a bizarre thing to do.'

She paused before asking her next question. She needed to be careful, but the conversation she'd overheard Dougie having might be important.

'Have you spoken to Christie Campbell?' she said. 'She knew Fraser, I think.'

'Yes, we have spoken to Miss Campbell,' he replied after a moment. 'She said she hadn't been in touch with Fraser for a while. She seemed quite a fragile young person. And when we spoke to her, her mother seemed very protective.'

That was interesting. Why had Christie not seen Fraser? And why was her mother so protective of her?

She said goodbye to Summers and rang off. His attitude was slightly confusing. Yesterday he'd wanted her help, but today he'd almost warned her off. But he had shared various bits of information with her that weren't yet in the public domain, and that suggested to Martha that the police weren't getting very far with the case. It was in exactly this kind of situation that Martha had always seen an opportunity. She wouldn't be treading on any toes if she took the investigation in a direction the police hadn't properly explored yet.

So, she needed to speak to Christie. She wouldn't tell Summers about the conversation she'd overheard. Not yet, anyway. And she still hadn't broached it with Dougie. It might well be easier to get information from Christie herself than her own son.

Martha put on her boots and jacket, the dogs jumping up at the sight. She loaded the mutts into her Subaru and drove off through the centre of the village.

When she knocked at Christie's house, her mum, Joan, answered the door. Turned out the lass had gone off to the stables and Joan told Martha that she might catch her there.

'Anything I can help with?' Joan said, a line forming between her eyebrows.

Martha remembered what Summers said about Joan being protective of Christie, and she didn't want to cause unnecessary alarm, so she thought up a quick white lie.

'There's something going on with Dougie. I'm not sure if it's this stuff with Fraser, but I wanted to see if Christie might shed some light. Teenage boys aren't exactly known for opening up, are they?' She gave Joan what she hoped was a weary smile.

Joan seemed satisfied, and Martha went on her way.

When she got to the yard, she slowed to a stop as a girl led a chestnut mare in from the field.

Martha leaned out of her window. 'I was looking for Christie. I don't suppose you could point me in the right direction, could you?'

The girl's mouth tightened and she shook her head. 'She went off on her own about an hour ago. Doesn't want company or bothers to tell anyone where she's going,' the girl said pointedly. 'I reckon she might have gone for a long ride up the Husky Trail.'

Martha thanked her and drove off, leaving the village by the back road; a single farm track with steep, grassy verges and not many passing places. A brisk hike around the old Husky Trail would clear her head. It would take her high up above the houses, giving a panoramic view of the mountains from its highest point. She hadn't been there for a while, and looked forward to seeing the majestic horizon stretching from the Arrochar Alps right around to the Menteith Hills. But more importantly, she would have time to think about how to question Christie.

'Shush you two,' she called to the back of the car, as the dogs began to whine, knowing they would soon be running along the trail.

She put on her hat and gloves as she got out. Although winter was almost over, the wind was biting today, as she gazed over the miles and miles of pine and spruce forest planted decades ago.

Selected tracts of trees had been felled, which always left the place looking like a war zone, until the replanted trees had grown and the undergrowth began to spread. Some areas had been replaced with native deciduous species, which displayed a variety of colours. The last burnished oranges had hung on and there was an empty but expectant feeling across the landscape, as winter began to turn its attention to spring, a few wild daffodils popping their yellow heads up from the dead undergrowth.

Skye and BJ leapt from the car and went barking off along the forest trail – a pale stone path winding away up the hill. Above her, clouds ran fast across a blue sky, and she knew that further up, where a lot of the wood was felled, the wind would bring tears to her eyes. Pulling the zip on her padded down jacket tighter, her knuckles grazed the matchbox outline in the breast pocket.

The hill ahead concealed the ruins of their croft, which lay on the far side. Would she ever get to a point where she could remember the brief but happy years of joy she had with her twins, rather than the sorrow of their loss? Her thoughts then turned to Dougie. She wondered how he was really coping with the loss of Fraser. Did it bring memories of the twins back to him? She'd not seen much of him this week. She felt a sudden need to hold him tight.

It was a beautiful, clear Sunday. As she walked, she felt her mind start to work the way it used to, when she was on a story. Skye barked up ahead. She hollered above his racket, giving a loud wolf whistle through her fingers when he ignored her call. He came racing around the bend with the terrier hurtling along behind. She could swear the damn dog was grinning he was so happy to be out. Must have been a deer.

Seconds later a girl on a black-and-white horse appeared around the corner of the trees. The beast was large, his legs and chest spattered with mud. The girl, whose face was also covered in mud, looked small up high on the horse and Martha wondered how she controlled such a big animal. Her blonde hair stuck out from under her hat and her eyes shone, clearly exhilarated to be out on such a blustery day. It was definitely Christie. Martha was pleased she'd not had to search long to find her. She grabbed Skye and slipped the old green lead around his neck, BJ quivering by her side.

'Sorry about the dogs,' she called out. 'Hope they didn't scare your horse.'

'It's fine,' Christie replied. 'Think they got more of a fright than we did.'

'Christie, isn't it?' Martha said. 'I'm Martha. Dougie's mum.'

'Oh, yes,' Christie said. 'Thought I recognised you. And I think I've seen these dogs before too.' She was almost breathless. The horse had sweat rolling down his neck and was blowing hard. 'We just had a good gallop along the top track,' she said.

'Look, I was hoping to catch you. I was just at your mum's and she said you'd be here.' Martha smiled warmly. It was awkward asking questions when she had to crane her neck to look up at the girl. 'I wanted to ask you about something I heard Dougie say yesterday. I think it might help with all this Fraser stuff, you know?' She gave another smile, and got an uncertain nod back. 'It was in the morning. I overheard him talking to you on the phone – something to do with the ritual…?'

Beneath the mud spatters, the girl's face drained of colour.

'I heard Dougie mention Fraser and something to do with a Crow Moon…' Martha cursed herself. This was impossible out here on the trail, with her on the ground and the girl up on a large horse. She was rusty. In the old days, she would have thought about all this beforehand. But she had to press on now. 'What can you tell me about it? It might help, you know…'

'I don't know anything,' Christie snapped. 'Why are you asking me? You should speak to Dougie, if he's the one you overheard.'

'But I know he was talking to you. He said your name. And it was pretty obvious how upset you both are about Fraser. It's difficult to talk to boys. I thought, you know, woman to woman…'

She was scraping the barrel now and she knew it. 'I know something went on, Christie, with the three of you. You, Fraser and Dougie. Can't you think? Anything could help.'

All the joy of her ride had gone from Christie's face. She looked desperate – almost terrified.

'I told you. I don't know. You'll have to ask Dougie.'

She started to move forward with the horse, but Martha reached out and grabbed the reins.

'Are you absolutely sure of that?' she pressed. She'd made a complete mess of this interview, but needed to get something out of the girl.

'Can you let go please?' Christie said, loudly. 'I need to get back home.'

The horse was restless, eager to get away, sensing his rider's mood. He picked up his feet, and Martha had to step back to avoid being barged off the path. Then he pulled away so strongly she had to let go of the reins, and with a strange, strangled whinny, he reared up. Martha staggered backward with a gasp, the beast's hooves so close, it was as if he was ready to trample her. Instinctively, she raised her arms to protect herself, just as Skye began to bark and BJ joined in, the cacophony accompanied by a sudden dark flapping. She dropped her arms, out of range of the horse now, and glimpsed a black shape diving towards Christie's head. The girl threw an arm up towards it, trying to control the horse at the same time. A scream escaped her throat as the bird swooped once more, clawed feet spread. But her horse had had enough. It bolted. Off at a gallop, down the trail, Christie clinging on.

Martha, breathing heavily, watched her go. The horse slowed further down the track, and Christie seemed to bring him under control. Martha scanned the skies. No bird in sight. Had she imagined it, in the panic of the moment? She suddenly felt unsafe out here alone. Something she'd never experienced in this landscape before. Not until this last week.

Martha turned to walk back to her car, picking up her pace.

She was sure the girl would be OK on her horse. She seemed to be very able. But she thought if she was her mother, she'd be worried about her being out here on her own.

Martha just wanted to be home now, and took a shortcut down a path marked *Do Not Enter*. She could see where it wound steeply down the hill; it would shave quite a lot off the walk, but her boots sunk into the mud. She hoped it didn't get worse as she descended.

She tried to refocus on the reason she'd come out in the first place. If Christie wasn't prepared to talk, she'd have to find a way to quiz her son about the conversation she'd overheard, and he wasn't going to like that one bit.

The dogs seemed subdued, keeping close to her, rather than running ahead. They'd been unsettled by Christie's skittish horse up on the trail, she thought. She dug into her pocket for dog biscuits for each of them, and her fingers caught against something cold and smooth. Puzzled, she pulled out the item: the bottle she had found in the woods last week. She'd forgotten all about it. She lifted it to the light and shook it. The sun glinted off the thick green glass and she could see tiny bubbles in the dark liquid inside. The cork stopper was rammed in tight, but picking up a sharp stone, Martha dug around the base of the cork until it loosened and she could pull it out. A strange smell she couldn't place rose from the bottle and tickled her nose. She pressed her thumb over the end and tipped it up, sniffing at the thick liquid that came out. It had a slightly metallic tang and there were dark lumps in it. She rubbed her thumb against her index and middle finger and watched the stain spreading.

It was ink.

CHAPTER NINETEEN

Hidden on top of the Garadhban hills, in amongst the razed tree stumps, and in his heavy camouflage jacket, he couldn't easily be spotted. But with his high-definition binoculars, he could see for miles. Zooming in, he watched the girl charging along the open section of the trail.

They'll find out and you'll get caught.

The taunting note mingled with the cold breeze that whistled loudly around him on the hill. He wished he could switch off the voice. Especially when he was enjoying watching the girl. On the softer ground they picked up pace, the lass leaning forward in her saddle. The horse's wild mane flying up as they raced flat out and without a care for injury. Her blonde ponytail flying out and bouncing off her back. Mud flew up, spattering them both, and when she pulled the horse to a walk, the animal's sides were heaving with the effort. The girl reminded him of another, many years ago. As she leaned down to pat the horse's sweating neck, he imagined her light fingers touching his own skin. He still missed *her*, after all these years. Freyja would have loved that damn horse too.

Focus on the girl. She's the next one. We need her.

As he pushed the wheedling voice aside, another figure came into view in the distance. Martha Strangeways was walking along the track with her dogs. From his elevated position, he watched both figures; they still hadn't seen each other. Then the dogs dived out in front of the horse and the beast briefly shied to the side of the track. He'd wondered whether the girl was angry that the dogs were loose. But she smiled when she pulled up to speak to Martha.

But then everything changed. Martha grabbed the horse's reins, and the animal suddenly rose up. The girl managed to hold on, but at the same time a bird swooped towards her. The binoculars were trembling in his hands. A buzzard? No. A crow.

And then the horse was off, speeding down the trail.

The voice whispered in his head now. Words he couldn't make out this time.

He focused in on Martha again. What was it about that woman? She kept turning up in places she wasn't meant to be. He'd have to be careful of her.

He had to avoid the police too. They'd been to his house twice already, doing door-to-door inquiries in the village. The first time he didn't answer, and the next he'd been out, and they'd left a card asking him to contact them. He'd need to be careful, especially with the next phase of his plan. It would take detailed preparations, but he had time before the next full moon.

CHAPTER TWENTY

Orla rang the bell to the manse a couple of times, but it seemed no one was home. But then Reverend Locke appeared around the corner of the house. Seeing her, he dropped his half-smoked cigarette, grinding it into the gravel beyond the step. In faded Levis and an old Bowie T-shirt, he didn't seem to be dressed for visitors. It was a Monday morning, she thought. And shouldn't a church minister not always be on duty?

'Hi there. Can I help you with something?' he said.

'Hello Reverend.'

Orla made sure her voice was throaty, and she noticed the way he quickly scanned her body as she pushed her sunglasses back over her hair. This was almost too straightforward, she thought.

'Call me Peter,' he replied. 'I keep the reverend stuff for church business.' His smile was easy. 'Unless, of course, you're here on church business.'

'Not at all, Pete. I could just use a friendly face. New in town and all that. I wondered if you had any decent coffee. I'm dying for a smoke, though, but I suppose you look down on that...?'

He laughed. He knew fine well she'd seen him stub out the cigarette.

Orla liked the sound of his shortened name on her tongue. She wondered how often he had an opportunity to talk to a woman with no strings attached. Most women round here would either be married or so ancient he'd not think of them as a potential partner, she supposed. Except for Martha, of course, and she'd never be interested in him or his church.

'Well? Got any coffee?'

'Aye, come around the back, and I'll stick the kettle on,' he said, leading her into the kitchen.

He actually had a fancy coffee pot that he put on the stove and ground the beans so the brew was fresh. She admired his muscled biceps beneath the old T-shirt. Wondered if he worked out. He was an enigma, Orla thought.

'Don't suppose I could use your loo?' she asked as the coffee bubbled.

He nodded and pointed down the hallway. 'Go past my study, then the stairs, and it's the room at the end on the left. Do you take milk and sugar?'

'God, no. The calories,' she laughed. 'Just black and strong please.'

In truth, she really just wanted a quick nose around the place, hoping to get a sense of the man. Was he brief-fling material, or worth something more…? As she passed his study, she heard his phone ringing in the kitchen. The low tone of his sonorous voice buzzed as he answered. Seizing the opportunity while he was distracted, she sneaked into his den. A large desk sat in the bay window, a worn leather chair tucked under it. The walls were lined with books and vinyl records. An old-fashioned record player sat on a side table. She could still hear his voice, so gave into temptation and had a quick sit in his chair. As well as two small inkwells, quaint in a wooden stand that obviously had held three at one time, there was an old, framed black-and-white photo of a pale-haired young woman. Orla reached out to touch it. The woman was pretty; a long plait snaking over her shoulder. She couldn't place the era it was taken, though; her clothes gave no indication. Was she an old flame? A mother, a cherished relative? Orla turned the frame over to see if there was anything written on the back to indicate who the woman was. She undid the catch, and as the frame opened a piece of paper fell out. Orla quickly bent to retrieve it and glanced at the handwritten text. Recognising the lines, she slid it into her pocket, and suddenly conscious that she could no longer hear Locke's voice, she put the photo back and replaced the frame in its position on the desk.

'What are you doing in here?'

Orla jumped up from the chair. How long had he been at the door?

Heart racing, she said, 'I'm sorry, Pete. I heard you on the phone and was so fascinated at this amazing old house I couldn't resist a wee snoop.' She pointed at the photo. 'Who is that? She's lovely.'

'My mother,' he said, wary. 'But she's been gone a long time. Now, do you want that coffee or not?'

Orla nodded and apologised again. When they returned to the kitchen she made sure to turn the charm up several notches, and that seemed to smooth over the awkwardness.

Half an hour later, she left the manse, happy with her work so far. She'd be seeing a lot more of Reverend Locke, she thought.

Once she was down the lane and out of sight, she slid the paper fragment from her pocket. *The Book of Shadows* was written in neat handwriting at the top, and beneath it the line, *As Ostara rises at Crow Moon*. The page was torn. The words were familiar and she suddenly recalled what Martha had told her, in confidence, about the lines of verse written on Fraser, the boy who had been killed.

The Book of Shadows

He draws me closer, and I am not certain now. Deep shadows seem to enshroud him at times. He says I am full of light and that is why he brought me here, to help him keep the past and the dark at bay. Such talk frightens me, but I try not to show it.

His mother does not like me though. He chooses not to see it, but I feel the graze of her stare. I hear the word she mutters beneath her breath when I pass. She calls me witch. He does not like it, but he says nothing.

He does not appear to be as kind now that I have been here for some weeks. He draws me away from the others, seems to like to keep me for himself. I am nervous now and have grown fearful. I hope to return home soon.

CHAPTER TWENTY-ONE

Holding the bottle of ink in her hand, the moments before her fall came flooding back to Martha – suddenly with more clarity than she'd had since it happened. The dogs had scarpered up the hill when she'd spotted the bottle, bending to pick it up as she'd climbed up the steep bank. Moments later she'd seen something moving among the trees, and that was when she had tripped and fallen.

Martha's mind shifted up a gear now, as she made her way home. If the bottle had been dropped so close to where Fraser was found, could the ink be the same stuff used to write on his body? It looked very old and the bottle was a strange shape – like a tiny hourglass. Was this significant, and should she bring it to the police's attention?

Every meagre line of inquiry into Fraser's death so far seemed to have led the police nowhere. She thought Summers needed all the help he could get right now. Apart from a bloke who may have seen another man in the woods, Martha herself was their only witness. Although they'd confirmed what the drugs were, they hadn't been able to trace the source yet and had even canvassed tattoo shops in Stirling and Glasgow to see if anyone had any info on the ink they were analysing from Fraser's body. This bottle might be of no importance. But she might hold in her hand something that could drive the case forward at last.

And it could also give her leverage with Summers, she thought. She'd never been one to stand on scruples when she knew she was on the trail of a story.

Monday morning saw her back at Police HQ in Glasgow, having called Summers the night before. This time the ogress on reception waved her through without a word.

Up in the open-plan office, Martha sat down opposite Summers, and laid out her proposal. He listened with a heavy frown on his face.

'Look, I'm on the ground out in Strathbran,' she said. 'My son knew the deceased, and his group of friends. I know the landscape too. And I have skills. Not to blow my own trumpet, but I've got ahead of the police on several investigations in the past. You can ask your colleagues if you don't believe me. There have been prosecutions that wouldn't have happened without the evidence I uncovered...'

'And you're definitely not working for any press outfit? Freelancer, touting a story?' He raised his eyebrows.

'Definitely not. This isn't about journalism. It's about finding out what happened to Fraser. And protecting my son and the kids of our village. It's been more than a week, and it looks like you've got nowhere. You need fresh eyes on this. And those eyes are mine. You just need to share what you have with me. And I'll share what I have with you.'

Summers heaved a sigh and stared at her for a long moment.

'OK, Martha, I'll make a deal with you,' he said at last. 'But I have to make it clear that if you go public with this, the whole investigation will be in danger. I'll do my best to keep you updated, but it's quid pro quo. You hear anything, or come across something that would help, and you *have* to let me know. Before the press. No tipping off your mates. In return, I'll trust you with information.'

Martha sat up straighter. 'No press. Understood.'

'Of course, it's a risk and if it goes wrong and you let me down – if anything gets out to the press that shouldn't – I'll be in deep shit and you'll be out on your ear. Is that all clear?'

'Abundantly,' she replied.

'So you said you'll share what you have with me. Does that mean you have something right now, or...?'

'I might have. I'm not sure,' Martha said with enthusiasm. 'It might be nothing, but when I was walking on the day I found Fraser, I found this bottle.' She pulled it from her pocket and placed it on the desk. 'I discovered it in my pocket yesterday, and it brought back a bit of my memory of what happened. It'll have my fingerprints all over it now as I wasn't thinking at the time. Just that it was an odd thing to find on the forest floor.'

She hadn't washed away any of the dirt off the bottle and had pushed the stopper back in tight after opening it yesterday. Her fingers were still stained with the contents.

He pulled a plastic glove from a box in his drawer, then picked the bottle up. 'It's probably just some piece of junk that has worked its way up through the earth, but I'll get someone to take a look,' he said.

'The thing is, I found it just up the hill from where Fraser was found, just a minute or two before I fell. And look,' she raised her stained fingers to show him. 'I got the top off it yesterday. It's ink.'

He stared hard at the bottle's contents, then put it back down on his desk. 'Now that makes all the difference,' he said. She thought she could see a tiny gleam in his eye. 'We'll get forensics onto it straight away in that case. And maybe you could show Ravi on the map more or less where you think you found it?'

'Yes, of course,' Martha agreed. 'Now, there's something else too. Just background really, but it might help.'

'Go on,' Summers said.

'You'll know that Fraser and Dougie were friends, knocking around the village together, backward and forward to our farm at Blacklaw on their bikes. Well Christie spent time with them too.'

'Christie?' Summers said.

'Yes, you said you'd spoken to her, remember? Well something happened between the three of them about a year ago, and after, she seemed to go off the scene. Probably just teenage stuff. But on

Saturday I overheard Dougie on the phone to Christie. They were talking about some kind of ritual. And about the poem and its links to Blacklaw and even to Fraser. It made me nervous. I don't believe in witchcraft and that kind of rubbish, but something has gone on with those kids. I went looking for Christie to ask her about it. But she clammed up on me.'

Summers looked sceptical. 'If we're sharing, Martha, I can tell you we've discovered Fraser was smoking weed. A few of his schoolfriends confirmed it. That might explain the kind of rituals they were taking part in ... And I'm sorry to say that your Dougie's name came up too.'

'What?' Martha was indignant. 'Dougie would never do anything like that. Fraser was a bit of a live wire – at least compared to Dougie – but I doubt they were into anything like that. Dougie knows my views on drugs. He wouldn't dare.'

Summers just looked at her. He didn't need to say it out loud: every parent thought their child would never do drugs.

'Look, we're already looking at Fraser's schoolfriends, and trying to find out what he got up to, to see if that gives us any leads. So we'll add what you've just told me into the mix. For now we're concentrating on the drugs found in Fraser's system. It's all speculation at this point, but one theory is that he was drugged just to knock him out while his attacker put that writing on his back. But then, while he was unconscious, he was sick and he choked on it, and was asphyxiated.'

Martha noted that Summers hadn't mentioned Dougie again. She knew the police would want to interview him about this soon, though.

'How's it going finding out who in the area might have been prescribed the Risperdal?' she asked. 'Someone must know where it's come from.'

'Patient confidentiality, Martha. As I've said before, if we had a suspect, that would be different. All we know for sure is that no one in his family has been using that medication.'

'How's the family doing?' she asked. 'They must be going

through hell.' She wondered if Summers knew she'd lost children herself. 'Is there anything else we can do to help them?'

'They're still in shock, Martha, as I'm sure you can imagine.' He paused.

'Any news on how the attacker moved his body? You thought he'd died somewhere else and then been dumped, correct? It's a pretty remote place and he was no lightweight.'

'We're thinking he may have been shifted at night when there was no one around to see. We're still working on trying to find any traces of tyre prints that weren't washed away in the rain. Now.' He put his hands on his knees. 'There's another way I think you could help us.'

'Oh yes?'

'Your lot from the press have started piling on the pressure.'

She nodded. This sounded familiar. The story vultures would be circling. If there wasn't some kind of breakthrough in the investigation soon, the family would think the police weren't doing their job properly, and a wily reporter would get over the doorstep, promising that some pressure from the national media would help make things progress a little faster.

'So I'd appreciate it if you could give me any advice you have on media handling. The heat is turning up now.'

'Of course,' she said. 'I'll have a think and let you know. And call or email if there are any press queries you're not sure about.'

'Thank you. And I'll keep you updated on the case, but on the basis that you're helping us with our inquiries, which technically you are. But none of this goes any further, OK?'

She smiled in agreement. 'I'll give you a shout if I think of anything else,' she said.

Summers stood up and slid open his desk drawer, taking out a squashed pack of Benson & Hedges before following Martha out of the office.

'I gave up years ago,' she said, a rueful smile playing at her lips as he offered her a smoke.

'I'm trying to cut down,' he replied. 'It's a bloody nuisance having to go outside these days for a fag break, but now is not the time to give up the smokes.'

CHAPTER TWENTY-TWO

Martha made Dougie a cooked breakfast when he got up on Tuesday morning.

'Smell of the bacon get you out of your pit?' she asked, smiling.

He sat down and watched as she served up the food onto two plates.

'You feeling OK, Mum?' he asked, with a frown.

She knew he was referring to her general allergy to domestic chores.

'Cheeky bugger,' she said. 'Just eat your breakfast.'

But he was right – this was unusual, and she did have an ulterior motive. She sat down at the table and watched her son demolish the full breakfast in no time. And just as he finished she spoke:

'I saw Christie the other day. Haven't seen her for ages, but she was out riding her horse.' She'd decided to start the conversation in a general way, so as not to put him on the spot straight away.

'Uh huh.'

'She seemed a bit on edge to be honest, and said that you two had been talking. About Fraser and something that happened when the three of you parted ways?' She left the question hanging in the air. She felt just a little bad about the way she'd framed this, but she didn't want to tell him she'd been listening in to his conversation.

'Dunno what she's talking about.' Dougie rocked his chair back on two legs. 'I haven't seen her for a while. Anyway, what were you doing out in the woods, Mum? You shouldn't be out there on your own at the moment.'

She noticed how he'd neatly changed the subject.

'I just took the dogs out for a long walk. I needed to clear the cobwebs.'

'For God's sake, Mum. Fraser's killer is still on the loose, and you're careering around in the forest on your own.' He was exasperated. 'You never think, do you?'

He'd been on edge for a few days, so Martha let this aggressive reaction slide.

'I had the dogs. And my phone. I was OK.'

'Yeah, well you weren't freakin' OK the last time. There's some mad bastard out there. As for the dogs, they're pets, Mother. What are they going to do, lick someone to death?' He slammed his cup down and stomped out of the room.

Martha stared at the empty doorway. Dougie's anger still hovered there. She knew it was really his concern for her. But there was something else there too. And she needed to find out what.

4

'You going out, Doug?' she called, when she heard him come downstairs just before lunchtime. He stood in the doorway, his face flushed, and she wondered if he'd been crying. 'Are you OK?'

He looked as though he was going to say something, glanced at her computer where it sat on the table and seemed to draw back, face suddenly white. Martha turned to the screen – she had the Feannag Dhubh poem on display.

'Yeah, just need to get out for a bit. That OK?' He didn't usually ask these days.

'Yes, but please be careful. You have got your phone on, haven't you?' He nodded. 'Are you OK, pet? You look like you've seen a ghost.'

'I'm OK, Mum.'

Only three words, but it was better than nothing. He pulled on his soft shell jacket and went out through the kitchen door.

Martha breathed in the scent he'd left behind him. Through the early-teenage phase, he had moved on to hair gel and deodorant, but now she could smell a funny, vaguely floral scent on him. Was there a girlfriend in the offing? Maybe it was Christie. The two of them feeling guilty over their dead friend. It seemed like only five minutes since he was a wee boy. When he was small, he often wriggled close, warm little body pressed against her stomach, and feeling her heartbeat, he had fallen fast asleep. Now he was all grown up. Shoulders broadening into a young man. With the worry of a murderer on the loose, she almost wished he was that little boy she could keep safe again.

'Cooey, only me!' A loud voice intruded – Orla announcing herself without even a knock on the front door. 'My God, that lad of yours is going to be a heartbreaker when he grows up.' She appeared in the kitchen. 'Handsome devil, isn't he? If only I was twenty years younger.'

She was brandishing a bottle of red wine. Martha didn't know how she felt about her friend making comments about the attractiveness of her teenage son, especially now.

'Just one, though,' Martha said, feeling like a drink might dispel the tension from Dougie's behaviour. Orla began to look for glasses.

'We can do selfies and stick them on Instagram,' she laughed.

Martha didn't know whether she was serious or not. 'I don't do Instagram, or any of that other social-media rubbish. I only used to look at it for work. It's unbelievable what people share on there.'

'Oh, lighten up, woman. What happened to the daring young Martha I knew, eh?' Orla set two glasses on the table.

'One of my son's friends has been murdered, Orla. I'm not feeling very light about it at all.' But Martha knew her pal was only trying to raise her spirits up, and she welcomed the buzz of Orla's frenetic energy.

'Sorry. I know I'm an insensitive cow,' Orla bulldozed on.

Martha shook her head and gave in. 'Yes, you can be.' It was said with a smile that broke the tension.

'Anyway,' Orla went on. 'What about that dishy minister? Pete. Seems like a lovely guy, and easy on the eye too.'

'For goodness' sake, Orla,' said Martha, laughing now. 'You're really pursuing him, then?'

'Maybe...' Orla tried to look coy. 'Anyway, I've got something to show you that I know you'll be interested in.' She paused dramatically.

'Come on, what is it? To be honest I'm focused on Fraser's death right now.' She gestured to her open laptop. 'I've sort of been co-opted into the investigation. Strictly in confidence, of course.'

'Have you now?' Orla raised her eyebrows. 'Well in that case you really need to see this. I knocked on the gorgeous Reverend's door yesterday – just for a friendly chat, you know. And while he was making us coffee, I made an excuse to have a look around that big old house of his. To see what I might be dealing with, if ... well, you know...'

'Where is this going, Orla?'

'Well, I had snoop around his study, and I found this.' She handed Martha a torn piece of yellowed paper. 'It was tucked behind a photograph of Locke's mother.'

Martha read the heading, then the line of poetry written on the piece of paper, and her heart quickened.

'This is a line from the poem – the second verse was written on Fraser's back.'

Martha quickly woke up her laptop and checked against the text there. She was right. 'As Ostara rises at Crow Moon' was the last line.

'I thought so,' said Orla. 'I remembered you showing it to me when I was here the other night. So why does our reverend have it, do you think?'

'And what does "The Book of Shadows" have to do with it?'

'So if you're part of the investigation now, will you take it to the police?' asked Orla.

Martha fixed Orla with a look. 'How exactly did you find it if it was tucked behind a photograph?'

Orla shook her head in mock despair. 'Alright, I was properly snooping. He had to answer a phone call, so I thought I'd take the opportunity. The photo was of a lovely young woman. I wanted to see who she was, so I might have opened the frame ... Then that fell out. I managed to pocket it before he saw.'

'He caught you?'

'In his study, yes. But I smoothed it out. It's all good.'

Martha shook her head. The fact that Orla had stolen the fragment from Locke's house, made it useless as a piece of evidence. The police would want to know how she had come by it and Martha could hardly tell them Orla had nicked it. But it did give her a bit of a new lead. And she knew who to ask about it.

'I need to make a quick call,' she said. 'I'll just be a few minutes. You pour the wine.'

She went into the living room and dialled the number for Helen Horne. When she answered, Martha explained about the torn page – although she didn't say where or how it had been found. She simply said she'd been handed it.

'Martha, this is serious,' Helen's voice was low, as if she didn't want to be heard. 'The Book of Shadows is like a diary that a witch would keep – in it she'll write down information about her spells, charms, the phases of the moon, and anything else relating to her craft. It's an extremely private thing, and the fact that what you have contains lines from "Feannag Dhubh" concerns me. This could be very dangerous. You must take care.'

CHAPTER TWENTY-THREE

NEW MOON

The village felt like it had been holding its collective breath all week. It was two weeks since Fraser had been found. People were waiting for news about him, but at the same time life was going on.

Christie had been at the stables all Saturday afternoon, and was walking home through Strathbran Estate, thinking about how she'd met Dougie's mum last weekend, when she'd ridden up the Garadhban track. Martha's interrogation had upset her, and Walter too. He'd bolted, and she still wasn't sure whether it was because of Martha or the horrible crow that had dived at her head. Or had it? She still wasn't exactly sure what had happened in those moments.

She couldn't stop thinking about the ritual. Dougie had said he didn't believe it was connected to Fraser's death, but she knew they'd have to speak about it again soon. Thinking about Fraser, she felt her eyes fill with tears. She wiped them away, and as she did she felt the vibration from her phone in her pocket.

It was a text from Dougie: as if he'd felt her thinking about him and decided to get in touch. But when she opened it, she saw he had another reason to message:

Need to meet. Mum looking at something about FD. Need to talk.

FD? Her heart sank. He must mean Feannag Dhubh. Christie looked around. Panic rose in her. The rite was only supposed to have been about giving Dougie some peace. She'd researched Ostara rituals to welcome in the spring and stuff about calming restless spirits that had met an unnatural death. She'd written it all down in her journal. Practised it at home. They'd decided to perform it under the Crow Moon at the moondial that night. The same moon was due to rise this month – two weeks tonight, in fact. She shivered. She knew the stories about the Feannag

Dhubh; she'd found out stuff about the mythology from the internet. But maybe she'd done something wrong – mixed up the rituals and caused something they hadn't meant to happen. The community online were divided about the legend of the witch: some said she was evil, but Christie didn't believe that.

She'd been terrified that night though. As the moon shone down, bathing them in its clear lunar glow, they'd begun the chant. The salt and crushed eggshells should have protected them, but when the black figure had come screaming from the trees, they had fled, terrified. She didn't know whether either of the boys had been back there since. She'd felt guilty for a long time, thinking back. And now Fraser had been … She couldn't even think the words. She wondered how Dougie was coping with this on top of everything else. That terrible fire he'd lost the twins in. Christie didn't think she would be strong enough to cope with such a hideous tragedy.

The air was cool where trees overhung the path and in the bluebell wood to her right as she walked. There was no sign of the delicate blue flowers yet. They would bloom in May, once the bright-green shoots had pushed through the cold winter earth, carpeting the woodland floor. She plugged in her headphones. She'd left it slightly late to head home, she realised, and quickened her pace – the daylight was already starting to fade. The clocks would go forward in a few weeks, she remembered.

Lost in her thoughts, she'd just passed through the stone gateway to the estate, when strong arms suddenly enclosed her from behind. Startled, then pleased, for a second, she thought it must be a friend.

'Dougie?' she said. But the grip that tightened around her was too powerful. The body smell too adult. She strained hard, trying to pull away, but whoever had hold of her, she couldn't get free. Her headphones fell from her ears and she could smell hot, sour breath on her neck.

'Stop!' She managed to get the word out before a rough hand

clamped over her mouth. Struggling, she tried to call out again, but the person dragged her backward towards the trees. A dog barked in the distance and breathing heavily in panic, Christie prayed someone would see them and help. She felt her legs trail helplessly through the mud; heart thumping against her ribs as terror rose in her throat. The man grunted with effort. She tried to kick her legs, but he squeezed her harder, making it difficult to breathe. He stumbled, pulling her through a field gateway, her hip hitting against the gatepost painfully.

Tears filled Christie's eyes, blurring clouds crowding the moon that had risen overhead. Stark branches of trees were outlined against the sky.

I'm going to die, she thought.

She didn't understand. Why was he doing this? Fingers dug hard into her sides and a harsh, chemical scent mixed with sweat came off him. They stopped and for a second his grip loosened, Christie kicking her legs as hard as she could and attempting a strangled cry against his hand. But the moment wasn't long enough for her to break free. She felt her phone slip from her hand then pain splintering through her skull, before darkness took her.

CHAPTER TWENTY-FOUR

Hauling the girl into a fireman's lift over his shoulder, the man staggered to the rusted quad bike and trailer, and dumping her on top of a torn tarpaulin in the back, he wrapped it tight around her so no one would know he had a body in there. A couple of weighted sacks secured the cargo. His heart was pounding; an adrenaline rush from taking the girl. The planning and sense of excitement had been building over the days he'd watched her coming and going. He'd even seen her walking on the far side of the road when he was in the old railway buildings. She hadn't known he was there, of course, as he watched from the abandoned shack. But the chance of being caught excited him like nothing had for a long time.

He'd known Fraser and Christie for some time – Dougie Strangeways too. Fraser had been harder than her though. It had felt more risky, creating the accident and then tricking him into drinking the drugged water. Then, after the work was complete, hauling his body back onto the trailer had required a superhuman effort. The witch said he might not be able to do it. But he was still strong. The girl would be more straightforward though. She was smaller, easy to subdue.

Come on. You've work to do. You need to get on with it.

'Yes, I am,' he said.

This girl was a different challenge. It had been a long time since his first. A very long time. And he'd hidden her so well, no one had ever suspected, at least not enough to do anything about it.

Here he was again though. They should never have played their stupid games. It was dangerous, and they'd opened a path to something they didn't understand. The whispers in his head had begun that very night, when they'd performed that ritual at the moondial. 'Take the girl and don't get caught,' that's what the voice had said. And now, with the police making inquiries about Fraser, there was an even greater risk. He'd have to take care. No one must find out yet. Not until he'd finished the job.

The sheep scattered as he drove through the middle of the flock – light fading as they headed into the darkness of the woods. Two weeks left and his plan was on track.

The Book of Shadows

I write this here as I have no other place to share my pain. My virtue is gone. I realise now his heart is truly blackened. I cried out when he hit me, my face pressed into the dirt in that dark and lonely place. He had no need to force me, and now says I am spoiled and cannot return home. I am tied to him forever and I must make the best of it.

I am in pain, but I must protect myself. There is a place I have found where I feel safe. Where the spirits reside and I am more like myself. I wish my mother had warned me what might happen here. I have been a fool.

CHAPTER TWENTY-FIVE

Christie didn't want to die. Shivering and stiff with cold, she stared wide-eyed into the dark. She knew she was inside a building. Its dense stone seemed to press the chill onto her as she lay, legs sprawled out awkwardly, on a dirt floor. Her wrists were tied, hurting with every feeble attempt to shift her body. Dense pain radiated across her neck and shoulders. She shook her head slightly, but the murky fog in her brain wouldn't clear. She didn't understand why she was here. She wondered what might be crawling around in the dirt beneath her. Tied up, she couldn't move very far.

'Help me!' she called. The place stank of mould, the fusty odour of an unused place. She could smell the faint scent of something charred too. Fear pooled in her stomach, its acid burn reaching into her throat. She retched, but nothing came up.

'Where am I?' she whispered. 'Mum...' Tears traced trails in the dirt on her face. 'Please, let me go home. Please.' Curling her knees up towards her chest, she felt as helpless as a small child as she stared into the shadows around her. She thought about Fraser. Was her abduction connected to him? Was it because of what they'd done? She sat back, feeling defeated, wondering if she'd get out of here alive.

The man squatted in the back corner of the building, watching Christie. He'd been there for a while, fascinated by the gentle rise and fall of her chest, her features free of all worry while she'd been asleep. It had been tricky getting her back here last night without being seen. Especially around the edges of the estate, where maintenance staff were busy finishing off for the day. He'd steered clear, taking a slightly longer route. Thankfully, no one came near this place now. Not since the fire in the steading, almost two years ago. He had to be careful though, as he believed whatever had been haunting him since that night at the moondial had insinuated its way into his thoughts.

The track leading to the farm had been overgrown, and there were no witnesses to see him with Christie, except the sheep. It was easier with the quad, but in her deep sleep, the girl had been heavier than he'd expected. He'd laid her down more roughly than intended, but she was still unconscious.

He'd watched her wake and cry. Not wailing, just silently sobbing and looking into the dark, frightened. A smile played on his face. He had all the power now. He enjoyed the moment – having control over someone else.

Worthless girl. She knows you.

He'd been feeling uneasy. His mind unable to settle. He wondered if she was right. He raked his hands across his scalp, pulling at his hair as though he could erase her voice from his head. He pushed his fingers into his ears, but her voice just became a whisper then. The kids had taken things from the church – the candles they had used – mottled crow egg shells gathered from fallen nests in the kirkyard. Things they'd had no right to. Things that tied him to their ritual. They had no idea. The crows he caught were manifestations of dark things, come to watch him. He had to be careful now. The voice knew his thoughts, she hid in their creases, and he didn't want to make her angry. This girl would be marked, with ink and words. Another verse and then one more to go. The witch had returned and no one was safe until he had banished her back to the dark place she'd come from.

The girl heaved in a gulp of dry air, the dust making her cough and almost choke. Desperate for a drink, her cries became louder; she sobbed, her fear suffusing the darkness.

'There's no one but me to hear you now,' he hissed. 'And the Feannag Dhubh.'

A sharp, shocked intake of breath. Christie fell suddenly silent, her petrified gaze fixed on the dark corner where he sat.

CHAPTER TWENTY-SIX

Locke looked surprised when Orla appeared at his door on Sunday afternoon, but he couldn't have been too annoyed with her about snooping around his house the last time she was there, because he ushered her inside and through to the kitchen.

'Hope I haven't interrupted anything,' she said.

'Not really,' he said. 'You've caught me between services. I use Sunday afternoon to prepare my weekly diary. Nothing that can't wait.' He gave her a cautious smile. 'Fancy a coffee?'

'That would be lovely,' she replied as she sat down at the table. She wanted to find out more about him. She sensed Martha wasn't his biggest fan, but she, on the other hand, was drawn to him. Yes, she was physically attracted to him, but there was something else – her journalistic instincts identified something odd there that she just had to uncover.

'Have you heard anything new about Fraser among your parishioners?' she asked carefully. 'I know Martha thinks the investigation should have moved on by now...'

'I haven't heard any more than anyone else,' he said. 'Tensions are high though, and people are worried about their children. The talk at the church door this morning was that the search teams are back and were preparing to go out again, so maybe they've found something.'

She watched him, grinding coffee beans in his fancy kitchen gadget. It looked incongruous – the rest of the house seemed to exist in a time warp. The kitchen units were old-fashioned, with worn lino on the floor. A satisfying hiss sounded as the boiling water poured over the coffee grounds and the intense smell of bitter chocolate and spice filled the room.

'I was intrigued by that picture of your mother the other day.' Orla could tell by the way Locke had looked at it that he had been close to her. Maybe this was a better way to bring him out of his shell. 'What was she like?'

'You mean the one you found when you were snooping?' His light-hearted tone belied a warning beneath. He clearly liked his privacy. And Orla wondered why.

'Tell me about your mum,' she said. 'I like to hear stories like this. She looked so young in that photo.'

He stared out of the window for a long moment. Then looked back at her. 'She left when I was young. So my dad brought me up alone.'

Orla held his gaze and waited.

'Now, as an adult looking back, to be honest I'm not surprised she walked out.' He rubbed his face briskly. 'Back then though, when I was a small child, it felt worse than if she'd died.'

'That sounds very difficult,' Orla said, watching him closely now.

'She was from Denmark,' he went on. 'My father met her when she was very young. Her own father was a minister in the Danish Kirk – similar presbyterian sensibilities to Scotland,' he smiled wryly. Then his face became sad again. 'For a long while after she left, I thought I could hear her talking to me. She had a very distinctive voice – with an accent, of course. It was like a phantom in my head. It went on for months, years even. It was quite scary for a young lad.'

'It must have been dreadful.' Orla reached out and stroked his arm. 'Did she just disappear? Was there no warning at all?'

'Nothing. I went to bed one evening and she was there. When I got up next morning, she wasn't. That was what I could never get over. If she was going to run away, why didn't she take me with her? That was the question I lived with my whole childhood.'

He explained how his grandmother had come to live with his father and him, taking over rooms at the top of the manse. A large, stern woman, he recalled her insisting they eat every meal in silence, and he'd stare, fascinated by the way she chewed every morsel of food, her jaw crunching with bovine determination. He mostly stayed out of her way, he said.

'Not that I would've been able to cause her much bother,' he continued. 'Things got so bad with my grief, I was medicated for much of the time.'

'That's terrible. What about therapy?'

'I remember going for a few appointments, but my dad favoured prayer over psychological help. And when that didn't work, my grandmother took me to some doctor in Glasgow, who gave me the pills. I still don't even know what they were...'

A noise outside the window alerted them to a large tabby cat staring in, mewing loudly.

Locke stood up and let it in, then opened a carton of milk and poured a little into a saucer. The creature wound its way around his leg, purring loudly, but when he leaned down to stroke its thick, peppery fur, it ran off, leaping back out through the open window.

'Please yourself,' he said.

The cat settled beneath a shrub in the garden, watching him.

'I didn't have you down as an animal lover,' Orla laughed.

'It's not my cat. Just comes here occasionally, looking for food.'

Orla took a sip of her coffee. 'What about your father?' she asked. 'Is he still alive?'

'Aye, but he's a curmudgeonly old devil,' Locke explained. 'He was the kirk minister here before me. Doesn't really think I've carried on the family business in the best of ways.' His smile was thin.

Orla put down her mug and said she needed to powder her nose.

'You know where it is,' Locke replied. 'No snooping this time...'

He was smiling, but again she heard the warning in his voice. A warning that made her more curious than ever. But she couldn't risk another foray into the rooms she passed on the way to the small bathroom at the end of the hall. She looked up the big staircase, into the dim of the upper floors. No, he would hear her footsteps.

In the bathroom, her eyes scanned for anything she could find. There was a cupboard under the sink, and a medicine cabinet over it with a mirrored door. She let the water run in the sink, quickly checked the cupboard – bottles of cleaning products – then carefully opened the cabinet.

She had very little time, so she quickly appraised the contents, making an inventory list: a sticky bottle of cough mixture, cotton-wool balls, cold remedies. Plasters. Painkillers. Everything you'd expect. But at the top, a paper bag, with the distinctive logo of a pharmacy. She reached up and pulled the bag towards her, and as she did so, its corner caught a bottle of vitamins. One hand on the bag, she darted the other out and caught the bottle just before it went clattering into the sink.

She let out the breath she'd been holding. Then examined the contents of the bag. Inside was a box. She read the label.

She had to breathe in again quickly.

Risperdal.

*

She walked back in the kitchen holding her belly.

'I'm so sorry, but I'm not feeling that great,' she lied.

'Hope my coffee isn't responsible,' Locke said, looking up.

'No, no. I risked some out-of-date yoghurt this morning, and I think it's disagreeing with me. So I'm going to make a move.'

Locke stood up and saw her to the door, and as she put her coat on and turned to say goodbye, she thought she saw a look in his eye and a slight incline of his head that might just have turned into a kiss.

But instead he squeezed her arm gently and said, 'Take care. I hope you feel better.'

For a second she felt a strange flash of disappointment. She nodded, and was about to tell him not to work too hard that afternoon, when a sudden commotion made them both step outside.

On the lawn in front of the manse the tabby cat and a large, black bird were rolling around in a squawking, hissing knot of wings and fur. It was unclear who was winning.

'Oh my God,' said Orla, as Locke ran forward with his arms out, shouting.

The fight broke up as suddenly as it had begun, the cat darting away into the bushes. The crow flapped off into the trees.

'How horrible,' Orla said, then hurried on her way, disquieted now, and keener than ever to get to Martha's to tell her about her discovery.

Martha shook her head at Orla as she finished telling her about her afternoon visit to Locke.

'I'm not sure what I'm more shocked by – your detective work or the fact that Locke has Risperdal in his medicine cabinet.'

Orla put down the big glass of water Martha had given her when she came rushing in through the door. 'What would you do without me, huh?' she said grimly.

'This could be an important development,' Martha went on. 'I'll have to take it to Summers. It might be a coincidence, but Fraser is found dead with Risperdal in his system, and then the same drug is found at the local minister's house…?'

'He just seems like such a nice guy,' Orla said sadly.

Martha stared at her friend. 'You know it's an anti-psychotic, don't you?'

Orla sighed. 'Yes, I do. But you should have heard him talk about his mum. Walked out on him as a child, you know. He said he was medicated back then – for the grief.'

Martha raised her eyebrows. That was an interesting detail. The distrust she'd always felt towards Locke was starting to get some colour now.

'Look, I do need to tell Summers what you found. But I'll do it in the morning. With this on top of the scrap of paper, I need some thinking time.'

CHAPTER TWENTY-SEVEN

Martha's chest tightened in panic when she opened the door and saw a uniformed police officer standing there. *Is it Dougie?* she thought, even though her rational brain told her that her son would still be in bed this early on a Monday morning.

'Can I help you?' she said, pulling herself together. After days of no apparent police activity, last night she'd seen renewed search teams out, and had assumed it was related to Fraser's death. Maybe the police had had a new tip-off?

'We're knocking on doors, trying to ascertain whether anyone might have seen or heard from Christie Campbell,' the officer said. 'We understand your son knows her.'

Martha's blood cooled. 'Christie? What's happened to her? Is she OK?'

'She has gone missing, I'm afraid, and we are concerned for her welfare. Search parties have been organised, but she didn't come back from the riding stables on Saturday night and her parents are extremely worried.'

'Good grief. No, I haven't seen her. I was speaking to her the other day. A week ago now, though. Out on the trails in the forest. She was on her horse...' Martha's mind was racing now. Not Christie too.

'My son, Dougie, is in bed. As far as I know he's not seen her. They were speaking on the phone, again more than a week ago, but I don't think he's seen her since.'

'OK, let us know if either of you hear from her, or think of anything that might help.'

As he walked away and she closed the door, her phone began to ring. It was Summers.

'I'm sorry to be calling so early, Martha, but I'd appreciate your help on something.'

'Yes, of course. I can't believe the news. Now Christie has gone missing! What *is* going on?'

'Oh, so you already know?'

'An officer has just been at the door. I couldn't tell him anything, unfortunately. He said she didn't come home from the stables.'

'That's right. We've tried her friends and the people at the riding place, but no one's seen her since she left yesterday tea time.'

'I noticed there was a search yesterday? I thought it was to do with Fraser.'

'Yes, they were out looking for her until it was dark. I'm here in Strathbran, at the Campbell house. We're organising another search as I speak. We need professionals on this who know what to do, and as quickly as possible.'

The line went silent.

'Do you think it's connected to Fraser?' said Martha at last.

'There's nothing immediately suggesting it is, but—'

'Oh, come on, man!' Martha interrupted, exasperated. 'How can it not be connected? She was friends with Fraser and Dougie. I told you that I'd heard her and Dougie talking about something – a ritual – and that it was connected with Fraser. Well I went looking for her the other day. She was riding her horse along the trails up in the forest. And she was very defensive when I brought up that conversation. There's something going on here, surely? Folk are going to be bloody terrified now, you know. Even if Christie's just gone off somewhere, which I doubt, people are going to be frightened for their kids.'

'I do realise that, Martha.' Summers sounded weary. She

understood his frustration, but she needed him to accept the connections. It was clearly time to reveal the pieces of information that Orla had discovered.

'Look, I said if I turned up anything I thought was useful, I'd share it with you. Well, there's some information I've come across that suggests there's someone you need to look into.'

'Hang on.' It sounded like Summers was moving outside. Out of hearing range of anyone else, Martha guessed. 'OK, go ahead,' he said after a moment. 'Who are we talking about?'

'Reverend Peter Locke.'

'What, the minister of the kirk?'

'That's him. Now, I'm not going to tell you who found this out, but I have it on good authority that a scrap of paper with a line from the Feannag Dhubh poem was in Locke's house.'

'That's hardly incriminating...' Summers began.

'That's not all though. Just last night this same source informed me that there's a pharmacy bag in Locke's bathroom with a pre-scription for Risperdal in it.'

'OK, now that's something important. And you should've called me the minute you found out.'

'I was going to call you this morning, but you called me first.'

'I'm available twenty-four hours, Martha. You know how it works. You should've called me.'

Martha was silent. He was right. And she would have to be careful if she didn't want him to end their deal.

'And you need to tell me how you came across this information so I can determine whether I can act on it.'

'Let's just say it was someone who visited him and happened to see that prescription. You'll have to trust me when I say they're an extremely reliable source.'

'We agreed you're not working for any media outlet,' Summers said. 'So you're not a journalist protecting your sources.'

'Can't you trust me on this one? I think you need to look into Locke.'

'I guess we could go round there and have a chat. And knowing he's on Risperdal is extremely significant. But we'll need clear evidence if we're going to search the property or bring him in for questioning.'

'Understood,' Martha replied.

She felt sick, the whole thing was far too close to home, but she knew she couldn't back out now. She couldn't leave this to the police. She was in too deep.

'Has that ink been tested yet?' she asked.

'I should get the results any day. I'll chase them,' Summers said.

Martha was troubled. She understood that Summers couldn't act on her information, because of the way Orla had discovered it, but she was certain that Locke should be treated as a person of interest.

'We need to crack on with this search,' Summers went on, 'and then I'm going to issue a missing-persons press release for Christie. I realise it will result in a media circus turning up here though. Any advice on how we can best handle that?'

'There's nothing you can do to stop it, I'm afraid. The village will soon be crawling with reporters. I assume you'll do an appeal for anyone that has information about her. I'd say get it on TV and radio ASAP, so you're on the front foot,' she said. 'And I think you really have to tell people about the poem now.'

'But that would suggest a definitive link between the two cases, wouldn't it?' Summers said. 'It would make the family think Christie was potentially in more danger than she may be in.'

'But she *is* in danger.' Martha couldn't help being short with him. 'I get what you mean about protecting her parents, but you're short on leads, and we both know that poem is key to all this. It's deeply connected to this place, and whoever wrote it on Fraser's back, and potentially killed him, knows Strathbran and its history. It's been too long without a breakthrough. You need to put something new out there. As soon as the press realise that another kid has gone missing from the same village as Fraser, they'll be here in droves. Even if there's no link between the two, they'll make one up. You need to show you're on top of both cases, doing everything you can.'

'Could you be there to help manage the press? From the sidelines, I mean? I know it's a lot to ask, but it might give us a bit of breathing space to get the search properly under way.'

It was a dilemma. Reporters knew they should always be the observer, never the story. But this was different. Martha was right at the centre of the action here. These were Dougie's friends who were going missing. He would be totally stressed out and she needed to be there for him. But she needed to find out what was happening too, who was kidnapping these kids. This wasn't just journalism – she wasn't breaking a story.

She thought of the way Christie had looked so carefree, sat up there on her horse the other day. Enjoying the wind in her face and a wide grin lighting her up. And then the way she changed at the mention of Fraser.

'I'll do whatever I can to help,' Martha said. 'We have to find her. And not in the way we found poor Fraser.'

The Book of Shadows

He made me say those words in church, and only his mother bore witness, her eyes sly with danger. She does not want me in her home, where she slips poison into his mind, but he insisted, and I believe he planned this all along. I am so alone here now.

He leaves me alone now my belly has swelled, though. I have a little more freedom to wander outside, to feed my beloved birds and watch the clouds dance over the hills. I slip away when I can to the place I have found, but I must take care. For if they find I go there at night, they will not like it. If they know what I do under the moon. But I must make charms to protect the life I carry now.

CHAPTER TWENTY-EIGHT

Monday passed and there was still no sign of Christie. A fresh team was assembled and a new search was under way early on Tuesday morning. Although Martha had managed to head off the first lot of press on Monday, as soon as the story hit newsdesks, more reporters and snappers had begun to arrive in Strathbran. This story was gathering pace. As she'd predicted, Fraser's name was being mentioned in the same breath as Christie's. Locals being questioned about what they knew, posed for serious-faced photographs next to the sign for the village. As she walked up to the hall, she spotted people out on their doorsteps, breath pluming in the chill morning air, chatting to neighbours in hushed, worried voices. Overhead, fingers of woodsmoke curved from the chimney pots. Winter wasn't over yet.

As she passed Fraser's house Jane MacDonald stopped her. 'Do you know anything?' she asked, her hand on Martha's arm, a pleading look in her eyes. 'Everyone's saying Christie's missing.'

'That's right.' Martha tried to look sympathetic. 'The police are doing a televised appeal for anyone with information about where she might be.'

'You don't think—?' Fraser's mum cut her question short. And they stood in silence for a moment.

'I'm so sorry about Fraser,' Martha said eventually. 'I didn't get the chance to speak to you at the service. Dougie is devastated, as you all must be.'

Jane nodded, trying to smile through eyes that brimmed with tears. 'You know what it's like to lose your child, Martha.'

Martha nodded, feeling her own eyes filling up.

'It shouldn't be like this,' said Jane, simply.

'I'm so sorry, Jane,' Martha repeated, appreciating how hard it was to know what to say to someone, even though she'd been through the same devastating tragedy. 'If there's anything I can do to help you, you know I will.'

She watched Jane's mouth tremble, on the brink of a wave of grief, and touched her shoulder. A tear slid down Jane's cheek.

She wiped it away angrily. 'What about our Fraser? They haven't even found who did it, and now they're off looking for Christie.'

They watched a police car drive past, and Martha said she'd better go.

She looked down the hill to the bare fields beyond the village as she crossed the road. A flock of what looked like crows were gathered, pecking at the still-cold earth.

Martha shuddered, remembering Helen Horne's warning about Fraser not being the last to be taken. The words from the last verse of the poem came into her mind: 'Starvation months are nearing end / She'll strike new lambs where no defend.'

Could the same person have taken Christie and Fraser? Or was this just a coincidence? She glanced behind her, towards the kirk and the manse beyond. Surely Locke couldn't be their man? There was something about him that unsettled her, but that was no reason to believe he was behind all this. Yet there was Risperdal in his bathroom ... She wondered how seriously Summers was taking the information she'd given him.

She crossed to the shop for a bottle of water. The village shopkeeper, Mrs Henderson, was clearly pleased with the extra business at her store. Martha watched as she told a few reporters looking for takeaway coffees what she knew, which was little other than gossip. She tucked her frizzy grey hair behind her ears and adjusted her glasses, in the hope someone might ask for a photograph or an interview.

'Of course, that girl was into weird stuff, you know. I can't remember when, but she came in here last year looking to buy large church candles and matches. Wouldn't surprise me if those kids hadn't been dabbling in Ouija boards or the like. This place has a dark history that many incomers wouldn't have a clue about.'

Helen Horne's words about the woman accused of witchcraft who lost her life on the spot where the moondial was built echoed in Martha's memory. She didn't believe in fairy tales. There was always a rational explanation for everything, she told herself. Mrs Henderson, and no doubt plenty of others, were just getting caught up in the moment, mixing the horror of a teenager's death with mystery and history. It was a potent mix that could fuel rumours if it got out of control. But she couldn't deny she was having a struggle not succumbing to the feeling that something eerie was abroad in Strathbran.

Leaving the shop, she headed to where the press had gathered around the village square. She recognised a few faces, people nodding to her and clearly thinking she was back working on the story, as they were; they didn't have a clue she was actually part of the narrative this time. It all felt surreal.

Her phone rang. DI Summers. He sounded harassed.

'Martha, thanks for holding them off for a bit. I appreciate your support. It's given us a head start so we got the new search teams briefed and out. I'm going to come down to the hall to hold a media briefing in thirty minutes. Could you let your friends know, so we can try to keep a bit of order?'

'I'll do my best,' she answered. 'I'm with them already. It's looking like the circus has come to town.'

She felt sympathy for the detective. It must be frustrating to have so little to go on and now that Christie was missing too, he'd be under immense pressure. She glanced round and subtly stepped away from the group.

'Any news on what I told you yesterday, about…?' She let her sentence hang. She couldn't risk any keen-eared reporter hearing a name.

'About the Reverend Locke? We visited him yesterday, saying we thought he might have a bigger picture of the community. Had a good long chat. Asked him whether he knew Fraser and Christie. He said the two of them and Dougie had played in a church band together a couple of years back. Is that right?'

'Yes, it is. When they were closer.' Martha hadn't made that connection. Locke would have seen them at least once a week. Known them pretty well.

'Well, it gave us the opportunity to see if he had an alibi. We said it was just a matter of course, asking where he was when Fraser and Christie went missing – because he'd revealed he had known both kids personally. Told him we were asking everyone who did...'

'And...?'

'Seems he can account for himself for the time periods – as you'd expect with a minister.'

Martha sighed, not sure if she was pleased or disappointed. 'But there's no telling exactly when they were snatched is there, so...' Martha tailed off. 'What about the Risperdal in his bathroom?'

'We're still looking into that. Look, I'd better go. See you at the village hall shortly.'

Martha rang off and looking around, she spotted a sensible guy she knew from the BBC Glasgow newsroom. He'd want to be in at the front, to get the first interviews.

'John. Long time, no see.' The journalist was smartly dressed, although the bright-green North Face jacket was at odds with his suit. It looked brand new; he'd probably bought it on the way out here, thinking the weather would be colder near the mountains.

'Martha Strangeways.' His whitened teeth made a wolfish grin against his clean-shaven jaw. His face was made for TV, Martha thought. 'It's good to see you. You got the inside track on this one already?' he asked.

'Not exactly,' she said. 'I live here. It's a bit odd having you lot turn up on my doorstep. DI Summers is calling a briefing in thirty in the village hall. Can you get the word round?'

John nodded. She knew he'd make sure he and his camera crew bagged the best spot before he told anyone else.

Martha caught a couple of other hacks and let them know about the briefing, and within moments, the herd was picking up its stuff and heading for the hall.

'What's going on, Martha?' asked Orla coming up behind her. 'What's the briefing about? Is there something new?'

'Summers wants to try to control the narrative,' said Martha. 'You know the drill.'

'So nothing about the stash in Locke's bathroom cabinet?'

'No. And you cannot – *cannot* – mention that to anyone yet.'

'Of course not,' Orla replied. Martha watched her light up a cigarette, her scarlet lipstick leaving a mark on the filter as she waved it about with typical melodrama while she talked. 'And I'm sure there's a reasonable explanation for it being there. I like Pete – he's ... interesting...'

'"Interesting"?' Martha stared at Orla.

She gave her a wide-eyed stare back.

This was getting complicated.

Fifteen minutes later, the old hall was half filled with media, all waiting. Through the windows Martha could see that a group of local people had gathered across the road outside too, watching for developments.

Cameras were at the ready as Summers appeared and stood behind a hurriedly assembled table. DC Walker was at his side, and it looked like they'd managed to find a junior press officer – a young woman in an overcoat was standing to one side, clutching a notepad and pen. Martha stayed at the back. This was the first media brief she'd been to since the night of the fire. She slid her hand into her pocket, fingers touching the box, a loose edge of tape against her fingers. She felt its contents jostle.

Summers' loud voice silenced the murmurs around the hall.

'We're here to ask for your help – and it's very important that you get the information clear and correct on this one. A teenage girl has gone missing from the village. Christie Campbell is sixteen years old and lives here with her parents. She was last seen leaving a local stable yard at around 6.00pm on Saturday to make the short walk home through Strathbran Estate. We have not been able to make contact with Christie since, and believe she could be in danger. We have found her phone on the estate, so she must have dropped it without realising. We're appealing for witnesses – anyone who has seen her shortly before or since 6.00pm on Saturday – to get in touch. We are also checking all the buses that have gone through the village in case she has gone off somewhere; as well as CCTV from train stations in Stirling and Glasgow.'

He didn't say so, but Martha knew that they would already have a detective looking through Christie's Instagram and Snapchat accounts, and that inquiries would have gone to her mobile provider to access any texts or calls she had made. If they hadn't already, the assembled media would soon be scanning any public profile she had on social media, to see what they could find out, or a photo to grab for their news reports.

The expectant silence was broken only by the clicking of cameras, giving Summers the chance to finish before they dived in with questions.

'Mountain-rescue teams are already searching the surrounding area. Christie is known to ride her horse around here, and particularly in the forest. We need to find her safe and well as soon as possible.'

The questions began. Would the parents give a statement? Would a picture be released? Did she have a boyfriend? Was there any reason to believe she might have been abducted?

And then it came:

Was this connected to the unsolved murder of Fraser MacDonald?

Glancing at Martha, Summers took a deep breath. 'We have no reason at this stage to believe this may be connected to the death of Fraser. We are following up a range of inquiries and hope to have news on that soon.' His voice was steady despite what Martha was sure must be inner turmoil. This was more than just a job to him, she thought.

A reporter standing beside Martha voiced what everyone knew wasn't being said: 'Aye, right. There seem to be a lot of young people go missing around here. Is there a problem you're not telling us about?'

The volume rose in the hall. Summers cleared his throat to speak, but the hubbub grew louder.

A sudden piercing noise grabbed everyone's attention. They all turned, staring at Martha, who had wolf-whistled through her fingers. Summers watched, a wry look on his face. He'd clearly not seen this happen at a press briefing before.

'Listen. You all know I'm a journalist. And there's a story here, for sure,' said Martha, suddenly realising that she held the room's attention. 'But this time I'm a worried member of the public. Someone who lives here. It's important that we let the police and the rescue teams do their job right now. I know this girl. She's out there somewhere, possibly alone and frightened. Perhaps lost. I know you've all got a job to do too, but let's do everything we can to help get her back.'

The TV reporter, John, chimed in. 'She's right. Let's stay around, report what we see and do what we can to help. At least give these people a chance to find her.'

The rest of the briefing went off without incident, Summers providing all the requisite descriptions, soundbites and responses. There was enough there for the various media outlets to chew on, Martha thought. He'd done well, considering.

'Thanks for that,' Martha said to John as the crowd began to move out of the hall.

'No problem. If you know the lass, you can return the favour and get me an interview with her and her family when she comes home, eh?'

Martha shook her head, smiling slightly. 'Aye, right,' she said.

He stepped away, exchanging a few words with Orla before turning away as his crew got ready for a live broadcast outside the hall. Martha hoped Orla was keeping her promises.

'Well, that was one way to get their attention,' Summers said, behind Martha. 'I didn't know you had such talent.'

'I'm used to calling dogs to heel,' she said with grim humour. 'This lot are no different really.'

CHAPTER TWENTY-NINE

With the search for Christie fully under way, Martha returned home. Her colleagues in the media would be busy writing their first reports, then trying to seek out new angles on the case, possible leads that the police hadn't yet mentioned. It was odd to have one of these very leads in her hands, knowing that she couldn't share it, that it wouldn't appear in a story under the byline 'Martha Strangeways' – it was odd not to experience the buzz of a scoop. But there was more at stake than her journalistic pride.

Locke was on Risperdal. Or at least he had Risperdal in his home. It was frustrating that Summers couldn't see a way to follow up on her tip-off. She knew his hands were tied legally, but couldn't he at least ask Locke whether he took the drug? Whether someone could have stolen his prescription? Maybe she could find a way if Summers couldn't. But then, that would drop Orla in it. There had to be a way around it. She'd written dozens of stories over the years about drug dealers and gang wars in the city. She remembered one in particular from a few years ago and wondered if she still had a copy somewhere in a cuttings file.

She climbed the stairs to the loft, which was split into two rooms – one that Dougie inhabited, and the other, accessed through Dougie's room, crammed full of the junk that had been in storage at the time of the fire. Martha wasn't often up here. Far from your average untidy teen, Dougie's shirts were neatly arranged on the clothes rack, the bed made. Rain pattered off the large skylight as she opened the blind. Out of the window the misty outline of Ben Lomond, the highest mountain they could see from their house, rose in the distance – Dougie had the best view up here. Her son's notebooks and recording equipment were on his desk. There was a floral scent in the air up here. The same smell she sensed on Dougie himself recently. She frowned, recalling what Summers had said. It did smell a bit like weed, but she didn't want to believe that he'd been smoking it. She ran a finger through the dust on his desk and took a guilty glance inside his notepad at a handwritten list. *Daily Goals*, it read.

Two hours guitar practice.

Music theory.

Weights – three sets of 10 reps 20 kilos, 50 press ups, 50 sit ups.

Revision.

How many seventeen-year-olds would be that organised? She felt a tug of affection for her gentle, kind lad. And gratitude too.

What she was looking for wasn't in his room though. She opened the door to the other side of the loft and stepped inside – the smell of dust and old books was heavy in here. The Velux skylight window had large cobwebs hanging from it, and boxes were piled everywhere – the detritus of several years of her life. From her single days at journalism college, with her Scots law and shorthand books, to boxes full of newspaper cuttings she had kept, many now yellowing with age. She hauled out a large box marked with the date from more or less the year she was looking for. Sitting down, she looked around at all the crap that had somehow ended up in here rather than a skip. It was a bittersweet feeling that she still had much of her history. She pulled cuttings out of the box, feeling their papery smoothness against her fingers. The scent of newsprint caught her nose.

Rain pelted hard against the window as Martha rifled through the cuttings. Seeing her byline again gave her an odd feeling, as did the photo they insisted on taking of her in front of a *Glasgow Evening Standard* backdrop the night she'd won Investigative Journalist of the Year for the fourth time running. She looked different then. More polished. Her black hair sleek, her make-up perfect. A slash of scarlet glistening on her lips. She never looked like that these days.

It took her a few minutes to find what she was looking for. She began to read the story, squinting in the dim light. Drug dealer Danny McMannus was an East End of Glasgow gang leader, suspected of orchestrating a number of shootings and arson attacks in a turf war several years before. She scanned the interviews, but apart from a trip down memory lane, nothing jumped out that would help in her current investigation.

She hauled out another box marked *Cuttings*, but when she opened the lid, it was full of photographs. An envelope marked *Orla & Me* caught her eye. Inside pictures of the two of them as teenagers, with big curly hair and eyeshadow to match their shoulder-padded outfits. Despite the make-up, there was something innocent and fresh-faced about the pair of them. She put them aside to show her friend later.

There were also pictures of Dougie, and underneath the first handful, images of the twins. She had photos of the boys on her computer, but hadn't been able to look at them since the fire. Martha held her breath as she gazed at the prints of her children, their smiling, innocent faces and matching outfits she'd so carefully chosen for them. Josh had a tiny cleft in his chin when he smiled. A minuscule difference from his identical twin, but she always noticed it. Sharp tears pricked at her eyes as she traced her fingertips across the precious photograph, leaving marks on the shiny surface.

As she wiped her eyes on her sleeve, she saw another photo lying face up on top of the box. It was a picture from a few years ago showing Dougie's smiling face, rounder than it was now. Christie stood next to him, her blonde hair framing her pretty features. And, arm around her shoulder on the other side, was a handsome lad, a few inches taller than Dougie. Martha looked closer at Fraser. A very different face from the one she'd stared into when she found him dead in the woods.

'The three of you together,' she said. She had no memory of seeing the photo before or recalling where and when it was taken. Judging by the ages the kids looked, it had to be a couple of years ago. She would still have been working then. Missing out on Dougie's life, she thought, sadly. She wondered whether Jamie or Dougie's dad had taken the photo while she was off chasing a story somewhere.

The trio looked so happy, and suddenly remembering Christie was missing, she shivered.

'Please God, let her be safe,' she said.

There was a group of people standing behind the kids, and though they were slightly out of focus, she could see a man in shirtsleeves – and wearing a dog collar. Reverend Locke. His dark eyes were looking over at the group of three as they posed for the camera. His smile was handsome, but his expression unsettled her. In fact his presence in the picture unsettled her. She wondered if this photo was taken when the three of them were in the church band. The timing was right.

She thought again of the meds Orla had found. Locke knew Fraser and Christie, and they'd both gone missing. He must be involved somehow.

She turned the photo over. On the back were the names of the three kids. Then underneath, scrawled in black biro: *Feannag Dhubh Tour 2016.*

A shadow suddenly descended on the window, coupled by a guttural croak. Martha looked up and gasped, jumping up, the cuttings and photos slipping from her lap.

A large crow was clinging to the window, staring in. It cawed loudly then took flight and disappeared. In the cloudless sky where it had been was a pale shape and she realised the Crow Moon was just days away.

CHAPTER THIRTY

Dougie was desperate for a smoke, but he'd have to wait. He couldn't stop thinking about that phone conversation with Christie. He wished he'd taken what she'd said more seriously. It was the last time he'd spoken to her. He should have arranged to meet, talk it through. Maybe then she wouldn't have...

He swallowed hard, a sick feeling in his stomach. Where was she? It was Wednesday now, and she'd been missing since Saturday. The village was in chaos, with police, journalists and search teams mobbing the place. He thought about Fraser. He was missing his friend like hell.

Fraser had introduced him to Gallagher. The guy worked at their school, as an assistant in the tech lab. But he'd been helping them with more than the school computers. They'd been getting their dope supplies from him by ordering via Snapchat. The beauty of that was the messages only lasted a few minutes and then they were gone, but you could organise a pick-up and leave the cash where you collected the gear. He'd never actually done it on his own, but he'd been there when Fraser had ordered dope.

It had started last summer. Christie pretty much did a runner after the night they did the thing at the moondial. They were all freaked out after that. Used to watching illicit horror films with his mates, Dougie knew that, boosted by the adrenaline rush, it was easy to convince yourself you'd seen things, that you were terrified. But he had seen that Christie was properly scared.

After that, rumours had begun to spread around school about witches in the woods, black magic and other shit. Maybe someone had found their candles and the egg shells and the salt ring at the

moondial. He didn't know. Christie had drifted away from him
and Fraser after that. And spent long periods away from school.
And he and Fraser had started smoking.

He texted Gallagher's number: *Can arrange a pick-up of gear?*

Dad had just given him his allowance, so he could buy a wee
bit and eke it out so he could get through the next few weeks.
When he had a smoke late at night with the roof window open,
it calmed his nerves, helped him to sleep.

On edge, he waited for the response. It dropped in after forty-
five minutes:

See you at 4 when I'm back from work. Don't be seen.

He picked up his guitar and started to play. So long as he was
doing normal stuff, Mum wouldn't notice. He'd definitely have to
be more careful to change out of his clothes if he'd been smoking,
before seeing Mum.

Gallagher was in the shadows when he arrived.

'Geez, man,' he said. 'You look like you could do with a
tranquilliser. You sure it's just weed you want a lick of?'

Throat in nervous knots, Dougie nodded, memories of Fraser
crowding in.

'You got the money?' Gallagher said, a sallow look on his rat-
like face.

He handed over the cash, taking the small bag. It was feather-
light.

'Bloody hell. That's not much, is it?'

'You want more, mate, you've got to pay. It's not like the shit
you buy on the web. This is good stuff.'

Dougie felt his skin crawl as Gallagher leaned closer into his
face.

'Heard what happened to your mate. Shame that. He owed me
money though. You gonna help out with that debt?'

Dougie shook his head. 'Nowt to do with me, pal,' he said quickly. 'I just need this to tide me over a bit.'

'Aye, right. See you next time though,' Gallagher smirked as he walked away. 'And we'll have to figure out a way to clear your pal's overdraft.'

Dougie wondered what the hell he'd got himself into.

CHAPTER THIRTY-ONE

'So, give me your professional opinion, Martha. What headlines would you be writing if you were covering this story?' asked Summers, when he turned up at Martha's front door on Wednesday. He seemed on edge, but she understood the pressure. 'We're trying to keep them away from Christie's parents just now. They've got enough to deal with.'

'They'll probably give you till tomorrow to find her, and then it'll really ramp up. Any more leads on Fraser?'

He shook his head. 'Is Dougie here?' he asked. 'I need to speak to him about Christie. Find out if he knows where she could have gone.'

'I think he went upstairs. This is all taking its toll on him, to be honest,' Martha said. 'But I've found out something you might be interested in.' She handed over the photo she'd found. 'It's Dougie, with Fraser and Christie. There's an unusual reference on the back.'

He read it and widened his eyes. 'That *is* interesting,' he said. 'Where did you get it?'

She explained she'd been searching in the loft. 'Is it something you can use? The three of them together – with Locke, and with the name of the poem on the back. The poem Locke had part of in his house.'

'You're right, Martha. But as I told you, when I spoke to Locke he mentioned that they'd been in a church group together. He volunteered the information. He didn't try to hide it.'

'Could it be someone else connected to that band though? That's when the three of them were closest, and if it's the same person who has taken Christie, then could Dougie be next on his list?' Martha could hear the fear in her own voice. 'It's clear now – the three of them are linked by the very words that you found on Fraser.'

'I promise you, Martha, I'm taking this seriously. I'll send someone round to copy this photo so we have it on file. But there's too much hearsay and suggestion involved here. I have to build a case on solid evidence, and I still don't have enough.'

'And what about the Risperdal? Have you found out anything yet? Approached Locke's doctor?' she asked.

Before he could answer, a noise in the hallway alerted them to Dougie coming down. He'd probably heard her raised voice.

'Have you found her yet?' Martha watched her son's gaunt face with concern. The disappearance of another friend had hit him hard, she knew.

'I'm sorry, Dougie, there's no trace of Christie yet,' Summers replied. 'Have you heard from her at all?'

'What are you talking about? Of course I haven't. Don't you think I would have said?' Dougie slumped into a chair, head in his hands.

Martha stared at him. He seemed particularly defensive. Overly so.

'We discovered her phone quite quickly. Looks like she dropped it just outside the gates to the estate,' Summers said. 'The thing is, Dougie, there's a whole string of messages between you two, Fraser too, going back more than a year. Some are from exactly a year ago and are about arrangements to meet near Blacklaw. Can you tell us anything about that?'

'We just did some daft game in the dark. And then Christie thought she saw someone and we all ran off. It's got nothing to do with this. It was ages ago and just kids' stuff. I don't know anything else,' the lad whispered through tears. 'You have to find her.'

Martha watched her son crumple before her eyes and wasn't sure how to stop it happening. She rubbed his back, tuning in to the vibration of his quiet sobs.

Dougie spied the photograph on the table. 'What's that?' he said.

Martha pushed the picture over and saw the fear and recognition on his face. She tightened her arm around his shoulders as he looked at his two friends. One dead and one missing.

Martha had a heavy feeling of dread as she saw the policeman out. 'I'll let you know if he says anything more,' she said.

Closing the door, she pushed her hands through her hair. Dougie's reaction to the photo was disturbing, and she wondered whether there was more to it – something about the trio that they didn't know yet.

CHAPTER THIRTY-TWO

Martha's instincts told her there was something about that photo – something that connected the kids and that damned poem. And she was sure Peter Locke knew what it was. He was in the photo, and he'd known all three when they were in the church band. And the reference on the back couldn't be ignored. She briefly contemplated contacting Summers again, but then dismissed the idea. She wasn't going to ask for his permission to question Locke. He'd visited him already, to no avail. She wanted to find out for herself what the man knew. And while she was there, maybe she could do a little Orla-style snooping. She grabbed her coat and called upstairs to Dougie that she was popping out.

As she left the house, she noticed a voicemail from Jamie on her mobile. She listened to it as she walked. He was asking her to call him, the sound of his voice seeming to reach her from the past. She would phone him later. And she could ask him for some advice about how to handle Dougie. She still needed him for that, at least.

Arriving at the manse, she couldn't recall ever being inside before. It was a lovely old Victorian villa with big stone lintels over the windows and a large garden stocked with shrubs and flowers. But as she walked up the drive and got closer to the building she couldn't help noticing the crumbling plasterwork and peeling paint on the window frames. On one of the upper floors, she could see a curtain rail hanging down, as if someone had pulled it too hard and not bothered to fix it. Looking around at the garden, it too seemed tatty and unkempt. As if no one had loved it for a very long time. The whole place gave her a sense of unease. She shuddered involuntarily and as she did so she spotted an old quad bike parked next to the rickety timber garage tucked round one side of the house. Odd. What would the minister need that for? she wondered.

Reaching the front door, she knocked, then waited. There was no reply. Undeterred, she knocked again, louder this time, and eventually heard a noise from inside.

Locke greeted her with surprise. 'Martha, hello. Please come in.' He opened the door wide. It seemed very dark inside.

She followed him into a tiled, echoey hallway, past a staircase made dim by a tall stained-glass window, and down a dingy corridor towards a large kitchen. There was a fusty smell to the house that caught at the back of her throat, and every piece of furniture she passed, every ornament, looked yellowed or worn. It was as though the place existed in a time warp from fifty years ago. She had the sudden urge to leave – to make some excuse and hurry back out the door. It was irrational, she knew, but all her senses were telling her there was some kind of danger here.

In the kitchen, Locke turned and invited her to sit down. It felt like he was standing a little too close. Like his smile bared too many teeth.

Martha swallowed down her panic and took a seat at the table, looking around. An ancient range cooker in pale cream dominated the room, its enamel work chipped and an old-fashioned kettle sitting on top. Its heat filled the kitchen. By the window a huge Belfast sink showed a few cracks, its curved brass tap glinting in the fading light.

'Can I get you a cup of tea?' he asked.

'No, thanks. I won't stay long. I'd just like to ask you about a couple of things,' she mumbled.

Locke looked at her quizzically. His hair wasn't slicked back today. It fell across his forehead.

'It's about a picture I've found,' she went on, pulling herself together. 'I'm interested to see if you know anything about it...'

She took the photo from her pocket, slid it across the table and watched Locke's expression as he stared at the image.

'Gosh, when was that taken?' he asked, picking it up. 'It's a bit of a surprise. Seeing that group together again.'

'That is you in the photo, isn't it?' said Martha. 'In the background.'

He picked it up to have a closer look. 'Yes, it's me, with Fraser MacDonald, Christie Campbell and your Dougie. Now, when was this?'

'Take a look on the back,' Martha said.

He turned over the photo. Martha scrutinised his face. She didn't know if Locke was aware of the writing found on Fraser – Summers was still refusing to make it public – so he wouldn't necessarily connect the title of the poem with that on the boy's back.

He smiled sadly. 'Such a nice picture of those young people enjoying themselves. 2016 – don't you remember, we did a couple of concerts that summer?'

'I remember the band. But I think I was working on some big stories at the time, so I don't recall going to any gigs.' She paused. Then pointed to the writing on the back. 'Do you know what Feannag Dhubh means?'

Locke darted a look at her with his dark eyes. 'I'm surprised you of all people need to ask about that,' he said. 'It's a myth connected to your old farm. Anyone round here from the older generations will know about it. Not so much the younger ones these days though...' He trailed off.

'I found out about its connection to Blacklaw,' she said, her confidence returning now. 'But why is it written here?'

'Ah, well, that's easily explained. The poem was set to music and the band played it as a song. It was part of the show we did that summer. Christie sang it. She was enchanting. You can't have been to that gig, then. You'd have remembered it, I'm sure.'

Martha watched him. He seemed rather unconcerned and relaxed.

She sat forward. 'Fraser is dead, and Christie is missing.' She tapped the table with her finger as she spoke. 'So you'll understand why I'm worried about my own son. I know the three of them were close. And having found this picture it's reminded me how tight they were.'

His expression was questioning. 'I understand your concern. But this is just an innocent picture, Martha. Taken of a group of friends during a happy time. I'm sure it's entirely coincidental that two of the young people have been involved in such tragic events. Do you think there's some other connection I should know about?'

His dark eyes were so penetrating it made her want to look away. She had to force herself to hold his gaze. Was he playing with her? Or was this all perfectly innocent, as he seemed to be suggesting? She thought back to what Summers had said about his visit here. Locke seemed to have alibis for when Fraser and Christie had gone missing. Had he played Summers in the same way?

'I don't know,' she replied at last. 'I was hoping you could tell me. And let's hope Christie is found safe. We don't need any further tragedy in this village.'

She was rattled, and now she wasn't sure what she'd expected to get out of this visit. Maybe she'd been foolish to come here. What was she even accusing him of? He was a community leader and had been involved with kids from the village for many years through the kirk, the school and the clubs. But she couldn't shake off the feeling that there was something he wasn't telling her. Neither could she rid herself of the quiet fear that seemed to creep round her body as she sat here. Was it possible he did know that lines from the poem were scrawled on Fraser? Who might have told him though?

She hadn't noticed until now that he wasn't in his church garb. Maybe that was why she felt there was something off about him – something unusual. Sat across the table from her in a T-shirt and jeans, his hair messed up and those dark eyes, she could see why Orla found him attractive. But it was a dark attraction. Something magnetic that you should avoid.

'Christie had been doing research about the Scottish witch trials,' he said after a long pause. 'She'd become quite obsessed with the Feannag Dhubh story. I suppose, with the local connection, it brought the reality of history closer to home. She was the one who found the version of the poem that was set to music and suggested they play it. They performed it really well.' He stopped. 'You should have been there.'

Martha frowned. Was that an accusation? She shook herself. There was nothing of that in his tone. But she wasn't sure now if she could even read his tone or expression.

'Do you think it could have anything to do with what has happened to the kids?' Martha asked carefully.

'I honestly don't know why it would.' He picked up the photo again. 'Would you mind if I kept this, Martha? It brings back good memories...' A smile played on his lips. She was suddenly revolted.

'No. No, I'd prefer to keep it.' She put her hand out. There was no way she was going to hand over something this important without talking to Summers again.

But Locke held on to the picture, moved it away from her hand even. She could feel her irrational panic rising again. 'I have a good scanner in my study,' he said. 'If you don't mind, it would just take a few minutes to make a copy now.'

She realised that this would be her opportunity, and quickly nodded. 'Of course. Make a couple of copies. I could give one to Fraser's mum as a keepsake. I think she'd like that.'

'Good idea,' he said and walked away with the image in his hand, down the corridor and towards the back of the house, leaving her quivering slightly in the huge kitchen.

Martha waited a moment and stood up, but as she did so she jumped so violently her chair scraped back on the tiled floor. A cat had leaped up onto the outside windowsill, its huge eyes staring directly into Martha's.

She sighed, feeling ridiculous, being spooked by a silly pet. *Get your act together, Martha,* she told herself, as she walked along the corridor, following the mechanical sounds of the scanner. The door to Locke's study was open.

'Could I just use your loo while you're doing that?' she asked from the doorway.

He looked up, almost guiltily, she thought. He had been writing something in a notebook on his desk.

'Of course. Down the corridor, past the stairs, then carry on and it's on the left.'

Martha continued as directed, scanning every inch of the place, looking for anything that might hint that Locke knew more about this than he was letting on. But there was nothing in the long corridor or on the dark staircase – of course there wasn't – and she found herself in the small bathroom. At least she'd managed to get in here. It seemed to be exactly the bathroom Orla had described. And yes, there was the medicine cabinet above the sink, where she said it was. Martha opened it gently.

It contained the usual over-the-counter pills and potions. But no pharmacy bag and no box of medication. She puffed out a breath and shuffled the contents of the cabinet around. But no, the Risperdal had gone.

She stood back and looked around the room. There was a cupboard under the sink. She opened it, poked around inside, but again, no medication. She sat on the closed toilet and screwed up her lips. Had Locke got rid of the Risperdal – suspicious that snooping Orla had found it? Or moved it to another room, maybe? She didn't have enough time to start looking around the house now, though. And the idea of wandering alone around this eerie, decrepit old manse, with the possibility of Locke catching her at any moment, chilled her blood.

She flushed the toilet, ran the tap for a moment, and was just about to open the door, when her eye caught sight of a small pedal bin in the corner. Hand still on the door handle, she reached out her foot and pressed the pedal with her toe. The lid popped open. There, scrunched up, was a paper pharmacy bag. Leaning over, she plucked it out. Nothing on the outside. Just an innocent bag that could have contained soap or deodorant or … She looked inside – there. She trapped it between two fingers and pulled it out. One of those curling paper receipts from a card machine.

She squinted at it. The ink was fading, the letters and figures faint. But across the top – the name of the pharmacy in Glenview.

She slipped it into her pocket, dropped the bag back in the bin, and opened the door. Then headed back down the corridor. As she passed the stairs, she found herself gazing at the stained-glass window again, then further up into the gloom of the upper floors.

'Here you are.'

Martha jerked back. Locke seemed to have appeared out of nowhere. He was holding the photo out towards her. His fingers brushed her own as she took it from him. Her heart raced at the contact.

'Can I take your mobile number?' he asked, with a smile. 'Just in case I think of something – I can let you know.'

She recited the number and he wrote it down on the back of his copy of the photograph.

She took a couple of steps towards the entrance hall. Then turned. She knew it was a risk, but she had to say something before she left.

'One other thing,' she said, heart banging now. 'Do you know anyone who takes a medication called Risperdal?'

He glared at her, eyes narrowed, then shook his head slowly.

'Well, it's been nice of you to visit,' he said. She noticed how quickly he moved away from her question. 'It would be good to see you at church sometime.'

'I think God gave up on me a very long time ago,' she said, moving towards the door. 'Thanks for the offer though.'

'Well, you never know. Many people lose their faith and then find it again when they need to,' he said, pushing his hair back.

'Maybe,' she said as he reached round her to open the door.

On the doorstep she turned to face him. 'Watch yourself with Orla,' she said, suddenly protective of her friend. This whole visit had unsettled her and she was more wary of Locke than ever. 'She's been through enough and she doesn't need to be hurt again.'

His expression darkened briefly. 'I think Orla is a big girl and can make her own decisions, don't you?'

She could feel his scrutiny on her back as she walked away from the house, thoughts churning over his reactions, especially when she mentioned the drug. Had she dropped Orla in it by asking him about it? Had she even put her in danger?

CHAPTER THIRTY-THREE

NEW MOON

Bats flitted around the rafters above Christie's head, as if attracted by her fear. The damp blanket that had been flung over her smelled like a wet dog, the wool scratched sharp against her skin. A metal dish and a water bottle with no top were balanced on the ground by her feet. Eyes straining in the gloom, she tried to sense if anyone else was there.

'Hello?' Her voice was a dry croak from breathing in the mouldy air. She felt her lips crack, tasted blood. Wrists tied, she could just reach the bottle and lifted it to her nose. It didn't smell of anything, so she touched the plastic to her lips, straining as she opened her palms to cup her hands around the bottle. Scared she might drop it and desperate not to let it slide from her grasp, she managed to tip it awkwardly and as much water spilled across her face and neck as went down her throat. It tasted odd, but she was too parched to care.

Hidden in the shadows, the man watched as she carefully laid the bottle down, balancing it awkwardly between her calves. She reached out to see what was in the bowl. There was a piece of dry bread, torn off a loaf from his kitchen. He couldn't remember when he bought it, maybe a few days ago, but it certainly wasn't fresh. She lifted and smelled it too, before throwing it away from her.

'You'll eat when you're hungry, girly.' He was annoyed at her ingratitude. His voice so low, he wondered if he'd said it out loud.

In a panic, Christie pushed herself back against the wall as far as she could, the water bottle falling over on the floor and its contents draining out.

'Please,' she cried out. 'What do you want from me? I just want to go home.'

Her voice was shrill. Angry. He didn't like that. He wanted her quiet and calm, so he could get on with his work.

Get on with it. Don't listen to her whining.

Christie's voice rose to a shout, 'Let me go. When my dad gets hold of you, you'll be dead!'

She slumped back with the effort of her outburst, head bent, crying.

Stupid girl. She'll learn the hard way.

The witch was right. Fraser was more straightforward. He'd gone off in minutes, although it hadn't ended well at all. He was glad he'd brought Christie here though, closer to where it all started. His forest shed where he'd taken Fraser was a few miles away, and now that winter was almost over, people might be walking near there. The rank smell of bird corpses tied to the fence should keep people away though.

Although she'd spilled the rest of the liquid, he was banking on Christie having swallowed enough of it. She'd have to lose consciousness soon, otherwise he'd have to find some other way to subdue her.

'Don't hurt me. Please.' Her words drawled slightly as the sedatives kicked in.

Christie's whispered pleas reminded him of someone else from many years ago.

Something scurried past in the dark. If there were rats in this barn, he needed to get on with it. Stop being distracted by these thoughts. He hadn't believed in ghosts. Not until he'd seen that dark shape fly out at those kids under the Crow Moon. They had no idea what they'd freed, but its presence had hovered by him ever since.

At last the girl had fallen on her side. He crept slowly over to where she lay. His small torch cast a beam around the space. He prodded her back. No response. At one time, sharp pins might have been driven into her skin. Witch pricking they'd called it. Trying to find places that didn't bleed to prove she was a witch. He didn't like the thought of that though. He switched on a larger solar-powered spotlight he'd bought from a garage months ago. It illuminated her prone body as though she was lying centre stage during a performance. Still breathing, he rolled her over, first onto her side and then, folding the blanket and spreading it in front of her, he pushed Christie onto her front. Her head was at an awkward angle, so he gently pulled the hair back from her face and straightened her neck.

You're running out of time.

He cut the back of her hooded jacket and T-shirt, uncovering her soft flesh. She'd been kept cool now for several nights inside the shed, and he'd leave her skin exposed when he was finished, to let the ink properly dry. Disconcerted at the thin bra strap across her back, he cut through that, taking care to keep the knife away from her skin. He didn't want to mark the perfect blank canvas that she presented. It was soft and pale, like calf skin, he thought, but better. She was skinny though, staircase ribs making him wonder if she ever ate anything. For a few seconds he looked at her.

Stop gawping. There's work to do.

He could feel the presence like an idle breeze at his neck.

Christie was out cold. He wondered whether she was dreaming. He wanted this one to be perfect before he moved on to the last. There wasn't much time left. Eleven days to the full moon. He took out the pen, checked its fine black tip and got to work.

The Book of Shadows

We must keep our joy secret. The boy is afraid of him, but I have discovered a fierce mother is hidden within me. From the moment I felt the boy's life ripple in my belly, I knew such love. I hoped it would change him. But he is harsh.

I say prayers for us both when he sleeps. He must not know that the ones I pray to are not his own gods and saints. I make offerings to my northern, ice-bound ancestors as well as to the elemental spirits of this place. To Mother Nature and the spirits of the earth, water and air. I mark time by the seasons and the changes in this beautiful place.

The crows flock to me, and he does not like it.

CHAPTER THIRTY-FOUR

'Give us your money. Come on, hand it over – now!'

The boys grabbed Sam on Thursday morning, shouting as he rounded the corner of the street near school. They waited for him most days, and he'd quickly learned to hand over the cash.

'Give us the fuckin' money now,' shouted Finlay, the bigger one, again.

Sam pulled three pound coins from his pocket, hurling them in Finlay's direction as he ran away as fast as he could down the road.

'Ye wee shite,' he heard one of them roar behind him.

He was fed up with being bullied – with being new and having no friends. He'd been a target of bigger kids in school before. The two who robbed him daily of his lunch money weren't even worth trying to fight. They'd kick the hell out of him and then do it again if he told anyone.

'Sedgewick!' Sam jumped. An English teacher was staring at him. 'Shouldn't you be in lessons already, boy? Get yourself into class this minute.'

Sam hoisted his bag onto his shoulder, head down.

'Yes, sir, sorry, sir.' He hurried in through the doors, heart sinking at the prospect of another day in school. There was nothing he liked about the place. No one had made any attempt to befriend him.

The school had been awash with rumours since an older boy died and a girl went missing. There were all sorts of mad stories flying around, mostly about drugs and a crazed serial killer on the loose. Sam hated it. There'd been reports in the local paper, and although they didn't mention drugs, his mum had used it as an excuse to give him the hard stare and a talk about the dangers of drug use now he was at high school. They'd been searching for the girl for days. Police cars and big trucks with *Mountain Rescue* written on the side still swarmed the village.

At first break, he headed outside, escaping the strong smell of teenagers in the corridors. He liked to stay out of the way. But as he rounded the corner, Finlay jumped out from behind a shed and pushed Sam hard, before yanking at his school bag.

'Got any more money, Spam Spedgeface?' he said, his lips pulled back over his teeth like an ugly, snarling dog.

'No,' Sam mumbled. 'I gave you everything I had earlier. I've got nothing left.'

'Give us yer phone then. It's probably crap, but I can get something for it at least.'

'I haven't got a phone.' Sam's eyes darted around, looking for an escape route or help.

'Don't even think about it,' said Finlay. 'Don't have a phone? What kind of dork are you?'

'I think we know who the dork is. You really should leave the first years alone, you little shit.' A sixth former appeared from behind the shed, smelling of smoke. He threw a cigarette butt down, before grinding it beneath his battered Converse.

Sam looked at the older student with gratitude. His green eyes smiled back at the kid. Finlay suddenly didn't look so sure.

'OK, Strangeways,' he said. 'Was just having a bit of fun, that's all. Right, Sam?'

'I saw what you were doing,' said the sixth former called Strangeways. 'Now beat it, you little shit, and don't let me see you bullying this kid again. Got it?'

Finlay let go of Sam's bag, throwing it at him before hurtling off, shouting expletives back at them.

'Wouldn't hang out around here, mate,' said the black-haired boy. 'Stay where you can be seen. Where it's safe.'

He winked at Sam before walking away.

CHAPTER THIRTY-FIVE

With all the stress of recent days, Martha warmed to the thought of meeting Jamie for a drink. On her way back from Locke's she'd decided to ask him out. She needed to quiz him about the drugs. His patients would use the pharmacy printed on the receipt she'd found, so maybe he could advise her about how to get some information on Locke they could actually use. She also wanted his help with supporting Dougie. She tried – and failed – multiple times, to get the lad to talk, about Fraser, about Christie, about how he felt. What he could remember that might help. Nothing was getting through to him.

It seemed like forever, with everything that had happened, but it was just a couple of weeks since Jamie had been at her bedside in the hospital. His face scarred from the fire, his eyes had still been warm as they looked at her. She recalled his voice as he said gentle words to her as she'd drifted in and out of consciousness. It was the past, she knew, but it might just be the future too if she'd let it. Dougie had been dropping hints for a few months now. She knew he'd be pleased if they got back together.

Jamie lived in Kilfintry, so they'd arranged to meet at The Kilfintry Inn. Martha figured if she was driving she wouldn't have much to drink. After a quick shower, she wiped steam from the mirror, noticing the shadows on her face and a few grey hairs creeping in. Her hair hadn't been cut for months. She blasted it dry before pulling it into an untidy ponytail. She dabbed on the same scent she'd worn for years, the Eau Dynamisante that Jamie had bought her, the patchouli base bringing back memories of long-forgotten evenings out. She didn't want to overplay it, but over her usual jeans she opted for a soft grey cashmere sweater he had also bought her. She hadn't worn it for a while. She slipped on her Puffa jacket, making sure the matchbox was tucked in the pocket. Jamie didn't know she carried it around with her, but it was a comfort, knowing part of her children was always with her.

'Just nipping out to meet a friend,' she called up to Dougie as she collected her car keys from the hallway. 'I've got my phone. Call me if you need anything.'

She waited. There was no response. She called out another goodbye, waited again. Still nothing. She sighed and closed the door behind her.

Martha waited in the car for a moment while the heating cleared the windscreen. She shook her head. What could she do with Dougie? As she pulled away, she saw a boy walking through the gloom down the hill on the opposite side of the street. He was short, and by his build, a few years younger than Dougie. But something about the boy reminded her of him. Maybe it was just because she was so worried about her son. Hood pulled tight, the boy passed the church opposite her house.

She pulled up next to where he was walking and lowered the window. 'Hi there. Are you OK, out by yourself?'

He nodded.

'Do you need a lift home?' she asked.

'No, I'm alright, thanks,' he said. 'Just on my way there now.'

'Are you sure? It's no problem.'

He nodded, and Martha watched as he walked away down the road. She didn't want to spook the kid by saying it wasn't safe, but she wouldn't want a child of hers that age to be out wandering the streets at dusk. Just past the bus stop he turned into the newish development of houses in Balloch Chase and disappeared. He seemed to walk purposefully, so she drove on. He was in the village under the streetlights; on his way home and safe. And he'd not got into a car with a stranger, so someone was bringing him up right, she supposed.

She switched on the radio and restarted her journey. After a few minutes of music, there was a local news bulletin: rescuers had been out all day again searching for Christie, it said. So they were still looking for the girl. There can't have been any news – nothing the police wanted to announce anyway. She'd check in with Summers again later.

She and Jamie had moved here because it was a close-knit community where they'd thought the family would be safe. It was within commuting distance for Martha when she was working at the paper. By the time they were settled in their new home out at Blacklaw, Martha was heavily pregnant. She'd enjoyed her maternity leave, spending a few weeks of bustling around the kitchen, her bump often getting in the way, or sat at the table watching sheep through the window peering back at her over the stone walls, as she waited for the twins' arrival. She had never taken time out like that. Life had been a treadmill for a long time and being forced to stop for a bit was alien to her. But gradually leaving daily deadlines behind and waking up to the gentle twist of a curlew's call, or the sheep calling to their lambs in the fields outside, had forced her to slow down and look at what was around her. She'd discovered that, from high points around the village, you could gaze east and on a clear day see the ramparts of Stirling Castle atop its ancient volcanic rock, and the Wallace Monument, which Dougie loved to climb up to.

Despite everything that had happened, this village still felt like home. She had grown up closer to the sea and still had her grandad's cottage in a tiny fisherman's village on the north-east coast. She hadn't been back for a while, but soon, she thought, she would go. Once things had settled down here. She sometimes got a strong craving to eat salty fish and chips out of newspaper, as seagulls dived overhead, licking greasy fingers while staring out at the North Sea.

Eyes on the road, she thought about Dougie. Why hadn't he answered when she called goodbye? Maybe he was just being a teenager. She wondered if her fear for her son wasn't irrational. Was she making connections where there weren't any? He was safe at home now. Although she was sure Fraser's mum had thought *he* was safe, even out on his regular morning run. Christie's parents must be going spare by now. God, what had happened to her?

The pub looked inviting. Misty rain was hanging low, giving

the lights a hazy glow in the darkening evening. She hadn't been in there for ages. They used to bring the boys on a Sunday occasionally. She'd forgotten about that. The little ones loved the teddy-bear-shaped chicken nuggets they served, with sausage and mash always Dougie's favourite.

Martha took a deep breath and pushed open the heavy door into the main bar. Low background music mixed with chatter from folk – Thursday night was specials night and it was busy. She inhaled the scent of beer mixed with earthy peat smoke from the fire. The smell of warm, cosy nights. The inn was a bit more upmarket than the boozer in her village, which was a spit-and-sawdust affair where women weren't exactly banned, but were frowned upon by the old-timers. Jamie was near the window, looking slightly nervous as she made her way through the tables.

He got up when he saw her and reached out for a slightly awkward hug, brushing his scarred face against her own as he kissed her. 'Drink?' he said. She smelled beer on his breath.

'Dry white wine please. Just a small glass. I'm driving.'

He took his empty pint glass to the bar with him and returned with a glass of wine and another pint, the amber liquid glinting in the firelight. He also had a couple of menus under his arm and handed her one.

'Wasn't sure if you'd have eaten or not.'

She hadn't intended to stay long, but seeing him again made her want to.

'Yes, that would be nice. Haven't had a meal out in such a long time,' she said.

Jamie breathed out and sat down opposite her at the table, his back to the rest of the crowd in the pub.

'Martha, it's good to see you. I'm glad you suggested this.'

'To be honest, I really needed a friendly face.'

'I'm glad you chose mine,' he said. And she was sure she saw a glint in his eye.

She relaxed a bit at this. And, after a halting start, their chatter became easier, and they both ordered food. She liked good seafood but the closest they had on the menu was scampi and chips, a Kilfintry Inn classic, according to the barman. Jamie went for the chicken pot pie.

The first glass of wine slid down a treat and although she planned to drive home, she agreed to another. The alcohol helped loosen her mood too. Everything had been such a stress. It was nice to sit and relax for a bit with someone who knew as much about her as anyone did – except for Orla.

She told Jamie that Orla had turned up in the village, renting a place nearby for a bit. Jamie had only met her on a few occasions in the time Jamie and Martha had been together, but he recalled the flirtatious blonde and laughed when Martha told him her mate had set her sights on Locke.

'Best of luck to the bloke,' Jamie said. 'I'd imagine Orla doesn't take no for an answer.'

Martha shook her head. 'She doesn't. But with him … let's say she might have bitten off more than she can chew.'

'Really?' Jamie swigged from his pint. 'Why do you say that? From what I remember of him, he seemed like a nice enough fella. And a minister and all that – has to be the gentle type, no?'

'You'd think,' Martha said, grimly. 'I've discovered some stuff about him since all this started with Fraser and Christie. Stuff that makes me very suspicious…'

Jamie put down his glass. 'I know that look, Martha Strangeways. What are you up to? Some editor's got you on this story, haven't they?'

Martha couldn't help but laugh. It felt good to hear his repartee again. 'No, no, it's not a job.' Jamie raised an eyebrow. 'But, yes, I am looking into the whole thing.' She put up her hand before he could object. 'In co-operation with the police,' she said. 'I sort of befriended that DI who interviewed me at the hospital.'

'What, Summers? The big guy?'

'That's him. He's letting me know what they discover, and in exchange I'm making my own inquiries, and feeding back what I find out to him.'

Jamie gave her a gentle smile. 'You're worried about Dougie, aren't you? That's why you're doing it.'

'He's really suffering, Jamie. A lot. You've heard Christie's missing?' she said. 'The poor lad's freaked out.'

Jamie nodded. 'Yes, I heard about Christie. It must be hard for him. Especially with what's happened to Fraser.'

'Exactly. I've got to do something to put an end to this. Not that it's helped much. Everything I've discovered seems to be a dead end or inadmissible.'

'Put an end to it...?' Jamie said, frowning. 'Do you expect another kid to go missing?'

'The thing is, Jamie...' She stopped, unsure whether she should share with him what she was about to say.

'The thing is...?'

'You need to promise to keep this to yourself, OK. It's not in the public domain yet, and Summers doesn't want it to be common knowledge.'

'Of course,' Jamie said. 'I promise.'

Martha took a deep breath in, then spoke in a low voice, so Jamie had to lean forward to hear her. 'Fraser had been doped and lines from a poem had been written on his back,' she said.

'A poem? That's weird.'

'It's even more weird than that.' Martha glanced around, checking no one nearby was listening in. 'The poem is connected to Blacklaw. To the moondial we discovered.'

'What? Blacklaw?!'

Martha signalled that he should keep his voice down. Then went on. 'There's something about that moondial. I've done my research – of course.' Jamie nodded. 'And I've discovered that it's the site of a witch burning in the seventeenth century.'

Jamie rubbed his chin. 'This sounds a bit familiar, now you say it. I'm sure I heard tell of this back when we lived there. Some old codger telling me Blacklaw was haunted. I didn't take any notice at the time. And nor should you now.'

'But it doesn't matter what I believe about the place. It's what the kids believed about it.' Martha lowered her voice even further. Jamie had to lean right across the table now. 'Apparently, Christie, Fraser and Dougie did some kind of ritual there, a year ago now. I heard Dougie on the phone to Christie about it before she went missing.'

Jamie frowned heavily. 'A ritual? What were they up to? Some kind of teenage Ouija stuff, surely? But harmless really.'

'That's what I'd have said. But get this: there was just one verse of the poem written on Fraser's back. In the version I've seen, there's one verse before it, and two after.'

'And you think that means...'

'That more kids could go missing.'

'And turn up dead with the verses on their bodies...? This is crazy, Martha. What does Summers say about all this?'

'He's not convinced. Like you're not. I can see.' She sat back, slightly irritated. 'But you know me, Jamie. I'd never spin something out of nothing. Look at this.'

She pulled the photo of Dougie with Fraser and Christie from her pocket and handed it over to him.

'It was in one of the boxes in our loft room. Bits and pieces we saved from Blacklaw.'

'I think I remember this,' he said, examining it. 'The kids were in a band, weren't they?'

'That's it. Now turn it over.'

Jamie did so. '2016. Sounds about right. And "Feannag Dhubh". What does that mean? My Gaelic is, well, non-existent.'

'That's the name of the poem.' Jamie's eyes widened at this. 'And I've found out that they played a song version of it in their band.'

Jamie couldn't conceal the worry on his face. 'Are you saying what I think you're saying?'

'If you mean, am I worried that Dougie's in danger, then yes.'

'I really hope you're wrong, Martha. Do you think Dougie knows anything more about all this?'

'I honestly don't know. I've tried everything to get him to talk. The police have been round asking too. He was so cut up about Fraser. And when he heard about Christie he lost it a bit. I'm not really sure what to do. I'm worried about him. And scared for him too. I want to lock him inside, never let him out of my sight. But of course, I can't do that.'

Jamie shook his head, and, reaching out, took Martha's hand. She appreciated the warmth, and closed her eyes for a moment.

Then she opened them again and looked into Jamie's. 'There's something more, though. And this will explain my comment about Locke earlier.'

Jamie pursed his lips. 'Go on.'

'The police did toxicology on Fraser, and found ketamine and a drug called Risperdal in his system. They think he was drugged. They found a puncture mark from a needle in his shoulder. And think he was given a spiked drink too.'

Jamie shook his head. 'This is seriously scary.'

Martha put her finger on the photo sitting on the table. 'Who do you see in the background here?'

Jamie glanced down. 'What am I looking at?'

Martha pointed to the blurred figures. 'Him. It's Locke.'

Jamie shrugged. 'It was a church band, so no surprise he's in the picture.'

'No, but when Orla was round there – on her seduction mission – she did a bit of snooping. And what did she find in his bathroom cabinet? A box of Risperdal.'

Jamie's mouth dropped open.

'And not only that. Another time, she looked around his study, and found a hidden scrap of paper with a line from the poem written on it...'

Jamie sat back. Picked up his pint and drained it. 'Risperdal's a strong antipsychotic. Does that mean Locke's had a spell of mental ill health?'

Martha raised her palms. 'Maybe. I went over there yesterday. Ostensibly to ask him about the photo – what he remembers. He told me about the band playing the Feannag Dhubh song. And he wanted to make a copy of the picture?'

'That's odd. Did he say why?'

'Just that it was a good memory. Anyway, I took the opportunity to go to the loo. I went into the bathroom and checked the cabinet, but the medication had gone.'

'Martha, you have to be careful...'

'I know, I know. But I did find this in the bin.' Now Martha produced the receipt.

Jamie took it and squinted at it in the dim light of the bar. 'I know that pharmacy. My patients use it.'

'I thought you would. I did ask him if he knew anyone that was taking Risperdal, but he sort of shut down the conversation on me.'

'I'm not surprised, Martha. You don't just tell anyone you're on an antipsychotic. Have you taken all this to Summers?'

'I have. But he's saying most of it's not admissible in court. Not enough to get a search warrant even. Summers went round and had a casual chat with him. Says Locke seems to have alibis for the time periods the kids went missing.'

'And they'd need to make him officially a suspect before any doctor or pharmacist would release information about prescription meds.'

Martha took back the receipt. 'I'm hoping this might help. But if the drugs aren't in his house, there's no longer a clear connection.'

'Plus, ketamine is definitely not on the NHS,' Jamie added.

Martha sighed and shook her head. 'So you've answered the questions I had,' she said. 'But if you do think of anything else – or hear of any Risperdal prescriptions being requested, will you let me know?'

Jamie nodded. 'And that was the only reason you wanted to see me – to quiz me as part of your investigation...?' He'd moved closer now, his knee meeting hers beneath the table.

She smiled and pressed hers closer.

By the time they made it out to the car park she'd had three glasses of wine, and although slightly tipsy, she insisted she was fine to drive home.

'You shouldn't be driving, Martha,' Jamie said. 'You're way over the limit. I'm calling you a cab.'

She shook her head. But she knew full well she'd had too much. She suddenly felt overwhelmed – by Jamie, by being there, by telling him everything that she'd been doing.

As they waited for the taxi to arrive, she leaned against him. It felt comfortable, and right. And, as the car pulled up and he reached to hug her goodbye, emboldened by the booze, she planted a kiss firmly on his lips. He leaned into her, hands finding their way under her coat and jumper, his fingers tracing her bare and still-bruised skin, as he moved closer and into a deeper kiss.

'Oh, Jamie. I'm not sure.' She pulled back, head spinning. 'I don't think I can do this now.' She stepped away, towards the cab.

'I'll call you?' he said. 'And tell Dougie I'm here if he needs to talk.'

She nodded, quickly getting into the car and securing the seatbelt. Her head was swimming, she wasn't sure whether from the wine or the kiss. They pulled away, and she turned to see Jamie standing in the mist outside the pub, watching her.

She remained silent for the short journey, then, at the bottom of the hill that led to the village, she said, 'Just drop me here, mate. I'm fine to walk.'

'If you're sure,' the driver said. 'No problem for me to take you to your door.'

'I need the fresh air,' she replied, handing him some cash.

A brisk walk up the hill would help clear the booze fog in her brain, she hoped, and although it wasn't a full moon yet, the sky was clear and the lights of the village twinkled in the distance. A cold wind rustled through the trees that lined the road. She listened. The rumble of the retreating cab eventually disappeared. Then silence. Her own breath seemed loud in the deep quiet of the night. Darkness drew in around her and, eyes wide, she focused on her steps, looking up towards the village.

Something drifted down, feather-light, and landed on her cheek. A few snowflakes caught on her eyelashes, blurring her vision. It was still only March. Winter not gone yet. A line from the poem slipped into her mind: 'In ink-dark forests floats mountain witch, / her feathered cloak as dark as pitch.' She recited it beneath her breath, thinking of all the strands of this weird case. Fraser's death, the poem, Blacklaw, the drugs, and now Christie missing. All the strands spinning like spider silk. How did they fit together, if at all?

A cloud peeled back, unveiling the moon. Martha felt a sudden breeze as though something was flying close to her face. Then it came again. And a third time. Wrong time of year for bats. Too cold. Another flutter. Something flitting past. Almost touching her. She threw up her hands to protect her face. Between her fingers, spotlighted beneath the moon, she saw ragged shadows, like those ashen feathers falling from the sky. And heard a *caw caw* – distant, but then close.

Seriously spooked now, she picked up her pace, recalling Helen Horne's words. The woman had told her to take great care, and Martha felt anything but safe right at that moment.

The Book of Shadows

He caught us singing today, and it was a disaster. They were folk songs from my homeland that my grandmother taught me as a child. Even my father, who was high up in our Lutheran church, did not object to his children learning their own folklore. Our traditions are ancient and should be honoured, he believed.

But today when we were singing and he *heard me, he was so angry. And when he found out about the poem from here that I have discovered, he was furious. This Feannag Dhubh – she reminds me of home.*

I am aching from his blows, but also from the fear I saw in my child's eyes – both for me and for himself. He is a wicked man who uses the name of his God to punish me. He cut off my hair and made me watch as he burned my thick braid on the fire. He knows I will take the blows for our child, and he uses this knowledge to punish me. I will make offerings tonight at the moon altar and ask the spirits once again to guide and protect us.

CHAPTER THIRTY-SIX

The eerie call of a fox barking echoed through the forest and over the hills. Low cloud nestled over a dense wooded area above Milton. Millions of trees, planted decades ago across moorland and mountains, stretched seemingly forever through fifty thousand acres of the Queen Elizabeth Forest Park. Hidden dips and gullies, bracken and deep fern underfoot, miles of space criss-crossed with a network of trails and smaller paths for mountain bikers, hikers and horse riders, all looking for an adrenaline kick. A haven for outdoor pursuits – lochs to paddle on and fish in. Miles of undisturbed country in between with places to leave a body – alive or dead.

The fox shrieked again. An owl, its pale outline emerging from the gloom, flew low across the land, hooting its search for dinner. Its wide eyes glinted in the dying light. Deer were alert for dusk predators, warm breath exhaling in plumes as their beautiful dark eyes peered nervously into the murk. Christie was so cold. She shivered, her head hurting with an intensity she'd never felt before. She opened her eyes owl-wide. There was nothing familiar in what was before her. Towering trees all around, their silhouettes frightening figures in the approaching dusk, making her heart race. Light continued to fade as though someone had turned down the dimmer switch in the sky. Her eyes reset, reacting to the nocturnal gloaming, and her brain kicked into prey mode. Cold air nipped at her bare back as she looked down at her muddy boots and filthy riding jeans clinging to her legs.

'Oh, God, where am I?' She was afraid, but at least she was no longer in that cold barn. Could smell fresh air at least. She had no memory of being brought to this place. The chill of night air stroked frozen fingers across her bones.

A sound bounced off the hills. In the distance Christie could see a mountain range outlined, layered in greys like a watercolour painting. But it was hard to get her bearings in this unfamiliar place. She tried to move. Her feet were no longer tied, but her hands remained painfully secured. She pushed straggling hair away from her face as best she could.

'Mum, please. Mum...' Her voice was croaky as she prayed into the empty night.

Trying to focus her scrambled thoughts, she'd lost all sense of time or reality. Was it days or hours since he took her? He gave her water, and she'd heard his voice. But she never saw his face. As night encroached, Christie could see an area in front of her that looked like dark water. She shuffled herself upright, her stripped back against a tree. She strained her ears, thinking she heard that sound again. A gentle wind rustled through the trees. Then what she thought might be the knocking sound of a helicopter whirring in the distance. Maybe she could hear dogs barking somewhere too. But too far for her to shout for help. Her throat was so dry her voice couldn't call out anyway. Overcome with exhaustion, she slumped back further against the tree, its sharp bark digging into her bare skin. Hope drained away. She'd die out here. Alone. She was desperate to see her mum and dad and her beloved Walter again.

As night intensified, Christie looked up. Iridescent green and white lights began to shimmer above her. Vertical lines of coloured cloud flickering. She wondered if she was dreaming again. Maybe this would be her end. As Aurora danced across the northern sky, she slid into an uneasy shivering sleep.

Bright lights swirled in front of her, purple and pink, orange and blue, everything spinning fast. She should feel sick, but didn't; she was dizzy, but it wasn't unpleasant, more like she was flying high in the clouds, through clusters of rainbows towards a warm light. Dougie and Fraser were at the clearing, the bright moon shining down. She could see herself and the boys, the candles lit, the white circle, and someone at the edge of the wood. A dark shadow watching them.

'Don't be afraid, Chris. It'll be alright.' A voice in her head, or coming from somewhere around her? 'It's not as bad as you think. You just need to let go.'

It was strange, the tone familiar, but she didn't understand. Then she was in church, playing her flute, its sweet sounds reaching up into the eaves, and she felt a sense of calm and beauty. Her breathing steadied. She was playing with no sheet music in front of her. She just knew the piece. It was the loveliest thing she'd ever heard, and as she looked towards the stained-glass window, a figure came alive and smiled at her, stepping out of the bubbled glass. A golden light illuminated a halo around a blue-robed woman with long red hair. Then she was out on the moor, riding her horse. Leaning forward in the saddle, her hair flying out behind, Walter's mane tangled in her fingers. It was glorious and she didn't want it to stop. Galloping on air, along a tunnel of trees, dappled sunlight flooding in and guiding them. She felt a strange sensation on her skin. A prickling, stinging, a sense of fear. Her eyes strained to see a figure ahead. She could hear words. '*While ashen feathers fall from sky, Under a ghealach Iàn Feannag fly!*' And a rush of jet-black birds flew up. A woman was standing in the light with her arms open.

'Christie, you're here, but it's not your time.' The woman's voice was soothing and calm. 'I know you called for me, but it's a long time until you come to this place. You must go back.'

She didn't want to leave. But the light pushed her back. It was over.

The Book of Shadows

He relented today and allowed an excursion. Perhaps he thought he'd gone too far when he hacked off my hair. The child rushed at him and was beaten for trying to defend me. We clung together and despite my own pain, I tried to comfort him and his burning face where the blow had made a bruise.

There is a great celebration for the Queen, and he allowed us to join others for a trip into the hills. The lochs sparkled, especially Loch Reoidhte, with its shape like a footprint. The boy was so happy. I was careful, but told him stories from my childhood, of giants whose footprints made dents so deep in the earth that they filled up and became oceans, and of the Norse gods. His eyes shone, but after a while his father said 'Enough!' And tried to extinguish our day. But we smiled in secret, and our spirits clung in union to those stories of hope and triumph.

CHAPTER THIRTY-SEVEN

Unsurprisingly, Christie's disappearance was once more on the front page of the *Stirling Advertiser* website on Friday morning. It was the biggest story right now for the local paper. Feeling she'd hit an impasse, and that the police had too, Martha was scanning the site for any new information, however insignificant. Yesterday, she'd taken a drive out along the track where she'd met Christie with her horse, but she'd found nothing. She'd been in touch with Summers too: there'd been no sightings, and CCTV at bus and train stations had drawn a blank. And he had nothing more for her on the ink or the drugs.

A small news report about a break-in at a local vet surgery a few weeks ago caught her eye. She paused for a moment, considering the story and wondering what might have been taken in the raid. The horse tranquilliser ketamine, perhaps? She felt the buzz of a potential lead. Summers hadn't mentioned anything about this, and it could be a new line in the inquiry, she thought as she dialled the number.

'Glenview Vet's. Leah speaking, how can I help you?'

'Hi, Leah. I'm hoping you can help me. I'm new to the area,' she lied, 'and was hoping to book my dogs in for a check-up and their annual vaccinations.' Martha had a vet for the dogs, but that didn't matter right now.

'Let me have a look at the book and see when we can fit you in then,' the receptionist said. 'I'll just need to take a few details from you if that's OK, about what type of dogs they are and how old, etc.'

Martha gave the information and an appointment was made for the following week. She must remember to cancel it.

'Do you look after horses too?' she asked. 'My friend is moving to the area and bringing her horse. She's looking for a good local vet who looks after equines.'

'Yes, we have a farm-animal vet on the team who does that.'

Martha gripped her pencil. Yes, her hunch had been right. 'Great,' she said. 'I'll give my friend your number ... There's just one other thing...' Martha paused. 'I heard that you had a break-in some weeks back.'

'That's right. It was in the newspaper and everything.' Leah sounded like she was enjoying the gossip. The perfect candidate to pump for information.

'Oh, really? What happened? No one was hurt, I hope.' Martha injected some concern into her voice.

'Oh, no, we're all fine, thank you. It happened at night, so no one was here.'

'But why break into a vet's? I just don't understand it...' Martha said encouragingly.

'Well, I probably shouldn't say this, but there's a growing drug problem around here. I suppose it spreads out from the cities. And although we think our kids are immune, unfortunately that's not the case. The high school has had a bit of an issue recently – not that they'd admit it. But both ourselves and the pharmacy in town were broken into on the same night. We had some supplies stolen, and I'm sure they did too.'

'I didn't know about the pharmacy. Which one was that?' But Martha thought she already knew. And her suspicion was confirmed. It was the pharmacy on the receipt she'd found at Locke's.

Putting the phone down, she wondered what this meant for the case. The vet's could well be the source of the ketamine found in Fraser's system. But could the pharmacy break-in be the source of the Risperdal? It was a bit of a stretch – Orla seeing the Risperdal at Locke's; Martha herself finding the receipt in what she assumed was the bag containing the medication. It might mean that the pharmacy had the drug in stock. And that could mean that Locke was in the clear.

Martha wondered whether the police were joining all this up like she was. Surely they knew about the break-ins, being so close to Strathbran. Any evidence they'd found at the time might be relevant to Fraser's death. She'd need to find out from Summers whether they'd put it all together. She sent off a text asking him to give her a call.

*

Summers rang a few minutes later.

'Anything for me, Martha?' he said. She thought she heard a little desperation in his voice.

'Well, maybe. Hopefully your guys will know about this already: two break-ins over at Glenview a few weeks back – the vet's and the pharmacy.'

'Oh, yes. We know about those.'

'Do you think that's where the drugs might have come from?'

'It's possible, Martha, although it may just have been opportunistic, rather than someone specifically looking for those two drugs. We definitely know ketamine was taken from the vet's, but haven't had confirmation of Risperdal going missing from the pharmacy.'

Martha paused for a moment before going on. 'Look, I'm pretty sure they do supply it.'

'Is this about Locke again?' There was a slight irritation in his voice now.

'Alright, yes. I paid him a visit. To ask about the photo I showed you. A friendly call from a mum concerned about her son.'

'Martha...'

'Look, I went to the loo while I was there, and ... and I might have looked in the bin and found a receipt from that exact pharmacy.'

'OK, it's a connection, but it's still nothing concrete. But maybe...' He trailed off.

'Maybe...?'

'Maybe it justifies asking Locke about the Risperdal.'

Finally, Martha thought. 'Today?' she asked.

Summers sighed. 'I'll get someone out there today, yes.'

Maybe Locke would be more willing to talk about the drug to the police than her. And if he lied and they found out, that would be incriminating, and they'd be able to get a search warrant ... But she was getting ahead of herself.

'Any more developments you can tell me about?' she asked.

'Yes, actually. We've had the results back on the bottle you found.' She pricked up her ears. 'The analysis shows it's ink – mixed with blood.'

'Blood?' Martha recalled the dark lumps when she'd spread it over her fingers.

'Not human blood. It's from a bird. And yes, it matches the ink used on Fraser.'

CHAPTER THIRTY-EIGHT

Christie's teeth chattered violently. She uncurled her legs, pain biting as blood rushed back into her stiff limbs. Hunger had left her wondering if her stomach had turned itself inside out. Even in her fragile state she was relieved to be alive. She smiled weakly; how pleased Mum would be to hear her girl was craving food.

The thought of Mum reminded her of the dream – the woman who had told her to come back. She'd spoken words from the poem – "Feannag Dhubh". And now, thinking of those lines, they made Christie feel weirdly resolute. She thought of the accounts she'd read of the terrible things women accused of witchcraft had been through. Everything that had happened – to Fraser and to her – seemed connected in some way to the poem and what had happened that night at the ritual. Maybe it was lack of food, the cold, being tied up here. But she was sure she was right. She shivered, recalling the shape that had rushed out at them from the shadows that night. Stay strong, she told herself. She would get through this ordeal and she would get home in the end.

She had no idea what day it was. Or how long ago that man had taken her from the building out into the woods. A blackbird was singing brightly in a mountain ash tree nearby, his yellow beak bright against the leaves and the few wizened red berries on which he was feasting. The elegant curve of his back, tail raised up to the sky, gave her hope. She was still alive.

With a massive effort, she pushed herself up onto her knees and crawled towards the pool of murky-looking water she'd seen last night through the gloom. The rough blanket that had been draped over her shoulders fell to the ground as she leaned forward. She plunged her still-tied hands into the water. It looked black but was surprisingly clear when she managed to scoop it up to her mouth. The sweet, peaty taste was heavenly as she gulped down what didn't pour through her fingers. She wiped her wet palms over her face to wake herself up, and pushing her wrists further into the cold water, she rubbed her sore hands together for what seemed like an age until she felt the rope gradually loosening.

The girl sensed something behind her and stopped.

'Please don't let him come back,' she whispered. She glanced around, praying that she wouldn't see the hideous man – that hissing voice in the dark made her cold skin crawl. He'd left her for dead, in the middle of God knows where, but she'd rather take her chances here, alone, than have that weirdo near her.

The air was frigid on the exposed skin of her back. A deer stepped out into the glade ahead of her. The animal was poised, wary and alert to danger, its large dark eyes looking nervously around as it picked its way off through the trees.

Thank God it was the deer she'd heard and not the creep who'd taken her. She slowed her breathing and tuned into the calm of the beautiful creature as she watched it disappear. She had to somehow get free, and try to find her way back home.

She looked down at the rope she'd managed to loosen in the water and began to work on it again, using her teeth to pull at the fibres. It tasted of filth and sweat. Tears of frustration welled up.

'Fucking hell. You're not going to beat me.' She said it out loud, in a rush of determination. 'I'm going to get home. I'm going to get home.'

Suddenly, the rope went slack and part of it fell away. She'd done it. She laughed in relief. Her arms were raw as she twisted her wrists around, blood rushing back into her fingertips. She slowly pushed herself up onto her feet, legs shaking, her head spinning as she clung to a tree for support. Hunger rushed at her. Mum would lay out the biggest breakfast. Bacon, eggs, sausages, pancakes, blueberries. Her mouth watered at the thought, and with her mum in her head she felt she could focus properly now. Christie picked the dirty blanket up, wrapping it around her shoulders. It was damp, but better than nothing. Slowly she stumbled forward through the trees, searching for a path. Praying he wasn't somewhere near, watching her.

CHAPTER THIRTY-NINE

DC Ravi Cheema hurried over to DI Summers' office in the corner of the open-plan room. The door was open so he knocked on the frame. His DI looked up at him with tired eyes. Ravi wondered how much sleep he'd had over the past couple of weeks.

'You're going to want to see this, sir,' Ravi said. He wanted to blurt it all out, but he knew it was best that Summers saw it for himself.

Ravi had been working on Christie's laptop and phone ever since the police had collected them from her house the day after she went missing. While the rescue teams continued their exhaustive search for the girl throughout the week, Cheema had worked on her broken phone, and had managed to retrieve some data. A search through it showed she'd been researching the Feannag Dhubh and had visited what looked like a local folklore website many times – hundreds of searches over a period of months. Looking up spells, charms and something called *The Book of Shadows* – some kind of witch's personal journal.

Ravi had reported all this back to Summers. He knew Summers was a bit of a dinosaur when it came to technology, but Ravi could see he trusted the new breed of detectives, like himself, and realised the force needed them more and more. He'd told Summers that it looked like Christie and Fraser might have got mixed up in some occult activities, and that it all started with her school project.

Summers had shaken his head. There was nothing there that proved a connection between the cases, he'd said. And nothing that would help them find Christie. Frustrated, he'd sent Ravi back to the drawing board. Over the last couple of days, Ravi had been running a special program that searched Christie's online activity. Most of it from about a year ago was what you would expect from a teenage girl.

But this morning, he'd found she'd received some pretty weird messages a few months before. And fortunately he'd managed to trace the IP address of the sender. When he saw where it was located, it had sent him running straight to the DI.

Summers sat in Ravi's chair and read the messages Ravi pointed to on his screen. Summers was shaking his head, and Ravi understood why. There were many dark places on the internet where people who looked innocent to the outside world could hide in the shadows.

'This person clearly knew their way around the web,' Ravi said as Summers finished reading. 'These messages are from a Hotmail address, but sent via a VPN, so whoever it was, was keen to make it difficult to trace where they were based.' Ravi paused, a bit out of breath.

'Go on,' Summers said, fixing him with a hard stare.

'But I've managed to get around all that. I know where the messages were sent from. It's a computer at Glenview High School, over the weeks leading up to when the girl dropped out.'

Summers slapped a hand on the desk, making Ravi jump a

little. But the DI didn't say anything, he just rubbed the other hand over his face.

'But I'd say it wasn't another pupil,' Ravi added hastily. 'This person had more knowledge than a kid would, I think. He – if it was a he – covered his tracks pretty well. More than your average punter, I'd say. But we've got the kit that can trace most domestic content. I mean it's harder when it's organised crime, as they're getting so sophisticated in what they can do now—'

Summers interrupted him: 'You're saying it might be a teacher who was sending a young girl these abusive messages and spreading these lies about her?'

Ravi nodded. 'An adult at the school, anyway.'

'Can you trace the actual computer it came from?' Summers asked, standing up now, and striding across the office. Heads started to bob up from behind computer screens.

'Yes, we can do that,' said Ravi, hurrying along behind his boss. 'We can look at the cookies and meta pixels through analytics. When people accept cookies, this can make their devices and personal data, including what they've been searching for, traceable. It's often used in marketing to serve up targeted adverts, but very useful in an investigation too. Each computer has a unique IP address and if we can get hold of the computer itself, we should be able to do a search on that and trace any untoward activity.'

'Brilliant,' said Summers, and turned to put a heavy hand on Ravi's shoulder. 'Excellent work, Cheema.' Then he clapped his hands. 'Everyone,' he called out to the office, 'we need a warrant to search the school, pronto. And we need to get out there – now!'

Ravi was left standing in the middle of the office, and watched as the team, depressed and dismayed for days, suddenly sprang into action.

CHAPTER FORTY

Sitting in the passenger seat as the car sped out of the Glasgow suburbs, Summers took a large bite of the ketchup-covered square sausage and crispy bacon bap he'd grabbed from the van outside the station while they waited for the warrant to be confirmed. He washed it down with tea. He wasn't sure when he would eat next.

They needed to get straight out to the school, but they would have to play it carefully. He didn't want the pervert who'd sent the messages to Christie alerted to the fact that they were on to him. If it was a teacher, they'd let the Campbells know, and get their family liaison officer, DC Davies, to see if there had been any out-of-school contact between a teacher and the girl.

'Dirty bastard,' he muttered under his breath.

Cheema looked over at him. It was the young DC's first big case, Summers knew. He'd told him he was his right-hand man on this – and his driver. Overhead, grey clouds were building again, sure to bring a downpour before the hour was out.

He was stuffing the last of the bap into his mouth when his phone buzzed in his pocket.

'Martha,' he said through a mouthful of food.

'Hi, Derek. Just checking in. Has anyone been out to see Locke yet to ask about the Risperdal?'

Summers shook his head to himself. 'Yes, I had one of the officers who's in the village pay him another visit. So yes, he has been asked – but was not at all happy about it. In fact, he wanted to know why we were asking him in particular about that drug, and said he hoped people were not spreading rumours about him...'

'Oh...' Martha said.

'Yes, oh. He's on to you, Martha, so I'd be careful around him. My officer pushed him, but he refused to confirm either way whether he had ever taken it himself. Asked if he was being questioned officially.'

'Damn it,' Martha replied. He could hear she was not best pleased. 'Any updates on those break-ins at Glenview?'

'No, but we're actually heading out that way now. Going to the school,' Summers said.

'What's happened at the school? Something to do with Christie? Fraser...?'

'We're just checking out some information related to messages that we've been able to access on Christie's phone.'

'OK. Great. Thanks for letting me know.'

She rang off, and Summers wondered whether he'd live to regret telling her about the messages.

The 1980s building had the visage of a concrete prison block rather than a high school for more than six hundred pupils. Kids came here from villages across west Stirlingshire, so there was a large area at the front that looked like a bus terminus. Summers and Cheema drove across it, disturbing a small group of crows, sending them flapping and cawing across the nearby playing field. Cheema pulled the car up right outside the front door, ignoring the yellow parking restrictions. It was half an hour after lunch so most pupils would now be settled in classes. Summers had made it clear to the whole team that their intention was not to cause too much disruption to the school day, for the kids at least. So the other cars who were with them were parked down the lane, ready should they be needed.

'Right, let's see what we can find out,' Summers said.

Rumours would spread about the police turning up at the school again, but that couldn't be helped. The school community was still reeling from Fraser's death and the fact that Christie was now missing. He was aware stories were spreading about who could be next. Hysteria hyped by media reports and local Facebook groups had mushroomed, with juvenile imaginations running wild through the classrooms too, no doubt. Summers was confident that the more bizarre elements of the case were not generally known, although they'd struggle to keep a lid on them for much longer. Summers just hoped they could find Christie before the witchcraft rumours really took hold.

'Good morning, officers. Can I help you?' The receptionist looked concerned as they showed her their cards.

'We have a warrant to look at the computers in the school,' Summers said quietly, Cheema nodding beside him. Summers handed over the paperwork.

The woman was flustered. She stared at the forms with an open mouth.

'We'd like to start with the IT department,' Cheema said. 'I presume there's someone who looks after all of the tech from a central point.'

'Yes, that's right,' replied the receptionist. 'I'll have to call the head teacher down though. We'll also need to make sure the IT suite is clear of any pupils before you go in.'

'I'd appreciate it if you could do that quickly,' said Summers. 'Staff will also need to be cleared from the IT classrooms. But they cannot be given a reason why. No computers must be tampered with.'

After getting no answer from the head teacher's office, she hurried off, leaving Summers and Cheema in the large, garishly painted reception area, among pupils' artwork that Summers hoped weren't self-portraits.

'Once we get in there, how long will it take to identify which computer was used to send the messages?' he asked Cheema.

'It shouldn't take too long, sir. The place likely runs on a central network and their IT support should be able to see activity anyway. That's why it's odd that this got through.'

'Unless it *was* the IT support,' Summers said.

The receptionist appeared at the end of the corridor, beckoning to Summers to follow her.

'You get on to that,' he told Cheema. 'I'll speak to the head teacher and you can call me when you find something.'

Seated in front of Geoff Haw, the head teacher, Summers took a long breath.

'I'll get straight to the point, Mr Haw. This is highly confidential, but we believe abusive messages and photographs were sent from a computer in your school to a pupil.'

Haw's face was a picture of shock. 'Do you think it could have been another pupil, Detective Inspector Summers?' he asked after a pause.

'It's possible, but more likely a member of your staff, according to my colleague. He's a cyber-crime specialist and will be able to trace which computer the messages were sent from. There's potentially more to this though. I understand the parents of the girl involved were in touch with your deputy head teacher about bullying and online abuse around the time these messages were sent, but the school seemed to have taken very little action in response to what was going on.'

Haw swallowed hard, his Adam's apple looking like it could choke him.

'It's very challenging. Kids have access to so much; it's hard to monitor everything that is going on. Many have smart phones, and we actually encourage that. Our school has large numbers of pupils travelling in by bus from rural areas across west Stirlingshire and we need to ensure the pupils can contact parents and guardians in case of emergencies. But these phones are powerful computers that they carry around with them all day in their pockets, so it's not always possible to know what they are getting up to. The school can only do so much.'

Summers nodded. 'We understand that, but the parents of Christie Campbell seem to have had very little support, and these messages could well be linked to her recent disappearance.'

At the mention of Christie's name, the teacher's face turned grey. Summers watched the penny slowly drop: Haw's school could be linked to something more serious than a bullied girl.

'We will do absolutely anything we can to help. We are all concerned about Christie. Is there no word on her whereabouts?'

Summers shook his head. 'I'm afraid not.'

'She was a troubled girl when she was here latterly,' Haw went on. 'And although I wasn't fully aware of all of the details, I know she left us halfway through the summer term.' It was clear Haw was now regretting how little support the school seemed to have given either the girl or her family.

Summers' phone buzzed before he had the chance to answer. Cheema.

'I'm in, boss,' he said. 'This is looking interesting. Someone in the IT department, a Joseph Gallagher, seems to have access to the whole system. I would say nothing could have taken place that he either didn't know about, or didn't actually do himself. We need to bring him in for questioning.'

'Joseph Gallagher,' Summers repeated. 'We'll find out where he is just now and if he's on site, we'll speak to him straight away.'

He turned to see that Haw was checking his own screen.

'Mr Gallagher has been absent for a couple of days,' he said. 'According to our records, he called in sick with a bug last Thursday and it looks as though he'll be off for the rest of this week too.'

'We'll need a home address, then, please.'

The head teacher looked as though he might protest, but seeing the stare Summers was giving him, he seemed to have a change of heart. He jotted the address down on a yellow Post-it note, passing it silently over to Summers:

Joseph Gallagher, 43A Dowland Drive, Strathbran, Stirlingshire.

Summers blinked. It was right around the corner from where Christie lived.

CHAPTER FORTY-ONE

Martha pulled up outside the school and watched as a few senior pupils strayed about. She could see a car parked outside the main reception and was sure it was police issue. Outside in the lane, there was a squad car, lined up behind another car – people sitting in the front seats of both. This looked serious, but it was clear Summers was trying to keep things low key. She wasn't sure how long that would work. The seniors walking down the lane were already taking a particular interest in the police car.

One of Dougie's friends emerged from the building and started to make his way across the forecourt. It was one of the lads she'd given a lift to and asked about Fraser when he was missing. As he walked past her car, she opened the window.

'Hamish,' she called over to him. 'Have you got a minute?' He stepped closer to the car, smiling when he realised it was Dougie's mum.

'Have you any idea what's going on?' she asked, nodding her head towards the police car.

'Aye. Apparently they've closed the computer labs and the cops are in there just now,' he said. 'Dunno if it's something to do with Fraser, or maybe Christie.' He continued on his way, saying he had a class to get to.

Martha sat for a moment, cogitating. Summers had said they were here looking into messages on Christie's phone. If they'd closed the computer labs, they must have traced these messages to the school. Were there other kids involved in this whole thing? In the rituals, maybe, all the Feannag Dhubh stuff? She knew herself how intense adolescence could be – the attraction some kids felt towards the occult and the unexplained. Towards the forbidden. Had it spiralled out of control? Could this be what Dougie was trying to hide?

She got out of the car and headed for reception. She would wait there for Summers to emerge. If there was some link to the school, then she wanted to know what it was. She needed to know what danger Dougie might be in.

She told the receptionist she was waiting for her son and sat in the chairs outside the school office, picking up a magazine, and flicking through it – all the while watching the doors, glancing out of the windows – keeping all her senses on alert. She heard the phone at reception ring, and saw the woman pick it up. Martha studied the page of the magazine, straining to hear what was said.

'Yes, Mr Haw. I'll get that information for the officers ... Joe Gallagher, yes? ... His whole record? OK, I'll print it off and give it to them when they come back through. Are they done with the computer lab yet?'

Joe Gallagher, Martha thought. It rang a vague bell, but wasn't a name she'd heard from Dougie. It was a large school, maybe this Joe was in a different year. But why would the police want his record? And then it dawned on her. Maybe Gallagher wasn't a pupil...

She stood up and approached the reception again.

'Sorry to be nosy,' she said. 'But I couldn't help overhearing you there. Who's Mr Gallagher? I don't think I've heard of him. Is he a new teacher?'

'No. He's a school technician. He works in the computer department, but...'

Before she could finish her sentence, Summers and Cheema emerged. Martha hurried over to them.

'Martha. I suppose I shouldn't be surprised to see you here,' Summers said. He seemed to be in a big hurry. 'I'm sorry, but we need to get going. Something's come up.'

'Is this something to do with Joe Gallagher?' Martha called across the hall.

This had the desired effect. Summers stopped dead in his tracks, turned and strode back to Martha. 'Keep your voice down, Martha, unless you want to cause a full-scale panic.'

'So you are looking at him in connection with Christie?' she hissed. 'He's the one who sent her the messages you mentioned?'

He nodded quickly and began to walk away again.

Martha kept pace with him. 'The press will be all over this.'

'Which is why I need to get to him before they do. Say nothing to anyone, Martha. I mean it.'

She nodded as he got into his car and pulled away.

Then she turned and headed back inside. Approaching the desk, she could see the head teacher talking to the receptionist in the office behind, a worried look on his face. She stepped round the desk and knocked on the door.

'Can I help you?' he said, opening it.

'I hope so. I was wondering if you have five minutes to chat about a member of your staff. Joe Gallagher?'

The head teacher's face paled to grey. 'Are you press?' he asked.

'I'm the mother of a pupil at this school. But yes, I'm also a journalist. I'm not working on this story though, I'm just a concerned parent.'

Beads of sweat had broken out on his brow. 'I'm sorry, but there's nothing I can tell you. If you want a statement you'll need to go through the council press office.'

Martha stared at him for a moment longer. It was clear Summers had told them the same as he'd told her: not a word to anyone about Gallagher. There was no more she could do here, so she thanked the head and made her way back out to her car, wheels spinning in her mind as she walked.

The vet's and the pharmacy break-ins had occurred here in Glenview, with drugs stolen from both. After the gossipy Leah at the vet's had mentioned a drug problem in the area, Martha had called a local newspaper reporter she used to work with to find out what he knew. He'd told her that the towns and villages of west Stirlingshire were certainly not immune to problems with school kids and drugs. His paper was even looking into gangs from Glasgow and Edinburgh running county lines – using young people to traffic drugs into rural areas instead of their home cities. Was that what this was about – teens getting out of their depth with drug dealers? And was the occult stuff about the Feannag Dhubh just a side show? And what about Locke – how did he fit into all this? Did he and Gallagher know each other? She needed more information about Gallagher, and knew exactly who to ask.

Back at home, she called up to Dougie, asking to speak to him. He appeared at the top of the stairs, a haunted look on his face, and his shoulders tensed up like he was expecting bad news.

'We're going out,' she said. 'We can't just sit here and do nothing. Let's drive along the forest tracks. See if there's any sign of Christie or anything that might help find her.'

He made a face. 'I dunno...'

'Come on. It'll do you good to get out.' He'd managed to go to school this week, but only on and off, and she wasn't sure he was able to concentrate on anything. Even his guitar had fallen silent.

She grabbed their coats from the rack in the hall and held his out towards him. Reluctantly he descended the stairs and took it from her. She called the dogs from the garden to get them in the car, and they headed off down Station Road, the route where Fraser had set off on his run just a few weeks ago.

She took the track past the sewage works, and then turned into the forest, hoping the gates would be open as the rescue team had been searching out here for a few days.

'Do you think they're going to find her?' Dougie asked. He sounded exhausted.

'I don't know, love. All we can do is help – and hope.'

They continued along the gravel road, huge pine trees lining either side of the track. They passed a small lake, only visible because they were high up in the four-wheel drive. When they came to a crossroads, Martha stopped, checking the map on her phone.

'There's so many tracks out here, it's hard to know which way to go,' she said.

It looked as though other vehicles had gone straight ahead, so she took a left turning, hoping her old Subaru would manage what looked like an abandoned path.

She knew this trip was probably a bit pointless. The police and search teams would have been very thorough already. But that wasn't the real reason she'd come out here. She needed to draw Dougie out, and a conversation in a car – both people facing forward, not each other – was often the best place to do this.

She allowed a few minutes of bumpy travel along the track, then asked the question that had been burning on her tongue:

'Do you know a Joe Gallagher from school?'

'Er ... not really,' Dougie answered.

She glanced across and could see how hard he was gripping the seat.

'Why do you ask?' he said.

'I was up at the school this afternoon and the police are apparently interested in speaking to him.'

'I've not really had much to do with him. He works in the computer department. Never struck me as too bright, to be honest. Most of the kids think he's a bit of a creep?'

'A creep? Why do they say that?'

'Just the way he is, I suppose.'

'Do *you* think he's a creep?'

'Maybe. I dunno...'

Hearing the wobble in his voice Martha sensed there was more, but decided not to press him for now. It was an odd fight in her mind – one she never thought she'd have to face: between her investigative instincts and being gentle with her son.

She knew he was in pain. Not just from Fraser and Christie, but from his little brothers. And she knew how he felt. Most of the time now, her grip on each day seemed tenuous. She only just got through. One day at a time, a grief counsellor had told her. She had to look out for Dougie too though. And she realised that doing so was probably the only thing that had kept her going. But now, with everything that was happening, he'd need her more than ever. With Jamie easing his way back into her life, perhaps they could all move forward together – supporting Dougie between them. Not the same family, but a family nevertheless.

She left a long pause before asking her next question.

'You know that picture, Dougie – the one with the name of the poem on the back?'

'Uh huh.'

'Have you remembered anything about it? Is there any reason at all why that would be significant?'

He didn't say anything and when Martha looked across, tears were sliding down his cheeks.

'Dougie, what is it? What's wrong?' She pulled the car to a halt and turned in her seat. 'Is there something you need to tell me? Whatever it is, it's OK, love.'

'Mum,' he gasped. 'It's all my fault. I think Fraser's dead because of me.'

'Why, Dougie? It's not your fault. I'm sure it's not...' Martha hoped that the doubt in her mind couldn't be heard in her voice.

She waited, watched him shake his head and open his mouth, but nothing came out. She tried to help him along a little.

'Look, I've found a few things out. You know me, always the journalist.' She tried to inject a small laugh into her voice. 'Were you three – you, Fraser, Christie – involved in something to do with the Feannag Dhubh? I know you played a song using the words from that poem about the witch who was burned...'

'That was the start of it, I suppose. Christie did a project about the witch trials. But then it got out of hand.'

He stopped, and looked out into the trees for a long while.

'I know about the ritual you did last year. I heard you talking about it on the phone to Christie.'

Dougie frowned at her. 'That was just daft kids' stuff, Mum,' he said. 'Christie had this idea that we could help lay restless spirits to rest by doing some chanting thing and lighting candles at the moondial behind our old house at Blacklaw. It was all a bit stupid to be honest.'

'What restless spirits?' Martha asked, a slightly sick feeling in the pit of her stomach.

'The ... the boys,' Dougie's voice had dropped to a whisper. 'I'm sorry, Mum. I was so cut up about the twins, Christie thought it might help. It seems so stupid now.'

Martha reached out an arm and pulled him towards her, kissing the top of his head. 'I know, love. I know...'

He sniffled into her coat. Then sat back up, wiping at his eyes.

'And this Joe Gallagher? Was he involved in any of that daft stuff?' she asked.

Dougie shook his head. 'No. No, not at all.'

But it seemed to Martha that he was making a huge effort to keep his eyes on the trees, and not to meet her gaze.

CHAPTER FORTY-TWO

Summers had to bang hard on the flimsy door several times before he heard shuffling footsteps. A chain drew back, the door opened a crack, and a slight figure with greasy hair peered through. The reek of cigarette smoke curled out. The man was the very image of a small-time drug pusher.

'Aye, what do you want?' A local accent, no warmth in his greeting. 'I've already told the police I don't know anything about that girl going missing. Didn't even know her from the school.'

Summers knew they'd already questioned Gallagher during their door-to-door inquiries. He didn't recall having seen the man at the village meeting they'd held, or volunteering to help with the searches.

'We're here about another matter, relating to your job at the school. Can we come in? We have a few questions.'

'I'd rather you came back another time,' Gallagher said, coughing loudly. Angry crusted sores blistered the corners of his mouth. 'I've been off work this week with a bug and don't feel like answering any questions just now.' He pushed the door half an inch as though to close it, but Summers quickly stuck his heavy boot into the gap.

'It would be in your interests to answer our questions voluntarily – here or else down at the station,' he said. 'It's your choice.'

Gallagher hesitated. 'OK, OK. The place is a right mess, so I'd rather maybe come with you. Gie us a minute and I'll get ma coat.' As he disappeared, the door opened further, revealing a grubby hallway with a series of doors leading off it. It had the odour of an unemptied bin and a sweet, smoky smell Summers recognised as weed.

Summers and Cheema looked at each other. Most people preferred to answer questions in their own place, rather than at the police station.

'He's got something to hide. We need to get in there and find out what. Let HQ know. And have a car sit outside here until we're allowed access,' Summers said in a low voice. Cheema nodded in agreement and typed out some quick texts.

Gallagher sat quietly in the back of the police car as they drove back to the station.

'Don't suppose I can have a fag in here?' he asked when they arrived. His eyes were glazed, sinking into his sallow skin. The same sweet whiff that they'd detected coming from his flat was now mixed with the odour of smoke and several days of sweat. Summers shook his head. He wouldn't let the bloke anywhere near kids.

'No-smoking policy across the force now,' he said. 'Not even allowed to smoke within the boundaries of the station. Has made quite a few people give up these last few years.'

Gallagher scowled and started sniffing as though he really did have a cold, although the earlier coughing fit didn't return.

'Am I goin' to need a lawyer, then? Do I get a phone call?' he asked when they got into the interview room.

Summers glared at him. His eyes were a bit clearer now.

'No, you're here to help us with our inquiries at this stage. Purely voluntary. We could have done this at your flat, if you recall.'

Gallagher scowled again. 'Can I get a tea with four sugars then?' He pulled out a chair and sat down heavily. 'A biscuit would go down a treat too. Got any custard creams?'

Summers asked Cheema to organise refreshments for their guest, and they left him to stew for a few minutes while they went back to the office to get updates from the rest of the team, who'd been focusing all their efforts on Gallagher and on Christie's messages while Summers and Cheema had been at Glenview.

They returned to the interview room with folders of new info, and a brew for Gallagher. Summers watched with a little pleasure as Gallagher burned his fingers trying to lift the steaming plastic cup from the table.

'Right. All set now?' Summers asked. 'Then let's get started.'

A worried expression briefly flitted across Gallagher's rat-like features. His small nose matched a pointed chin that sported several days of straggly hair. He could have done with a good wash too. Summers wondered at the quality of the staff Glenview employed.

'We've some questions about the computer network at Glenview High School. We understand you have full access to it, to enable you to monitor the pupils' activities.'

Gallagher nodded. 'Aye, that's right. Full access. No one can do anything in that school without me knowing about it, at least on the school's network. There is also a private network monitored centrally that the head teacher and the deputies use. I don't have access to that one.' He was confident now, Summers thought. Wanting to show the power he imagined he had.

'We are looking into some messages sent to a pupil a few

months ago that came from the school network. The one that you have *full* access to.'

'What messages would those be? Those kids are daft. They think that they can look up porn sites and surf their own social media when they're in the classroom. Of course they can't. We've put controls in place, but the silly little buggers try anyway, not knowing it sends up a security flag every time they do. I know what every one of them is doing, and when and where they're doing it.'

'These were emails to a girl, mentioning witchcraft. Threatening her. She was doing a school project and had joined discussion groups on various websites. One in particular that we're interested in, which we think you might know something about: ravenmaster-spells.co.uk. Someone in the discussion forum there managed to get hold of her email address and then sent her things that freaked her out. Horrible pictures of animal sacrifice and devil worship. They were sent to her directly from a computer in the school. Do you know anything about that?'

Shoulders tensing visibly, Gallagher's cheeks flushed.

'Nah. I wouldn't know anything about that. Must have been before my time. You'll be wanting to speak to the previous incumbent about that.'

He sat back, letting out a long, foul-smelling breath, as though they were wasting his time. 'Can I go now then? We done?' he asked with a smirk.

'Unfortunately for you, Mr Gallagher, we're just starting. Those messages were sent after you had started at the school. We checked. You'd already been there for six weeks when this activity took place. It led to a pupil being bullied and almost suffering a breakdown. She has since left the school.'

Gallagher's expression told Summers he knew exactly who they were talking about.

'I don't know anything about that. It must have been a pupil sent those messages. You know some of them are really bright and probably know more about the system than I do. Wouldn't be surprised if the wee buggers have managed to get hold of the passwords somehow and hacked into the system. Kids these days...' He trailed off, sweat starting to bead on his brow. 'I'm not feeling too well actually. Been off this week, as I said. Think I'd like to go home now if there's nothing else.'

Summers looked at Cheema.

'Actually, we'd like you to stay here and answer some more questions. This all took place after the school day, and on one occasion at the weekend, when there were no pupils in school. We're checking with the school admin right now to see if your security codes were used to access the school building at those times.'

Gallagher slumped back in the chair.

'I want a lawyer then,' he said, looking defeated.

CHAPTER FORTY-THREE

Martha was out with the dogs on Saturday morning when a call came in from Summers. She'd texted and called him the previous night, with no response. She guessed the Gallagher development was keeping him busy. She hurried to answer, keen to hear the latest.

'Martha...' Summers paused. 'There's no easy way to say this. We need to speak to Dougie.'

Martha was instantly on alert. 'What about?'

'Look, we really need to speak to him directly. You'll need to be present, of course, as he's under eighteen, so you'll hear everything we have to ask him. Can we come to the house now?'

'Yes. I'm just out with the dogs. I'll go straight back.'

'We've already called Dougie—'

'You've spoken to him?'

'We had to check the number. He said he's at home, so we've told him to stay put.'

'How did you get his number? I don't remember giving it to anyone...'

She heard Summers sigh on the other end of the line.

'Derek, please – give me something. You know I'm desperate. I know much more about this case than any ordinary witness. I'm working with you, aren't I?' She could feel herself shaking, her heart tapping unevenly in her chest.

'OK, OK, I'll just tell you this: it's about Joseph Gallagher. He's been in custody since yesterday, and we've seized his phone. We've been working through it overnight and trying to get in touch with all the contacts he's spoken to in recent months. Dougie is one of them.'

An array of emotions ran through Martha's head at high speed. Dougie had only yesterday told her that he didn't really know Gallagher, and now it appeared that he'd lied to her.

'But...' she began.

'I can't say any more, Martha. We'll see you at the house shortly. Make sure Dougie doesn't go anywhere.'

The call ended and Martha looked at the woods around her, still leafless, dark and damp.

Silence prevailed.

It was broken by the sudden cracking caw of a crow.

She turned her head towards the noise, but the bird was nowhere to be seen.

As she approached the house, BJ started to yip with excitement and soon she could hear Orla's voice. She quietened the dog with a biscuit and as she got closer to the garden, she realised that was Orla talking to Dougie.

'Oh, who's been a naughty boy then?' Orla said. 'I can smell it a mile off, Dougie. Now what *would* your mother say?'

Martha stopped beside the garden wall and listened.

'Please, don't say anything to her,' Dougie was saying. 'She'll not like me smoking. She doesn't know,' he said, faint hope in his voice.

'I'll make a deal with you then, young man,' replied Orla. 'I'll not tell your mum if you do two things for me: give me a drag of whatever it is you're smoking, and tell me what's going on with you.'

Martha couldn't believe what she was hearing. What the hell were the two of them smoking?

'I know something's up,' Orla went on. 'You've been looking seriously stressed recently, and your mum's told me how difficult things have been for you, with one friend killed and another missing. If you need someone to chat to – other than your mum – I've got a good ear. And maybe I could help.'

There was a pause, neither of them spoke for a moment.

'Ah, now that's some pretty good shit,' Orla said with a laugh. There was another pause. Then Orla said, 'No, that's enough for me on a Saturday morning.'

A second later something small and white sailed over the wall and landed right at Martha's feet. She stooped to pick it up. It was the butt of a roll-up. Martha gave it a sniff. A strong scent of weed was coming off it.

As she did so, she spotted another, similar, roll-up butt in the grass a few feet away. And another under the bush at her side. Instinctively she looked up. The window to Dougie's loft room was directly above her head. Her mouth dropped open. Had Dougie been smoking weed all this time?

'The police called this morning,' Dougie was saying to Orla. 'They said the guy they have in custody, Joe Gallagher, has my name in his phone and they need to speak to me about it – with Mum there. I'm sure they think he took Christie.' The words rushed out. 'Fraser and me bought weed off him, but now he's told me I have to pay off Fraser's debt now he's ... now he's...' Dougie couldn't finish the sentence. 'Mum will go ape shit when she finds out.'

Martha raised the latch on the gate and opened it. Orla had her arm around Dougie's shoulder.

'Yes, she really will go ape shit,' Martha said. They both turned, astonished.

'What exactly do you think you are doing, smoking that stuff in my garden?'

They both stepped back.

'Does someone want to tell me what is going on here?' Martha demanded.

'Dougie just got himself upset, that's all,' said Orla.

'Mum, it's the police. They want to speak to me.'

'They're not the only ones.' She held out the butt of the joint to Dougie. 'This is yours, I believe?'

Orla moved back, eyes wide at the anger in her friend's tone. 'Of course not, Martha. Don't be so bloody ridiculous. I was having a cigarette out here, that was all. Dougie must have been standing downwind and got the smell on him. You need to calm down.'

Martha saw Dougie briefly catch Orla's eye with a look of gratitude.

'Please don't lie to me, either of you. You don't smoke roll-ups, Orla. And anyway, I've just stood on the other side of that wall and listened to everything you've just said. Dougie, get up to your room and clean yourself up. The police are on their way and you'd better have some damn good answers for them, after what I've just heard.'

Dougie scurried into the kitchen and up the stairs without another word.

'And as for you,' Martha said to Orla, 'sod off back to your lover. I'm so furious I can't even speak to you right now.'

'Yes, I can tell,' Orla said bullishly. 'And I'm not going anywhere when my best friend is in bits.'

She pulled Martha into a hug. And Martha let her, feeling suddenly weak.

'You need to lay off Dougie, you know,' Orla said into her hair.

'I'm not surprised if he has the odd smoke. None of this is normal for him, you know.'

Martha took a deep breath, then hugged Orla back, tightly.

'I'm sorry for snapping. But it's this whole situation. Dougie's involved somehow. He seemed on the point of saying something yesterday – he told me it's all his fault that Fraser died – but then he clammed up. And now this Gallagher thing has come to light and Dougie is linked to him in some way.' She stood back. 'Did I hear right just now? He said he and Fraser were buying weed from Gallagher?'

Orla nodded, smoothing Martha's mussed-up hair.

'And Gallagher's trying to get him to pay Fraser's debts?'

'That's what Dougie said. I couldn't believe it myself. Who is this Gallagher?'

'A technician at the school. The police arrested him yesterday. Summers is on his way over to speak to Dougie. They found his number on Gallagher's phone.' She hung her head. 'Oh, Orla. have I had my head buried in the sand all this time?'

'No, you haven't. You've been grieving. And that's different. The problem is you've always been in control of everything. But you can't direct any of this. Not what happened to the twins and Jamie. Not how Dougie's dealing with it. And certainly not what's happened with Fraser and Christie. You can only try to manage your reactions to it all. I bet you've never talked properly to anyone have you? About the twins, or Jamie?'

Martha shook her head. 'I can't,' she murmured. 'It's too hard.'

'Well, I'm here now to help you. Sooner or later, you're going to have to confront what has happened to you all, because it's the worst that ever could happen. You'll have to find a way through it. You have no choice. And remember you still have a son, Martha. That's the most important thing right now.'

Martha nodded. She knew Orla was right.

'But Jane MacDonald doesn't have a son anymore,' she said. 'And I just pray that Christie's parents still have a daughter.'

CHAPTER FORTY-FOUR

The black Labrador always ran off in the woods, chasing deer or any imagined prey. Bill Baxter was a former gamekeeper, and he'd never had a dog so disobedient. He knew the land well and they walked for miles, now he was retired and had plenty of time. He loved being outdoors, but didn't shoot anymore. He'd done enough killing, and hauling of deer and game birds from the moor, in his forty years working on the Strathbran Estate.

'Harris! Here, boy.' The beast was way up ahead on the track. Tail held high, trotting along at a steady pace.

A red kite soared overhead. Riding the wind, its high-pitched call whistled across the forest, distinctive crescent-shaped tail catching the updraft as it drifted in the clouds. Bill stopped, head rolled back, watching the magnificent bird against the canvas of sky and clouds. He could have watched it all day. With Ben Lomond in the distance, it was a glorious sight. He was glad to see the beautiful creatures back in the sky again, where they belonged. He'd been sad to hear about a spate of bird poisonings in other parts of Scotland. One estate manager had even been prosecuted for it.

Bill knew well the positive impact on local economies Highland estates and their game businesses had, but he had always thought that a huge part of his job was about preserving the land, and not just for the pheasant and grouse. He was out of that world these days though, and could simply enjoy the peace of the countryside, escape to these wild places and watch the wildlife. Shooting with a camera rather than his gun.

The dog barked some way off.

'Harris, come! Where the hell are ye?' he called, increasing his pace along the stony track. His aching hip meant he couldn't move fast, but the tone of Harris's bark said he'd found something interesting. The dog had gone off the path and into the trees, his loud yelp echoing across to the far side of the forested glen.

'Calm yersel, boy. What have you got there?'

The dog was in a small, sunlit clearing surrounded by dense pine, his tail stiff, the ruff on his neck standing to attention. There was something there, and the dog was stubbornly refusing to move. Bill would have to cross a forestry drainage ditch to see what it was. He placed his walking crook with care, stepping over the small stream gathered in the ditch, his boots bouncing on the cushion of bright-green sphagnum moss that covered the forest floor. Although an able man for his age, Bill was miles from the village out here and not likely to meet anyone if he tripped.

Grunting with effort, he ducked under the lower branches of the pines. The air beneath the trees smelled damp, and small green shoots had started to peek through the carpet of orange needles, signalling the approaching change in the seasons.

Harris looked up, eyes shining and saliva dripping from his jaws. Bill squinted as a low mound came into focus under the trees.

He narrowed his eyes again – and he realised he was looking at a person.

'What's happened here?'

Moving closer, he could see tangled blonde hair. A girl. Lying awkwardly on her side, her top ripped and back exposed, she was facing away from him.

'Oh, bugger.'

He'd heard news reports all week about a local girl going missing. Just this morning, the Friday bulletin had reported that hopes were fading that she would be found.

He put out his hand, touching her arm and pulling her over onto her back. She was a young lassie, her face bruised and filthy. He cleared her hair from her face, then felt for a pulse, as his own raced.

'Oh, my word.'

There was a faint beating in her neck, and her eyes opened slightly.

'Help me ... please help me,' the girl whispered through cracked, bleeding lips.

Bill pulled out his phone. There was hardly any signal, but as a former first-aider his mobile was still registered to piggy-back on any available network.

He dialled 999, muttering 'Thank God' as the call started to ring.

CHAPTER FORTY-FIVE

Martha hurried to the door when she saw Summers arrive. She'd sent Orla on her way, and Dougie was still upstairs. She wanted to quiz the DI before he spoke to him, so she ushered Summers into the kitchen and closed the door.

'Look, I'll tell you what I've found out from Dougie,' she said, holding her hands out. 'But I really need to find out what you know too.' She looked pleadingly at Summers.

'Go on,' he said. She noticed he hadn't promised anything.

'Yesterday, he denied knowing Gallagher at all. But today, I've discovered that him and Fraser were buying weed from the guy.'

'That seems to be right. Gallagher has admitted to selling dope to Fraser. And both Dougie's and Christie's numbers were on his phone, so we're assuming, as they were all friends...'

'I think it's gone a bit further than that,' Martha said. 'Dougie says that Gallagher has been putting pressure on him.'

Summers frowned. 'What kind of pressure?'

'Apparently, Fraser clocked up a debt with him. And now Fraser's dead, Gallagher expects Dougie to pay it back.'

'Well, we can add that to the list of possible charges,' Summers said.

'So you think he's your man?'

Summers pulled a chair out and sat down. Martha had too much nervous energy to do the same.

'We're still putting it all together. But we think we'll have a case.'

'Does this mean he's behind the break-ins at the vet's and the pharmacy? That would link him to the drugs in Fraser's body, and with Fraser and Christie's numbers on his phone...' Martha's mind was busy making connections.

'We're checking Gallagher's fingerprints and DNA against all local unsolved cases, including the break-ins. You may be right that that's where he got the drugs. But there's much more compelling evidence.'

Now Martha did sit down. She nodded at Summers to continue, staring hard at him.

'We searched his flat. He had photos of a number of the kids from Glenview High on his personal computer. And we know he'd been sending emails from the school server to Christie. He also tried to persuade other girls to send photos of themselves. We don't yet know if anyone actually met him though. It's something else we're checking out.'

'Dougie said everyone at school thinks Gallagher's a creep. But this goes way beyond creepy.'

'It does. And we can link him to Fraser's death too. We found a stash of ketamine in his car – under the spare wheel in the boot. He claimed he's been using it himself and bought it from a dealer. But you might be right about the break-ins. That could well be where he got it from. We've charged him with the online offences and possession of a class-A for now, so we can keep questioning him.'

Martha realised Summers was trusting her with far more detail than he really should. 'I appreciate you telling me all this, Derek,' she said. 'What about the Risperdal? Did you find that?'

'Well, there's the thing. Gallagher is denying knowing anything about that, and we've found no traces so far. We're waiting for confirmation of any prescribed drugs he might be on, but, like you say, he might have got hold of it by breaking into the pharmacy. So, circumstantially, it all stacks up. We think Gallagher probably subdued Fraser with the drugs while he completed the writing.

When we showed him the photos of the lines we found on Fraser, he denied all knowledge, of course. He did look genuinely shocked though. Maybe seeing it like that made him realise the game was up.'

Martha frowned. There seemed to be a lot of holes in this case that still needed filling in.

'We're certain the online stalking with Christie was him, though,' Summers continued. 'We've pinpointed it right back to times he was known to be in school. He thought he'd covered his tracks. Not well enough, it seems.'

'Has he given you any hint about where she might be?' Martha said. 'Dealing drugs to kids and sending them messages online is one thing, but escalating to abduction and murder seems a bit of a leap. Not unheard of but…'

'That's what we're focusing our questioning on at the moment. He's saying he never met her outside school and has no idea where she might be. And our teams are still flat out looking for her, I can assure you. Nothing we've turned from his house or car has given us any leads though. Which is incredibly frustrating.'

Martha pondered all this for a moment. She wanted to feel positive, relieved that Gallagher was behind bars, and not going anywhere soon, but doubt nagged at her.

'What about the photo?' she asked. 'The one with Fraser, Dougie and Christie? It shows them all together. And it mentions the poem. You have a copy.'

Summers nodded, an uncertain expression on his face now.

'So, did you show him it? What did Gallagher have to say about that?'

'We didn't, Martha. Not yet anyway. To be honest, I'm not sure how it fits with what we now know about the man.'

Martha stared at him, slightly aghast. He couldn't just dismiss the Feannag Dhubh part of all this, could he?

'Look, two of the kids in that picture disappeared, and my son is the third. Fraser had lines from the bloody poem on him – a poem

Christie was studying and that is mentioned on the photograph. Gallagher knew all three kids – he had their phone numbers. You need to ask him about the picture – about the poem.'

Summers tapped his fingers on the table. She wondered if he was now a little irritated.

'To be honest with you, Martha, we need to concentrate on the facts: on the solid leads and evidence we've now uncovered. I just don't think all this stuff with the poem is the best angle to pursue right now. We need to find Christie; that's our priority.'

Martha slumped in her chair. 'Of course it is, of course. But … something's not adding up for me.'

Summers looked like he was struggling to remain patient.

'What about Locke?' she said. 'Does Gallagher have any connections to the church?'

'I know you have a hunch about the Reverend Locke,' said Summers. 'But I think you've got that one wrong, Martha. Gallagher's our man. Everything points to him. We have solid evidence against him. And he's connected to Fraser and Christie – and Dougie, of course. Who I need to speak to.' He rapped the table with his knuckles, clearly wanting to get on.

'And they were all in that photograph,' Martha said pointedly. 'Will you at least get your guys to look at it again? See if there's any connection to this bloke? Just put it in front of him and see how he reacts. Mention the Feannag Dhubh to him. It can't hurt, now you have him.'

Summers sighed. 'We can, but it's not a priority.'

Martha could see she was trying his patience now. 'I hope it's him, I really do,' she said. 'But I can't help feeling there's some other angle. What about the ink bottle? That's solid evidence. You said the ink was definitely the same as the stuff used on Fraser.'

'We haven't asked Gallagher about that yet, but we will. And yes, we will keep exploring all angles. But it does look as though Gallagher's our man, Martha. And Dougie has a connection to him that I need to speak to him about. Now, is he here?'

Summers stood up, clearly marking an end to Martha's questions, and as he did so, Dougie appeared in the doorway, making Martha wonder what he'd heard.

'Dougie,' Summers said. 'Right on time. I wanted to ask you a few questions, if that's OK?'

Dougie nodded, his pale features colouring.

'I'm sure you'll have heard that Joe Gallagher – the IT technician at your school – has been taken into custody.'

Dougie nodded again.

'Well, we've examined his phone, and your name was on it. I believe an officer called you earlier to tell you this. Do you know anything about Gallagher?'

'I ... I don't know,' Dougie began.

'Dougie,' Martha said, in a warning tone. 'DI Summers here needs to know what your connection is to Gallagher. Tell him what you told Orla and me. There might be some small detail you know that will help the police find Christie.'

'Joseph Gallagher is in custody, so you're safe,' added Summers. 'And you're not in any trouble. Honestly.'

'Fraser had bought weed for us from him,' Dougie said, holding tightly on to the doorpost, avoiding his mother's eye. 'But I didn't really know the bloke myself, except from school.'

'But he's been in contact with you since then, hasn't he,' said Martha.

'Yes,' Dougie admitted. 'He said Fraser owed him money. And now he was dead, I had to pay it back.'

'When did he say this, Dougie? Do you have texts or emails from him?'

Dougie looked down to the floor, then up at Martha. 'No,' he murmured. 'I went to buy weed from him last week. He gave me less than I paid for and said that's how I'd pay Fraser's debt.'

Martha put her hand over her mouth. The idea Dougie had met with this guy so recently chilled her to the bone.

Summers left a pause before speaking again. 'Are you sure you don't know anything else about Gallagher that might help us find Christie? The place you met him, anywhere he deals from, that kind of thing...'

'I don't know anything about where she is!' Dougie said in a rush. 'For God's sake, don't you think I'd tell you if I knew?!'

Summers' phone rang, interrupting the conversation. He looked at the screen, then walked into the hall to answer it.

Martha grabbed Dougie's arms, and held him. He was shaking hard, trying to hold back the sobs. She pulled him to her.

'Is she alive?' she heard Summers say into his phone.

She looked down the hall. Summers was leaning against the wall, almost for support. She stared at Dougie, and he stared back.

Martha looked back at Summers. He nodded, grunted, nodded again. 'Good. Good,' he said. 'Yes, me too. I'll be there as soon as I can.'

Martha watched as he let the arm holding the phone drop to his side, and then looked up, staring at the ceiling for a moment. She wouldn't have been surprised to see him slide down the wall to the floor.

'Has something happened?' Martha called down the hallway. 'Has ... has Christie been found?' She almost dared not ask.

Summers turned and came back into the kitchen.

'They've found a girl in the forest. I need to go. And not a word to anyone.' He pointed at Dougie, then at Martha.

'But is it Christie?' Martha demanded, her voice thick with concern. 'Please tell us you've found her alive...'

'I need to go. And I repeat, do not tell anyone about this. We cannot have this news getting out until we've confirmed her identity and let her family know. Is that clear?'

They both nodded silently. He examined their faces for a second. And then he relented.

'It looks like it's Christie,' he nodded. 'And hopefully she's alive.'

CHAPTER FORTY-SIX

When Bill's call had got through to the emergency services, police had immediately alerted mountain rescue, still keeping him on the line.

'The lassie's in a bit of a state,' he said. 'Cuts and bruises. She's filthy and she feels awful cold. But she's breathing.'

They told him to try to get her into the recovery position and then wrap her in anything he had spare to keep her warm. He took off his heavy Barbour jacket and scarf, tucking them around her, the scarf beneath her head. Thankfully, it wasn't a wet day and there was some warmth in the weak sun shining overhead. She was out of the path of a biting wind coming off the Lomond hills, and Bill positioned himself to take the brunt of the cold blast. The police didn't keep him long on the phone – it was important to make sure his phone battery didn't fail in case the girl took a turn for the worse before the mountain-rescue team got there.

'I've been working around this land for forty years,' Bill told the police officer before they rang off. 'You'll need a four-wheel drive and most likely a helicopter to get her out quickly.'

'Thanks for the heads-up. You'll receive a text from mountain rescue. Just respond "yes, I'm here" and they'll be able to pinpoint exactly where you are. OK?'

'Aye, will do,' said Bill.

He knelt down beside Christie and stroked the hair gently back from her face. 'Poor wee thing,' he said as the dog held vigil too.

He and the dog stood guard until help arrived, the old man wondering what had led this fragile girl out into the wilderness in the state she was in.

Bill was starting to feel cold himself when the roar of a Land Rover engine finally announced the arrival of the rescue team, almost an hour after he'd made the call. Although she wasn't awake anymore, he kept speaking to the girl, hoping she'd know she was safe now. He struggled to his feet as they approached, waving his arms so they knew exactly where she was. 'Over here,' he called.

A Police Honda CRV followed on behind, its tyres crunching loudly as the driver pulled up on the track.

'Bloody good job you were out here, eh, Bill?' said the rescue team leader, getting out of the Land Rover. The old gamekeeper was well known in these hills.

'Aye, John. Used to spend a lot of time out in these parts, but hadn't been up here for a while. Thank God I decided to come out this way today. And Harris has such a good nose.'

Brightly clad in Gore-Tex uniforms, the rescue team started unloading equipment from the back of the van. John crouched down beside Christie, quickly feeling her pulse.

'She's breathing, but her temperature's low, and it looks like she's got a few superficial injuries,' John told DC Walker, who'd followed the rescue team into the forest, on DI Summers' instructions. 'I reckon we'll be needing the air rescue to get her out.'

John removed Bill's jacket carefully, wrapping Christie in a silver space blanket so she was swaddled like a baby. Hypothermia would be unusual at this time of year, but if she'd been exposed to the cold for a few nights, and was in shock, they needed to get her into hospital as soon as possible.

DC Walker was more concerned that she couldn't be roused now; according to the old man, she'd shown no more signs of coming round again since he first found her, well over an hour ago. Her clothes were torn and ligature marks and deep scratches were clear on her arms. She hadn't done that to herself, he thought. And he knew there was a possibility of sexual assault, given the state of her torn clothing and injuries.

It took very little effort to lift her between them. But as the emergency medical technicians placed her on a stretcher, the space blanket fell away, and Walker caught a glimpse of markings on the skin of her back.

'Shit,' he said. 'Hang on a sec.' Pulling a phone out of his pocket, he held the blanket up and took a photo, before dialling through to Summers.

DI Summers answered after two rings.

'It looks like it's definitely Christie Campbell,' Walker said. '... No, she's unconscious, but alive. We're getting her airlifted out and over to the Queen Elizabeth, and we're doing everything possible to preserve evidence. But there's another thing, sir.' He paused.

'Well, what is it?' Summers was impatient.

'There's that writing on her back. And I don't think it's a tattoo. It looks like more lines from that poem.'

Summers was silent for a moment. It was the same as Fraser, Walker knew.

'Get photos on your phone and send them to me.'

'Already done.'

'OK. And we need every scrap of evidence we can get, so ensure the ambulance crew do everything to protect her clothes and the scene. Thank God she's alive though...'

The helicopter was loud as it came closer, appearing over the tree line. There was plenty of room to land on the track five hundred yards down, at a clearing for turning lorries during tree extraction.

'Got to go, sir,' Walker shouted over the deafening noise of the helicopter landing. It whipped up a frenzy of small stones and dirt from the track.

The paramedic jumped down, moving quickly over to where the girl lay on the stretcher. DC Walker watched the rescue team leader, arms moving as he explained over the roar of the engine what the girl's condition was, before they stretchered her into the helicopter. Just a glimpse of her pale face showing above the blankets, then an oxygen mask was clamped over her face, before the doors closed behind her. The rotors began to whirr even more loudly, the dust and storm force causing a minor maelstrom in the trees around the site.

A scene-examination team was en route, and the area where the gamekeeper found Christie had already been cordoned off. The old man sat in the back of the police vehicle with his dog. Shocked and cold, now the adrenaline rush of finding the girl had worn off. Thank Christ he'd found her, Walker thought. Another night out in the middle of the forest and it would have been a body extraction. The helicopter rose, turning in a wide arc and heading south towards the city, its flight path taking it right over the girl's home village.

Derek Summers' blood pressure was pounding as he came off the phone to DC Walker. If Christie had the same markings on her, then this was the breakthrough they needed in Fraser's case. It was clear that whoever had taken Fraser, had also abducted Christie too. They'd need to get Gallagher to crack and admit what he'd done.

He immediately called DI Cath Davies, the Campbells' family liaison officer. She'd make sure the family heard first that Christie had been found alive. He trusted Martha not to tell anyone – and hoped Dougie wouldn't either.

The examination of the girl was key now. And he prayed she would regain consciousness soon and be able to identify her attacker.

CHAPTER FORTY-SEVEN

The snazzy new hospital building towered over the south side of the city, all glass and sharp edges. It had been christened the 'Death Star' by locals.

An emergency team was on hand when the flight touched down on the rooftop helipad. They quickly brought the injured girl inside, where she was taken straight to the ITU for a full assessment. The usual frantic Saturday rush had already started to build in the ED waiting room.

'We've been advised to handle her with extra care,' one of the nurses said. 'There's a possible link to a murder case, and police are on their way now.'

A hush fell over the team as they worked steadily, checking Christie over, first making sure all her vital signs were improving. She had warmed up during the trip and been given IV fluids to help stabilise her.

A senior nurse trained to carry out a forensic examination had also been called to attend. When the consultant was satisfied the girl was safe to be moved, she was transferred to a quiet room, a police officer already stationed at the door.

The sky outside was Glasgow grey, matching the solemn atmosphere around Christie, when staff nurse Sarah Boyd arrived. Sarah could see instantly the girl had been roughly handled. Her arms were covered in abrasions, her fingernails torn and blackened with dirt, and the clothing on her upper frame had been shredded, her bra straps neatly cut through with a sharp blade. The girl's thin wrists were raw and bruised from restraints.

'Poor thing,' she said, her mind turning to what else the girl might have suffered. 'But at least you're alive. That's something.'

Her body temperature had been raised closer to normal levels already, and her breathing was stable beneath the oxygen mask. Given the undoubted trauma she had been through, and although she was unconscious, she'd been sedated so that she could be assessed before any attempt was made to wake her. A female medical photographer was on hand too.

'You know what we need to do,' Sarah said. 'Let's take it slowly. As much time as we need. OK?' The young woman nodded, her face focused on the task ahead. 'I'll ask you to take a picture of each new wound or mark and we'll note every one in turn.'

It was slow, careful work. It was sometimes hard not to be emotional, but Sarah knew how important it was to make sure they got this right. She had to be professional, treat the patient with care and compassion, but also preserve the evidence for later. She'd also need to examine Christie in case of sexual assault. The girl's upper clothing had been partially cut away, but there was no evidence yet that her riding jeans had been removed or interfered with. They were torn and covered in mud, the smell indicating the girl had wet herself at some point. Hardly surprising given she'd been missing for a week. A miracle actually, that she'd been found alive.

Collecting every bit of evidence, each piece of clothing was gently removed, Sarah's gloved hands handling the items as carefully as possible before depositing them into evidence bags. The girl's trousers, which clung to her slight frame were cut, peeled away and bagged too.

She needed to be turned to examine her back. Sarah had been briefed about what she'd see, but was startled when the light revealed several lines of black, inked text, which started just below the girl's shoulder blades and continued down to just above her buttocks. It was far more extensive than she had imagined it would be. And so strange. Suppressing a shiver of distaste at the thought of what the girl had been through, she trailed her gloved fingers gently over the words. Her pale back was smooth and the writing was neat, with just a few smudges where it had bled slightly into the girl's alabaster skin.

In shadows Feannag Dhubh doth hide
While winter frosts o'er land reside
But as dark seasons yearn to turn
Through kirkyard murk grave worms do churn
Hide all treasures, Keep them safe
For things that gleam her eye will crave

Sarah read the fancy script and looked up to catch the eye of the photographer.

'What on earth is it?' she said. 'It's so macabre.'

'I don't know,' the girl said. 'I've never seen a tattoo like this though.'

'I don't think it's a tattoo,' Sarah said. 'Someone has deliberately written this stuff on her, but it's not permanent, thankfully. She won't be left with this on her for life.'

Just as well, she thought. The line about grave worms churning made her skin crawl. Sarah looked more closely at the words. Whoever inked them had done so with a steady hand. Maybe it was a tattoo artist? She signalled to the photographer to take detailed photos, of the whole verse as well as close-ups of every single line and nuance.

Then she scrutinised the girl's arms, and saw there were some older cuts there, made with something sharp. She sighed, shaking her head gently. This pretty, delicate lass clearly had issues at some point in the past, and she wondered whether they'd led her to here. She continued her examination with extra diligence.

⚓

An hour after Sarah finished her careful process, Joan Campbell entered the hospital room where her daughter lay. Lips pinched tight, tears slid silently down her face. The woman had aged over the past few days. Hand reaching out as she approached the bed, she covered her daughter's bruised fingers with her own, squeezing them gently to feel the warmth.

'Oh, Chris,' she whispered. 'My girl. What happened to you?'

DC Davies accompanied the Campbells. Christie's father stood mute, staring at his daughter, unsure what to do. She was alive, but God only knew what she had been through. The last few days had been hell on earth. The police officer pulled up chairs and guided Joan into one of them.

'The doctors will be down to see you soon,' she told the anxious couple. 'The main thing is she's alive, and scans have shown no internal injuries or breaks. She's been unconscious since she was found. But she was very cold and probably in shock. You should also know that they have found some writing on her back,' she added. 'We never made this public, but Fraser was found with similar writing on him. We believe they're lines from a poem – a different version on him and on Christie.'

Joan looked bewildered as she sat staring at her child, stroking her hand where it lay over the covers. Her father nodded and then sat down, feeling a rush of emotion, but wondering what else they might have to hear. They waited in silence.

CHAPTER FORTY-EIGHT

It was early Saturday evening, and dark, but Martha was outside the village hall with a few reporters from the nationals. Rumours abounded that a girl had been found in the forest. Martha was keeping tight-lipped, feigning ignorance, but keeping her eyes and ears open and checking her phone every few seconds for texts or calls from Summers.

A car drove up near the green, and someone waved at Martha. It was DC Walker, who she'd met at the hospital a few weeks ago now. She moved over to the car, aware of the other reporters' eyes stalking her, keen to see if there were any developments. There was a change in the atmosphere – everyone knew something had happened, just not exactly what it was yet.

'Martha, DI Summers has just called,' Walker said in a low voice, so Martha had to lean on the edge of the car window. 'He wanted me to confirm to you that it is Christie they've found. She's being airlifted to Glasgow as we speak – alive, but in a poor way.'

'Thank God for that,' she replied. 'Is there any info on what happened and where she was found?'

She could feel the press pack across the road staring at her and the policeman, wondering if tomorrow's Sunday morning splash would be good or bad news.

'Up in Milton Forest. I was there.' Walker paused for a moment. Gathering himself. 'It's a few miles west from where we were searching last night, quite far out, on one of the less-used trails. She's alive.' A smile played on his lips. 'But severely dehydrated and not conscious. She was airlifted and she's in hospital. The office is informing the newsdesks of all this right now, Summers says. But could you let your pals know there'll be a news conference at 8.00pm at the police station in Glasgow?'

Martha nodded. 'Yeah, no worries.'

He drove off down the road as she turned back to her former colleagues. They were all looking at their phones, and she was guessing the good news was already being messaged through to them from their desks.

'Well, the good news is they have found her. Alive, thank goodness. Going to be a news conference at 8.00pm at Police HQ.'

'Cheers, Martha. You coming back on the job then?' asked Craig, crime reporter on the *Scotsman*.

'Ach, don't know about that. I seem to have got myself mixed up in this one though.' She felt like she was already back in the thick of it.

'Had someone taken her, do you know?' Craig asked. 'The only information the desks have is that she's been found alive. Did that cop have anything more? Is she likely to survive?'

A few others gathered around, listening. Martha would have to be very careful. She didn't want to jeopardise the investigation by sharing too much.

'They still don't know if someone abducted her, but it sounds like she'll be OK, I think.'

'I heard they'd arrested someone from a local school. You know anything about that, Martha?' another reporter asked.

'Did the police actually find the girl, or was it someone else, by chance?' said another journalist.

'Like I said, guys, they've found her alive and she's been medevacked into the city. Just be grateful that they've got her and we'll have to see what comes next.'

Martha's concern was all for Christie, but she could see her ex-colleagues weighing up the better story – what would sell more papers, whether the lass was alive or dead. She shook her head, realised that the break from frontline reporting had changed her perspectives. Life was so precious, she thought, saying a silent prayer that the girl would be fine.

She watched as the buzz whipped across the media scrum. Reporters and photographers packed up and began to head off to the conference, a few of them already filing copy down the line, hoping it wouldn't already be out on social media before they had the chance to announce it. Martha was glad for once she wasn't reporting this story.

She watched as the cars drove away. To her old colleagues this story was coming to its close – with Christie found and a key suspect in custody, it looked like things were about to be tied up nicely.

Martha wasn't so sure.

She looked around her, at the houses huddling together around the village square, the warm, yellowy lights in their windows making the place look a cosy and safe place to be. But the light of the moon that had just appeared above the hills was cold and eerie, creating deep, unnerving shadows on either side of the road as she hurried home to Dougie.

CHAPTER FORTY-NINE

Sunday morning in Strathbran felt a bit more hopeful. The rescue teams had been stood down and the tension in the village had already begun to release – relief about Christie spreading like a wave as the news came in that she was alive and recovering in hospital.

Summers was back in the village to thank everyone for their support with the searches. Volunteers had worked tirelessly to find her and although it was a stroke of luck that led to her discovery, everyone was grateful that she was safe at last. And alive. A public meeting had been called in the hall at 10.30, and Martha found Summers at the door when she arrived a few minutes before it started.

'How are you doing?' she asked. He looked tired, but a little lighter in mood than he had for a while.

'Well, you know how it is. Glad to have found Christie, but there's still a lot of work to do. And Gallagher isn't giving us anything.'

'What, nothing? Has his solicitor told him to make no comment?'

'No. That's the strange thing – he's talking, he's just not admitting to anything.'

Martha nodded at her neighbours as they filed into the hall. She touched Summers' arm to move him further away, out of earshot.

'What about Christie? I presume they've examined her? Was there...' Martha lowered her voice as more people arrived. 'Was there writing on her anywhere...?'

Summers nodded sharply. Martha breathed out through her nose. She wasn't sure if this was good or bad news.

'And was it...?'

'The third verse of the poem? Yes, it was,' Summers murmured.

Martha shook her head. 'Did ... did anything else happen to her while he had her?' she asked carefully.

Summers looked thoughtful. 'If you mean what I think you mean, then no. The hospital has confirmed there was no immediate evidence of sexual assault on the girl,' he said.

'But would the photos he sent to her last year imply some sexual motive? I've not seen them of course, but I presume you have. And, you know, it would be unusual if an online predator had taken the risk of moving into the real world and then *not* taken the opportunity while he had the chance. Why take such a massive risk and abduct the girl if he hadn't intended to physically assault her?'

'You're right – it would be unusual. But the examiner is very experienced, and she says Christie wasn't touched apart from the injuries from being roughly handled and the writing. He'd obviously had to remove some of her clothes to do that, but it doesn't appear that there was a specifically sexual motive,' Summers said. 'And as far as Fraser was concerned, there was nothing to indicate that kind of interest in him. His top had been cut away at the back, same as Christie's, but as I say, just to do the writing. And it does look like Gallagher's online interests were in girls, not boys.'

Martha sighed, disgust making her stomach sour.

More cars were arriving now – people from the surrounding countryside coming for the meeting. The hall would be packed.

'Also, we now know Gallagher had his disclosure checks in place and he doesn't have a prior record,' said Summers. 'He wouldn't have been able to work at the school otherwise.'

'That doesn't mean he isn't guilty of something, just that he's never been caught before,' said Martha. 'I've covered enough hideous court cases to know that when perverts go after victims, it usually involves sex.'

'It could be that there was a sexual act, just not actually on these kids themselves,' Summers said pointedly. 'But we haven't found physical traces of sexual activity on either Fraser or Christie. What we do have is a lot of circumstantial evidence against Gallagher. He'll be assessed by a forensic psychiatrist at some point. That might reveal something more detailed about his past and his motives, or at least how he's justified his behaviour to himself.'

'Has he said anything about the poem?' Martha said.

'We showed him photos of Christie's back. He denies any knowledge of it. He even asked why we keep asking him about the poem. He's a good actor, I have to say. Anyone would believe he has no idea about that writing.'

'What about the ink? Any evidence of that from his home?'

Summers shook his head. 'But we have checked his medical records now. No sign he's ever been prescribed Risperdal. So he must've got it from an illegal source – maybe the pharmacy break-in, although we still can't pin that on him.'

'So you've got no hint, no indication why he might have written those words on them?' Summers shook his head. 'Nothing in the poem that can be connected to Gallagher in any way...?'

'Nope,' Summers replied. 'Maybe a combination of drugs – and we know he had ketamine, probably Risperdal and definitely cannabis, and who knows what else – ended up causing extreme hallucinations. Some of the messages he sent Christie are really very dark, so it's not a leap to think maybe he had become obsessed with the poem and all that witchcraft stuff. That's how he met Christie online, after all, on discussion groups about the occult.'

Martha nodded her head. But the more she heard from Summers the stronger her feeling that all this just wasn't adding up.

'At least now he's in custody, no one else will be at risk,' Summers went on. 'We just have to keep pressing him, and keep searching anywhere connected with him. We'll find something, I've no doubt about that.'

She wondered whether Summers wasn't taking the easy way out. She'd seen it before when police had a suspect in custody – particularly a strong candidate like Gallagher – they could become a bit blinkered, a bit close-minded, forgetting about the details that might lead them to the real culprit.

'And what about the photo I found? Did you show it to him?'

'No, not yet. It's an option, but I honestly don't think it's relevant now. Maybe it's just a photo Dougie kept and has nothing to do with any of this?'

'Unless Gallagher was the one who took it, maybe. No one has recalled taking it so far. And what about Locke? Any connections with Gallagher there?'

He shook his head. 'Martha, Gallagher's our man. I'm convinced of it. If I had a small interest in Locke, the events of the last couple of days have cleared him in my mind. He's just a local minister who might be taking some medication.'

Martha looked at Summers hard. She could see she wasn't going to change his mind. Not without more evidence.

'Shall we...?' Summers pointed to the door.

A weak sun was trying to break through the clouds as Martha walked back down the hill to her home after the meeting. After thanking the rescue teams and everyone who'd been involved in the searches for Fraser and Christie, Summers had patiently answered everyone's questions – giving as much information as he could and being clear where he couldn't go into further detail.

He'd confirmed the news that Gallagher was in custody. Martha knew that was going to be virtually impossible to suppress, as rumours had begun to spread since Friday. All the people she had spoken to – parents from the school, Gallagher's neighbours in Strathbran, everyone – described him as a loner and a bit of a weirdo. There was surprise that he'd ever got a job at the school, but when pressed, no one could pinpoint a particular reason why they said that. Martha herself knew he'd been dealing drugs to kids, but no one else had mentioned it, and she was thankful, for Dougie's sake, that titbit hadn't done the rounds yet.

It was clear the guy was a scumbag. But was he responsible for the death of Fraser and the abduction of Christie? Martha just wasn't sure.

A large black crow, feathers glossy in the morning light, pecked at the remains of a dead rabbit in the road – its ear flapping incongruously in the breeze. The bird regarded her as she got closer, then took off into the sky. She watched it land, precariously balancing on the weathervane at the top of the kirk tower. The faint outline of the swelling moon visible behind it.

CHAPTER FIFTY

Orla watched Locke weave between the headstones as he crossed the grass of the graveyard. He disappeared into the dark arched door of the kirk.

Orla followed in his footsteps and turned the old iron handle on the kirk door. It creaked as she pushed her way inside. The cool of the building greeted her as she entered – the atmosphere created by the hooded, lintelled windows and the shafts of light penetrating through the gently coloured glass. There were fresh flower displays, prepared she supposed by a women's guild committee. The large white lilies at their heart were too funereal for her tastes – the strong, bitter scent of the deathly bloom caught her nose. She preferred wild flowers. Snowdrops, bluebells, pale-yellow primroses and tiny wild daffodils that grow in abundance in spring.

Orla was quiet, watching as Locke knelt at the altar. Hands in prayer and head bent, he took a moment before lighting a candle and placing it in front of the cross.

'Hello, Pete.' Her voice cut through the heavy silence of the kirk. He looked for a moment as if she had upset his equilibrium, a frown briefly tightening his brow.

'I was just leaving the meeting at the hall and I saw you come in here,' she said. 'I was wondering if you fancied a coffee.' She gave him a broad smile and moved closer to him. 'I could really do with someone to talk to. A few confessions I'd like to make.'

Her senses were on a hair trigger as she touched his arm. She was conflicted. She didn't discount Martha's suspicions about him. She'd fed them herself when she'd found the medication and the slip of paper hidden in the photo frame, after all. But when she was in his presence, she felt intrigued, and drawn towards him.

'Well, we don't do confession in this church,' he said, no trace of the irritation she'd seen briefly flare. 'But we can do coffee.'

'I didn't see you at the meeting, but I suppose you must have heard about Christie? Her family must be so relieved.'

'Yes. Indeed. I'm sure everyone will be. Things may start to settle down now.'

'I'm not sure about that. I mean, the police may have someone in custody, but they still haven't said they know who killed poor Fraser, and, of course, where has the girl been all this time? The detective inspector was very tight-lipped just now in the meeting. I hope she'll be able to help them get to the bottom of this once she comes around.'

She followed him down the aisle and back out through the door. He seemed pretty quiet, almost unresponsive. She wondered where the flirty guy had gone.

'We can take a rain check, if you're busy, Pete,' she said. 'I could come back later for that coffee. I don't want to interrupt you.'

'It's Sunday service this afternoon and I do need to prepare. You're always a welcome interruption though,' he said. He ushered her through the gate and across to the manse.

His kitchen was warm as he handed her a mug of coffee and she took a seat at the table.

'Oh, did Martha show you that picture she found?' Orla asked. She knew the answer to her question, but wanted to see Locke's reaction herself. Martha had found it odd, given what had happened to two of the kids. 'It was you with Dougie, Fraser and Christie. She was certain it was connected to what's been going on.' She was careful not to mention that Feannag Dhubh was written on the back of the picture. The police still hadn't made public that lines from the poem had been written on the kids' backs. She'd heard it from Martha but wasn't supposed to know herself.

Locke's expression darkened again for a second, but he quickly replaced it with a smile.

'Yes, she has quite the imagination, doesn't she? I don't think Dougie was ever in any real danger though.'

'Oh, why do you say that?'

'I think Martha has been through a lot in recent years and that must affect her perspective. She seemed very on edge when I spoke to her. It was almost as though she was accusing me of something, but even she wasn't quite sure of what. She needs to be careful she doesn't overstep the mark. This community has a history of unfounded accusations ending badly.'

'Goodness, that sounds dark,' she said, squeezing his arm.

Was he talking about the witch trials, she wondered. Why refer to something centuries ago as if it had an influence today?

'She's just overprotective of Dougie,' she said. 'You know how it is with mothers and sons.'

'Indeed. I was only fortunate to have that protection from my mother for a short time.' He seemed reflective, sad. 'I learned to value my mother only after she was gone.'

'But you still have your dad, right?'

Locke looked out of the window. Then back at Orla. His dark eyes seemed to lock on to hers so she couldn't look away. She felt her heart rate pick up slightly.

'He's never really been there for me. Not when my mother left, or really at any other point in my life.'

Orla was surprised. He'd said very little about his parents so far, although the few comments about his father had been loaded with an undertone of dislike. For someone who preached the word of God, he surprised her at how ungenerous he seemed to other people sometimes.

'He was born in this village, like his father before him, and he'll die here too,' Locke said. 'The sooner the better as far as I'm concerned.'

CHAPTER FIFTY-ONE

Dougie hurried down the stairs late on Sunday morning. He wanted to get out of the house while his mum was at the meeting at the village hall. She'd put him on the spot the night before, quizzing him for ages about Gallagher and how much Dougie knew about his connection to Fraser and the drugs. She'd also asked him if he knew about Gallagher's links to Christie. And then seemed very keen to know if Gallagher knew Locke at all. Dougie could not imagine the two of them as mates, and had said so, but his mum had kept asking, trying to find out if he'd ever seen them together, whether Gallagher was around when they'd had the band a couple of years ago.

And as if that wasn't enough, then Orla had turned up, and she'd started going on about Reverend Locke too. She seemed obsessed with the bloke. His mum had started telling Orla to keep away from him, that she didn't like him, and it had turned into a bit of a silly argument. But then the wine had come out, and that had given Dougie an excuse to go to bed. But he'd had a sleepless night wondering what else might come out and how much trouble he'd find himself in. He decided he needed some breathing space, so this morning he had packed some spare clothes in his bag, along with his phone and a few other bits and pieces, intending to go off for a couple of days to clear his head.

He and Fraser had found an old shepherd's hut about five miles into the forest. They used to go there for a smoke on summer nights. It was on the edge of a hidden pond and they'd chill there with their tunes, watching the resident heron fishing on the water. No one else knew about the place and they'd stocked it with a few tins of beer and other supplies ages ago, so he'd be fine there for a couple of days. He missed Fraser. It would be good to be in a place they'd spent time together.

He'd written a note to Martha, saying he was off to his dad's. He hoped she'd find no reason to call him there. If she did he'd just face the music when he got back. Right now he just needed to get away.

He heard the familiar click of the front gate. His mum must be home. He quickly put the note on the kitchen table and slipped out the back door. His bike was already waiting, propped against the wall. He wheeled it out and was pedalling down the track behind their house as he heard the dogs bark a greeting to his mum.

'Hi,' a voice called as he turned at the track by the primary school. 'Thanks for helping me the other day.'

Initially confused, Dougie then recognised the kid – it was the one he'd seen being bullied at school the previous week.

'You're alright,' he said. 'What's your name?'

'Sam. Sam Sedgewick.'

'Well, Sam Sedgewick, I'm Dougie. Don't you let those kids hassle you, alright? Any more trouble from them and you let me know.'

Sam nodded. 'Where are you going?' he asked, a hopeful note in his voice. Dougie smiled. The kid wanted to keep him chatting.

'I'm off into the woods.' He pointed off towards Blacklaw. 'Need some alone time. A friend of mine died, and I just want to think about him, you know?'

Sam's face twitched. 'Is that the boy called Fraser? The one they found?'

'That's him,' Dougie said. 'He was a great mate.'

Sam looked uncomfortable now, like he didn't know what to say.

'Got to go,' Dougie said. 'See you soon,' and he rode away up the track, his head down, legs pounding the pedals.

He was sweating by the time he reached the far side of the woods. He stopped at the spot where Fraser had been found. Where his mum had fallen. The place was deserted. Police tape still fluttered in the wind. He stood astride his bike for a few minutes, thinking about his dead friend.

'I'm sorry, mate,' he whispered. 'I wish I'd been there for you.'

He'd nearly cried when he heard they'd found Christie. A rush of Snapchat messages had announced it even before his mum had told him. At least she was safe now in the hospital. He felt so relieved, but still thought there was a lot of shit that was yet to hit the fan. They'd already found out about him and Fraser buying drugs from Gallagher. And he'd told them Gallagher said he had to pay Fraser's debts. He'd been looking up penalties online and was worried that any chance of getting into uni was now screwed. Especially if he ended up with some kind of criminal record. He also knew that Fraser wasn't the only one Gallagher was selling weed to. And Snapchat hadn't stopped since Friday with people saying what they thought Gallagher had been up to otherwise. Who he'd sent messages to and what they'd contained.

He felt in his pocket for his phone. He should probably turn off the 'find my friends' service so his mum wouldn't rumble he wasn't at his dad's.

It wasn't there. Shit. He remembered putting it down while he stuffed his bag with clothes. He must have left it on the bedside table. Well, it was too late to go back now. Maybe it would be best to just disconnect for a bit anyway. But what if his mum did check to find where his phone was? She probably wouldn't, he tried to reassure himself, not if she thought that he was at his dad's. Dad had been away on holiday and only just come back, so it was natural that Dougie should go and spend some time with him, and she knew he could get to school from there as easily as he could from Strathbran. She'd probably be pleased he was getting out of the village after everything that had been going on.

He left the spot in the woods where Fraser had been found and crossed the bridge, turning right and up towards Blacklaw. He didn't like going past his old home, and when he and Fraser went to the hut this way, he always looked in the other direction, or made some joke or tried to race Fraser – anything to distract himself and stop him looking at the burnt remains of the farmhouse where his little brothers had died.

An engine whined in the distance as he rode hell for leather down the track, trying not to look either at Blacklaw, or up at the small hill where the moondial was. When he did look up, he saw a vehicle on the horizon, coming towards him from the opposite direction. Dougie kept his head down. He hadn't expected to meet anyone and didn't want to stop and talk. In particular, he didn't want to be seen by anyone who knew his mum and could say they'd seen him here. Fortunately, it had just started to rain, so he pulled his hood up, tightening it around his face and squinting into the wind as he battled a squall that had rolled over Blacklaw ahead.

The noise of the engine got closer, bringing a man on an ancient quad bike into Dougie's line of sight. He breathed out in relief. He couldn't see his face, but he guessed it was just some farmer checking his hill sheep. He shifted his bike over to the right-hand side of the track and slowed down slightly. They should be able to pass each other without having to stop.

But the quad didn't seem to slow, and Dougie realised it was going to hit him. It seemed like the man might not have seen him. Was he blind – didn't he know he was heading for a collision?

'FUCK!' Dougie screamed at the last minute, as he rammed on his brakes and swerved.

But there was nowhere to go. The bull-bars at the front of the heavyweight vehicle slammed into Dougie's bike and knocked him over the handlebars and into the ditch.

He glimpsed the trees surrounding the moondial just before he hit his head. Above him dark shapes swooped and dived. His eyes swam in and out of focus, as a horrid flapping of wings seemed about to smother him. They parted for a moment and a face loomed above him.

And in that split second he realised he recognised the man.

Then everything went black.

CHAPTER FIFTY-TWO

Martha's old news editor, Neil Wilson, had an industry reputation for being a tough bastard. He loved to tell people he kept the heart of a cub reporter in a jar on his desk.

Luckily, Martha knew his bark was mostly worse than his bite, and that he'd mellowed very slightly since a heart attack three years ago. Calling him on Monday morning, she greeted him warmly.

'Martha,' he cried, warmth in his voice. 'So when do you plan to get your arse back into work? You should be back where you belong.'

She laughed. 'Typical: straight in for the kill.'

'Seriously, though, when are you coming back? I hear you're making your own news out in the sticks.'

She gave him a potted version of her involvement in the case. She tried to downplay seeing Fraser's body and how close Dougie was to him and Christie. She didn't want some back-office reporter chasing her son down. 'They've got this Joe Gallagher in custody now though,' she went on. 'And I think the police seem pretty convinced he's their man. I wondered if you had any more info on him?'

'Oh, right, I get it,' Neil said. 'You're not phoning in with a story then? You want to know what we know?' He laughed, and Martha joined in. 'I'm afraid we only have the details the police have provided us with. We're doing some digging, of course, so I'm hoping that might change in the next day or so. You're local to the school – do you know anything about him...?'

Martha realised she had to be careful here. 'All I've heard is that he's a bit of a loner, and the word "creep" is being used a lot. But that might just be in retrospect. You know how it is in these cases.'

'I do. Well, if you sniff anything useful out, be sure to tell me first. We might be a bit further ahead if you were back in your old job, Martha. And if you fancied a few shifts, just to see how you feel about the old place, let me know. Be good to get the inside track on the quiet life you're living out there – murders, abductions and the like.'

'We can maybe meet up for a drink when things settle down, at least for old times' sake. And will you let me know if you hear anything about this Joseph Gallagher? It's more of a personal interest to me, Neil, given how close to home this all is.'

Martha was thoughtful as she put the phone on the table. Perhaps it was time to move on. She could certainly do with starting to earn again. But she didn't know if she could be drawn back into life as a staff newspaper journalist, at least not on the same terms. The job could never come first again though, she'd learned that the hardest of ways.

She sat down, the memory of that last time she'd seen her twins, almost two years ago now, coming back in all its awful detail. Leaving the boys in the care of their dad, she'd walked out into the deepening night, her last words for the penned-in dogs, before she got into the car. She'd wiped a fine sheen of ice impatiently from the windscreen with gloved hands. It was only a few days until bonfire night and there'd be a fine display on the village field, where they'd been building a wood stack for weeks. They'd planned to wrap the boys in snowsuits and take them to see the fireworks, she thought now with a smile. Three-year-olds were too young for sparklers just yet.

Her key had slid into the ignition, and as she plugged her phone in, the bluegrass notes of the Be Good Tanyas singing 'In My Time of Dying' blasted from the radio. She loved to play it loud, especially when Dougie was in the car. He called it 'barn music'. She was cutting it fine with the time, so had put her foot down as she drove along the now-deserted A811, thoughts tuning in to the story. Several women had been attacked over the previous four months. Her police contacts had said the attacker knew what he was doing, and in spite of forensic evidence and CCTV gathered at each scene, there had been little progress, allowing him to notch up several more victims.

At the press conference, after ten minutes of being bombarded with questions, Chief Superintendent Masterton got to his feet. 'I want to thank you all for your assistance. Clearly, we will be working around the clock on this investigation, but tonight our thoughts are with this young woman's family. We will do everything possible to catch the man responsible,' he'd said.

As he turned to leave through the grey door at the back of the room, Martha already had her phone glued to her ear, calling through to Neil who was still at his desk, waiting. Just as Neil answered, she'd felt a hand settle on her shoulder. Expecting her photographer, she turned to see a uniformed officer. He'd gestured at her to follow him, his face solemn.

'Hold that thought, Neil,' she said into her phone. 'Looks like I might get a bit more. Call you back soon.'

She'd cut the call. Ushered into a back room, she sat down. She'd lost her photographer for now, but no matter. It was the story she was after. A senior officer would be through in a minute, she was told. The dingy place smelled of unwashed socks and misery. As she'd waited Martha's thoughts raced. Who was the girl? Where was she from? What more did they know about the attacker? She wondered why they'd singled her out, hoping she'd get an exclusive for tomorrow's front page. Moments later the door opened with a creak and another officer – a large man with prominent eyes, but the same serious expression as the first – came through.

'Martha Strangeways?' His voice was sober, almost apologetic.

She nodded, not catching his name in an uncharacteristic moment of confusion. Why did he know who she was? 'I'm sorry to have to inform you of this, but there's been a fire at your home.'

The officer had held her as she'd screamed at the news her babies were dead.

She looked out of the window, across the fields. She still had Dougie. She had to remember that. And she could never go back to making the job more important than him.

❧

She had texted Dougie last night, asking if he'd got to his dad's OK, but he hadn't responded. Typical. Now he was in the city, she wouldn't hear from him till he was back home and looking in the fridge for food. Teenagers. She sighed, glad he was out of the way for a bit at least. And he was safe. That was the most important thing.

She still had the feeling that things were unfinished though. The ritual Christie, Dougie and Fraser had performed at the moondial, in order to appease the spirits of the twins, and the Feannag Dhubh poem and what had happened at Blacklaw centuries ago were all clearly important in the case. Yet none of that seemed to figure in the picture the police were building around Gallagher.

Martha opened her laptop and found the poem again. Fraser had the second verse on his back, and Christie the third, according to Summers. He'd made no mention of the fact that the first verse of the piece was missing. Where was that? she wondered. Could there be someone else missing? Someone they didn't even know about yet?

She tried to stand back from the case. It was often useful to forget the details and try to see things from another perspective. Could the culprit be someone from outside the area? Someone who'd visited and seen an opportunity. But twice? When she'd talked to people around the village, during the searches and subsequently, no one had mentioned noticing any strangers behaving oddly in the area recently. And it was the wrong time of year for tourists. No, it seemed that whoever had taken those kids had knowledge of the local area, and the folklore, albeit obscure, connected to Strathbran. And everything pointed to someone they knew, or who knew of them.

Martha sighed. There was plenty about Gallagher that fit the bill, she had to admit. And he was in custody, so Dougie should be safe. But somehow she didn't feel that he was.

She thought about the ink. That weird-shaped bottle, like a tiny hourglass – each drop inside counting down to something. She'd found it close to where she'd found Fraser, and they knew it had been used on him. But that was a while before Christie went missing. If the same ink had been used on her then whoever had taken her must have had more of the stuff. Summers had said they'd not found any in Gallagher's flat, but maybe he kept it elsewhere. But Summers had also told her that Gallagher claimed to have no knowledge of the poem, and was shocked to see the lines written on Fraser's and Christie's backs.

Perhaps he was telling the truth.

CHAPTER FIFTY-THREE

'Lord knows what she's been through.' Mrs Henderson was telling a customer all about Christie when he entered the shop. He shuffled unseen down the far aisle. Close enough to hear, but not to get drawn into the chatter.

'Our kids aren't safe these days.' Sandy Price, a local man with kids of his own, the man knew, was vocal. 'They might have found her now, but there was a bloody maniac on the loose. Killed one kid, and before the police tracked him down, he'd kidnapped another.'

'And it wasn't even the police that found her. It does make you wonder, Sandy. What *have* they been doing?' Mrs Henderson said.

He listened to their banal chatter; knowing more than anyone else about what was going on. It gave him a delicious feeling of control. A third person was now missing too. Someone who had come to him quite by chance over the weekend – just when everyone thought they were safe. No one seemed to know about that yet though. He was surprised. He'd been waiting for signs that another search was imminent.

'They found her up one of the old tracks on the way to Loch Katrine.' Bea Henderson's nippy voice had always grated on him. 'Not that far off the West Highland Way, they reckon. Who knows how she got out there? You get all sorts on that walk coming out from Glasgow,' she speculated, as though a local person kidnapping Christie was unthinkable.

He had left her miles from the walking path. The woman didn't have a clue, and he was tempted to tell her to shut up. He was glad Christie was alive; she was obviously stronger than she had looked. Anticipation washed over him – about what might happen next.

'And the bloke they've arrested is someone from Glenview High,' Sandy said. 'What the hell are things coming to that a teacher might be involved?'

'Not sure if it's a teacher – just a member of staff I think,' Mrs Henderson replied. 'And he lives here in Strathbran.'

'Are they sure they've got him then?'

'Seems so...' she replied.

He latched on to the thought. It was good that they had someone else in the frame. They'd be proved wrong, of course, but it would give him time to complete the work before the full moon, which was due in just six days. Tick, tock. Time was running out.

Police had swarmed over the village for weeks, but so far it seemed like they hadn't made the right connections. He knew Martha Strangeways was asking around – and she seemed to be gathering all the right pieces of the puzzle. But now the police had someone else in custody; he was sure that would confuse the woman no end. He grinned to himself.

He wondered whether they'd questioned the girl yet, tried to get her to identify anyone. She'd only heard him whisper to her before the drugs kicked in. And he was sure she'd not seen him. He'd been nothing more than a shadow. He doubted she'd even be able to tell the police where she had been. In fact, he was sure of it. She was so deep under when he moved her that he'd wondered if she was already dead. But once he'd got rid of her, it was no longer his concern.

The police must have worked out by now that Christie and Fraser were linked. He really wanted credit for that, even if they didn't know who he was. They'd find his work, the beautiful lines he had etched so carefully across her pale flesh.

Coming across the Strangeways boy had been a stroke of luck.

Unless someone, or something, unseen really was helping him. It was perfect. He'd had to think quick – took him to the hut in the forest where he'd kept Fraser. He was a striking boy, like his mother. He wondered how she would cope when she realised her boy was taken too. Regret momentarily skimmed over him. If he could just complete the poem and dump the kid before Saturday's full moon, there might not have to be another death after all.

He dropped the paper and loaf of bread he'd been going to buy. That awful woman at the counter was gloating, pretending she knew it all.

'We don't know if she just wandered off. I mean, you know Joan pulled her out of that school after there was trouble. She'd been dabbling in things she shouldn't have been. It's happened in this village before though. Long ago. That lass was tempting fate.' The local appetite for scandal and gossip was only made stronger by what had happened these last few weeks.

'Stupid woman,' he said under his breath. 'You have no idea.'

She called his name after him as he made to leave, having spied him in the shop security mirror. 'Nothing you wanted today?' she asked.

Ignoring her, he let the door bang shut behind him.

Be careful. You're not done yet.

The warning was soft in his head.

He noticed a police car parked outside the Campbell house as he passed. He wondered who might come to his door to ask questions next. He'd lie low for a bit, stay out of the way as much as possible. He had much work to do.

CHAPTER FIFTY-FOUR

He stood out as he entered the Radisson Hotel on Argyll Street in Glasgow on Tuesday afternoon. He'd swapped his dog collar for jeans and a battered leather jacket, his dark hair pushed back from his handsome face. He was carrying a motorbike helmet. Orla admired him as he looked around for her, unaware of the admiring glances of a couple of women on reception. His eyes lit up when he spotted her, and she recalled the feeling of him pulling her close the previous day when they'd said their goodbyes. For this meeting she'd pulled her blonde hair back from her professionally made-up face, and she'd chosen skinny jeans and a bright-pink polo-neck jumper that showed off her perfect proportions.

She'd listened to Martha's doubts about the man. And she'd had no defence when, on Saturday night, Martha had listed the reasons Orla should nip this relationship in the bud. She knew he wasn't all he seemed – but that was part of the attraction. There was a sense of danger to him. She saw it as he walked towards her across the hotel lobby, smiling.

'You look ... well, different,' Orla said. 'Come here on a motorbike?'

'I did,' he grinned.

'I'd never have expected a minister of the kirk to be a biker,' Orla smiled. 'Not until I met you, anyway. Somehow it fits.'

'Hangover from my rebellious student days.'

'What happened to your hand?' She noticed the knuckles on his right hand were skinned.

'Came off my bike yesterday,' he said, dismissing her concern with an easy smile. 'Getting a bit old for it these days.'

'I've booked a table for late lunch in the bistro,' she said.

The place was cosy, intimately lit with candles, and they settled into a booth, Orla ordering a bottle of wine.

It wasn't long before the conversation turned to Christie. Orla knew he'd just come from the hospital. She asked how the girl was. 'And I'm not asking as a journalist, I promise,' she added.

'Hopefully she'll make a full recovery,' he told her. 'Although it's doubtful she'll recall much of what has happened to her.'

'I'm surprised that they let you in to see her,' Orla said. 'I'd have thought only family and police would be allowed anywhere near her yet.'

His expression was ambiguous before he said, 'Being a minister puts you in a very trusted position...' There was an odd look in his eye as he said it, and Orla laughed nervously.

She decided to divert the conversation to lighter topics, and started talking about herself, and her TV career.

'I always knew I wanted to be on telly,' she said. 'Same as Martha knew she wanted to be an investigative reporter. She's never taken any bullshit, you know. Not since we were teenagers. I've missed her these last few years,' she added.

'Losing her children the way she did must have been horrific,' he said. 'It's my job to help people come to terms with death, and I would have been happy to be of assistance, but she certainly didn't seek anything from the kirk.'

'She's always been very self-contained,' Orla said. 'Her mother and her twin sister died before she was a year old, so she was taken into care as a baby, then adopted. It was investigating her birth family that made her want to be a reporter.'

'That explains quite a lot about her determined attitude,' Locke said, smiling. 'I've certainly experienced that side of her character.'

Orla didn't want to stray onto that territory any further. She knew Locke had an idea why the police had asked him about the Risperdal, and she didn't want the finger of suspicion to point at her.

'What about you?' she asked. 'What made you turn to God?'

'As I told you, it runs in my family I'm afraid. Didn't have much choice in the matter.'

They spent the rest of the meal exchanging stories of their youth – misspent and well spent.

Finally, Locke looked at his watch. 'We should probably get going,' he said. 'It'll take about forty minutes to get back out to Strathbran at this time of day.'

Orla stretched her arm across the table. 'What do we have to get back for, Pete? Unless you've a wife or a dog hidden away. Why don't we make a night of it?'

He hesitated, staring into her eyes.

'I'm a married woman in name only,' she said, 'if that's what's worrying you.'

A smile played on his lips. 'OK,' he said. 'If you're sure.'

'I've already booked the room.'

She took his hand and led him towards the lift.

CHAPTER FIFTY-FIVE

Dark shadows fell across her pale cheeks, but Christie was awake and propped up in her hospital bed late on Tuesday afternoon when Summers arrived to interview her. Gallagher was still being held on suspicion of abduction and murder, and although a blanket with Christie's hair and blood and the rope tying her hands had been recovered near where she was found, forensics hadn't turned up any evidence yet that might indicate where she had been kept.

After greeting her and her parents, and finding out how her recovery was progressing. He sat down on the chair next to her bed. 'I need to ask you a few questions, if that's OK?' he started. 'The nurses have told me I can have a few minutes with you, but if you feel you want to stop, just tell me. OK?'

She nodded. 'I'll help if I can. I don't know if I remember much though.'

'That's OK. Just tell me, in as much detail as possible, what you can remember of the night you were taken?'

She took a deep breath. 'I was walking back down from the stables and had just passed the gates to the estate, near where the woods are. Someone grabbed me from behind.' Her eyes shimmered and she swallowed. 'His hands were over my mouth, and there was a horrible smell on them. He dragged me away, and I tried really hard to get free, but he was just too strong.'

'Are you sure it was a man, Christie?' Summers asked, determined to get all he could while the ordeal was still fresh.

'Yes. But I didn't see him at all, and at first he didn't say anything. Not then. It all happened quite quick. I don't know where he came from.

'I was thinking about Fraser, you know ... feeling really sad about what had happened to him. I had my headphones in, playing music, and then all of a sudden ... He was very strong. I don't think a woman could have grabbed me like that. I remember a horrible smell from his hands and then I must have blacked out.'

'And what about afterwards? When you woke up?'

Her soft features tightened as she tried to remember, her lips pressed together in an effort not to cry. She was trying hard to hold it all together, to concentrate.

'I woke up in some kind of stone building. It smelled ... like mould and dirt. My hands and feet were tied. I was so cold, and it was dark. I was really thirsty. I started crying for my mum.' Christie glanced over to where her mother sat, hands clasped tightly, silently watching her daughter as though fearing she might disappear again. 'There was a bottle, and I managed to grab it and drank what I could.' Her voice started to crack.

'It's OK, Christie, take your time,' DI Summers said. He was almost holding his breath, trying not to scare her, but needing to draw everything he could from her.

'I heard a noise and called out. I thought it was a rat or something. But then I heard a whisper. Someone talking. It was horrible, but I don't know what he said.' She slumped back onto her pillows.

'Did you recognise his voice?'

Christie shook her head. 'And I didn't see him. It was so dark and he wasn't close to me. He was just a shape in the shadows.'

'I know you were friendly with Fraser,' he added gently. 'You can't think of anyone connected to you both that could be in any way involved, can you?'

She shook her head. Then a worried look crossed her face. 'I know about the poem, written on my back. Mum told me it was the same with Fraser – there were lines written on him too. It was the Feannag Dhubh poem she said. We used to perform a song version in the church band. Reverend Locke was here before, visiting. Maybe he would know more about the poem? He knows a lot about stuff like that.'

Summers was surprised. 'Locke was here?'

'Yes, a couple of hours ago. Wasn't he, Mum?' she asked, seeming unsure now.

Summers looked over at Joan Campbell and she nodded.

'That poem though,' Christie went on. 'We all used to play the song. I used to sing the words. Dougie played guitar ... It's not there now though, is it?' Her mum shook her head and squeezed Christie's hand. The ink had been removed from her back and was being analysed. Summers wondered if it would match the ink on Fraser.

'Detective, can I ask you a question?' Christie said.

He nodded. 'Of course. Anything.'

'You ... you don't think Dougie could be in danger too, do you?'

'No, I don't,' Summers said. And it was true. Despite Gallagher's protestations, he was still convinced he was responsible for the death and kidnappings. He was sure they would find more evidence – something irrefutable.

'But anything you tell us might help keep you both safe, Christie. And other kids. You've been so brave. But Dougie is OK. I saw him with his mum at the end of last week. He was really worried about you, and I'm sure he'll be glad to know you're feeling better.'

'I hadn't hung around with Fraser or him for ages. I know he and Fraser were still quite close though. I sometimes saw them together in the village,' she said. 'And sometimes with that man from school.' Her mouth trembled on the edge of tears. 'But that had nothing to do with me, and I wouldn't want to get anyone in trouble.'

No one had yet told Christie about Gallagher's arrest.

Summers had made sure the Campbells didn't mention it. He'd told them she wasn't ready to hear it yet, but what he really wanted was for Christie to name Gallagher herself, unprompted.

'You've done really well, Christie,' Summers said. 'We'll finish up now. Cath here will remain with you and your mum and dad, so if there's anything else you remember, just tell her, and I can come back and see you, if that's alright.'

The girl nodded, eyes huge in her pale face.

'The man from school' could only be Gallagher, thought Summers as he left the hospital.

CHAPTER FIFTY-SIX

HALF-MOON

'Dougie!' Martha called up the stairs when she came back in from taking the dogs for their morning walk on Wednesday. As she'd walked, she had been looking forward to seeing her son back. Giving him a hug. She hadn't heard from him since he'd gone off on Sunday, but that was typical of teens, she supposed. His scrawled note – *Gone to Dad's. Back Wednesday morning. Lv U x* – was still in the fruit bowl on the bench. He had a guitar lesson pencilled on the calendar for today. He wouldn't miss that. He was practising a new piece of music written by his mentor Peter Stewart and had been excited at the prospect of performing it at Easter.

Presuming he was crashed out upstairs, headphones in, she went back through to the kitchen and sat down with her laptop, scrolling with unease through the various news reports about Christie.

'Relief as Missing Girl Found'. 'School Technician Arrested on Suspicion of Murder'.

Summers had messaged her the day before to let her know that

Christie had woken up that morning and he was questioning her
that afternoon. God knows what she'd been through. Or whether
she would be able to name the person who'd abducted her. Martha
had to stop herself messaging Summers to find out what he'd
learned. The police had still not found where Gallagher had
supposedly kept both Fraser and Christie, or how he'd abducted
and shifted them. She knew from Summers that Gallagher had an
old car, but from what Martha could gather, nothing off-road –
nothing that could have got to where either Fraser or Christie had
been found.

It was another hole in the picture the police were trying to
build of Gallagher. Another reason for her to doubt whether they
had the right man. He might have been dealing dope, and he
might have sent Christie, and other kids, hideous messages, but
she couldn't make any connections between him and the poem,
the ink and the legend of the witch. Martha's instincts told her
this was all wrong. It seemed to her that Summers and his team
had simply discounted all those leads. That they regarded the
legend as just that – a fiction. And that the kids had been messing
around with fairy tales.

None of it sounded like a fairy tale to her, though, and the
thought that someone dangerous might still be out there made
her skin crawl.

'Dougie!' she called again after five minutes. There was still no
response.

She climbed the stairs, to see that the door at the top of the
loft ladder was still wide open. Dougie usually kept it closed. The
rungs creaked as she pulled herself up – her injuries still making
themselves known. As soon as her head and shoulders were above
the hatch, she looked around. But she could see no sign of her son.

'Where are you?' she said aloud, climbing up into the room.

She pulled her phone out and called Dougie's number. There
was a buzz from somewhere in the room, and she spotted
something light up in the corner of her eye. She turned. His phone

was on his bedside table. Strange. Wherever he was, he had left his phone behind – which he never did.

Returning downstairs, heart beginning to race. She texted Jamie: *Dougie with you?*

He called her almost straight away.

'Hey. No, he's not here. I've just finished morning surgery. I haven't heard from him today. I assume you've tried his phone.'

'Yeah. And it's in his room. I thought he'd come in while I was out with the dogs. But there's no sign of him here.' The sinking feeling deepened in her stomach. 'I haven't seen him since Sunday. He's been at his dad's. Trevor would have dropped him back here before he went to work. That's what he usually does. Anyway, Dougie must have come back because his phone is here.'

'He's probably just gone round to a pal's. Or maybe the shop?' Martha could hear his concern too. 'The news that Christie's OK must have been a massive relief for him, anyway.'

Martha agreed, but she had to suppress a creeping sense of disquiet. She agreed to keep Jamie posted.

'I can come around later if you like, but text me when he's back.'

'Will do.'

She rang off, and as she turned, she noticed Dougie's outdoor jacket and rucksack were not at the bottom of the stairs. She would've expected to see them there, where he usually dumped them when he came in.

Returning to the kitchen she tipped her coffee, now cold, into the sink.

By late morning, Dougie still wasn't back. Martha called Trevor, but there was no reply. So she fired off a text to him, then drove around the village, stopping at a few of his friends' homes. No one had seen Dougie. He was supposed to be on study leave, but she'd checked with the school, to see if he'd gone there for some reason

– although she couldn't imagine why he'd not take his phone. No one there had heard from him either. Where was he? She phoned Jamie again.

'Have you heard from Dougie?' she said without even a hello, her anxiety more pronounced now.

'No. Hasn't he come back yet?'

'No. I've been out looking for him. His jacket and rucksack are gone, but like I said before, he hasn't got his phone with him. I've got a horrible feeling about this. He's been really erratic recently. He was with me when Christie was found, but seemed totally on edge. Jamie, I don't know what to do.'

She was trying hard to keep her escalating paranoia in check when her phone buzzed with an incoming text.

'Hold on,' she said. 'It's a text from his dad.'

She read the message with a sinking heart. Put the handset back to her ear.

'Oh God, Jamie. Trevor says he hasn't seen Dougie at all. He didn't go to his dad's on Sunday. Where has he been? And where the hell is he now?' She was frantic.

Jamie was quiet for a minute.

'Have you tried the locator app,' he said, 'to see if you can pinpoint where his watch is?'

'Eh? How do you do that?'

'Don't worry. I'll do it. I don't think I ever disabled the feature from when we first got him his smartwatch. I'll see if it's working. If he's somewhere with Wi-Fi or data, we might be able to find out where. Give me two minutes.'

Martha's stomach churned as she waited for what felt like forever, her phone to her ear.

'His phone is definitely there, isn't it?' Jamie said at last. 'Right where you are. Are you sure he's not in the house?'

Puzzled, Martha went methodically into every room in her house. Her anxious calls dropped into silence. At the top of the stairs she peered up the loft ladder and shouted out again.

'His watch is not showing, which means it's not connected to his phone or any kind of signal,' Jamie said. 'Let me have a think if there's anything else we can do to trace his watch signal. I'll ask Gemma in the surgery if she knows.'

He rang off, and Martha climbed up into the dark of her son's room. A faint buzzing started.

'Shit, shit. It's his phone.' She rushed over to pick it up, thinking irrationally it was him, but then saw that it was Jamie calling.

'Where've you been, Dougie? Your mum is worried sick.'

'It's me,' Martha said. 'I told you his phone was in his room. There's no sign of him. Something's really very wrong.'

'I'm on my way now, Martha. Stay put till I get there.'

Once Jamie had rung off, she stared at the screen of Dougie's phone. The battery light was flashing, and the screen showed a number of texts, including a couple from her since Sunday, and missed calls. Martha didn't like it. The phone was down to two-percent charge, but the ringer was on silent. She didn't understand. And when she didn't understand she became very scared.

CHAPTER FIFTY-SEVEN

Orla brushed the knots from her hair. They'd had a late breakfast in bed and Locke was now in the shower. She did wonder whether his parishioners were missing him. But she didn't care. He was hers for this short while. She scrolled through her phone, half listening to the TV news on in the background. She heard the water stop, and turned to watch him appreciatively as he walked towards her, a towel wrapped firmly around his trim waist. Leaning down, he kissed her neck.

'Hey,' he said.

'That's a very impressive tattoo,' she said, her fingers tracing the outline of a large, sleek raven taking flight, its dark angel wings rippling over the skin of his chest. She'd been surprised the

previous day to see that a kirk minister was so heavily tattooed –
there were extensive designs on both his front and his back. 'I
was wondering what was under those robes of yours,' she
murmured as she got up out of bed, ready to take her turn in the
bathroom.

He grabbed her and pulled her close, into a kiss. 'Well, now
you know.' He spun her round, making her scream, drips of water
cascading from his hair and down over his back. As they turned
Orla caught sight of their reflection in the mirror – her face full
of delight; and between his shoulder blades, lines of text. She'd
noticed them the night before, and thought they were written in
a foreign script. But in the mirror, she could see it was English.

'What is that?' She ran a finger over the lines on his back.

'A secret from my student days,' he laughed. 'Something my
mother loved and father would have killed me for.' There was a
strange note to his voice.

'Your favourite song or something?' She squinted to see if she
could make out the words.

He raised his eyebrows and turned so she could have a proper
look at them.

Orla frowned as she realised. 'You had them written on you
backwards...?'

He smiled grimly. 'My father used to make me write this out
over and over again when I was a child. The same as his mother
used to do to him. Kind of a warped family tradition, you could
say. I had it done backwards as a sort of a two-fingers to him. My
father would hate to think I'd defied him like that.'

An uneasy feeling was taking hold of Orla. She was suddenly
very aware that she was nearly naked and alone in a hotel room
with this man. She took him by the shoulders and looked again
in the mirror.

She was right. She'd seen these lines before.

She gasped involuntarily, and hoped it sounded like she was
impressed rather than shocked.

She'd found the missing first verse of 'Feannag Dhubh' – tattooed across her lover's back.

CHAPTER FIFTY-EIGHT

A burning smell roused Christie with a start. She was still safe in her hospital bed though. The window wasn't open, so it hadn't come from outside, and as soon as she woke up, she couldn't smell it anymore. She thought she must have dreamt it.

Not much else about her ordeal had come back to her. The doctors said her mind was protecting her while she got better.

She pulled herself up in the bed and rubbed her eyes. It was Wednesday, she realised. Last night they said if she was well enough, she could go home today.

'You OK, Christie?' DC Davies peered through the door, then came to stand next to the bed.

'Yes, I'm fine. Just woke up suddenly. I could smell something in my dream, I think. It was weird, I could almost taste it. I got this really strong sense of being somewhere there had been a fire.'

'It could be a memory coming back to you.' Cath pulled up the chair next to the bed. 'Do you think this was to do with somewhere you'd been before we found you in the forest?'

Christie thought hard. She remembered stone walls, a dirt floor. Drinking from a bottle. A shadow in the corner ... it began to move. And then there was a low whispering. She'd strained to hear the words, to recognise the voice ... And yes, that was what she'd smelled. Like a fire doused with water.

She shuddered. Closed her eyes, then opened them again and looked at Cath, who was examining her closely.

'Yes. Wherever I was held smelled of burning ... Not like it was *on* fire. But like there'd been a big fire there sometime before.'

She saw the officer pulling her phone from her pocket. Christie realised she must've told her something important.

'I'm just going outside to make a call, OK? Let me know if anything else comes back, won't you?'

Christie nodded. 'Can you ask a nurse to come in to see me? I'm feeling much better. I'd like to go home today.'

'Will do. You definitely look like you're on the mend.' Cath gave her a smile. 'Let's hope they say yes.'

CHAPTER FIFTY-NINE

When Summers arrived at her house he could see that Martha was agitated. When she'd called him, he'd been on his way to the village to investigate a new snippet of information Christie had recalled, and given to Cath Davies, so he said he'd come straight over.

The dogs scurried ahead of them to the warm kitchen, where Martha introduced him to Jamie – her ex, she said. And Summers realised this was the father of the twins who'd died.

'Now – tell me again what you said on the phone.' He sat down at the table.

'Dougie is missing,' she said, clearly trying hard to control her panic. 'I've not seen him since Sunday. He left a note here saying he was going to his dad's in Glasgow and would be back today. And when he didn't come home, I called his dad. He's not been there at all.'

Summers frowned, but let her go on.

'I called Jamie here. And I've been on to all his friends, and the school. And no one has heard from him. I want to speak to Christie. She has to know something.' There was a wild energy about her. 'It's happening to Dougie like it happened to her...'

'Martha, Martha.' Summers put his hands out. 'We have Gallagher in custody. Dougie's not in danger from him.'

Martha gripped the edge of the table and closed her eyes for a moment. 'But what if it's not Gallagher?' she said. 'What if you've got it wrong...?' There was desperation in her voice.

'There's new evidence: he did break into the vet's surgery in Glenview. We've found his prints there. And we've confirmed the ketamine we found in his car came from there. So we've charged him with that. It's just a matter of time until he confesses to taking Fraser and Christie.'

'But what about the Risperdal?' Martha shook her head at him, as if in despair. 'And the ink? Is it the same ink on Christie as you found on Fraser? I found the bottle before Christie went missing, remember. That's important. Have you found any type of ink at Gallagher's place? And you know that there's a definitive link to Locke with the Risperdal. I told you that.' She fixed him with a wide-eyed stare. 'Derek, are you completely sure you're not missing something here? My son has gone missing – *while* Gallagher has been in custody. Dougie is connected to the abductions of the other two. And they're all connected to Locke. You have to take this seriously!'

'I am, Martha, but are you sure he's not gone somewhere to clear his head or something?'

Jamie cut in. 'Look, I shouldn't even be telling you this, but I've checked Locke's medical records.' He looked at Martha. 'After you told me about him having Risperdal. He is registered at the practice I've been working in. But there's no prescription against his name for that drug.'

Martha looked at him, astonished. 'But Orla saw it...'

'She must have been mistaken, Martha. I'm sorry. I don't think there is a link there.'

'You see, Martha, I don't think there's a need to worry too much.' Summers decided to ignore, for now, the fact that Jamie had accessed private medical records. 'Gallagher is under lock and key. Put it this way – Christie came home from hospital today. I wouldn't allow that if I thought the perpetrator was still at large.' He paused for a moment, looking at Martha. 'We're slowly piecing together what Christie knows. It just takes time to pull all the evidence together. You know that. I honestly don't think there's any reason to believe Dougie is in danger. But he's a young person who's taken off somewhere, so I'm happy to try to find out where he is.'

'I'm really worried. He wouldn't just go off like this. And he's been really badly affected by what happened to Fraser and Christie...' All attempts at reassurance were falling on deaf ears, Summers could see. 'Are you absolutely certain it's Gallagher?' Martha repeated. 'Have you found out why he wrote that poem on them?'

Summers glanced at Jamie.

'There's a couple of things to tidy up, so we're not quite there. Gallagher hasn't admitted to the writing yet, but it's only a matter of time, I believe. You suspected there could be more victims, as there were more verses, and you were right. As I told you, Christie was marked with the second verse of the poem. We also found ketamine and Risperdal in her system, as we did in Fraser. So, exactly the same MO.'

'Yes, but there was one verse left – and now my son is missing. Don't you think you're being a bit blinkered, Derek? That it's just possible you might be wrong?' Martha's fear was palpable now.

'I'm convinced Gallagher's our perpetrator, Martha. Dougie is not at risk, in my estimation. There'll be some other reason he's gone missing. And we can look into it for you, of course.'

Summers watched the struggle on her face.

'I know there's sense in what you're saying, Derek, but I just have this feeling that Dougie's connected to it and now he's gone.'

Summers nodded. He understood her concern. 'As soon as I leave here, I'll make a call to the station, and we'll get someone looking for Dougie.'

'Thank you,' Jamie said, taking hold of Martha's hand.

'Now, there is something else I wanted to tell you,' Summers said, 'before you hear it from someone else. I'm actually just on my way to Blacklaw Farm.'

Martha instantly looked up. 'Blacklaw? Why?'

'Christie had a recollection. She had a strong memory of the smell of burning or something burnt. And she thinks she smelled it where she was held captive. The only place that there's been a major blaze in recent years is—'

Martha's voice was all sorrow when she finished his sentence: 'At our farm.'

CHAPTER SIXTY

The long shadow of the gravestone loomed over the child hiding in the kirkyard. He was trying to stay out of sight, but not doing a very good job of it. Looking for tools in the workshop, the man heard faint snivelling noises amongst the shrill calls of the crows riding the breeze around the kirk tower.

'Is there something wrong, boy?'

They were in the oldest part of the kirkyard, where many headstones crumbled like bad teeth; some toppled over where the ground had given way. He had always found the place soothing. Some people worried about being near the dead. Refusing to step on the graves; superstition overtaking common sense. The boy looked up, tears streaking his plump cheeks, snot shining on his top lip under a bloodied nose. The hood on his waterproof jacket was torn.

'Has something happened to you?' The man wondered if the child couldn't hear properly.

Afraid, the boy pushed back against the gravestone.

'Let me help you up and have a look at the damage,' he said, holding out his hand.

Unsure, the boy wiped his face on his sleeve, sniffing loudly, and then reluctantly took the hand offered to him. The man pulled him to his feet.

'What's your name? Shouldn't you be in school?'

'S-S-Sam,' the boy stammered. 'I can't go in like this. Anyway, they took my money.'

The man was puzzled. The child looked about eleven or twelve years old. An innocent, he thought. A new opportunity.

'You come with me. We'll get you cleaned up and see what we can do about those bullies,' he said to Sam, handing him a large white handkerchief from his pocket. Taking the child's bag in one hand and holding his hand in the other with a firm grip, he led him through the avenue of yew trees to the back gate. They walked up the hill towards his house.

'We'll get you sorted in no time,' the man said, for once managing to turn the volume down on the voice that swirled in his mind.

4

Sam had warmed up next to the fire. Bookshelves lined the walls; the place smelled of old stuff. A framed photo of a large woman watched him. Her dark hair was cut blunt to her ears and a thick string of pearls looped tight against her chunky neck. Her black eyes stared out at Sam. He didn't like the look of her. The man put a plate on the rough table in front of him with a digestive biscuit on it. Nothing fancy, but that was fine. He'd slowly heated milk in a pan, spooning three heaps of thick brown powder into a mug, muttering under his breath as though someone was talking to him. Sam wasn't worried. The man had rescued him.

Sam had never had proper cocoa before. When she remembered, Mum bought him diluting chocolate you mixed with hot water out of the kettle. This was much nicer. It made Sam feel much better.

'So tell me what has happened today, Samuel?' the man said when they were settled. He insisted on calling the boy Samuel. 'Such a good biblical name,' he said. 'Your mother must be a God-fearing woman, is she?'

Sam said he didn't know. His mum didn't go to church, but she was always working hard he said, seeing the man frown.

'Your father, what does he have to say about you not going to school?'

'Oh, I don't see my dad much,' Sam replied. 'He moved to Ireland after the divorce.'

The man's expression darkened. 'What has been happening then?'

Sam explained about the bullies. 'I just put up with it. But today Finlay punched me, and I fell and bust my nose.'

'What do the school and your mum say about this?' His voice was firm, direct and quite scary. He wasn't angry exactly, but there was a menace Sam wouldn't have crossed. Up close, he was pretty old, but nothing like his own grandad – a jolly, friendly figure. This man was anything but.

'I haven't told anyone. I threw some coins at Finlay last week, and he said he was going to get me. There was an older boy at school who helped me too, and I knew Finlay would be annoyed about that. So when he came after me today, I was kind of expecting it. I didn't know where to go, so I just went and hid in the churchyard.'

'Well, you're safe here for now. But we'll need to deal with those bullies. That can't be allowed to continue.'

Sam liked that. The way the man said 'we'. Someone else had his back.

'Who helped you at school?'

'I think he was called Strangeways,' he said, remembering the older boy had a funny name.

An odd look flitted across the man's face, and Sam concentrated on his hot chocolate, which tasted good. He felt OK. But also that it was probably time to go home, if the man would let him. He put his mug down and said thank you but he'd better leave. His mum would be worried.

'I'll give you my phone number and you can send me a message anytime,' said the man. 'I'll text you when we can meet.'

'But I don't have a phone,' the boy said.

'You do now.' He handed Sam a small mobile, and the boy was too surprised to say no. 'You must keep this secret. OK? It's very simple to use, and there's a sim card in it and my number, so if you want to call me, you can.'

Sam didn't know what to say. He didn't want to take it. But then thought he'd better show that he was grateful.

'OK, thank you.' He turned it over. It was an old-fashioned one.

The man handed over a charging lead and plug.

'Put that away in your bag, Samuel, and keep it safe. I'll see you soon enough. It would be good to meet up tomorrow, as there's a place I'd like to show you. You'll have to tell your mum that you have made a friend and are going to their place for tea. You can give her the number of your new phone and tell her it's your friend's, so she can call if needed.'

Sam felt slightly panicked. This was all too much. He didn't know this man. Not really. He moved over to the door.

'Remember what I said, Samuel, and make sure you go to school from now on,' the man told him. 'And it would be better if you didn't say where you've been today. It might get you into trouble, and then you wouldn't be able to come back here if you needed help.'

Sam was worried, but agreed it was probably best if Mum didn't know where he'd been hanging out all day.

CHAPTER SIXTY-ONE

The ruined farmhouse squatted on the horizon as they drove up the lane. They bounced over potholes, until they turned off a junction and up an even more rutted lane.

'Jesus, why would anyone want to live up here? It's the middle of bloody nowhere,' Summers moaned, grunting as the seat belt locked again, jamming his large frame firmly to the seat.

'They'd done a rare job of renovating the place, sir. Some would say it was paradise living out here,' Walker replied. 'You definitely need a four-wheel drive though. Hadn't been lived in for years until Martha and Jamie bought it. Such a shame about what happened to their bairns.'

As they turned into the yard, Summers considered the woman he had come to know over the last few weeks. He doubted help had arrived quickly this far out on the night of the fire. He knew she wasn't here at the time. He could understand why she was worried about her son now, after what he knew she'd endured before.

The remains of the farm were visible from all around. The fire that night must have looked like some ancient hilltop pyre from another age. A line of high mountains in the distance made for a spectacular backdrop. The grass ahead hadn't been cut for a long time, and they could both see that a smaller vehicle had flattened it in places in the overgrown yard that used to frame the house. The fields on either side were fenced moorland, housing a mixture of scrubby-looking sheep, with a few shaggy Highland cows. Tyre tracks were clearly visible in the muddy yard.

'We'd better stop here,' Summers said, indicating the side of the path. 'It looks like there have been visitors. Martha said she hadn't been up in a long time, so we'll want forensics to examine these tracks.'

They stepped out of the car. Dried manure was spattered on the walls where livestock had taken shelter against the stone buildings. Summers grimaced. He was a city copper through and through – never fancied the rural beat. The stone walls of the house still stood, but rubble was piled next to the main building and roof slates had fallen and smashed. A torn piece of curtain, which once bore brightly coloured cartoon characters, was caught in the fence and flapped in the wind. The place felt eerie.

'Let's start in here,' Summers signalled to the byre, and pulling on some gloves, he turned the large round handle on the barn door.

It scraped over the dirt floor as he opened it, and they stepped inside. Walker propped the door open with a rock and switched on a torch, its powerful beam illuminating the interior.

Summers sniffed a few times. The stench of dirt and mould mingled with the unmistakable whiff of smoke. 'What do you reckon?' he asked Walker. 'Seems to me this could be where she was kept.'

Half-height internal walls created pens where livestock must have been housed at one time. As Walker swept the torch beam across the space, Summers could see that the dirt floor had been disturbed. Partial shoe impressions were pressed into the soil. And then, there, in one of the pens, a larger disturbance, as though someone had been sitting or lying there.

'Over here, Walker.' Trying to stick close to the wall Summers trod carefully across to where something lay. A discarded plastic bottle with dregs of liquid in the bottom. He took the torch from Walker and methodically scanned the whole pen.

There: a ragged thread of blue jersey material caught on a nail in the wall. Summers carefully removed it, and dropped it into the bag Walker had already taken from his pocket.

'Christie's hoodie?' Walker said.

'Exactly,' Summers replied. 'I think we've hit the jackpot. Get on the phone to the forensics team now. We don't touch anything else until they're here.'

CHAPTER SIXTY-TWO

Martha stood among a stand of trees, on a piece of higher ground on the other side of the farm from the moondial. From here, she had a good view across a couple of fields to Blacklaw, but was sure she would remain unseen. She held on to the trunk of a tree, her fingernails pressing into the bark while she waited for Summers and Walker to emerge from the byre.

When Summers had stood up from their kitchen table and made his way out to the car, where Walker was waiting, Martha had got up to follow him, grabbing her coat in the hall. He turned and put up his hand. 'You can't come with us, Martha. I'm happy to share information with you. But you can't be part of this. We're visiting a potential crime scene. I can't allow it.'

'If Christie was held out at Blacklaw, there's a chance Dougie could be out there now too,' Martha said. 'I have to find my son, Derek. I have to—'

'Martha,' Summers interrupted sharply. 'I don't believe he'll be there. But if he is, we'll find him, won't we? Either way, you're not coming. And that's final. Understood?'

Jamie had come up behind her and placed a hand on her shoulder. 'Understood,' he said. And Martha had nodded in grudging agreement.

But as soon as the officers' car had disappeared down the lane, Martha had shrugged her coat on and grabbed her keys.

'Martha!' Jamie called from the door as she got in her car. 'What did Summers just say? He doesn't want you crawling all over a crime scene.'

'It's alright, I won't be on their crime scene. I won't even be on the farm. I'll just be...'

'What will you just be?'

'Watching. I just need to see if Dougie's there. Surely you can understand that?'

Jamie stood silently. He did understand. She tried to give him a smile but her face felt too tight.

She hadn't followed the police car. Instead she took a circular route out the other side of the village, looping round until she was coming at Blacklaw from the other direction. She'd pulled her car up by a gate on the side of the road, climbed over it, then hurried across a field, and then another, until she was in the stand of trees she'd often taken the dogs through when they'd lived at the farm. She had been just in time. The two police officers were standing in the yard. They seemed to be looking at the ground. Tyre tracks, thought Martha. Someone had been there. And then the men had entered the barn.

Now, she felt like she'd been waiting for days. Did the fact they hadn't come out mean Dougie was in there? Alive? Or...? She couldn't even allow the next thought. Perhaps there was nothing in there and they were just carefully searching.

And then, a movement at the barn door. Walker emerged. Then Summers. They closed the door behind them. Both wore blue gloves. They made their way across the yard towards the car.

She pulled her phone out and called Summers, watching him. A second later he took out his phone too.

'Martha...'

'Are you there yet?' she asked, as if she were still at home. 'Is Dougie there?'

'No sign of Dougie, Martha.'

She slumped against the tree, her arm wrapped round its trunk.

'But it does look like Christie was here. We've found a scrap of her clothing. We'll bring forensics out here to comb the place. I'm sure they'll find something to show Gallagher was here.' Martha suppressed a sigh. 'And by the way, I've called the station and we have officers asking around the village for Dougie. You just sit tight...'

Martha thanked him and ended the call. Then hurried back to her car. She needed to speak to Christie.

❦

'She's out seeing her horse,' said Joan Campbell when Martha arrived at the door. 'She was absolutely desperate to go, so Cath, our family liaison officer, agreed to take her down to the stables for ten minutes. I don't know what we'd do without that woman.'

At that moment, a car pulled up beside Martha's, signalling Christie's return. She got out and came up the path, cheeks rosy and eyes shining; the visit to the stables seemed to have done her good.

Martha gave her the biggest smile she could manage. 'I'm so pleased to see you home, Christie,' she said. 'How are you feeling?'

Joan ushered her daughter into the house, and Martha followed, watching. She thought she could understand what the woman had been through. She felt that she was going through it right now.

'There have been detectives out at my old house, Blacklaw Farm,' said Martha, once they were sitting in the living room with cups of tea. 'They told me there are signs that's where he took you.'

Christie's smile faded.

Cath Davies looked hard at Martha. 'How did you—?'

'Dougie's gone missing, Christie,' Martha interrupted. She couldn't let the officer stop her. 'I thought he went to his dad's on Sunday, but he didn't turn up there. No one's heard from him. Has he been in touch with you?'

Joan's hand went to her mouth. She stared at Martha, confusion and fear in her eyes.

Christie trembled slightly. 'No, I've not heard from him since … since what happened.'

Martha tried to control her voice, tried to speak calmly. 'If there's anything you know, Christie. Anything that might help us find him – you must tell me. I'm so worried.'

Christie looked at her mother, then at Cath. 'But … but I thought you'd caught someone. I thought it was over…'

'We have, Christie. There's no need to be scared.' Cath stood up. 'Let me just make a call.'

'Look, Christie. I think there might be something to do with Blacklaw in all this.' Martha sat forward, impatient, looking hard at Christie. 'It seems you were kept there. And you and Fraser and Dougie – you were out there last year, weren't you?'

Joan Campbell looked at her daughter, baffled. Christie stared into her lap.

'You remember, you said something about a ritual. At the moondial?' Martha pressed. 'What happened that night? You have to tell me what you know. It's important if we're going to find Dougie.'

The girl seemed alarmed by the rise in Martha's voice.

'I ... I don't know.'

'Come on, Christie. Please. Dougie could be in great danger.'

'Martha. I know you're worried, but can't you see, Christie's upset. She's been through so much,' Joan said.

Christie shook her head. 'Alright, yes. We went there on the night of the Crow Moon, almost exactly a year ago. Me and Dougie and Fraser...' Her voice broke on her dead friend's name.

'OK. And what were you doing there?' asked Martha, struggling to stay gentle.

'It was to help Dougie. Because of the twins.' Christie darted glances from Martha to her mother. 'There was this ritual, to do with the Feannag Dhubh. I sort of researched it. We had to light candles and recite the poem. To bring the witch to life and help them find peace. Your ... your twins. For Dougie.'

'Oh, Christie,' said Joan.

'Dougie told me something similar,' said Martha. 'But he called it kids' stuff. Nothing serious. Is that what you think?' she probed, watching Christie carefully.

'I know Dougie says that, but ... but something happened. Something really happened. It was awful. A black thing – a figure – just sort of appeared. In the middle of the ritual. I know it sounds unreal, but it flew out from the moondial at us. Like it didn't want us to be there. We were so scared, Martha. We just ran. And I'm sure it was chasing us.'

Martha stared at the girl. Christie stared back.

'Honestly. That's what happened.' It seemed to Martha that her eyes were pleading with her.

Something clicked in Martha's mind.

'Are you sure someone else wasn't there, Christie?' she asked, sitting on the edge of her chair. 'Someone who was watching you, maybe? Someone who maybe pretended to be chasing you?'

Christie shook her head. 'I ... Maybe there was. I didn't see anyone, but...' Her expression changed as she realised what

Martha was suggesting. 'You don't think...?' She put her face in her hands, and her shoulders began to shake.

Joan Campbell stood up and swept her daughter into a hug. 'That's enough now, Martha. I think you'd better go.'

Martha stood up, still looking down at the distraught girl.

Joan gave her a hard stare. Her message was clear, so Martha made her way to the door.

'I hope you find Dougie, Martha,' Joan called after her. 'I really do.'

Cath Davies was outside on the phone as Martha walked to her car. She ended her call and put her phone in her pocket as she saw Martha coming.

'Can I have a quick word?' She was frowning.

Martha looked down, waiting to be told off. 'You've just called Summers, haven't you?' Cath nodded. 'And he said you should tell me to take it easy on Christie. That I shouldn't even be here?'

'Almost exactly what he said. You need to leave this to us, Martha.'

Martha didn't reply, lest she say something she shouldn't.

'Summers wanted me to let you know something else, though.' Martha looked up. 'Some of the officers have been doing a door-to-door round the village, asking about Dougie.'

'And?'

'A kid has said he saw him on Sunday morning. On his bike.'

Martha could kick herself. She hadn't thought to look to see if Dougie's bike had gone.

'Which kid?' she asked, stepping close to Davies now.

'Summers didn't say his first name. But his surname's Sedgewick. Youngster apparently. Knew Dougie from Glenview High.'

Martha was already at her car and jumping into the driver's seat. She heard Davies call her name, and saw her raise her arms in despair as she drove away.

Martha knew Moira Sedgewick vaguely. She lived with her boy at the bottom end of the village, in a cul-de-sac of more modern homes down past the primary school. She was at the house in minutes, and rapping on the door. Probably too hard.

Moira answered, looking a little surprised. 'Oh. It's Martha, isn't it? Dougie's mum?'

'Yes, that's right. The police have just been here, I think? Saying your boy saw Dougie?'

'They have. He was very helpful.'

A young lad, about eleven or twelve, still in his school uniform, appeared behind Moira in the hallway.

Moira put her hand round his shoulders. 'This is Sam. Sam, this is Martha – she's Dougie's mum.'

'Hello, Sam. I ... I just wanted to thank you for helping the police,' Martha said, trying to look relaxed and smiley.

'That's alright.' Sam looked at her uncertainly.

'You saw him on Sunday morning, is that right?' The boy nodded. 'Did he say anything?' she asked. Despite her efforts, she could hear she was sounding intense. 'About where he might be going?'

'He was on his bike,' Sam said slowly. 'Going up that track.' He pointed in the direction of the primary school. 'He said he wanted to think about this friend.' Sam paused. 'That boy Fraser.'

Martha nodded. 'And did he say where he was going to do that?'

'In the woods, he said. The ones up that way.' Sam stepped out onto the front path now, turning and gesturing out of the village. Martha looked where he was pointing. It was towards Blacklaw.

'Are you sure he didn't say anything else, Sam?'

'That I should tell him if anyone bullied me at school.'

It was as if a hand gripped Martha's heart. Even when he was upset, her Dougie had been looking out for this kid.

'Thank you, Sam. You've been really helpful. I'm sure Dougie will see you at school soon.'

Martha hurried away down the path, before she burst into tears.

CHAPTER SIXTY-THREE

The silence in the car was leaden between them as Martha and Jamie turned down the Blacklaw track just as dusk fell. This wasn't going to be easy. Pale fingers of mist stretched across the fields. The moondial mound stood proud of the surrounding land; an island in a sea of fog. An eerie loneliness seeped into the car. Martha became aware of every breath she took, and it was a huge effort to keep focused on the track ahead.

It had taken a bit of time for Martha to persuade Jamie to come out here with her. He was still at her house when she returned from seeing Sam Sedgewick. He opened the door as she got out of the car.

'Any word?' she'd asked.

'No. I was just about to ask the same question.'

Inside, she'd dropped into a chair in the kitchen. 'The police have been doing a door-to-door in the village. Came across a kid from Dougie's school who said he'd seen him on Sunday morning. On his bike.'

Jamie sat down too. 'Which means he had no intention of going to his dad's.'

'Exactly,' Martha replied.

They'd stared at each other for a moment. She wondered if she looked as weary as him.

'I went to see the kid. Sam Sedgewick his name is. Lives down near the primary school. He pointed out where he'd seen Dougie. On the track heading out to the woods and Blacklaw.' She drummed her fingers on the table.

Jamie put his hands behind his head and looked up at the ceiling. 'You think Dougie was going out there, don't you?'

'I don't know, Jamie. Maybe. The kid says Dougie told him he wanted to go to the woods to think about Fraser. If he was on the path by the primary school, he would've had to ride past Blacklaw to get out to the woods.'

'So...'

'So Christie was definitely held at Blacklaw. I called Summers – they found something that confirms it: a scrap of her clothing. He has crime-scene folk out there examining the place.'

'Well, that's good. If Dougie has been there, they'll certainly find out.'

'I'm not so sure they will. They're focused on looking for things that connect Gallagher to the place. That's what Summers said. I mean, they'll find Dougie if he's there tied and gagged or someth—'

A sob blocked her throat. It was suddenly hard to breathe. Jamie grabbed her hand, and she held on. The moment passed. She would not think of Dougie like that. She would not.

'We have to go out there and look for him, Jamie,' she said as she recovered.

'I don't know, Martha. They'll turn us away as soon as they see us.'

'Not now. This evening, after they've gone. They're searching for traces of Gallagher. Not Dougie. So we have to do what they're not doing. Don't you see?'

Jamie nodded.

And when the sun set, and Martha made for her car, he came with her.

'You OK?' Jamie said now, a quiver in his voice.

Martha shook her head, trying desperately to hold back exhausted tears. This was hard for them both, but Jamie had been here that night. He'd crawled from the wreckage of their home having failed to drag their children to safety. She looked across at him as they pulled up to the yard. An intense feeling of sadness enveloped them both, and she felt into her pocket where the matchbox was tucked tight.

'Not really,' she said. 'You?'

He shook his head. Swallowed.

Even the dogs were quiet as they got out of the car. Skye especially, was unusually subdued as Martha opened the boot.

'Come on, boys,' she said, laying her hand across the collie's warm head.

He looked up at her with his odd-coloured eyes, and it felt to her as though he also carried the sorrow of this place. She knew he'd be picking up on their frayed emotions. Martha felt like she was unravelling. They had to find Dougie. She couldn't bear it. Jamie came around the car and without saying anything slipped his hand into hers. It, at least, felt warm and comforting.

There was crime-scene tape hanging off the gate to the yard. It looked like it had been put up and taken down again. There was tape across the door to the byre, though.

'Looks like they've finished everywhere but in there,' said Martha, pointing. Jamie nodded.

They walked in silence around the rest of the buildings, taking in the ruin of the place. There wasn't much left of the house itself other than the walls and a couple of blackened window frames that by some miracle hadn't disintegrated. The roofless gable end stood out black against the still-pale sky above. An icy wind blew across the bare fields, making the hawthorn next to the house scrape the bare fingers of its branches against the blackened stone. A lonely sheep bleated into the quiet air.

Jamie had brought a big torch with him. He swung it round to light up the darker shadows as they stepped across the threshold into the charred remains of their former life. It was unrecognisable as a home. The floors had mostly burned away. Nothing remained of their furniture, their things.

'I can't think Dougie would have come in here,' Martha said. 'He'd have taken one look and ... and ... Oh, God, Jamie. Where is our boy?'

She looked up through the open space where there'd once been a roof, desperately trying not to shed the tears in her eyes. There were several remaining rafters, reaching out towards each other across the void. And as she looked, a black shape dropped from above, and landed on the burnt tip of one of the beams. A crow.

And then another, flapping down and landing in the same place on another limb. And after that another, and another. Until there were not enough rafters, and the birds had to line up beside each other. They fidgeted and turned. Shuffling, cawing briefly, twitching their heads. Settling in for the night.

Their beautiful home had become a roost for the crows of Blacklaw. For a moment it was as if every bird was staring down at her, threatening, defensive. Martha was gripped by a sickening fear. She was an intruder.

A scuffle of paws at her feet made her gasp and stagger back. Skye suddenly took off barking, out of the shell of the house, through the yard and off up the track beyond.

'Skye!' Jamie called, but the dog had got the scent of something.

Before long his urgent barks sounded from the hill behind the house. Martha hurried back out into the lane, the terrier at her heels.

'He's up at the moondial, Jamie. There must be something there.' She set off at a run along the muddy track, gulping in the thick, cold mist that swayed around her, the fear she'd felt in the ruin of her house now mixed with anticipation of what she might find.

By the time she reached the stone steps, Skye was standing at the top watching her.

'What is it?' she asked him. 'What have you found?'

He turned and started to run in circles around the stone structure, barking and barking, as if he was possessed. In the twilight his eyes looked wild, ringed with white, his tongue lolling, saliva coming off it like silver sparks. Jamie arrived beside her, and they climbed the steps together.

'What is that?' Martha said when they stepped into the clearing at the top.

She dropped to her knees on the moss to examine the remnants of some kind of white grit forming a disjointed circle around the obelisk. Jamie cast the torch around, then bent down and parted the long grass.

'Look.' He trained the torch on a candle, then another nearby. Then a glass jar, another candle, another jar.

'Christie told me today about what they were doing,' Martha said. 'They were here. Under the Crow Moon. Almost exactly a year ago to the day. Doing a ritual for the twins.'

Jamie looked at her. In the misty light of the gloaming his scars were prominent, his face seemed to be pulled into a permanently sad expression.

He turned away from her and pointed to an area where stones had been laid to make a small fire pit. There were still a few charcoaled remains.

'Was Dougie coming here for this year's Crow Moon?' Martha said. 'But why? I just don't understand.'

BJ started to whine then shot off into the undergrowth, barking frantically, his *yip, yip* echoing around the empty place.

'This place seems to have infected him with something,' said Martha, following him to the edge of the clearing.

The dog was frantically digging at something, his face covered in damp earth. Jamie waded into the bushes, reached down and was pulling BJ back by the collar, when he stopped. Froze.

'Shit,' he said. 'Is this Dougie's?'

He lifted up a black, mud-covered backpack. Martha saw panic in his eyes.

'He was here.'

CHAPTER SIXTY-FOUR

Sam kept the phone hidden. He'd waited until after dark last night before he turned it on. He made sure the sound was off, so if the man texted him, Mum wouldn't ask questions. He'd been quite insistent that Sam shouldn't tell anyone, and he was slightly afraid of what would happen if he did, so decided he'd keep it a secret for now at least. Mum had brought him a phone too, at the supermarket, a better one with a bigger screen and the internet on it. She gave it to him after dinner last night. A surprise. He'd gone from having none to having two, and he'd been looking at YouTube videos of dogs already.

'No social media though, Sam. You're too young for that yet,' Mum said. 'And I've set up a locator on it. That means I can track wherever you are, so you won't be able to go missing without me finding you. Isn't that great?'

He realised then the reason his Mum had given him this present. He knew she had been really upset about all the stuff with Fraser going missing and then being found dead, and that girl Christie disappearing, and being found miles away. She was worried something might happen to him too.

'Yes, that's good,' he muttered. He would rather have had a dog. That would keep him safer, he thought.

The text message came through on Thursday morning when he was at school:

Meet after school today?

Sam was unsure. The man had helped him. And it was good to know someone had his back, especially with the bullies from the school bus around most days. After thinking about it for a while, he texted his mum saying he'd been invited to a friend's house after school. She texted back, seeming pleased he'd made a friend, and said to keep his phone on so she'd know where he was. She added a smiley face and a love-heart emoji. He felt a bit sick as the day wore on at the thought of lying to her. He messaged that he could see the man, but only for a couple of hours. He was told to meet beside the old railway buildings. The man signed the message 'Peter'.

Peter was already waiting when Sam walked down the hill from the bus stop after school.

'Where are we going?' Sam asked.

'I just want to show you somewhere. It's a secret place,' the man said, a tight sort of smile on his face. 'I think you'll like it.'

'Is your name Peter then?' Sam asked.

'It's as good a name as any.'

They walked through the back lanes unseen; most people indoors, having their tea. Eventually they reached a gravelled area leading to the woods. Sam spotted a quad bike parked in a corner. Peter got on and told him to get on behind him and hold on. Sam wondered where they were going. They seemed to ride for miles, the cold wind making his cheeks sting. After bumping noisily along a smaller track for a while, they stopped outside a corrugated-iron shed. It looked abandoned, and he could see paintwork peeling away from the metal like dead skin.

Sam followed Peter around the corner to the front of the building with a growing sense of alarm. Tied to the fence were rows of what looked like black rags moving back and forth in the wind. Moving closer, he realised with dread they were birds. Dead crows. All hanging upside down, tied onto barbed wire with orange twine. Fluttering with no life or sound. Their glassy eyes stared; their beaks hanging open like they might call out for help. Sam caught his breath in a sob, and the man turned to look at him.

'You're not afraid of a few dead birds, are you, Samuel? They're to keep the devil away. In some places they say they're ghosts of the dead.'

His words struck pure terror into the boy. He didn't like dead animals. This was horrible. Even the air smelled of death. Sickly and sweet.

'I think I'd maybe rather go home now,' Sam said, his voice halting and unsteady.

'I don't think that's necessary. They can't hurt you, child.'

Peter walked into the shed, and Sam had no choice but to follow him inside. As Peter closed the door behind them, the boy wondered if he'd ever see his mum again. Why did he agree to come here? Lips quivering, he looked around, hoping an escape route would open up.

Then he realised he hadn't turned off his new phone, the one from Mum. It was on silent as he'd had it in his bag during school lessons. If he didn't go home, he hoped she'd be able to find him here, now very glad of the locator app Mum had been so pleased with. He felt he was at least connected to her, and that helped.

'That's the point, stop interfering,' the man growled, as if someone had just said something to him.

Sam looked up nervously. Peter wasn't speaking to him, was he?

But now the man looked at him. 'Hungry?' he asked.

Sam nodded, even though he wasn't really. He took the can of cola and the packet of crisps the man offered him, and sitting down on a box in the corner, he opened the crisps, putting them half-heartedly into his mouth. He tasted just salt. They were slightly soft, as though out of date.

'Eat up, boy. Thought you were hungry,' the man said.

'I am.' Sam's voice was a whisper.

He had to hold back tears again, sniffing loudly as the man started to read from the Bible in front of him. Sam hoped if he just sat and listened, the man who called himself Peter might let him go home.

A noise sounded from the other side of the wall, like an animal moaning. The man looked up.

'Stay here,' he said. 'It's probably just a fox.'

He pushed past and went outside. Sam heard the noise again – this time it sounded like a person.

A few minutes later, the man came back in.

'All sorted,' he said, an ugly grin on his face. 'That one won't be bothering us again.'

Sam felt horrible. What had he done?

'I'm worried Mum might come looking for me if I'm not back soon. She's been really freaked out with these older kids going missing, and it's starting to get dark.'

'You're right, Samuel. You're a clever boy. We must not be too impatient, but I think you wish to learn, and you know I can help you.'

Sam was relieved when the man told him to gather his things before they headed back out into the now-dark night. The air was stiff with cold; damp mist curled around the trees. He was glad to climb back on board the old quad, all the earlier sense of excitement gone and replaced with a need to get as far away from here as he could. He wanted to be home. But he wouldn't say that. He needed to make Peter think he wanted help. But he never wanted to come here again.

The Book of Shadows

My heart is broken to hear him weep so. He cared so well for that baby bird. In secret, of course. A Corvus chick fallen from its nest. When he brought it inside, held gently in his small hands, it peeped a tiny 'craw' that made us smile. I told him of the great god Odin, who kept two ravens at his side, to represent his thought and memory. Huginn and Muninn. The Raven God sent his familiars out across the world to gather news.

My child named his chick Hugo and loved it. I did not have the heart to stop him. Despite all my boy's carefulness, I am sorry to say that beast of a man found it. To terrify the child, he crushed the poor thing to a scrap of feather and bone in front of his face. He is a brute. But I must endure, for my boy is broken, and I fear he is too soft for this harsh place.

CHAPTER SIXTY-FIVE

FULL MOON

A knock at the door made Martha practically fall over herself to get to it. It was only Orla. Martha slumped back against the wall in disappointment.

Orla came in and wrapped her arms round her friend.

'I was hoping it was him. Come home…' The tenderness from her friend broke down Martha's defences and she began to sob.

'You've still not heard anything?' said Orla, escorting Martha into the sitting room.

'Nothing. And the police still seem to think Gallagher's their man.'

'They've mobilised the search and rescue team again,' Jamie said. 'When we told them last night that we'd found his bag at the moondial, they went back to Blacklaw. They found Dougie's bike this morning.'

'It was in a ditch in the lane just past the house,' said Martha. 'I don't know how anyone missed it.'

'Anyway, it convinced them that Dougie's missing around here somewhere, and not gone off on a jaunt,' Jamie went on. 'They're going to do a sweep of the forest around Blacklaw.'

'But they still don't think it's linked to Fraser and Christie,' Martha said, throwing up her hands. 'Summers is convinced Gallagher's responsible for that. Like it's just some massive coincidence that Dougie's gone missing like the other two. I despair. I've been sitting here all day just waiting.'

The truth was, Martha had spent her time trawling through everything she had discovered over the last few weeks, looking for some detail that might lead her to Dougie. Summers had given her a stern warning. 'I don't want to hear you've been anywhere near those search teams, Martha. You'll hamper their efforts.' She knew he was right. And she wanted to be at home, in case Dougie turned up.

'OK. Martha ... Jamie,' Orla looked at them both carefully, and Martha could see that in the blink of an eye she'd transitioned smoothly from her friend to the professional journalist. 'I don't think enough is being done. It's clear the police are going in the wrong direction. And they're being too slow to react. We need to put some pressure on. We have to speed things up now.'

'Yeah, I think you're right,' Martha nodded, seeming to gain energy from the thought of doing something proactive. 'I guess I could speak to the newsdesk at the *Standard*.'

Orla put a hand out. 'You leave this to me. We'll go to the BBC. This needs immediate action. And as wide coverage as possible.'

It was strange to Martha to give up control like this, but she felt a small warm spot in her chest as Orla went out into the hall to make a call. Amidst her fear, it was good to have someone looking after her like this. She huddled up against Jamie on the sofa, listening to Orla's brisk tones – it was clear she was calling in a favour.

'Right,' she said as she re-entered the room. 'Sorted. They're going to send out a camera. He'll be here in an hour, and they've asked me to front it. You OK with that?'

Martha nodded, her mind whirring. She knew their history would soon be out in public – the fire and the twins, re-examined and pulled apart. But she didn't care now. She just had to do everything she could to find her son.

She got up and went into the kitchen, busying herself with making tea. Orla followed her through.

'Listen Martha, there's something else I need to tell you. It's a bit weird, to be honest.'

Martha turned, frowning.

'It's about Pete. We met up in Glasgow a couple of days ago. Spent the night in a hotel.' Orla smiled faintly.

'You know, Orla, I've said my piece about Locke.' Martha didn't have the energy to think about Orla's love life right now. 'You're a grown-up, you just do what's best for you—'

'OK, but it's not that. It's … well, of course I saw him naked, and … he has tattoos. There's a crow on his chest.'

Martha frowned and stared at her friend, interested now.

'And on his back there are some lines of poetry. They're written backwards, but yesterday morning I caught sight of them in the mirror. It's—'

'From the Feannag Dhubh poem,' Martha finished.

Orla nodded slowly. 'It was the first verse.'

Martha felt dizzy and grasped the kitchen counter for support. Her brain was racing, trying to place this piece of information into the rest of the puzzle. But it wouldn't fit.

'And you waited a whole day to tell me…?' she said, shooting a glance at her friend.

'I just couldn't let myself believe he'd done anything so … so awful. I was sure it must be some coincidence. He's lived round here his whole life, after all. I've been agonising what to do about it, because I knew as soon as I told you—'

'—that I'd jump on it?'

Orla nodded, looking down shamefully.

Martha shook her head. Getting angry at Orla and throwing around recriminations wasn't going to help Dougie. She needed to think what this meant.

'Why backwards?' she suddenly asked, to herself as much as Orla. 'And you're sure it was a tattoo, not written in ink, like on Fraser and Christie?'

'He said it was something to do with his father. Sounds like he had a horrendous time when he was a kid. His dad used to make him write it out over and over – like lines as a punishment, I suppose. So having it tattooed on himself backwards was a sort of act of rebellion. So you can see why I thought it might just be an innocent coincidence…'

'His father was the minister here before Locke, I think,' Martha said. 'I never knew him, but I've heard he wasn't the nicest person to be around. Very old-fashioned, and pushed a lot of people away from the kirk because of it.'

'Pete told me the same thing. No love lost between them, apparently.'

Martha recalled Locke's reaction to the photograph she'd found. Maybe that's why he'd seemed weird. Had Christie's passion for the poem and the folklore woken something within him? Could it have prompted him to extreme acts several years later?

She contemplated going to Summers with this news. But she thought she knew how that would play out. No, she had to focus on this interview Orla had set up. That had to be the quickest way to getting Dougie found.

'Sir, you need to see the news. The evening bulletin,' Walker said, as he came into Summers' office, picking up the TV control.

Puzzled, the detective frowned at Walker – then saw the haunted face that appeared on the screen.

'We're going live now to rural Stirlingshire for the latest update on a case of murder and abduction,' the presenter said.

Martha stood outside her house with Jamie. Her fist was clenched tight around something. The camera panned to Orla.

'The parents of the latest teenager to go missing are with me to make an urgent appeal for information,' she said. 'This follows the murder of Fraser MacDonald four weeks ago and the recent abduction of Christie Campbell, who thankfully was found alive last week in the forest ten miles from the village of Strathbran. We come to you live from the same village today. Martha, what can you tell us about what has happened?'

The camera zoomed in on Martha's face, exhaustion and worry buried deep.

'My son, Dougie Strangeways, has been missing since last Sunday. I have recently found out that both Fraser and Christie, along with my son, were involved in some kind of incident together exactly a year ago today near to the place where my twins died in a fire.'

Summers and Walker watched in silence as Martha struggled to maintain her composure.

'Jesus Christ,' Summers said.

'Take your time, Martha,' Orla said on the screen.

'I have been pleading with the police to help find him for days, and we are desperate now.' She looked straight at the camera. 'If you or someone you know is holding my son, Dougie, please, *please*, let him go. He has been through enough. I am begging you. Let him come home.'

Orla came back on screen, her emotions only just being held in check.

'As Martha said, if anyone has any information about the whereabouts of Dougie Strangeways, please call the number on screen now or contact the police on 101.'

A photograph of Dougie grinning into the camera appeared on the TV with a BBC helpline number running across the bottom.

Summers shook his head. 'She really believes that Gallagher's not the killer. I just hope we're right and she's wrong.'

CHAPTER SIXTY-SIX

It was early on Friday morning when Summers rapped on the front door. Martha had been up for more than an hour. She'd managed scraps of sleep through the night, each time waking in a panic, thinking she'd heard Dougie's voice.

'Have you found him?' she asked as she threw open the door. But Summers was already shaking his head and putting up his hands. 'I'm sorry, Martha. The search went on late last night, but they've found no sign. They're just regrouping now, ready to go out into the forest again.'

She felt herself slump, and walked through to the kitchen, collapsing into a chair.

Jamie came down the stairs. He'd spent the night in Dougie's room. The living-room door opened and Orla appeared. She'd slept on the sofa.

Summers looked at them as they rubbed their eyes and grunted out greetings. 'I'm pleased to see you have people here to support you, Martha,' he said. Then looked at Orla. 'And I'm surprised, but pleased, to see you here.'

'Why's that, Detective Inspector?' Orla said, putting on her best disarming smile. 'I'm Martha's oldest friend. Didn't she tell you?'

Summers turned his mouth down and nodded. Then sat down and looked from Orla to Martha. 'What was that about last night, Martha – going on the news? Why didn't you tell me? I thought we were working together.'

'So did I, Derek. So did I.'

He frowned. 'Something you want to say?'

Martha didn't want this confrontation; she didn't know if she had the energy for it. But Summers had come to her door, first thing in the morning. And maybe having it out might move the dial. Might help them find Dougie.

'Alright, Derek.' She had to control her voice. 'I'm convinced that whoever abducted Fraser and Christie is still at large – and has abducted Dougie too.'

'Martha—' Summers began, but she held up her hand.

'I know you have lots of evidence pointing to Gallagher. But there are lots of holes in your case too. Things that don't add up. Am I right?'

Summers nodded.

'I'm not saying Gallagher wasn't part of all this,' Martha went on. 'But I'm certain there's someone else involved. Someone dangerous...'

Summers sat back. 'You're going to tell me you think that person's the Reverend Locke, aren't you?'

'There are just so many unexplained connections between him and the kids – and the poem. He had a piece of it in his house. He had Risperdal—'

'We've been through this. You didn't even see that drug yourself. It's just hearsay. How do you know whoever saw it can be trusted?'

'I can help you with that,' Orla said. She had been standing, leaning against the worktop, but now she took a seat at the table.

Martha exchanged a glance with her. Orla knew she'd kept her name out of the case.

'It's alright, Martha,' she said. 'If this is what it takes...' She turned to Summers. 'It was me, Inspector. I saw the Risperdal in Pete's ... the Reverend Locke's medicine cabinet. I'm happy to make a statement, if it helps.'

Summers stared at her a moment with a heavy frown. 'It might have helped if you'd come forward earlier.'

'Would you have believed me?'

Summers didn't reply.

'And there's something else about Locke you should know.'

'And what's that?'

Martha bit her lip. Orla looked down at the table for a moment.

'I've been ... sort of dating Peter Locke these last couple of weeks. This week we ... well, let's just say I saw him with his shirt off.'

Summers opened his hands, his palms up, as if to say, *so what?*

'He has the first verse of "Feannag Dhubh" on his back,' Martha rushed out. 'Orla saw it in a mirror. Locke had it tattooed on himself – backwards. In mirror writing.'

Summers looked at Orla.

'It's true. Exactly what Martha says. Pete told me it was an act of rebellion against his father. He was the minister here before Pete. Apparently the old man used to make Pete write the poem out as a punishment.'

Summers took in a deep breath. 'I can't deny, this is ... well, interesting information. Information I wish I'd had earlier.' He looked sternly at Orla, and then at Martha.

'Look, to me he's just a lovely guy,' Orla said. 'But with a troubled past. He's told me stuff about his mother disappearing when he was a kid. Just walked out, he said, never to be seen again. He grieved for her as if she'd died. His father tried to fix it with the power of prayer, or whatever, but in the end his grandmother took him to a doctor. He was medicated for long periods of his childhood.'

'Did he say with what?' asked Summers.

Orla shook her head. 'No, he didn't. And I feel bad for telling you, because I really don't want to believe he can have done stuff to these kids. But since I saw those lines on his back, I just don't know anymore. I can't help thinking Martha might be right about him.'

Summers looked down at his hands for a moment.

'Derek, please,' Martha said. 'Can you just entertain the possibility – he's clearly a damaged guy, with access to the drug, who knows the kids, who knows the poem, who has the damned thing written on his own back...' Her voice was rising. Jamie placed a hand on her shoulder.

'OK, OK,' Summers said. 'Yes, I agree, this all does place him under some kind of suspicion. We'll pay him another visit.'

'Today?' Martha said putting her hand out and gripping Summers' wrist.

'Right now,' Summers replied, standing up.

Martha gave Summers and Walker, who was sitting in the car outside, one minute's lead, and then jumped into her own car to follow them, ignoring Jamie's protests.

'Please, Jamie,' she said. 'Dougie might be in the manse or something. Or there might be some trace of him there. You stay here, in case there's news of him.'

'I'm coming with you, though,' Orla said, getting in the other side of the car.

Martha didn't argue, and sped off down the lane after Summers and Walker.

She pulled into the manse drive to see the police officers standing by the open front door. She scrambled out and approached them. Summers turned, and she prepared herself for his bark, ordering her away. But he simply shook his head at her.

'The door was open when we arrived,' he said. 'And no one's responding to our calls.' His face was tense. Walker's too. Summers nodded to him, and Walker took a step inside. 'Wait here,' Summers hissed at Martha and Orla. Martha stepped forward herself, only prevented from following them by Orla's hand on her arm.

The seconds ticked by, then she heard the word 'clear' shouted by Walker. And then by Summers. They were moving from room to room around the ground floor. Through the open door she then saw Walker climb the stairs, Summers bringing up the rear.

'I'm going in,' Martha said, shaking Orla's hand off her arm.

She hurried through the hallway and down the corridor that led to the kitchen. She looked in the living room, scanning for any sign of Dougie, and saw that a chair was turned over and the hearthrug was skewed and rucked up. She backed out of the room and went to the next door – the study where Locke had made copies of the photograph when she was last here. There was more mess in here. Papers were strewn across the floor, a table looked pushed out of place. Stepping inside, something crunched under her foot. Shards of glass lay on the floor. And nearby, on the carpet, a photo frame, pieces of glass still hanging on to the corners. She could see it held a photograph of a young woman. There'd been some kind of struggle, she thought. She looked back down the corridor. Did it start in the living room and then continued in here? Locke and ... Dougie?

She moved further into the room, looking around, her heart beating fast. No blood, no scraps of clothes. No Dougie. She could hear footsteps above her. The word 'clear' repeated again and again. He wasn't in the manse, she thought. She closed her eyes, dizziness taking over, the fear multiplying in her belly. She put her hand out to support herself and touched the edge of the desk under the window. Took a few deep breaths. Then opened her eyes again.

And saw, sitting beside a big old-fashioned blotter, a wooden stand holding a small glass bottle, and spaces for three more.

'Derek!' she called. 'You have to see this.'

She heard heavy feet thundering down the stairs. A moment later Summers appeared in the study doorway.

'The house is empty,' he said. 'No sign of Dougie that we can see. But there's been a scuffle. Here and in the living room.'

Martha stepped back and pointed to the desk.

'He has the ink,' she said.

Summers walked forward and stared at the glass bottle, an exact match for the one Martha had found in the forest.

Walker entered the room. 'Get on the radio,' Summers told him. 'We're looking for Reverend Peter Locke as a matter of urgency. He's now a person of interest, if not a suspect.'

CHAPTER SIXTY-SEVEN

The man who called himself Peter had been sending Sam messages throughout the day at school on Friday. There was something about them that scared Sam. He didn't like the way Peter talked about his mum, as though she was a disappointment. He wanted to meet again after school, but Sam didn't want to. So he messaged back that he couldn't. That he had too much homework. But then Peter said he had to come. And threatened to tell his mum where Sam had been and how he'd skipped school. It all felt overwhelming. He'd thought the man wanted to help him, but now he wasn't so sure. He'd have to go to see Peter today. But after that he would ditch the phone and stay away.

He called Mum at lunchtime, and she sounded a bit miffed when he asked if he could go to a friend's place this afternoon as well. He made up a name and gave her a vague address on the other side of the village. She'd agreed in the end. He knew she was pleased he was making friends at last. It made him sad that it wasn't true.

'Keep your phone on,' she said, before the rang off.

He met the man in the same place as yesterday, and they'd walked to where the quad bike was parked. Although they'd made the journey before, Sam couldn't track where they were going in the forest – the trees whizzed past in a blur of green and brown, and the cold wind made his eyes water. Storm clouds frowned on the horizon, warning of bad weather to come later.

When they reached the dilapidated shed, the boy shivered and looked away; the dead birds were still strung along the fence like ghastly decorations. As he was ushered inside, he thought that he'd never find his way home alone from this awful place. He was stuck out here.

Peter began to read Bible verses to him again. It went on for what seemed like hours. Sam really wanted to go home, but it didn't seem like the man's monotonous droning about God was about to end anytime soon.

'Samuel, are you concentrating?' Peter glared at him.

Sam's stomach plummeted to his shoes. 'Yes. Yes, I am.'

'What did I just tell you then?'

'Er, something about Jesus?' Suddenly grateful for the gloomy interior, Sam hoped the man wouldn't detect the lie.

'Now, Samuel.' Peter's voice was a dangerously low hiss. 'I don't think that's true. You haven't been listening to me, have you?'

'I need to get home. Please. Mum is going to be back early from work.' Again, he hoped the man couldn't tell he was lying.

'Your mum doesn't come home this early. I've seen you letting yourself into the house after school.'

Sam blinked, more scared than ever. Had this man been watching him?

He shivered, and thought of all those poor birds, half rotted and swinging from the fence outside. 'She ... she's coming home earlier today,' he tried again. 'She just had a lot of work on, but it's done now. We're going to have dinner together. I *have* to go, or I'll be in trouble ... Please.'

'You can't go,' Peter said. 'You must stay here – it's a special day. The final full moon of winter rises tonight, Samuel. It's called the Crow Moon.' Peter smiled, but Sam looked back at him, horrified. The fear he'd had ever since he'd met this man was coming true. He wasn't going to let him go. Sam was trapped here.

Moving closer, Peter clamped a hand on Sam's neck. Sam's shoulders slumped under the weight. He could feel Peter's damp breath at his ear. Wind made trees scratch their branches against the walls of the shed. Sam felt tears welling.

Peter stared at him hard with dark, dark eyes. 'I hope you haven't told anyone about me, Samuel. Have you?'

Sam shook his head vigorously. 'No. No, definitely not.' He wished he had though.

'Alright.' Peter gave him another long stare. Then he took his hand from Sam's shoulder. 'Let's get this place warmed up,' he said. Then turned, and busied himself getting a fire going in the stove in the corner.

Sam watched the paper and twigs starting to catch, in minutes the glass lit up with yellow flame. The firelight caught a glint in the man's eye that Sam didn't like.

'Now,' said the man sitting down again. 'We *must* continue with our lessons, Samuel.'

Sam shook his head, as the man picked up the Bible again. It was well worn. Like him. His nails were long and yellow, the joints of his fingers gnarled like a tree. He wore the big coat again, the collar grazing his unkempt beard.

After what seemed like an age, Sam cleared his throat nervously. It was getting dark outside now.

'I ... I really should go home. I'm sorry, but I can't stay for the, er, Crow Moon thing. Mum will be worried about me. She wasn't expecting me to be away for so long today.'

The man stopped reading and stared. 'Did I say you could speak?' A dangerous edge sharpened his words.

Sam shook his head, tears threatening to spill.

'Go away,' Peter said to something over his shoulder, brushing his hand at the air, as if batting off an insect.

Sam was confused. He wasn't talking to him, was he?

'I really do have to go home. We could meet again another night if you like—'

The old man suddenly lunged towards him, his large hand connecting with a painful slap against Sam's cheek. Sam was almost knocked from the chair.

'You're going NOWHERE, boy. DO YOU HEAR ME?!' Peter roared.

Flecks of saliva hit Sam's face, and his hand flew up to the heat coming off his swollen cheek. Terrified, he looked around at the door. Could he make a run for it?

'You have lied to me, boy, and now you will learn the hard way,' Peter bellowed, shifting forward to hit Sam again.

Sam ducked down just in time to avoid the blow and darted away. The man reached for him, twisting round, but caught his leg against the table and started to fall. Sam saw his chance to make a dash for the door. He knew Peter hadn't locked it, and he scrabbled at the handle, hearing the man hauling himself back up behind him.

'I'll get him, don't you worry,' Peter growled.

Overcome with terror, Sam didn't have time to grab his bag, but he knew his phone was zipped safely inside his coat pocket. Heavy breathing close at his back, the boy hauled at the door with both hands. It opened suddenly and he threw himself outside, running and not daring to look behind him.

Strong gusts of wind raced through the clearing into the boy's face, as he scampered across the path, now lit partially by the rising full moon overhead. Sam headed into the viscous dark of the forest, tripping over branches and stumbling through ditches, not sure where he was going and sucking air into his chest, worried it might split open with fright.

'You'll never find your way out. Come back here now!' the man shouted behind him. But Sam kept running, branches scratching like fingernails at his face, knowing his only chance was to get as far away as possible.

The wind roared through the trees, and Sam looked up as clouds raced fast over the moon. There was no time to be afraid of the dark. He had to keep going, get as far away as possible.

Rain began to fall now, a few big drops at first, and then heavier and louder. It was soon pouring into his eyes, plastering his hair to his head. He careered into a thick stand of pines, and staggered to a stop, falling exhausted against a tree trunk.

Panting hard, he curled up tight against the shelter of the tree, and as he did so, something soft brushed against his face. He looked up. Ribbons were tied to the branches above him, and chimes were playing in the wind. He was amongst the trees on the Fairy Hill near Aberfoyle. He was that far from home. Outside the hollow he'd tucked himself into, the forest sounded under siege from a storm. But here, it was as if the dense trees were closing in around him, keeping him safe. He began to breathe more steadily, and, eyes straining into the dark, he pulled the phone out of his pocket.

He could see three texts and two missed calls from his mum.

The battery showed only eighteen percent and the signal bar swayed between one and three pips. He concentrated on pressing the right buttons. The line crackled against his ear, and then he heard his mum's voice, faint and frantic at the other end.

'Sam, Sam. Is that you? Where are you? Please come home.'

'Mum. Can you hear me? Please help me, Mum. I'm lost in the forest. Help.'

The signal died and the phone line cut off. Panic engulfed him once again, and he curled up against the tree, unaware that the brief flare of light from the phone had been seen and someone was coming towards him through the woods.

*

You MUST get rid of him, she gasped in his ear. Everything leads back to you.

The man knew exactly where the kid was, in the only part of the forest where wind chimes played in the trees – near the Fairy Hill. He knew the boy would bring the police right there. They'd find his hideout sooner or later. He had to get this done though. It was the only thing that would send the witch in his head back where she came from. He'd completed the writing on the Strangeways boy before he'd collected Sam, and now he needed to get rid of them both and banish her back to the darkness. Sam had turned into an added complication which he'd now have to deal with, or the whole thing was in danger of being discovered too soon. Looking up, he could see the Crow Moon beginning to rise. He was running out of time. He held the syringe in his right hand and trod as carefully as he could over the soft carpet of pine needles. The raging noise from the storm battering the woods helped to mask his approach.

*

A large figure in a flapping black coat was the last thing that Sam saw.

CHAPTER SIXTY-EIGHT

'You'll need to calm down, madam,' the 999 operator told Moira Sedgewick. 'Start at the beginning.'

Words tumbled out through her tears – her son was missing and his phone had gone dead. He said he was going to a friend's, but hadn't come home. And then he'd called her, terrified.

Within fifteen minutes Moira was opening the door to two police officers.

'Have you checked with his friend, Mrs Sedgewick?' the officer asked.

'No. He told me the road, but I can't remember it. But that doesn't matter now, because Sam called me just before I called you. He sounded frightened. He said he was lost in the woods and then he got cut off. I've got that locator app on his phone, but it doesn't seem to be working. Maybe his phone is out of battery, but if he's in the woods, he could have fallen or anything.' Her voice rose several notches. 'Please, please, you have to find him. It's wild out there and he sounded so, so scared.'

Summers was standing in the doorway to the village hall. The cloud had been building all afternoon, and the rain had blown in an hour before, just after it had got dark. It was the worst possible time. Now they were looking for two missing kids, and their potential suspect, in the dark and wet and wind.

He'd called in more bodies from the surrounding area and from the city, and the centre of the village was now illuminated by flashing blue lights as they all began to arrive. Word about

Martha's TV appeal the evening before had already run around the place, and he'd decided to draw on that, and made an appeal for help from the public to find the two lads. He was keeping the information about Locke quiet for now. But he'd briefed one team of officers to search the village for any signs of him. They'd visited the cottage where Locke's father lived. But no one was home there. A forensics team was already in the manse, examining the scene of the struggle. Martha had asked him whether he thought what they saw was the signs of Dougie putting up a fight. Summers couldn't tell her that wasn't the case. He felt a sickening tightness in his chest. He'd had it only once or twice in his career – when he'd got a case badly wrong. He just hoped he could right that wrong this time.

Dozens of people were turning up at the hall, pushing through the rain, which now gushed down the street, bubbling in torrents as it tried to escape into the overwhelmed drains. The lights of the hall seemed to be drawing them in, Summers thought. The news that another kid, this time a young boy, had gone missing too, was bringing folk out in droves.

Summers had briefed the rescue team, and they now organised the volunteers into groups, making sure they had clear instructions about what their roles were and that no one else went missing or got hurt. The search and rescue team would tackle the outlying areas, with locals confined to the relative safety of the village and its immediate surroundings. Although Sam had said he was lost in the forest, the village was surrounded by dense woodland and the rescue team thought he might be disorientated, and was actually closer to home than he believed. Someone had made some hastily printed handouts for the volunteers to use, with photos of both Dougie and Sam. The volunteers, many of them most likely parents, Summers thought, listened intently to the brief from the police, their faces pinched tight with concern.

Sam and Dougie's faces stared out from the posters stuck to a board at the front of the hall.

Martha stood near the back door of the hall, Jamie on one side, Orla on the other.

'What can we do?' she asked Summers, approaching him as the groups of volunteers filed out. 'And what's happening about Locke?' She was fighting to control the desperation in her voice.

She had spent the day driving through the lanes surrounding Strathbran, Glenview and Aberfoyle. First with Orla beside her, then Jamie. Neither had been able to persuade her to sit down and wait at home, leaving the police to do their job. She knew what she was doing would probably have little effect: scanning the hedgerows, woods and fields on either side of the road, stopping occasionally and walking down a side track; collaring the odd farmer or dog walker and quizzing them about a teenage boy with dark hair. But the movement of the car, the changing views, the wind outside and the noise of the engine seemed to stop the fear overwhelming her. Sitting still at home she thought she would drown.

She'd driven home reluctantly at dusk, Jamie persuading her that driving around in the dark was pointless. And when they'd arrived at the house, Orla was waiting with the news that Sam, the very boy who'd last seen Dougie, was now also missing.

Summers lowered his voice and gently drew Martha to one side. 'We have a team hunting for Locke. But I don't want that to be general knowledge. We need all these people to be focused on finding the kids.'

Martha nodded. She understood that.

'You could join one of the search parties, Martha,' said Summers. 'If you think you're up to it?' She realised she must look exhausted. 'Don't go off on your own though.' He raised a finger at her.

'No, no, I won't,' she assured him. 'Look, Derek, be honest with me. Do you think Locke has them both? That kid Sam had nothing to do with the poem or the ritual or any of it. He knew Dougie by sight, but that's about all I think.'

'We don't know right now. We have to look at what's right in front of us. The kid has a phone on him and I've got Ravi trying to track the signal just now. The problem is this weather, it's knocking a lot of the phone masts haywire so he's finding it hard to get a trace. His mother says the phone went dead when she was talking to him, so that might be the reason.'

'And Dougie? What's your plan to find him?' A sob caught her unawares. She felt like her body was out of her control. Jamie held her to his chest.

'We'll find him, Martha. I promise. My hunch is that when we track Sam's signal and get to him, Dougie won't be far away. But we're searching for both of them.' Summers pointed at the posters at the other end of the hall.

An officer approached and pulled Summers to one side.

'We'll go and start looking,' she said to Jamie and Orla, taking a huge breath and pulling her hood up as she moved out into the pouring night. 'I should have brought Dougie's phone. It was charging. I'm going to go back and get it. You join one of the search parties and text me to say where you are, so I'll come and find you.'

'Shall I not come with you?' asked Jamie.

'No, you go with Orla. I won't be long, and I'll meet you once I get a text to say where you are.'

Jamie and Orla moved over to a group of people gathered around a dark-green Land Rover. Martha turned towards home. The darkness seemed somehow deeper than ever as she left the village square with the flashing blue lights of the police cars, and the headlights and torches of the search teams.

She could hear her feet on the road, the patter of the rain on the tarmac, the gurgling of water in the gutters. The wind pulled at her hood. She put her hand up to hold it, but too late, it was tugged off by a sudden gust. She turned her face away from the driving rain, and saw, in a ragged hole in the clouds, that the moon was full. The lines of the poem, which she'd read so many times she knew it by heart, came back to her. She shook herself, pulled her hood tight over her head and pressed on.

And nearly walked into a slight white figure that appeared suddenly out of the murk. Martha stepped back in alarm, forgetting about her hood now, which was once more pulled from her head.

It was Christie Campbell she saw, her heart pounding in her chest. She was wrapped up in a long white ski jacket.

'Martha. I'm so sorry about Dougie. And now this other kid. I'm just going to help. Mum said I'm not well enough, but I have to do something.'

'I appreciate it. I'm sure Dougie does too.' Martha made to walk on, but Christie put her hand on her arm.

'I think they're missing because of what we did,' Christie said. 'The ritual at the moondial. It's a year ago tonight.'

Martha's frustration flared. 'It's too late for myths and legends, Christie. Dougie and Sam are out there somewhere. And whoever has taken them is dangerous, and we have to stop him.'

Martha shrugged off her hand and hurried on down the road.

'The witch is dangerous too,' Christie called after her in a thin voice. 'She's why all this is happening.'

CHAPTER SIXTY-NINE

Locke had been searching for his father, Elijah, all day.

He'd woken up that morning to the sound of heavy fists pounding on the front door of the manse. He'd tumbled out of bed and down the stairs, pulling on his clothes as he went. What could have happened that someone was banging so urgently? Opening the door he'd been met by his father, a crazed look on his face, his eyes glassy. Peter's stomach turned over. He remembered that expression from when he was a child. It never boded well.

'What's up, Father? What's happened?'

Elijah pushed past him into the hall. 'It's today,' he growled. 'It's today she has to go back…'

'What are you talking about?' said Peter, following his father as he walked on further into the manse. 'Father, listen to me. Have you been missing your medication again?'

He found him in the living room, looking around, as if he didn't know where he was.

'Father, maybe we should get you home and have you take a dose of those pills. Then we'll make you comfortable and they'll start to work. That's why the doctors prescribed them for you. They know what they're doing.' Peter stood beside his father and put an arm round his shoulders.

But Elijah, always strong, threw his son's arm off so violently that he sent Peter flying. He grabbed the back of a chair to stop himself falling and knocked it to the floor, his feet scrabbling at the rug beneath him.

By the time he'd recovered, his father was out of the room and in the corridor, shouting, 'Where is it? What have you done with it? I need it now. Now!'

He was in the study, clearly searching for something. 'Tell me what you want, Father, and I'll find it for you,' Peter said, approaching him more cautiously this time.

'Yes, I'm trying to find it!' Elijah said over his shoulder, as if someone else was standing behind him.

He moved around the room, nodding. Then looked at the doorway and grunted an acknowledgement. Peter looked in the same direction. There was no one there. Of course. He knew there wouldn't be.

Elijah picked up a paperweight that was holding down a bundle of papers on a side table. He threw the weight aside, smashing it into the table in the process, and picked up the pages.

'Not those,' said Peter, rushing over and trying to grab them from his father's hands.

But Elijah shoved him off and stared at the handwritten sheets. Then at Peter, and back at the pages. 'This is her,' he said. 'This is her writing. That witch of a mother of yours.'

'Don't call her that,' Peter shouted, feeling the heat rise in his face, and grabbing for the papers.

'What are they? Letters?'

'Stories. She used to write me stories. I still read them.'

'Ungodly nonsense, no doubt,' Elijah said, and tossed the whole sheaf in the air.

As they fluttered to the floor he picked up the photo frame that sat on Peter's desk. He stared at the image for a moment, his face flickering as if a stream of emotions were passing through his mind. Then something else seemed to catch his eye: the inkwells sitting in the wooden stand on Peter's desk. His mother's special set she'd brought with her from Denmark, made of Holmegaard Kluk glass. She'd used this ink to write the stories that were now scattered across the floor.

'Yes, I see it,' Elijah said to someone, and pulled a bottle from the stand. And Peter only now noticed that there was just one left. Where were the other two bottles?

His father held the bottle to the light and shook it. 'Top that up,' he murmured. Then turned and looked Peter in the eye. The photo frame was still in his hand. He dropped it to the floor and stamped on it as he strode from the room.

'What do you need that for, Father?' Peter said, hurrying after him. 'Top it up with what?'

Images of all the cruel and vindictive torments his father had inflicted on him as a child – and on others – began to crowd in. Followed by a nauseating realisation. He broke into a run, but Elijah was already mounting the quad bike and speeding out of the drive, round into the lane at the back of the manse and towards the woods.

There was no point following him on foot or in a car. Panting with panic, Peter sprinted over to the tumbledown garage and threw open the doors. He shrugged on the jacket and pulled on the helmet that were both placed on the seat of his motorbike, and without bothering to lock up the garage or the house he roared away, after his father. Hoping he wasn't too late.

*

It was night by the time Locke returned to the village. He was frozen and stiff from hours on the bike. And he still hadn't found his father.

As he entered the square, he saw a stream of rescue and police vehicles parading out in all directions. His stomach tightened and he prayed they'd have more luck than him. He knew he needed to tell the police his fears. He'd hoped to find his father first, but he'd failed. He'd go back to the manse and call them. He had DI Summers' number.

But as he passed the kirk, he noticed a faint light in one of the windows. He stopped his bike. It was Friday – there were no services. And he'd not been in the village to unlock the doors this morning. There was a woman who acted as church warden, and she had a key, but he couldn't think of a reason she'd be in the church this evening. He dismounted and hurried down the path, pulling out his keys.

He didn't need them. The door was unlocked. The cloying scent of beeswax and lilies was strong as he pushed it open, his hand trembling slightly. Although rain hammered on the roof, it was otherwise quiet inside. He stepped into the aisle. The large candles either side of the altar were alight, guttering in the breeze sneaking in through the front door. Peter frowned. Who would've been in here to light them?

As he moved toward the front of the kirk, he passed the small door that led to the crypt below, the oldest part of the church – the only remains of the ninth-century Pictish building. Behind the door, a small stone staircase led down into the earth below, where a barrel-shaped vaulted chamber contained ancient remains within an aumbry, or stone cupboard. Tiny slit windows let in light along the east wall, where the ground fell away into a meadow, and there was a worn stone gargoyle, the lines of the crow it depicted reflected in the gothic architecture on the kirk's roof.

The small door was slightly ajar. It was generally kept locked. Locke only went down there when taking visitors on a tour of the building. A breeze blew through from the open church door to the crypt door. The uneasy feeling he'd had since seeing the candles was turning into a sick fear.

He knew there was a torch in the vestry, so he quickly retrieved it, checked it had working batteries and then shone it through the gap in the crypt door. The staircase snaked away downward and around a corner.

'Hello?' he called, his words echoing. He breathed in the cold, damp underground air that streamed up from below. 'Is someone down there?'

Silence. Locke took a few steps into the narrow passage. When, out of nowhere, a face appeared around the corner, eyes squinting into the bright light of the torch beam. Locke jumped back, shocked.

'Father?!'

The old man's head was grazed and dirty. His outdoor jacket was soaked. Locke had never seen him look so disorientated.

'Father?' he said again.

Elijah Locke used the thick rope attached to the wall by rusted iron rings to haul himself up the steps, the metal ringing against the stone wall and his weight.

'What were you doing down there...?' Peter asked hesitantly.

Elijah mounted the last few stairs and pushed hard past his son.

Peter looked down. Elijah's boots and trousers were covered in mud and he'd dripped water all over the floor. His face was scratched as well as the nasty graze to his forehead. The expression in his eyes was even more crazed than it had been that morning.

Elijah gripped the back of a pew, apparently regaining his breath. He was fumbling with something in his hand. It was a mobile phone.

'Father, what *is* going on?' Peter feared the answer to his question. 'You've hurt your head. Let me see. Do you need a doctor?'

He moved towards his father, but without warning the old man spun round, glaring at him.

'Why were you in the crypt?' Peter asked again. 'And how did you even get in? I keep the door locked.'

'Do NOT question me!' Elijah's eyes blazed with anger. 'Leave me now.' He waved his arms wildly, lurching towards his son.

Peter couldn't tell whether he was going to attack him or hug him, and he backed away, towards the crypt stairs. But then he froze.

Peter, my darling boy. I never wanted to leave you. You were my world.

Peter could hear her voice. It was clear and close. But it was in his own head, surely? He'd imagined it, hadn't he? None of this made sense. He hadn't heard his mother's voice since he was a boy.

He turned and glanced at the darkened staircase.

'Oh, Father ... what have you done?' He stepped towards the door.

Without warning, the full weight of the old man barrelled into his back, propelling him forwards, towards the altar. The blow knocked the wind out of him, but he managed to keep on his feet. As he turned, though, Elijah hit out at him. But Reverend Peter Locke was no longer the defenceless child he had once been.

'What have you done? Where is my mother? Where is Dougie Strangeways?' The suspicions that had been brewing all day were breaking through. 'What did you do to Fraser ... to Christie?' he shouted, competing now with the wind that roared through the door, while rain hammered against the stained glass, threatening to smash through.

'I had to do it,' his father shouted back. 'I kept Freyja in the dark all these years. I've been protecting this place from her. I've been protecting YOU. But those kids let her out again. She escaped. I've been trying to send her BACK!' he screamed.

His words made no sense to Peter. The old man had totally lost his mind.

'What do you mean, you kept my mother in the dark?' Locke cried. 'Where has she been? Where is she now?'

'She's HERE, you fool. She's been here all along, and you never realised it. You thought she'd just left – gone back home to Denmark, or wherever. And I let you believe it.'

Peter grabbed at his father's arms. 'What do you mean? She was here? I don't understand.'

'You never did, you fool. Your mother wanted to take you with her when she left. I found her book. She was planning to run away with you. But I couldn't allow that. Her leave ME? Never.'

Peter grabbed a pew for support. Did his father mean...?

'She thought I didn't know what she was up to,' Elijah went on. 'But I saw her at that moondial. With her spells and filthy rituals. I should have known she was a witch when I first met her. She thought she could keep you both safe with all her unholy practices.'

'She wanted to take me with her...' Peter felt a terror, but also a warmth. She hadn't abandoned him. But if his father had stopped her, did that mean...?

'What did you do to her?' Peter's rising voice echoed in the high vaulted chamber of the kirk. When he looked at the old man, it was as though hell was burning in Elijah's rheumy eyes. He grabbed the old man by the arms and shook him hard.

Elijah threw Peter's arms off him with horrifying strength. 'I squeezed the life from her as she pleaded for you,' he said with a sneer, miming his hands around a delicate throat.

Peter was struck dumb. He'd murdered her. His father had killed his mother...

'But those kids, they set her free. To taunt me.' Elijah's eyes were filled with fury as he thumped his palms against his temples. 'And I can't stand it anymore. She has to go back to the dark.'

A sudden rage took hold of Peter and he hurled himself at his father. But Elijah was too fast, too strong. He ducked and lurching forward, smashed his head into Peter's stomach, sending them both flying, and into the tall brass candleholder on the right-hand side of the altar. It swayed, crashing to the ground. The candle jumped out, its flame catching the holy cloth, then setting light to the carpet running along the front of the church.

Heavily winded, Peter grabbed onto a pew and pulled himself to his feet. Something warm trickled down his face and his fingers were sticky – blood was pouring from a gash in his head.

'Why were you in the crypt?' he shouted. 'Who's down there? Dougie?' He was aware now of the flames running along the carpet and spreading back through the narrow hallway into the rear of the church.

Ignoring him, Elijah hauled himself up and limped heavily towards the front door. It seemed he was injured, his steps were the slow, exhausted lumber of an old man. Peter saw him slump into a pew, pull his phone from his pocket and the small screen lit his face as he pressed at it. What was he doing?

Plumes of smoke were quickly filling the building, flames leaping up and reflecting off the holy scenes in the stained-glass windows. Peter managed to stand and began making his way to the front door. But then, above the rising tide of the blaze, he heard a faint, childish cry. It came from somewhere behind him. Someone else was here.

Then her voice again:

Save the boy, Peter. Help him. He shouldn't be down here with me.

The cry came again, from the direction of the small staircase and he turned and stepped back down into the crypt, coughing violently, his eyes stinging from the smoke.

'Oh, dear God, what has he done?' he said as he entered the darkened stairwell that led below.

The Book of Shadows

He calls me 'witch' now. I don't know where this will end. Beneath the persona he uses at the pulpit, his anger is a constant flow of lava. We must sit and watch, and I swear I smelled brimstone on his words on Sunday. The village is afraid of him too. I see how his eyes shine with the power of it.

If he were to find this book he would take it from me, so I must take care. I have recorded all my thoughts here, as well as words to help protect us.

His mother watches my boy and they have threatened to send him away to school. But that would break him. And me.

I will go to the moondial, light candles, spread herbs and use sacred water to invoke protection. I fear it will not be enough, but I must try.

CHAPTER SEVENTY

Martha walked quickly through the driving rain. She'd collected Dougie's phone, and as she'd left the house, Jamie texted to say he was with a group searching gardens, and they were starting in the centre of the village, so she should join them there.

She looked out for the search party's torches as she walked but as she passed the kirk she stopped, pushing back her hood. The stained-glass windows were illuminated with a swaying light that sent shadows out across the graves. Who was in the church, she wondered. Everyone was out searching for Dougie and Sam, weren't they? Unless it was Locke. He was still at large.

She looked back towards the village hall. She should find someone and let them know. But what if Locke had Dougie in there? She pushed the heavy kirkyard gates, leaving them clanging behind her as she hurried up the path towards the main door.

Getting closer, she heard noise from inside. Voices. She couldn't make out what they were saying, but it sounded like an argument. Martha hesitated, unsure now whether it was safe to check what was going on. She didn't recognise Dougie's voice. But that didn't mean he wasn't in there. As she approached, she saw the church door was ajar. Water flooded down across the slates from above, overflowing the gutters over the front entrance. She listened, straining her ears.

'What have you done?' she heard someone shout. Male voices, but distorted by the wind. Could one be Dougie? She felt a sudden feeling of dread as the clouds cleared, letting the bright full moon shine briefly. Martha glanced around. Thought she saw a dark shadow flit in front of a row of gravestones and disappear around the back of the kirk.

Her phone vibrated, and the voices inside the building rose

once again. She hesitated, unsure whether to turn back and go to Jamie or Summers and tell them what she'd found, or whether to push through the door to the kirk and see if it was Dougie inside. The sense of dread settled in her stomach. The phone buzzed again. She looked. It wasn't Jamie. It was an unknown number. With trembling fingers she pressed the message. And gasped.

A close-up photo of Dougie filled the screen. His face looked distorted, eyes terrified in the bright flare of a camera flash.

'No!' she screamed into the night.

CHAPTER SEVENTY-ONE

Rain pummelled Martha as she grappled with her phone, trying to clear the water from the screen. Her mind was frozen. Terrified, she looked again at the image of Dougie and thought her heart would break. Was this a photo of him inside the kirk, or was he elsewhere? She couldn't tell. Should she run and alert the police? Or see if he was inside first? She shook herself, trying to clear the fog of panic. No, she had to check inside. She couldn't miss this chance to find him. But she could let Jamie know.

She stood in the porch and, fingers shaking, forwarded the photo to Jamie, tapping out a message with it:

At church. Someone's inside. Just got this pic of Dougie from unknown number. Show to police. COME NOW.

She pressed send and rushed at the half-open door. A roaring sound momentarily stunned her as she entered. Flames were licking up the walls where the tapestries hung, and a scorched smell hung in the air. The whole of the front area of the church was on fire, and it was spreading quickly.

A large figure loomed towards her, black against the golden flames. 'What's happened?' she called out as he approached. Was it Peter Locke? No. This was an old man. Dishevelled, his face gashed and filthy. As she came closer she recognised him. It was a man she'd seen one day when she was out with Orla. They'd gone back to see where Fraser had been found and the man had been on the bridge in the woods. She remembered Skye's unusually aggressive reaction towards the man. How he'd glared at the dog.

'YOU!' he bellowed as he got nearer. 'Your boy started this,' he snarled. 'And I've finished him – under the Crow Moon.'

It took a second to sink in to her brain. Then her body took over, and she hurled herself towards him. 'Where is he? What have you done?' Martha clawed at his soaking-wet coat, trying to grab hold of him.

But he was braced for her impact, and knocked her sideways. As she went down she grabbed on to his coat again, her legs getting in his way. He crashed into her, falling down hard onto the stone floor. She heard the thud of his skull as she tumbled against a pew, hitting it with her cheekbone, wood splinters scratching across her face.

The old man had landed face first and his body was horribly still. He was lying across her legs, a dead weight. She pulled and struggled as she tried to get out from under him. The place was ablaze now. Flames reflected in a pool of blood that was spreading across the stone beneath the old man's head.

Fire raced to the rows of pews at the far side of the church. It stretched up the walls, dancing against the windows. A bang, and glass rained down from above. She turned her head as shards showered her hair. The air was becoming thick with smoke, the heat intense. She had to find Dougie before it was too late. Where, here in the kirk, could he be?

With a massive push, she managed to roll the old man over and then hauled her legs out from beneath him. Fingernails scrabbling against the blood-covered stone floor, she pulled herself to her feet, still half squatting as the smoke thickened the air above.

Something moved through the dense black cloud – a dark figure bundling through a doorway at the side, flames all around.

A man. He was carrying something. He stumbled, almost going down onto his knees, before he managed to right himself and stagger forward. It was Peter Locke, and he was carrying something. A body. It hung over his shoulder. He was desperately trying to make it to the front door.

'Dougie!' she called out, but her voice was carried away with the roar of the flames now engulfing the building.

Martha couldn't breathe, every gasp clawing in more of the thick black smoke. Locke passed her now. She staggered after him, desperately trying to see if it was Dougie he was carrying. But Locke fell, close to the door. The intense heat felt like it was stripping her skin. Every breath an agony in her chest, as she yanked her scarf up over her face, and squinting through the smoke, lunged to where Locke lay. The body had fallen clear of him and was half propped up against a pew. Sandy-coloured hair was plastered to a small head and his face was filthy, a trickle of dark blood across his forehead.

It was Sam. She stared at him, frozen for a second. So where was Dougie?

Sam moved, coughing, his eyes flickering open. And she suddenly thought of the box tucked tight against her heart. Her babies, all that remained of them. She couldn't leave another child to perish in a fire.

Martha grabbed Sam's arms, stumbling backward towards the door, every choking breath an agony, her eyes streaming as though needles were stabbing them. Bright-orange flames just feet away now. She fell again, crawling over the stone threshold and out through the studded door onto the slabs in the porch. The rain pelted her face as she collapsed, holding tight to Sam's hand at her side. She could go no further.

But what about Dougie? She pushed herself up, and turned to the open door – it blazed orange now, the heat coming out in waves. She'd risk anything for her boy, but if she had any chance of saving him, she needed to know whereabouts he was in there.

She pulled her phone from her pocket and tapped on the last message. There was the photograph she'd just received. She used her bloodied, blistering fingers to zoom into the corners and the edges of the image. She thought she saw branches. Maybe clouds. He wasn't in the church when this was taken.

There – a shape in the background. It was faint, but she knew what it was – the stone obelisk stretching up to touch the moon.

She knew where to find Dougie, she thought, as the smoke and heat engulfed her.

CHAPTER SEVENTY-TWO

The sky above the kirk was lit up like a huge bonfire, sparks dancing high and floating in an angry cloud that drifted over the full moon. Jamie and the search party he was in looked at each other in disbelief. What now?

And where was Martha, he thought. She should be here by now. It didn't take that long to walk to her house and back. He pulled out his phone and noticed that the text app was flashing. He'd missed a text. It was from Martha, sent a few minutes ago.

His heart lurched as he saw the photo of Dougie. He had to read the message with it twice, his brain was so scrambled:

At church. Someone's inside. Just got this pic of Dougie from unknown number. Show to police. COME NOW.

'Shit,' he said, and grabbed the police officer who was with their group.

He showed him the picture. 'Martha has just received this photo of Dougie. And she's saying she's at the church.' Without waiting for a reply, he rushed off in the direction of the burning building.

'Jesus Christ,' he said out loud, unsure if he was praying or exclaiming. 'Not again. Please not again.'

A wail of sirens caught on the wind. Other people were now

running towards the kirk too. Jamie saw Summers ahead of him, his bulk thundering along with the effort. Jamie came up behind.

'Martha's in the kirk!' he called as he caught up. 'And someone sent her this.' He thrust his phone in the detective's face.

Orla caught up with them too. 'Oh God, no!' she said as she saw the image of Dougie's distraught face. 'Does that mean Dougie's in there?' She pointed towards the church.

Jamie grabbed her hand and they raced towards the blaze, the heat intensifying as they got closer. Frantic now, Jamie scanned the crowd, but he could see no sign of Martha. A fire engine had already arrived from Aberfoyle and was blocking the road in front of the building. Some of the firefighters had been out helping with the search for the boys and they must've called it in. The sound of a second one en route could be heard in the distance. The roof of the church had already started to collapse at the far end. Firefighters were silhouetted against the flames, breathing apparatus covering their faces, while others already had water pouring in through giant hoses that snaked their way between the gravestones.

'Don't let her be in there. Please. Don't let her die,' said Jamie out loud. He rushed past Summers and up to the church gates.

'Stop, Jamie, you can't go in!' Summers called.

Trying to hold back his horror, the intense heat making his already scarred face crackle with pain, Jamie managed to get halfway along the path before being stopped and restrained by a police officer. He struggled, the towering blaze now reflected in the eyes of all those watching helplessly. It was as if his soul was on fire. He couldn't bear to lose Martha too.

Slates collapsed in a waterfall and the metal crow finials on the roof toppled into the flames from the disintegrating roof. Jamie struggled against the restraining arms of the large officer.

'Stop, sir,' the officer said. 'Let the firefighters do their job.'

A burst of shouting and screaming amongst the chaos, and then through the smoke, a shape emerged from the porch.

Covered in black smoke, a firefighter carrying a small body in his arms. Paramedics rushed to take over as the child was lowered gently to the ground.

Suddenly, a crash announced the collapse of the stone tower. Jamie crumpled, all hope gone. If Martha was in there, then she must be dead. He knelt down, hands over his face, and wept. He felt a hand on his back, and he looked up, barely able to see through his tears, as another figure appeared from the porch, a second body over his shoulder, long black hair hanging down over the firefighter's back as he placed the stricken person onto a grass-covered grave.

'Martha,' panted Jamie with relief.

He broke free of the police officer and rushed over to where she lay. He dropped down beside Martha, her face as black as her hair. Jamie touched his fingers to her throat and was relieved to feel a faint throb of life. Then some of the fire crew appeared at his side, and pushing him aside, hurriedly placed an oxygen mask over her face.

Jamie was on his knees, tears streaming. Summers appeared and put his hand on Jamie's shoulder.

'Thank God she's alive,' he said.

As they lifted Martha onto a stretcher a small yellow box fell from her pocket.

Jamie bent down to pick it up from the grave. He'd keep it safe for Martha.

CHAPTER SEVENTY-THREE

Martha came to with a jerk, her eyes snapped open. She was staring at a metal roof. Something was clamped tight over her face. She was in an ambulance. But she couldn't feel it moving. She began to cough, trying to pull the mask off.

'Woah, calm down, Martha, you're safe now.' A man in a green paramedic's suit leaned over her. 'We're just doing a few checks, and then we'll get you to hospital.'

'No...' she croaked. 'My son!'

'Your little boy is safe,' he said.

Confused, she started clawing again at the mask. 'Not the boy in the kirk. My son. Dougie.' She struggled to sit up, but the straps from the stretcher were tight across her body. She felt a grip tighten on her hand.

'It's OK, Martha. I'm here.' It was Jamie.

A frenetic bout of coughing overtook her, and she shook her head. She was desperate to say something and pulled at the mask. Jamie leaned over and lifted it.

'What is it, Martha? What do you want to say? You're safe now.'

'It's Dougie.' A fractured whisper. 'That picture. He's at the moondial.' She tried to sit up.

'You can't go anywhere. It's not safe.' The paramedic gently tried to push Martha back. 'We're taking you to hospital.'

'NO!' She struggled, throat in agony. 'Jamie, look at it. Look behind his head.'

She watched as Jamie pulled his phone out of his pocket and found the photo. He brought the phone closer to his face. Then he stared at her. 'You're right.' He turned to the paramedic. 'She's right. The other boy who was missing – her son. We know where he is. I have to go. I have to show the police.'

The paramedic pushed open the back door.

'No, Jamie, please...' Martha used all her strength to wrench off the mask and wriggle out of the restraints.

Jamie turned and stared at her. She saw him understand what she wanted to say.

He turned to the paramedic. 'Look, I know this is unconventional, but I have to take her with me. It's her son. She has to be there. I'm a doctor. A GP. Give me the portable oxygen, and I'll take responsibility for her.'

The paramedic shook his head. 'I can't force her to stay, and I'm not advising it, but if you say so... '

Summers' face appeared at the open ambulance door.

'It's Dougie,' Jamie said, as they unstrapped Martha. 'He's at the farm. We have to go there NOW.'

Summers looked momentarily confused.

'You're sure?' he said. 'We were all over that place two days ago with the search. There was no sign of him.'

'I know,' Jamie said, 'but we're sure he's there now. Have another look at the photo I showed you.'

Martha reached into her pocket for her phone, and it tumbled from her shaking fingers onto the floor. 'In the background. The moondial,' she rasped, before another bout of coughing paralysed her.

Jamie pulled out his own phone and opened the photo Martha had sent, Summers leaning over his shoulder to see.

'Fuck,' he muttered. 'Let's go then.'

Jamie pulled Martha up and taking the portable oxygen tank and mask from the paramedic, led her out and over to Walker, who was waiting beside a police car. They raced down through the village, blue lights flashing and sirens blaring, Martha having coughing fits in the back, and Jamie administering oxygen as best he could.

The rain had stopped by the time they reached the farm.

'Go past,' Jamie instructed Walker, who was driving. 'The moondial is another five hundred yards further on.'

Surrounded on all sides by a shroud of mist that had emerged from the ground into the cold night, the raised earth was bathed in an ethereal glow from the full, bright moon. Propping Martha up between them, Summers and Jamie moved as fast as they could towards the skeletal trees that encircled the place. The scent of recently soaked earth was heavy from the fields and undergrowth.

'There's a path, leading to a staircase. It goes from the back of the garden,' Jamie said, following Walker, who swung his torch beam in an arc until he picked out the steps.

At the top, they could see the stone structure standing in a bright pool of lunar light. In its shadow, a curled-up figure lay face down. Walker shone the torch on to him. They could see he had his hands tied.

'Dougie,' Martha whispered, her voice breaking.

The torch beam caught his back. His top had been cut away. Lines of copperplate script had started to blur across his bare skin, some words now missing as they'd dissolved in the rain.

Fires blaze ... Blacklaw Braes
... Moondial rouses dead ...

Under ghealach làn Feannag fly

... rises at Crow Moon

'Mum,' Dougie rasped. 'Muuum.'

'I'm here, Dougie.' Martha pulled herself away from Jamie's grip and struggled up the steps to her son.

She reached him just as the others did, and sat by him, cradling his head in her lap.

'It was Elijah Locke,' Dougie whispered. 'Elijah Locke,' he repeated. And again, as he slipped into unconsciousness.

Martha stared up at Jamie, then Summers and Walker. Their shocked faces turned into pale masks of tragedy by the cold, silver light of the Crow Moon.

CHAPTER SEVENTY-FOUR

One person didn't make it out of the fire alive that night. Elijah Locke's cremated body was pulled from the wreckage the following day.

And a few days after that, the police and specialist fire forensic investigators discovered another body. The remains of a woman were discovered hidden beneath the floor in the crypt.

'The body was protected from the blaze by the thick stone in the crypt,' Summers told Martha as she recovered at home after more than a week in the hospital.

'It was a woman, probably in her twenties, and she'd been buried only a foot or so beneath the earth floor, obviously for some time. There were fragments of cotton clothing and blonde hair attached to the skull. The examiner also discovered fractures to the laryngeal cartilages, which would indicate strangulation as the most likely cause of death,' said Summers. 'When the forensics team went into the crypt to investigate, they could see the earth was uneven in that area, so they decided to excavate. She certainly didn't die of natural causes and shouldn't have been buried there, that's for sure.'

'Do you have any idea who she was?' Martha croaked, her throat still recovering from the smoke.

'We found a small book hidden in a crevice in the wall near the body. Looks like it was some kind of journal. It has *The Book of Shadows* and the name Freyja Rohde Locke written inside the cover alongside a page with the Feannag Dhubh poem written on it.'

Martha raised her eyebrows. 'You mean...?'

'We believe she's Peter Locke's mother. And there's this.' He handed Martha a piece of paper. 'That's a scanned copy of the final entry,' he said.

It is cold out here beneath this bright moon. I exhale shallow breaths in plumes of fear. An owl screeches, and I see her ghostly outline catch the moonlight as she glides by. I have no fear of her, but of what is to come. I have done all I can to safeguard my child, but dread this feeble circle of protection will not hold. I am sorry for you, son. I've tried so hard to appease him. I hope that one day you will understand. Be brave, my love. Stay true. I hear him coming now and I am afraid.

Martha read it through, her mouth moving as she voiced the words that had been written so long ago. 'God, that's so sad. She must have been petrified knowing he was going to kill her.'

'We've opened an investigation into her death, of course,' Summers explained, 'and as Orla told us, Freyja disappeared years ago when Peter was a boy. We've been interviewing the older people around the village – who remember Elijah and his wife when he was the minister. The story he put about was that she had left him and gone back to Denmark, but even at the time people thought that was odd. Apparently she doted on her child.'

'That's so sad, Derek. So all those years, Peter thought his mother had abandoned him, when she had been killed and buried in the very kirk he prayed in every day.'

'Our Danish colleagues are already looking for any indication that she may have returned home. According to those old enough to remember her, she lived a sheltered life here, but because Elijah was so feared locally, no one questioned his version of events. The police at the time wouldn't have carried out an investigation unless she had been reported missing, so it's unlikely there will be any records of her disappearance.'

'I always thought Locke was strange,' said Martha. 'But perhaps he was simply troubled – not dangerous.'

'We're also doing another thorough search of the manse. Elijah and Freyja lived there with Peter. And Elijah only moved out when Peter took over the ministry.'

Martha thought of the poor woman buried in the crypt with her throat crushed. Freyja Rohde. Such a pretty name.

'Peter will be a match for the DNA if it's her,' she said, and Summers nodded in agreement.

'How's Dougie doing?' he asked.

'Good, yes. Pretty much recovered. He's back to school today.

I thought it was too early, but he insisted. Wants to get back to normal I suppose.'

When Dougie had come round in hospital the day after they'd found him, he'd been able to tell Summers the story of how Elijah had run him off the road with his quad bike, then kept him in a shed somewhere, giving him water that made Dougie feel drugged. He recalled snippets of memory – being hauled out onto a trailer. Travelling through the woods. Being carried over the old man's shoulder, then left at the base of the moondial as the rain poured down.

'I hear Peter's still in a bad way,' Martha said. 'It was him I saw after the old man knocked me down. I thought he was holding Dougie hostage or something. But now I think he was trying to save Sam. He was rescuing the child from his own father.'

'He suffered severe smoke inhalation and has been put into an induced coma in ICU,' said Summers. 'They're not sure if he'll pull through. He doesn't even know his father died in the kirk.'

'Yes, I know,' Martha said. 'My friend, Orla, is giving me daily updates on his condition.' Her chest hurt like hell as she hacked up a cough.

'And Sam?' she asked once she'd recovered.

'He's doing well,' Summers said with a small smile.

Sam had told the police about the old man who had helped him at first, but then frightened him. He kept dead birds in a hut in the forest, not far from the fairy tree, Sam had said. He'd also mentioned hearing someone moaning nearby when Elijah had taken him there. Now they knew it was Dougie.

'Sam said the old man called himself Peter. Elijah was clearly trying to put the blame on his son. There's something wicked about that,' Summers said. 'We found the hut a few miles outside Strathbran, in the forest. Dozens of dead crows strung up outside. There was also an empty box of ketamine from Glenview Vet's, and Sam's school bag was there too. Gallagher caved and admitted the vet break-in when we told him we found his prints there. And he claims he'd put most of the stock, apart from the quantity we found in his car, at the old railway buildings in Strathbran. Elijah Locke must have got hold of that somehow.'

The text message with the photo of Dougie had come from an unregistered mobile phone, Summers told her. The police assumed it was Elijah's but anything on him was gone in the blaze.

'Locke had my phone number, Derek. He wrote it on a copy of that photo the day I went to see him. Could his father have seen that?' she said. She wondered if the old man wanted her to find her son alive after all. Why else would he send the image?

'Does this mean there's no longer a maniac on the loose?' she asked.

'I think it definitely does,' said Summers. 'Since Dougie identified Elijah as his attacker, we've directed the whole investigation at why he might have done all this. We've stripped his cottage from top to bottom and we've found various notebooks and papers with the poem written out over and over again. Along with random scribblings about Freyja being a witch, in league with the devil, and sister of the crows. All sorts. We're piecing it together now, but our theory is that he believed Peter's mother was a witch, and that her spirit had returned to Strathbran. This ritual of writing on the teenagers looks like his attempt to banish her once again.'

'In the church he said to me that my boy started all this, and he was finishing it, under the Crow Moon,' Martha said. 'So that seems to make sense. He thought the kids released Freyja's spirit by doing that ritual at the moondial a year ago.'

'It all seems very farfetched, I know,' Summers went on. 'But we've discovered a few things that might explain the old man's state of mind. We found boxes of the Risperdal at Elijah's cottage – prescribed to him...'

'And not to Peter...' Martha said.

'Exactly. We went to Elijah's doctor. He was being treated for a condition called paraphrenia. According to his GP, it's a form of schizophrenia that can cause paranoid delusions and hallucinations. The Risperdal controls it, but if you stop taking it...' Summers opened his hands. 'Sam said the old man did act strangely at times, as though he was talking to someone who wasn't there. If Peter does regain consciousness, and if he's in a state to be questioned, we might find out more about Elijah and what he believed about all the Feannag Dhubh stuff. But when that might be, we just don't know.'

He paused for a moment, and gave Skye, who was sitting at his feet, a good scratch behind the ears.

'There's something else I need to tell you, Martha.'

She raised her eyebrows, concerned at his tone now.

'Our forensics team has been out at Blacklaw again. Giving it another sweep, in light of all this new information. And they found something.'

'What?'

'They looked at the outbuildings where we now know Christie was held, but they also examined the ruins of the cottage and the garden, in case there was any other evidence. They found what was left of a cigarette lighter hidden in the undergrowth. It was pewter with the initials "E.L." engraved on it and a lock symbol.'

He paused.

'Elijah Locke...' Martha said.

Summers nodded. 'It's being examined for traces of the accelerant that was found at the croft during the initial investigation.'

Martha didn't know what to say. She shook her head, trying to take in what he was telling her.

'Are you saying the fire might not have been an accident?' she said at last. 'And that Elijah might have started it? But why?'

Summers placed a steady hand on her arm. 'We don't know. Domestic fires are sometimes examined by police personnel who don't have intensive training, and unless there was reason to believe this was suspicious they might not have asked a specialist to examine the scene. In light of this find, though, we'll be reopening the case.'

Martha stared at him. For once lost for words. Her heart contracted. She thought of her matchbox and its precious cargo. All that was left from the first vicious fire that had devastated her family. In that box was all that remained of her babies. The only way of knowing they had been there at all were the six small teeth that had been found. The police couldn't even say whether they belonged to both her boys, or just one. Discovered amongst the ruins of their bedroom, three small, rounded incisors, two top and one bottom, a tiny pointed canine and two baby molars. She'd carried them everywhere with her since that dreadful day. She thought she'd lost it on the night of the kirk fire. But Jamie had found it and kept it safe.

CHAPTER SEVENTY-FIVE

Several weeks after the kirk had burned down, a forensic technician working in the upstairs area of the manse hollered down to DC David Walker.

'Walker, you'd better come up and see this,' he called.

They were taking their time to examine the house. Trying to solve the puzzle of what had happened between Elijah, Freyja and Peter Locke. Recent events meant the old mystery of Freyja's disappearance had resurfaced. Unpicking the connections would take time, if it ever became clear at all.

As Walker went towards the stairs he looked around the place – it was like entering a time warp. Everything was old-fashioned: the worn upholstered chairs, dark mahogany furniture and somewhere the heavy ticking of a grandmother clock. It had passed through the hands of three generations of the Locke family, but, Walker thought, it seemed unlikely much had changed.

'Walker,' the voice called again.

Walker wondered about Peter as he made his way up several flights of stairs. What kind of life had he had here with his overbearing father and a grandmother that people recalled as being monstrous? The Lockes had originated at Blacklaw, the police had recently discovered – the farm Martha Strangeways owned.

He climbed the last set of stairs to the attic, its treads threadbare, the heavy air dust-laden and gloomy. Dark wooden doors added to the dour atmosphere. Peter had clearly only occupied the lower half of the old property, and the kitchen seemed like the only place with any warmth.

Walker stepped through a narrow door, expecting to see the technician in his suit, but instead saw a hole in the wall, plasterboard ragged all around it. Walker ducked his head. There was another room on the other side.

'In here,' the technician said. 'You won't believe it.'

Walker bent down, stepped through and was taken aback to see a figure over by the tiny window, sitting in an armchair. The skin was shrunken and leathery, strands of grey hair hanging over the face, a thick choker of dusty, discoloured pearls incongruous at the throat of the rotten body concealed in now-tattered, but probably once quite formal clothes. The lips were pulled back in an obscene grin over stumps of yellowed teeth. As though she died laughing.

Walker stared at the hideous sight for a moment. Then something clicked in his mind. He recognised that choker, those pearls – even the clothes were familiar. He'd seen them before. In a photograph recovered from Elijah Locke's cottage.

This was Netta Locke. Elijah's mother and Peter's grandmother.

'Good God,' the young policeman said. 'I wonder who knew she was here.' He looked around the room. There was no door. The plasterboard must have been put up after she'd been placed here.

'But there's something else,' the technician said. He very carefully tipped the corpse forward and beckoned Walker over.

The mummified skin across the woman's back was bare. The familiar lines of faded text were written across it. Walker picked out enough words to recognise the first verse of 'Feannag Dhubh'.

A large tabby cat walked into the room, its brush-like tail stuck up high as it purred loudly around the legs of the corpse in the chair.

EPILOGUE

A cold wind blew the day Martha set out for Blacklaw. Snow still clung to the mountains in the distance and in pockets through the woods, where daffodils bloomed bright in clumps on the threshold between winter and spring. The death of the old season and the birth of a new one that she hoped would, within weeks, bring light and warmth. Overhead the disintegrating April moon was already visible in the wintry sky, and as she looked up, Martha watched a ragged black crow outlined against the fading disc that hung between grey clouds. The bird cawed loudly, and a small group of its fellow corvids lifted from the treetops, calling in unison. The Crow Moon had signalled the end of winter and the end of a nightmare.

Martha had changed over recent weeks. Physically, she was thinner. And a bright white streak had begun growing through her hair.

'Trust you, Martha,' Orla had said. 'I spend a bloody fortune on cosmetics and hair dye, and you spring a Mallen streak and look instantly amazing.'

Martha made her way through the woods from the village, pausing for a moment on the slope by the river bank, a carpet of rotten leaves beneath her feet. Dougie and Jamie had gone ahead with the dogs and were already waiting on the bridge. Orla was at her side. When she had hesitantly told Martha she was pregnant, the news had come as a shock, but Martha was genuinely pleased for her friend. She hoped it would work out with Peter Locke, but knew that Orla would make a wonderful mother and already had seen something new and magical bloom within her.

It was peaceful, the sound of water trickling below and the wind through the bare branches of the beech leaves above them. A robin was singing – his sweet, high-pitched trill made her smile as she stopped at the spot she had fallen weeks ago. She looked at the place where Fraser's body had lain and wondered briefly how his family were coping.

Summers had been giving her regular updates about the case. The notebooks he'd told her about, filled with Elijah Locke's disassembled thoughts, contained mentions of both her and Dougie, as well as Fraser and Christie, along with warnings of witches and crows. It seemed as though Elijah Locke had been watching the three teenagers at the moondial that night of the Crow Moon the previous year, and had chased after them. His illness bringing on paranoia that they'd raised the dead, they'd then become the target of his delusion.

'Come on, Mum,' Dougie shouted.

His voice was now becoming that of a young man, she thought. Over the past few weeks, they'd reached a quiet understanding. She'd told him and Jamie about the new investigation into the fire. As hard as it was to accept, they might never actually know the truth – whether it was an accident, or a deliberate act of violence against their family. But Martha knew they needed to deal with it together.

They crossed the bridge, went through the kissing gate and up the track towards the farm. The now-derelict buildings were still marked by fire, but she could see no trace of what else had gone on there. The sheep lifted their heads as they passed, and a curlew whistled across the moor.

She felt for the box in her pocket.

Jamie had been shocked when he discovered what was inside. Six small ash-stained teeth. All that remained of their twin boys, lost to the fire at Blacklaw Braes. 'Oh Martha,' was all he'd said, before he'd pulled her close.

It was now time to let it go for good. They'd decided to bury it, not in the churchyard, where a small stone bore their names, near the now-ruined kirk, but under the tree in the field behind their home where their boys had loved to play.

She had a small pot of wild yellow primroses to plant too. For Freyja. The lost mother who'd been found in the crypt.

Martha's fingers slid over the battered matchbox for a final time before she laid it and the ghosts of her children to rest amongst the wild daffodils emerging on that windswept hillside.

Later, Martha sat at the kitchen table. Everyone had gone out and the house was empty. A spider was busy spinning a new web at the window, and the dogs were settled at her feet. Sam was coming round later to take them for a walk.

She sipped her tea. The ink scratched on the paper as she began to write on the blank page.

ACKNOWLEDGEMENTS

I finished the final edit of this book under a rising winter full moon, and that seems as it should be. Many years of work, rewrites, sleepless nights and a large dose of magic have gone into the making of this book.

It started with a simple idea – six human teeth in a matchbox, given to me by Stuart and Louise at my first ever crime-fiction retreat at the wonderful Moniack Mhor in the Scottish Highlands. That was the day Martha's story came into being.

Many twisted threads of Arbriachan magic have been stitched into these pages on my visits to that enchanted place since. Plot twists and the wonders of nature have been worked out while walking those hills, as well as the forest trails of my home in the Trossachs, or watching the crow, who until last October, visited our garden daily. He came to us, looking unwell, for several days last year. As though saying goodbye.

I have to thank my fabulous publisher, Karen Sullivan, and the whole Orenda team for their ongoing belief in this book, and West Camel for his astounding calm, editing wizardry and a sprinkling of extra crow feathers.

And of course to my agent Euan Thorneycroft: thank you.

For that early inspiration and ongoing support, I thank the whole Moniack Mhor team and especially Rachel, Angie, Kit and Charlotte.

And for generating that first creative spark, I salute Louise Welsh (and for so much ongoing support and friendship), Stuart MacBride and the brilliant Val McDermid – without whom Jamie might have been forgotten.

The crime-fiction community is known for its warmth and support, and without their encouragement this book would not be here. So huge thanks to my friends Yrsa and Oli, Mari and Mo, Karin Salvalaggio, Kevin Wignall, Lilja and Margrét, Jacky Collins, Kelly Lacey, Vic Watson and Simon Bewick, Karen Campbell, Ewa Sherman, Susi Holliday, Trevor Wood, Carolyn Jess Cooke, Sandra Ireland and Heleen Kist.

Special mentions for supporting my sanity and for great wine and book-chat nights go to fiction queens Alison Belsham and Eve Smith.

I have to thank Jenny Brown and Jo Dickinson for early encouragement and amazing opportunities, and I can't forget the Bloody Scotland Pitchers class of 2019 – Cheralyn, Libby, Elissa, Bob, Ann and David. Can't wait to read all of your brilliant books!

My work mates who have kept the flame alive when I've been juggling too much include retired Strathclyde police detective Davie Morrison, who I thank for his expert advice, Natasha Augustus, who I thank for proofreading and Dr Robert Gibb, who I thank for forensic psychiatry advice. Thanks also to the awesome sisterhood that is Lisa Dransfield and Lisa Morton and all the Athena women. Brigid and Lee too.

My crime crew united by trips to Moniack Mhor include Tricia, June, Elaine, Heather, Lou, Sandra, Edith, Stu, Gillian, Anne, Sarah, Amanda, Sylvia, Anthea, Claire and our wonderful and never-to-be-forgotten Kim. Thank you.

Also, the small and beautifully formed G2 writers group: thanks Colette, Charlie, Sandra, Mhairi, Midge, Sheila and Nicola and the lovely ladies of Edinburgh Writers Forum, Jane and Kristin.

I thank my mam, Mollie, to whom this book is dedicated, for everything you do and for the many nights of me reading excerpts I'd just written for your critique. Always honest whether good or bad.

To my life partner in crime, Ian, thanks for the support and all the tips on mountain rescue, body extraction from tricky places and everything else. I couldn't do this without you.

To my lovely boys, Finn and Brodie, thank you for your endless support and love. And lastly thanks to my darling Bagel Jørgensen (BJ), who has sat by my side throughout the writing of this book.